TO CATCH A THIEF

"You are a woman of honor guarding one of Egypt's most ancient treasures."

"You know the ruby's true purpose?" Panic welled up inside her, but Karida fought it down. This was now no mere matter of the gem. Nigel planned to steal the treasure of the golden mummies.

He snorted. "Of course. I've known all along. Malik told me."

"You were working with him? Of course. He had supposedly hired on as your servant. And you ran off and left him to his punishment."

Satisfaction filled her as Claradon paled. Then he gave a shrug. "Such is the way of thieves—those foolish enough to get caught are punished." He stepped forward and took her hand, very gently unfurled her fingertips. His heat was like an inferno. The ruby lay on her palm, its teardrop base pointing upward like an accusing fingernail. "And you have been caught."

Other *Leisure* books by Bonnie Vanak:

THE SCORPION & THE SEDUCER
THE SWORD & THE SHEATH
THE PANTHER & THE PYRAMID
THE COBRA & THE CONCUBINE
THE TIGER & THE TOMB
THE FALCON & THE DOVE

The Lady & the Libertine

Bonnie Vanak

LEISURE BOOKS NEW YORK CITY

*For my readers. Thank you for taking a chance on my books.
I hope you have enjoyed my Khamsin series, and they have
swept you away to another time and place. May your lives
always be filled with love and laughter.*

A LEISURE BOOK®

April 2009

Published by

Dorchester Publishing Co., Inc.
200 Madison Avenue
New York, NY 10016

ISBN 10: 0-8439-5976-2
ISBN 13: 978-0-8439-5976-5
E-ISBN: 1-4285-0648-9

The name "Leisure Books" and the stylized "L" with design are
trademarks of Dorchester Publishing Co., Inc.

Printed in the United States of America.

10 9 8 7 6 5 4 3 2 1

Visit us on the web at www.dorchesterpub.com.

The Lady &
the Libertine

Chapter One

Khamsin camp, Eastern desert of Egypt, 1908

He would not be the virile groom tenderly deflowering her on their wedding night.

He would never cause a sigh of passion to wring from her slender throat as he caressed her virgin breasts, now hidden beneath the modest white kuftan.

The sparkling ruby dangling between them stood out like a blood droplet against a snowy bank. His hands, accustomed to stroking the skin of whores, were not worthy of touching her.

They were, however, quite capable of stealing the ruby, as they had swiped other priceless Egyptian antiquities.

Crouched beneath the shade of a cigar-shaped ben tree, Nigel Wallenford, rightful Earl of Claradon, studied his prey as he clutched an oily rifle in his sweating palms. The silent woman picked up scattered seeds on the ground. Karida was her name. She guarded the ruby he needed to complete the key and locate the treasure of the sleeping golden mummies. All week, during his visit here on the pretext of buying Arabian mares, he'd heard her relatives praise her virtue and honor as if she were not a living, breathing woman but a limestone statue. Nigel wouldn't have cared if she was as corrupt as he; he cared only about the ruby.

Ben trees, acacia trees, and yellow-green plants peppered the water source near the Khamsin camp. The burning yellow sun played off jagged mountain peaks and peach-colored hills of sandstone. A cooling breeze chased away the sultry afternoon heat shimmering off the tawny sands. Black mountains and endless desert ringed this part of Egypt's eastern desert.

Jabari bin Tarik Hassid, the Khamsin sheikh, thought Nigel was currently at the water source to kill desert hares, but he had chosen the spot to pursue Karida. Each afternoon since his arrival, she came here to gather seeds. Like a good hunter, he'd learned her habits, knew her movements. Like a hare struck down by a bullet, Karida would never know what hit her. The ruby would soon be his.

Karida kept stealing glances at him. Her face, hidden by a half veil out of courtesy to the visiting al Assayra tribesmen, was expressionless.

A good hunter knew how to disarm his prey, make them feel false security. Nigel set down the rifle and offered his most charming smile. He gestured to the bullet-hard seeds she dropped into her goatskin bag but kept his gaze centered on the ruby. His fingers itched to swipe the stone. *Soon.* "Are those for eating?"

Karida blinked, as if startled to hear a human voice. "Samna. Cooking oil." Like her Uncle Ramses and the rest of her family, she spoke perfect English. Yet her accent was odd, as if she'd lived somewhere other than here in Egypt. "I'm marrying tonight. This will be my last time gathering the seeds." She gave a little sigh, as if pondering her fate.

"Do you love him?" Nigel blurted, then could have kicked himself. A rude question. But he was a foreigner; maybe she'd forgive him.

"I do not know him." Karida gave a little laugh, as sweet and musical as the jingling of gold bracelets. "I was informed I was chosen as a bride, but I don't know who has chosen me. All the al Assayra warriors are honorable and noble, however, and so my husband will be." Her large, golden-brown eyes, so exotic and mysterious, seemed to pierce him. "He will never lie to me or steal, and he will be admirable all his days."

Nigel stared at Karida in sudden bleakness, feeling the shadows of old ghosts smother him. She was so damn perfect, an angel compared to the demon lurking inside him. His gaze dropped to his hands, and he rubbed them violently against his khaki trousers, knowing he wasn't fit to touch her.

You would never marry me. I can't father your children. My own sire lied about my birthright because I was sterile, and though I was older, I could not give him an heir like my twin brother. I wouldn't give you my heart, but I could steal away yours.

Or worse. I could kill you.

Screams echoed down a rocky mountainside in Nigel's mind, then silence. Nigel tensed against the memory, guilt swallowing his soul until nothing remained but an inky darkness. He could just shoot Karida, take the damn stone, and leave her corpse here, festering in the blistering heat. One more crime to add to his list.

She glided over to a small brown rock to pluck out the few seeds scattered there. Each movement held an inborn grace. As sinuous as a serpent, so lovely. Unlike Nigel, Karida was not scarred from painful surgeries to fix an arm that would never work quite right. Her skin was flawless, her body smooth and unmarked.

Her exotic gaze centered on him as she straightened. "You won't see many hares at this time. It's too hot. Like the scorpions and the vipers, they like to hide."

"Like Englishmen should," he joked. "Ground's hot enough to poach an egg."

His gaze dropped to her feet, and he wondered if her toes and ankles were as perfect as the rest of her. Fabric billowed in a sudden gust of wind as the gods answered his prayers, revealing a flash of shapely ankles and well-shaped feet in silver sandals. Nigel licked his lips, imagining his fingers stroking her delicate skin and tickling her toes.

As she moved toward one of the trees, his eyes caught a sudden movement in the rocky sand. "Christ, watch out!" he yelled.

He raced forward, hooked an arm about her waist, swept her off her feet, and waltzed her away as if they were dancing in a ballroom. The goatskin bag tumbled from her fingers and fell to the ground with a smack just as the viper's head emerged from its sandy nest. Fangs struck the bag instead of her ankle.

Trembling, she remained in his embrace. Nigel became aware of those soft breasts pressed against his chest, the rapid pounding of her heart. A fragrance of orange blossoms and almonds filled his nostrils. For a wild moment, he wanted to rest his cheek against the top of the scarf covering her head and stay there, holding her in his arms.

Reluctantly he set her down and turned, watching the snake disturbed from its afternoon nap. He hunted for a rock to kill it.

"Use this."

Karida handed Nigel a nearby stick he'd seen the Khamsin use for shaking acacia leaves loose to feed their camels and sheep. He grasped it, and his fingers tentatively brushed hers. Nigel trembled violently at the sizzling contact.

Drawing in a sharp breath, he curtly told her to stand back. He lifted the sturdy pole to strike the viper. It lifted its head and, for a moment, its cold, beady gaze seemed to reflect the blackness inside him. Then Nigel struck. Again and again he beat the snake, even after it lay motionless on the ground. Blow after blow, the misery and self-loathing inside him exploded like gunpowder.

A gentle hand tugging on his jacket sleeve caused him to stop. "That's enough, Thomas. I think it's past dead."

Her gentle, teasing tone caught him off guard, almost as much as her use of his false name. Nigel tossed away the stick and turned to stare at her. Dryness filled his mouth.

Bloody hell, she was beautiful. Pure as polished ivory. Radiant as the sun. His gaze dropped to his hands. Hands that killed more than just snakes. Nigel scrubbed them against his trousers.

"Are you all right?" he asked hoarsely.

Karida gave a little nod. She stared back with frank interest. Rapt, he leaned forward. Was it his imagination, a trick of fading sunlight, or did her eyes widen as if she liked what she saw and wanted him as well?

His pulse quickened. Nigel wished he could see more of her face. Was her mouth thin and flat? Did she have a wart on her nose? The flimsy veil was a fabric barrier between his curiosity and answers. *Take it off*, he silently ordered. He began chanting in his mind: *Take it off.*

Karida unhooked the veil and let the fabric flutter down. Breath hitched in Nigel's throat.

Good God. No warts. Nothing but honey-toned smooth skin, a face sculpted by the Egyptian goddess Isis herself. A pert nose, full lips in a cupid's bow, elegant cheekbones, and the most startling caramel eyes he'd ever seen. As her long fingers smoothed over her cheek and she tilted her head, he watched with rapt fascination. Such grace. Her every movement was elegant as an ibis taking flight.

His gaze fell to her rounded chin that nonetheless hinted of stubborn pride. The contrast between her graceful femininity and the arrogance of that little chin stirred his blood. She looked like a fighter. He wondered if she would prove such in bed, wrapping her limbs about his hips as he drove into her, nails raking down his back as she hissed and bit in a fury of desperate need. Blood surged hotly through his veins as he indulged this wild imagining. She was his bride and, on their wedding night, she shyly removed her robes to bare her lovely body for his pleasure.

Nigel's lids lowered, and he daydreamed about cupping her breasts with absolute reverence, their heaviness resting in his palms as he gently kneaded, showering her with tender, adoring kisses. Making love to her through the night, he coaxed shrill cries of pleasure from those rose-red lips, waking up to her in the morning and knowing she was exclusively his, that he'd forever marked her with his passion and she'd never forget him . . . even though he was a lying dog and she was a beautiful princess.

He shook free of the daydream as she reattached her veil. He turned away, knowing she was a woman of honor bound to marry a man of honor. A sweet innocent like Karida would never lower herself to be with him. The women in his bed were always whores, or liars just like him. His gaze dropped to his thieving fingers. It was time to do what he must. He was in desperate need of money.

In a desert cave was locked a map leading to stolen treasure as vast as King Solomon's. Nigel had the scorpion charm and needed only the ruby, the missing stone atop the stinger, to acquire the map. He soon would return to England, find proof he was the true heir, and drop this absurd masquerade as his twin; the title would be his, the earldom of Claradon, and afterward he'd seek the treasure and become wealthier than the pharaohs.

Tension knotted his stomach as he remembered a hopeful, gaunt face waiting for him in England. Little hands, calloused and scarred by hard labor, eyes far too sad. Damn it all, he was a sinner, not a saint, but he'd get that gold and for once in his miserable life do something right.

Karida had turned to retrieve her dropped goatskin bag. Nigel fished in his pocket for the fake necklace that would replace the treasure around her slender neck. He swallowed hard, but his hand shook violently as he reached out to her.

Silently, he cursed. *Just do it, damn it.*

He had taken but a step forward when he heard a distant thunder. Again, Nigel silently cursed. Too late.

Karida whirled, pivoting like a ballet dancer he'd once seen on stage. Her gaze went strangely flat as a small cluster of Khamsin warriors rode up. Clouds of dust swirled around their horses' hooves. A proud, regal-looking man clad in the indigo *binish* and loose trousers of a Khamsin warrior dismounted with grace. It was Nuri, Karida's father. He gave Nigel a friendly nod.

"Karida, it is time to prepare for the marriage capture."

"Yes, Father." She gestured to Nigel. "Thomas abandoned

his watch for the desert hare and caught a viper instead. He saved me."

Gratitude and praises were showered on him, making Nigel's stomach churn with disgust. He accepted their thanks but ruminated in dark amusement that he should learn from the viper's fate. Get too close to Karida, and he, too, would lose everything.

He went to collect his rifle and the goatskin of water he'd brought, turning both physically and mentally away from Karida. Money was all that mattered. Women did not. Especially a woman he could never have, with a full, sensual mouth made for kisses and startlingly clear eyes as exotic as the pyramids. He had one last chance: tonight when she was wed. After that, she would depart with her husband and forever escape the grasp of his dirty hands.

By tonight he'd have the ruby in his possession, and by tomorrow he'd have forgotten her name. So he fervently hoped.

Today was her wedding day, and they were staring at her again.

Back straight as the palm tree shading her, Karida bint Ali Sharif kept her gaze focused upon nothing. Better to pretend aloofness among the other brides awaiting the marriage capture, especially when she was the object of their gossip.

Hot color flushed her cheeks. Whispers rang like shouts in her ears as the women waited for the men to arrive:

"How can any warrior want her? They say she is incapable of bearing children."

"Scarred, and she can't conceive. My mother says she does not bleed each month!"

"Poor Karida. This is the only way she can find a husband. Such a burden to her parents. I wonder if they regret her coming from England and becoming part of their family."

The whispers she could endure. Gossip was hurtful, but she'd endured far worse. Hunger. Beatings. Cold, stark prison walls. Her heart squeezed nonetheless. She was approaching twenty-three, and no Khamsin warrior wanted to marry her. They regarded her as an oddity: the foreigner brought from England by their sheikh's bodyguard, Ramses, who told them she was related to the earl of Smithfield, his wife's father. Even after Ramses's brother Nuri took her into his family, the others treated her differently. Prospective grooms rejected her after hearing the whisper that she was incapable of bearing children. This marriage capture, arranged by the Khamsin sheikh, was indeed her only chance.

Never mind the stares. They always stared at her. For the first year at the Khamsin camp, Karida had gotten even by stealing from the tribe, resorting back to the ways of the English workhouse where she had lived. She had lied and stolen until the day she'd swiped a pretty ruby necklace from her Uncle Ramses. Expecting a beating like she'd gotten in the workhouse, she'd cringed when Nuri discovered her crime. Instead he had taken her to Ramses, who gave her the ruby and charged her with the important task of guarding both it and the treasure map it was said to unlock. He challenged her to change and become a person of honor, because he trusted and believed in her. That was ten years ago. She now stood to marry a man of honor. No one else would do.

Vibrant energy thrummed through the camp's more than one thousand tribal members. Women fetching water in goatskin bags or making cheese from goat's milk were laughing and talking more than usual. The delicate aroma of jasmine scented the air around the brides.

Men from the al Assayra tribe would soon "raid" the Khamsin maidens. That Bedouin tribe, which lived near the western oasis of Bahariya, had sent warriors here to select eligible women. The Khamsin allowed this marriage capture in order to honor the al Assayra's tradition, but each previously selected maiden would give her silent consent by offering her hand when a warrior approached. Afterward the men would carry off their "captured" women. The warriors would pay their would-be brides' fathers the *kalim*, the bride price. Then the wedding feast would commence, and then the warriors would take their wives to their tents and consummate the marriages.

Karida's heart raced with hope. One man among the al Assayra had requested her hand. She dared to hope it was Kareem, the younger brother of the sheikh. Karida had met him when she and her uncle visited Bahariya and she'd seen the very tomb whose treasure she protected. Kareem's arresting features and piercing brown eyes had sparked a fire in her like a match set to kindling.

Kareem had been impressed by her knowledge in the art of Bedouin jewelry-making, and he had charmed her with his courtly manners and winsome smile. He was only nineteen, home on leave from Oxford. Gossips said he was kind and noble, a fierce warrior in battle, and eager to acquire a bride. He'd seemed to divide his attentions between Karida and another girl, but Layla tended to talk too much. His personal and loyal servant, Saud, had secretly told Karida that Kareem definitely approved of her. Saud's dark eyes danced with mirth as he told her this, and Layla was not now among the waiting brides.

Giggles filled the air. The gaggle of women lounged beneath the cluster of date palms, their hands adorned with intricate patterns of henna. Kohl and other cosmetics were applied to their faces, making their eyes appear huge and mysterious. This was a corral of potential brides, waiting for capture.

To Karida's relief, the conversation switched to the upcoming nuptials and the consummations to follow.

"What do you think it's like? Will I know what to do?" one bride-to-be asked.

Farrah, a girl about two years younger than Karida, tossed her head. "My sister told me everything. It's like a horse mating. The man's stalk becomes stiff, like a camel crop, and he mounts you as you open your legs. He pushes his stalk inside you. It hurts the first time, and you bleed, but then it gets better and you eventually like it."

"How much does it hurt?" another anxious bride asked.

"It depends upon how large the stalk is," Farrah replied. "I hear the more power a man has, the larger the stalk."

"Kareem's stalk must be very large," whispered a third girl, and the others giggled.

"He is a sheikh's son. Of course he is powerful," said another. She nodded toward a man standing beneath a nearby date palm. "Are the English powerful as well?"

Karida's heart skipped a beat as she recognized Thomas, the English visitor who had saved her from the viper. He was alone, studying nothing, and yet she sensed he was studying everything. Even her.

"He is very handsome," ventured Farrah. "And virile. I saw him ride out earlier with our sheikh. He sits very well on a horse."

"How large do you think his stalk is?" asked one bride.

Their gazes whipped over to the Englishman. Karida's heart gave a violent thump as Thomas glanced at her, smiled, and then looked away.

Remembering how she had briefly unveiled before him, she flushed. Her breathing grew uneven as she remembered how she had felt in his arms when he'd whisked her away from danger, her soft body pressed against his hard one. Yet his eyes, green as Nile river grass, had shown flashes of a haunting loneliness that echoed her own.

She had never met such an intriguing man. His khaki suit, starched white shirt, brown tie, and shoes dusty from sand made him look like any ordinary Englishman. He had sharp, chiseled features. Sunlight picked out auburn flecks in his thick brown hair. Broad shoulders hinted at arrogance born of breeding. His full mouth, square chin, and dark brows showed a man capable of holding his own among her tribe's fierce warriors.

When their gazes had collided at the spring, she'd read the naughty dare in his eyes. With brazen recklessness, she had answered the demand. It had been worth it to see his eyes widen with bold interest. For a wild moment, she wished he were the one she would marry and give her body to.

Foolish! Would he want her if he saw her naked?

"I wonder if he would care," she murmured.

The other women glanced at her. "What?" Farrah demanded.

"Nothing," Karida replied. "Just thinking aloud."

A thunder of horses' hooves pounded the pebbled sand. Karida rose to her feet and shaded her eyes. Dust clouds in the distance darkened the air as the sound increased. She joined the other giggling girls who had also stood. Her heart thudded as a group of twenty men on beautiful Arabians rode through the camp center, their robes of deep purple and white flowing behind them. Ululating yells split the air. Women threw their hands up and screamed as the horsemen galloped closer. A phalanx of Khamsin warriors on either side waved scimitars and shouted along.

Anticipation shone in the brides' eyes. Delighted shouts and squeals of laughter erupted in a storm of sound as the men on their fine horses circled. Frantic hope beat inside Karida. This was it; she was about to become a captured bride. True, she was scarred and could not have children, but she still had value and much to offer.

The forgotten dream surfaced once more. A handsome, strong warrior on his white horse swept her away to his bridal tent. He would be noble and honorable, never lie, cheat, or steal. He would defend and protect her, fall upon his sword if she bade it, and make love to her beneath the moon and the stars as the silks in his enormous tent billowed in the breeze. For once, she would have someone who loved her for who she was, not caring about the ugly scars marring her beauty, not pitying her for being a bastard hidden away in the desert like a shameful secret.

Karida's pulse quickened as the riders guided their mounts closer, each cantering over to a giggling girl who offered her hand. Each man lifted his willing captive into his saddle, swinging her before him and galloping away. The stuff of romantic dreams happened here before her wondering eyes. She, too, wanted desperately to be one of the chosen few.

Finally, nearly all the men had ridden off. The Khamsin gathered around, cheering and yelling. The last al Assayra warrior on his mount seemed of prodigious height and carried himself with grace and pride. He unfastened the veil covering the lower half of his face, and Karida's heart raced. *Kareem*.

He had striking features, high cheekbones, a full mouth, and an arrogant but charismatic air. Seeing Karida standing alone, he guided his mount toward her. The breath caught in her throat. Karida willed her trembling limbs to relax as her heart raced with eager anticipation. Her mind chanted words of hope. *Oh, please, pick me. Yes, pick me. Here I am . . .*

His dark eyes blazing, Kareem approached on his white steed. A joyous tinkling sound came from the little silver bells adorning the colorful purple and gold tassels on his horse's harness. Kareem gave her a reassuring smile, murmured a greeting, and reached down for her hand. Her fingers trembled as they brushed against his tan skin, so close, just within touch. Her new life, her new hope; someone truly wanted her . . .

Outraged cries filled the air. Kareem pulled back, confusion furrowing his brow. He stared at a woman pushing through the crowd, determination in each of her pounding steps.

Karida's heart sank. *Oh God, not Rayya.* Layla's mother. *Please, no . . .*

"As is my right in these matters, I lodge a formal protest. Karida is flawed," the woman called. She pushed her daughter toward the prince. "Take Layla instead."

Kareem's features hardened into a threatening scowl. "How dare you insult my bride?"

"Sire, Karida is *najes.* Unclean. She will never bear children."

Karida's heart pounded wildly as Kareem's frown turned into a pensive look. Rayya persisted.

"A future sheikh needs sons. Layla will give you fine sons. She promises to be like myself, strong and fertile. Karida cannot bear children. I have proof she is not fertile," the woman insisted.

Behind her, Nuri struggled in the secure grip of Uncle Ramses. He rained a string of violent curses on Rayya's head.

Regret darkened Kareem's face. He looked torn. Karida knew whatever he did, he must choose and choose now or the contract would not be binding. The prince clucked to his horse, turning the Arabian away. He took the hand of the silent Layla, who gasped as he pulled her up onto the mount. The white Arabian snorted as Kareem settled his bride into the saddle, and loud ululating yells ripped through the air as he galloped away.

Shame brought a blush to Karida's cheeks. Her hand, still outstretched, quivered like silken tent drapes in a hard desert breeze. She let it drop and pretended not to care.

A thousand stares increased the heat in her flaming cheeks. She wanted to shrink back beneath the towering palm and bury herself deep in the sand. Pride forced her to lift her head high instead. She would never let anyone see how deeply she hurt.

The shouts died away, and people gradually drifted off. Karida returned to her carpet beneath the cool palm tree and concentrated on staring straight ahead. She'd pretend as if it never happened. As if nothing mattered. Her chest felt hollow with grief and regret.

When all fell silent around her, she finally dared look. Eyes that refused to shed a tear regarded the sweep of sand and trees. No one was there . . . except Thomas, the Englishman, still leaning against the nearby date palm. Hands in his pockets, he regarded her with quiet intensity.

Fresh humiliation poured through her. She lifted her chin, daring him to say something equally cruel as the murmurs and whispers. He merely regarded her with a sad smile, as if he understood. Then he made the most astonishing gesture, one recalled from her distant past in England. The Englishman touched his forelock in a grave salute of respect. As if she were an equal, as if she were a woman worthy of respect. Flustered, she looked down at her feet.

When she looked back up, he was gone. A desert wind had swept him silently away.

Chapter Two

Laughter spilled through the camp. Lamb stew with rice and tomatoes was consumed as the wedding feast, and musicians played a wild polyrhythmic beat on their instruments. Crackling flames from several campfires leapt into the air, sparks dancing on the night wind. As the only English visitor, Nigel sat in the honored circle of men that included the sheikh of the Khamsin tribe and Sheikh Zahib of the al Assayra tribe, Kareem's eldest brother.

A short distance away, Karida sat with her family. Her face remained veiled, her carriage stiff. Nigel knew what it was like to be rejected and shunned. He also knew the necessity of pretending to the world it mattered not one whit.

He pushed aside his feelings. They were dangerous. Just as dangerous as the man slithering toward him, eyes dark, flat, and cold, wind billowing the dresslike *thobe* at his ankles. The man was posing as his servant, but Malik bin Wardi was his partner for this heist.

While exploring for treasure in the Eastern Desert, Nigel found a cave with an ankh and a jackal carved on a rock wall. Malik, whom he'd hired as a digger, confessed in a moment of drunken camaraderie that the symbols marked a secret room hiding a treasure map. For generations, apparently, Malik's family robbed tombs and hid their stolen finds in another. This last sacred tomb was "filled with golden mummies." Malik's ancestor had cleverly placed traps in the tomb to thwart grave robbers like himself, drawn a map to detail the easiest way to find it, and sealed the map inside a secret room inside the cave. From father to son, all the secrets of the tomb's treasure were passed down for use at a later date—passed down until Ali, Malik's father, had altered tradition. Ali refused to tell Malik of the tomb's location or its secrets. Instead, he'd begged protection from the Khamsin when he was threatened by other robbers who desired the treasure, begged protection and claimed to realize that what his family had done was sacrilegious. Ali had given the Khamsin a ruby, the missing half of a key to open the map room. All Nigel needed was that ruby to complete the scorpion amulet key. Then he could recover the treasure map and find the tomb. Karida guarded it.

Nigel trusted Malik as much as he'd trusted the viper he'd killed earlier that day, but he also knew how to keep the man tethered. He'd said if he caught Malik taking the ruby, he'd chop off all his fingers one by one.

Malik asked in English, "Sir, I have seen to your horse for the night, as you asked. Is there anything else you require?"

"Yes, return to my tent and fold my laundry. Immediately," Nigel instructed.

Cold anger entered the man's eyes, but it was matched by the steel in Nigel's own. Malik finally bowed and left, fingering the curved knife at his side.

"Malik?" Nigel called out.

The man turned.

"If you fail to keep to your word to keep everything clean, you know what your punishment shall be." Nigel held up his hand and waggled his fingers.

Malik swallowed hard, bowed, and scurried off.

On his right, Ramses bin Asad Sharif, the sheikh's bodyguard and Karida's uncle, shot Nigel a questioning glance. "More sweet tea?" The warrior held up a clay pitcher and gestured toward an empty, handleless cup. He regarded Nigel with frank interest.

Nigel nodded.

"That little mare you rode and are considering for purchase is very sturdy. Is everything meeting your expectations with her?" Ramses poured the tea and then replaced the pitcher on a low, round copper table in the middle of their circle.

Nigel nodded.

"You are a man of few words these days, Thomas. On your last visit with Jasmine, you were very talkative." Speculation bloomed in Ramses's amber-colored eyes.

Nigel shrugged.

Ramses studied him and put a hand to the hilt of the long sword always at his side. "How is Jasmine, our beloved Badra's daughter? Have you married yet?"

Bloody hell. Ramses asked the question in Arabic. The Khamsin warrior's gaze was sharp and assessing.

Nigel spoke flawlessly in the same language, lying. "We will marry soon, but first I must return to London to settle old business." In truth, he did have old business to settle—finding proof that his brother's title was legitimately his. The plan was with the consent of his twin. Hell, it had been Thomas's idea. Thomas, who was now living in Cairo with Jasmine, his bride. Thomas, who had locked all the estate funds into a trust that could only be used for repairing the country home and tenant cottages their father had neglected, maintenance of the London townhouse, and as a small allowance for their mother. Nigel would be just as broke as before.

"Congratulations." Ramses's broad shoulders relaxed, and his hand left his sword hilt.

Overhearing the remark, the other men in the circle turned to Nigel. He answered their questions easily, asking polite questions about their families in return. The talk shifted to children.

Ululating yells broke out to the accompaniment of wild drumbeats from the musicians playing near their small circle. A laughing dark-haired girl no older than fourteen ran toward them, threw back her head, and yelled. Then she dashed up to the circle and squatted by Ramses's side. The warrior's fierce expression softened. He chucked her beneath the chin.

Nigel's heart twisted unexpectedly at the clear affection between father and daughter. He thought of the sad, hopeful face that awaited him in England.

"Fatima, why aren't you with your mother and the women?" Ramses asked.

The girl's lovely face creased in a pout. "I couldn't care less about weddings and fuss," she declared in English. "I want to go with Tarik and Asad to see to the al Assayra's horses. Please, Father, *must* I stay with the women?"

"Yes," he told her, giving her a gentle push. "Time enough later for horses. Try to be a lady for once. Your mother would be pleased with your company."

Fatima rolled her eyes. "Yes, Father." She pushed to her feet and bolted away, dust eddies kicked up beneath her racing feet.

"Children." Ramses sighed, but there was pride and warmth in his voice. He glanced at Nigel. "You will soon know how trying they can be."

"Yes, I look forward to finding out," Nigel responded.

His gaze flicked to Karida. "Your niece possesses an admirable dignity. She will make some worthy man a very good wife—a man who understands her inherent value. What will happen to her now? Will she remain here?"

A guarded look covered Ramses's face. His eyes became chips of flint. "You are asking many questions, Thomas."

Nigel thought quickly and offered his most charming smile, one that had softened the steeliest curmudgeons. "Forgive my curiosity. I can't help but think of my beloved Jasmine and the snubs she suffered in England. I wish the best for Karida, and I hope the future holds only joy as it has for my bride-to-be."

Ramses's gaze was steady. "You gave up a great deal in England to live here with Jasmine: the money you made for your English estate, the lifestyle of being an English earl . . ."

"Giving up those things is easy when the return on my investment is far greater," Nigel replied.

A reluctant smile touched the Khamsin warrior's mouth. It vanished when he glanced at his niece.

Sheikh Zahib leaned forward, following his gaze. "Fear not, Ramses. I am certain a good man will be found. One worthy of your brother's daughter."

Ramses's bearded face became a grimace. "Only the finest would do. Karida is an exceptional woman, pure and moral. A lie never passes her lips, and she sets an example for all Khamsin women."

Again, their praise made her sound more like a statue carved from limestone than a woman, cold but pure. Nigel glanced at the silent Karida. Interest flared. He would wager much that a living heart beat beneath all that honor.

"You chose well in giving her the ruby to guard the map," Sheikh Zahib said gravely. "The treasure of the sleeping golden mummies must never be disturbed. My brother, Kareem, has sworn an oath to guard the tomb with his life, Ramses, as your niece guards the tomb's map. Their marriage would have been a perfect bonding of our two peoples, but my brother is stubborn and guards his own heart as zealously as anything."

Ramses stiffened, as if the sheikh's talk of the treasure bothered him. He glanced at Nigel.

Nigel pretended absorption in his tea but said, "Hearts are far more dangerous than lost tombs. And hide many more secrets."

Zahib gave a deep, rich laugh. "Wise words from the honored guest. But this tomb has extremely dangerous secrets. Traps for the unwary, whose dangers are known only to Kareem, Ramses, and Nuri's daughter. Ali, the tomb robber who stored the treasure there, reputedly took knowledge of the secret traps to his grave and did not pass it on to his sons."

"I have heard of such traps." Nigel gave a casual shrug. "Ancient Egyptian tales to scare off explorers. Tales of traps and curses? Rubbish. Nothing more."

Silence descended like a dark cloud. Nigel glanced up to see the flames flicker eerily over Sheikh Zahib's face. "Do not discard the warnings so lightly, my English friend. Traps and curses carry more power than you can imagine. And the tomb of the sleeping golden mummies has them all."

Malik didn't warn me about that. Cold sweat broke out on Nigel's forehead, and he gave a respectful nod. He was tempted to believe. Bloody hell, how would he maneuver past all that and grab the treasure?

I'll find a way.

"Sheikh Zahib, with all respect," Ramses murmured, "it is not good to speak of that which should lie undisturbed beneath the sands. Many lives have been lost for that treasure."

Zahib dusted off his hands and stood. He began a long speech in Arabic about the joy of the occasion and then gave a blessing for all the new brides and bridegrooms. As the speech ended, a loud ululating yell split the air. The crowds cheered. Startled, Nigel cheered as well. About time. The sheikh was a windbag.

He glanced once more at Karida, his mind working rapidly. Tonight, whatever it took, he would have that ruby in hand. Even if she was a rejected bride surely mourning beneath her facade of celebration.

Guilt surged through him, but Nigel ignored it.

Karida endured the feasting with stoic strength. From a distance she watched Thomas, the Englishman who had looked her over so boldly. Deep inside, she yearned for some measure of attention from him again. He seemed the only person in camp whose opinion of her remained seemingly unchanged. Even her parents had fussed over her, despite her assurances all was well. She wanted to flee.

It could be worse, of course. She could still be in the workhouse, suffering from cold and hunger. Or in prison.

A violent shiver raced up her spine as her thoughts drifted back to her life in England. Her name had been Anne Mitchell. She'd been twelve and a thief. The workhouse mistress had dragged her away to a dark cell after discovering the money she had stolen. That inky black space was crawling with rats. She'd screamed and banged on the door, begging for release. A day later, when the mistress opened the door, two scowling policemen by her side, Anne had bolted. She'd run up the stairs, into the kitchen, and outside, but then she'd tripped over stones ringing an outdoor fire used to heat water for washing. Pain seared her as she'd fallen onto the glowing coals, the smell of her own flesh charring as she writhed and screamed—

They hadn't thought she'd live. She was tougher than they thought.

Then Lady Cardew arrived at the hospital. Every day she'd brought Anne delicious food, from warm muffins dripping with butter to real meat pies. She'd corrected Anne's speech. "We are going to make you into a presentable young lady," Lady Cardew had said.

When they released Anne from the hospital, Lady Cardew took her to a large townhouse in London. A sour-faced butler admitted them and brought them into a fancy room. Lady Cardew told her to sit straight on the settee as she went to talk with the earl of Smithfield and a bearded man named Ramses. Anne had heard them yelling. Terror made her palms clammy as they entered the room. The ostrich feather on Lady Cardew's hat bobbed as she flounced, but it was scraggly, and her pink gown showed threadbare patches.

The earl of Smithfield, dressed in a black suit, looked kind-faced. She'd liked him more than Ramses, the shorter, dark-bearded man. Ramses scowled and was dressed in odd indigo clothing, with blousy trousers tucked into blue boots and a coat that hung down to his thighs. A long sword was strapped to his waist. Anne realized he was the earl's son-in-law. He looked as if he'd like to use his long sword on Lady Cardew.

The earl sat beside Anne and smiled.

Anne trembled, wondering at her imminent punishment. At the workhouse, the mistress always beat her with a long cane when she stumbled over reciting sums at school or fell behind in her work picking apart oakum rope. Anne had gotten even. Silent as a ghost, she'd stolen the hag's coins.

"What a proper young lady you are," the earl told her. Then: "Anne, you're going to have a new home and new parents."

Lady Cardew sniffed. "I want three thousand for the brat and not a farthing less."

"Silence!" The earl turned, his voice commanding. "You'll get your money. Tomorrow my solicitor will have it ready."

"It had better be ready, Lord Smithfield. Or she goes back to the workhouse." The woman left the room then, slamming the front door behind her.

The intimidating Ramses stared at Anne. "She will live with my people, Landon. You shouldn't keep her here." He'd spoken perfect English, albeit with a heavy, musical accent.

"I can give her a good home," the earl said, but Anne heard the hesitation in his voice.

"And the shadow of her parentage will always darken her future. How can you be assured that her mother will not return and demand more money for her? She will be safe with us. My brother and his wife recently lost their only daughter. They pine for another child, and Anne will fill their hearts."

The earl looked directly at the bearded man. "Katherine must know."

Ramses looked away. "I will tell her. Katherine has a good heart and loves children. This one belongs with the Khamsin. Not here in England where innocent little ones are mistreated."

"Sir?" Anne had tugged at the earl's sleeve. "Why is Lady Cardew so angry?"

"The . . . lady is your mother." The earl looked away, his

mouth tight. "We, er, didn't know of your existence until she brought you here."

Lady Cardew was her mother and had abandoned her to the workhouse? She had clearly fallen on hard times, and now she was demanding money from the wealthy earl in exchange for Anne. Which meant . . . the earl must be Anne's father. Now Anne understood why Lady Cardew had been so nice, polishing her as one would polish a dull penny to make it look shiny and new.

But suddenly Anne was very happy. Even if Lady Cardew had sold her to the earl like she was a secret no one wanted discovered, the earl looked kind and he was her father. *I have a father. I'm somebody's daughter at last!*

"Papa," she'd said, smiling and holding out her arms.

The earl's face fell. He drew back, and Anne was stricken. He didn't want her either.

"Tell her, Ramses," the earl said thickly, turning away.

Tell me what? "What's going to happen to me?" she whispered.

The dark-bearded man squatted down before her. He suddenly didn't look so menacing. "Child, do not be afraid. You will have a lovely new home in Egypt, with people who will love you dearly and give you everything you need." He looked emotional as he patted her hand. "Wherever you go, you will never know want."

But she would never know her real father either. Anne looked at the earl, who refused to return her regard. His stony-faced stare was aimed at the wall.

He must have heard about her many sins, and that was why he didn't want her. She was one of his sins, too, best kept hidden away. Shame crept over her like a blanket.

"What's Egypt like?" she asked.

"It's very far from here and warm. Not like England. Would you like that?" The bearded man sounded anxious.

She needed a home, and her father didn't want her in his

grand house. But maybe she could make him change his mind. Maybe she could make him see what a little lady she might become. To start, however, she would have to go quietly along with the plan to hide her in the warm land far away.

Anne had nodded as Ramses patted her hand. They'd decided she would be called Karida, "Untouched," in her new life. She would journey to a strange land where no one would yell at her or force her to work as she shivered from cold and cried from hunger. Best of all, she'd not go to prison for what she'd stolen.

She had looked at the earl, anxious to see if he approved of her decision. The earl remained silent, staring at the wall. But perhaps he would come to visit her. She'd be on her best behavior and would impress him so much he would eventually change his mind and ask her to live with him.

I will make you proud, and you'll come to this Egypt to get me. You will want me, she promised him silently. *One day.*

That day had never come.

"Daughter, are you well?" Nuri looked at her with a strange combination of pride and sorrow.

"I am," she told her adopted father.

He loved her, as did his wife. But he was not her real sire.

Karida fingered the ruby that lay between her breasts. As a gift for guarding the ruby, after ten years she was to receive a large sum of money—what would have been her wedding dowry. Now that she'd been forsaken by Kareem, it would be crucial. The money would enable her to return to England and open a small shop to sell the Bedouin jewelry she adored crafting. Then, she hoped, maybe, just maybe, her real father would be proud of her and finally accept and acknowledge her.

As the wedding celebration ended, Karida pushed to her feet and started for her father's quarters. Nuri intercepted. His dark brown eyes were troubled, his manner gentle. He steered her toward the lee of a tent for privacy.

"My beloved daughter, I am sorry. Kareem intended to

make you his bride. He professed his apologies and insists on making generous payments of the *kalim*." Nuri looked away. "More than was agreed. He said it was a matter of honor, and he will pay."

Honor. She wanted to laugh. Kareem's honor. Not hers. He was paying for a bride he did not want.

"He is wealthy enough, Father. I trust you will put the money to good use," she said.

"I've asked Ramses to make arrangements to keep it safe for you. It is yours."

Lines were carved into the man's careworn face, and Karida pasted on a brave smile of her own. She couldn't maintain it as he continued to speak.

"Kareem was so confident of having you, he asked me to move all your belongings into the bridal tent."

Oh, dear God. All blood drained from her face.

"Where . . . is he sleeping tonight?" she managed. She forgot her own pain at seeing her father's grief and worry.

"Karida." He began a long speech about how special she was, how important to their family. If he could shield her from all the world's hurts, he would. But she was an adult now and not a child.

"Kareem is a good man. He did not wish to grieve you, so he has left with his bride already. The tent he arranged for you . . . it has all your belongings. I will have them moved back to our tent now. I did not get a chance—"

"It's all right, Father," she assured him. "I will sleep there tonight, alone."

"But . . ." His handsome face searched hers.

"It will be less obvious if I simply go quietly there. We'll move my belongings back tomorrow. Discreetly."

Let me have my dignity. Please, it is all that is left.

Her father sighed and nodded. "Let me escort you, and we will pretend all is well."

It was not well and never would be. But Karida held her

chin high as she passed the line of bridal tents set on the camp's far edge to give the couples privacy.

At the last, the most lavish tent, he pulled aside the flap. "Have I ever told you how very proud I am that you are my daughter, and how much I love you, even though you are not of my blood?" Nuri's gaze was sad.

She touched his arm. "I love you, too," she whispered. "And I am proud to belong to your family."

Karida went inside alone, not daring to breathe until the tread of his sandals assured her of his departure. Lamps burned on low sandalwood tables. The large, low bed was piled with silk pillows. She sat on the bed and buried her face in her hands. Around her, she heard the sounds of other couples retiring to their tents.

Laughter and then hushed noises filled the night air. The sounds of rustling clothing, soft voices. The bridal couples were preparing to consummate their marriages.

Karida shut her eyes, trying to squeeze out the sounds. From the next tent came a man's low groan, a woman's excited moan, which escalated into a high pitched, brief cry of pain. Soft masculine murmurs of reassurance . . .

Remembering the conversations of the women before the marriage capture, Karida blushed. Someone was now a woman, she realized. A wife. And if they were blessed, in nine months she'd be a mother.

Karida climbed out of bed and undressed. Naked, she stared into the mirror hanging on the tent pole. Flickering lamplight spilled over her lower abdomen, the thatch of dark curls covering her womanhood. Shame filled her as she stared at the mirror in utter disgust, and her mind played over every woman's expression when she emerged from the baths and they saw her body, what Layla's mother had seen and caused her to shout out her protest: the ugly ridge of burn scars across her abdomen. She felt the pull of old scar tissue. Some areas were completely numb, others hurt slightly when she moved. That pain, coupled with the fact that her monthly courses were not always monthly, made the other women tell her she could never carry a child.

Karida dressed quickly, attaching her veil and hiding her face. Desperate for fresh air, she ran from the tent. Sand and pebbles crunched beneath her sandaled feet. Silver moonlight dappled the palms around the camp. Gooseflesh sprang out on her arms as the raw cold of the desert night bit into her flesh.

She walked toward a cooking fire. Someone had rekindled it. Flames crackled and arched upward. Karida's anger and grief poured out in a flood; warmth dripped down her cheeks. She brought a hand to her veiled face, and it came away wet.

A sob escaped, but she choked the next one down. With a vicious gesture she scrubbed her eyes dry.

"He wasn't worthy of you, you know. So stop crying," came a voice in Arabic, as deep and smooth as the velvet night, as dry as hot sand.

Jerking her gaze up, Karida stared at the man by the fire. Shadows surrounded him. His body was a silhouette, but she knew who he was: Thomas. The Englishman resembled a statue in the stillness.

"Don't let them see you like this." The softness of his tone nearly shattered her rigid resolve against more tears. She lifted her chin.

"I'm not crying."

"No, you aren't, not now," he observed. "But you are chilled. Your wedding finery isn't adequate covering for the night."

He moved closer, with the slow grace of a prowling leopard. He stepped close enough for her to inhale the light fragrance of a spicy cologne and a unique masculine scent all his own. He stood half a head taller than she. Beneath the casual elegance of his khaki suit, she sensed a hard-muscled body as finely tempered as a Khamsin scimitar.

Karida glanced down, realizing with mortification that she still wore her wedding robes. A bitter laugh escaped. "I am not a bride. I only look like one."

"You do indeed look like a beautiful bride. The sheikh's brother is an ass."

"Or a viper."

Her little joke caused a chuckle, deep and throaty. She liked Thomas's laugh. Then her spirits fell again. "Kareem did what he must. Layla is a better choice for a future sheikh than I am."

"When he left with her, Layla looked like a frightened horse ready to bolt. I doubt he'll find any satisfaction to-night." The Englishman drew closer.

"Even the most frightened mare knows she must do her duty," Karida rejoined.

"A duty that can be quite pleasant with the right touch," he murmured. "Do you know what's best for calming an anxious mare?"

"Release it to run wild?"

Another small chuckle followed and a shake of the head. "Touch," he answered. "You calm a nervous mount with touch. Not one that's rough or overbearing, just a gentle caress, a soothing stroke." He lifted a hand as if to touch her, but it trembled. Anguish twisted his expression. He jerked his hand away.

Remembering the feel of his body against hers earlier in the day, Karida licked her lips. She edged closer, and her long-ing gaze collided with his. Her breath hitched.

Thomas raised his hand once more, slid it around the nape of her neck. It felt oddly comforting—and erotic. A shiver born of need raced through Karida. Fingers bearing slight cal-luses massaged her neck muscles.

Karida reluctantly pulled away. Thomas's brilliant green gaze was thoughtful.

"How can you be so beautiful?" he murmured. "Like a per-fect jewel."

She trembled at the heat of the look he gave her. He jammed his hands in his pocket and stepped back, staring at the sand as if ashamed.

"Let me walk you back to your tent," he muttered. Then he frowned and stooped to recover something. A small gasp fled her lips as he straightened and held out his hand. In it was her ruby necklace.

"You dropped this. Be careful. I believe the catch is loose," he said.

Karida thanked him.

As she went to attach the chain, he stepped forward. "Allow me," he murmured.

She lifted the long mass of her hair, quivered as his fingers fastened the clasp and brushed the back of her neck. Heat shot through her as she felt those fingers linger upon her skin, and then shame turned her cheeks scarlet. She remembered talk of the Englishman. Thomas, this English nobleman, was betrothed to Jasmine. This must stop. Now.

She turned, and he gave her a long, thoughtful look. Flustered, she started off toward her tent, but Thomas's long legs easily kept pace. They passed the line of tents housing the new brides and grooms. Moans and sighs filled the night air. Sounds of wedded bliss. Not hers.

"Are you leaving soon?" she asked, desperate to fill the silence between them and shut out the sounds of lovemaking.

"As soon as I can. I must return to London. I have family duties to attend," he said. "Obligations. If I could, I would like to stay."

"You must return . . . your *betrothed* will be waiting for you." Karida emphasized the word.

They reached her tent. Thomas lingered, his gaze resting on her with an odd sadness. "Good night," he murmured. "I wish you all the joy in the world."

Karida gave a small nod, removed her shoes, and ducked inside her tent. She felt like crying again.

The lamp was still burning as she'd left it, but something was amiss. Instinct warned her of the intruder even as he rushed forward. Thomas's servant, Malik. She cried out as his fat fingers ripped away her necklace, stinging the flesh on the back of her neck that Thomas had caressed so tenderly.

"Bitch," he snarled, swaying on unsteady feet. "It's mine. The ruby belongs to me."

Karida scrambled backward, but he caught her. He pulled out a lethally sharp dagger, waving its curved blade as he dangled the ruby before her. The scent of wine befouled his breath. He was intoxicated and dangerous. Her mind raced over strategies.

She raised her voice, hoping to alert others. "Malik, your father gave it to the Khamsin to protect and keep that treasure safe. You dishonor him. You're nothing more than a thief who desires to take the treasure of the pharaohs. You will be punished."

"I deserve the treasure. I'm Ali's eldest son, and if he hadn't gotten scared and come to the Khamsin for protection, the treasure would be mine by right of passage from father to son! The ruby belongs to me."

"I will never let you escape with what is mine to guard!" she shouted.

Shrugging, he raised the dagger, but a hand seized Malik's wrist before he could do anything further. Karida gasped. She had not heard Thomas enter the tent.

"Don't," he said mildly in Arabic. "I have two rules: Never go out in the Egyptian noonday sun, and never hurt women, children, or puppies." And with a loud smack, the Englishman's fist connected with Malik's face. Karida's assailant crashed backward and to the ground.

Karida stared at Thomas, who looked troubled. "You were outside and heard?" She went to offer her hand in thanks. He stared as if it were a viper, then shoved his fingers through his hair.

"I almost wish I hadn't," he muttered, staring at the unconscious Malik. "Why were you so foolish, you dolt?" After a moment he glanced at her. "Are you all right? Did he hurt you?"

Karida squatted down and retrieved her necklace. "He took this from me and said it was his."

Thomas swore softly in Arabic, studying the ruby dangling from its broken chain. He beckoned to her.

"The clasp is broken. I'd better repair it," she said.

"We can fasten it by tying a knot. It's safer on you, for now." He lifted her hair, pushing it aside and doing as he said.

Karida felt a stab of pity for the Englishman, who stared at Malik, who was beginning to stir. "What will happen to him?"

"I'm not sure. I think it will be very severe." Karida hugged herself, remembering the traditional punishment for a thief.

The somberness in Thomas's eyes aged him. He glanced at her, jamming his hands into his pockets. "I am . . . sorry," he said.

She blinked, confused. "For saving me?"

He shrugged his broad shoulders. "That it could not be otherwise." A pulse beat wildly at the base of his throat as he studied her. "You are truly beautiful," he said.

Karida's face warmed. No man had ever looked at her this way, not even Kareem. But Thomas had a fiancée in Cairo, and Karida refused to dream.

"Thank you for saving me again," she said quietly. "Is there a way I may return the favor?"

He stepped close enough for her to see the hardness of his jaw, the yearning in his eyes. His mouth was firm yet sensual, his lower lip full. Karida scolded herself. She must not think of Thomas's mouth, warm, wet, and taking hers.

Shock stiffened her into immobility as he closed the space between them and lifted her veil to expose her lips. His eyes glittered with frightening intensity. "Yes, you may. One kiss, damn it, before I leave."

As his mouth descended, she regained her senses. She stepped back and delivered a hard slap to his cheek. His green eyes widened, and he rubbed the mark her palm had left.

"Only a dirty desert jackal, a man without honor, would

act like this when he has a fiancée waiting for him in Cairo," Karida whispered, deeply disturbed he had dared to touch her in such a manner. But even more troubling was her reaction. She had wanted his kiss, longed for it. Turmoil raged inside her. Where was the woman who'd long ago vowed to be upright and moral?

Thomas's face became hard. He gave a slight, mocking bow. "I am what I am." There was no apology in his tone.

Voices sounded outside her tent. Karida went and pulled aside the flap, letting in her father, uncle, and several armed warriors.

"Others heard shouts and came and got us. Karida, what has happened?" Nuri lowered his scimitar.

Still shaken, she could not reply.

Thomas stepped forward. "Your daughter came out to the cook fire to get some air. When she returned to her tent, I escorted Karida for safety. As I left, I heard Malik accost her and rushed inside to help." Some unknown emotion flashed across his face. "I could not allow harm to such a woman of purity and honor."

Karida clenched her fists at his slightly mocking tone. He knew she had been tempted by his kiss.

Showers of gratitude fell on Thomas, who murmured modest protests. Malik groaned as he gained consciousness. Karida felt like groaning along with him.

"Get up, thief," Ramses said, poking the man with the toe of his boot. He rested the tip of his razor-sharp scimitar against Malik's neck.

Karida's assailant opened his eyes to regard the faces all around him. His attitude became desperate. "Please, don't. I am sorry. I beg you . . ."

All murmurs ceased as the tent flap jerked aside. Men nodded in respect as Jabari entered. The tall, dark-haired Khamsin sheikh took in the scene and looked at Ramses, his bodyguard and second-in-command. After Ramses explained what had happened, Jabari gestured for warriors to haul Malik to his feet.

"This is your second offense. I gave your family the protection of my warriors when your father came to us for help. We dispatched your enemies and treated you as one of us. As one of us, you are subject to our rules and my command."

"Please," Malik whimpered.

A frown creased Jabari's brow. "You asked for mercy, and I granted it when you were caught stealing a golden dagger. I warned you there would be no mercy the second time. You know the punishment." He glanced at the grim-faced Ramses, who clenched harder the hilt of his scimitar. "As befitting a thief, your left hand will be removed."

Karida saw Thomas back away. Blood drained from the Englishman's face, and he looked as if he would retch. He clearly had no taste for desert justice.

Jabari pronounced, "This will be done tomorrow at sunset."

Chapter Three

They gathered in a wide circle the following afternoon as the sun sank into the mountains. Karida swallowed hard as she stood beside her father. The disaster of her failed wedding had faded in light of Malik's theft and the return to camp of a tight-lipped Layla, escorted by her angry father and brothers. Gossip said Kareem had returned the bride, the marriage unconsummated, because she had confessed the shocking news that she was pregnant with another man's child. A hasty marriage was reputedly being arranged for her with the father, a peasant from a local village.

Layla certainly lived up to her mother's prediction of fertility, Karida thought without malice. She felt only pity for the girl.

As she shuffled her feet, waiting for Malik to be brought forth, Karida thought of Thomas, who had vanished as silent and swift as a desert mirage. He was already on his way back to Cairo, not staying to witness Malik's punishment. Her father had informed her of the Englishman's departure over their breakfast of goat's milk and yogurt.

Two muscled warriors brought Malik forward, forcing him to his knees. Karida grasped the ruby about her neck, reminding herself that this was a thief's just punishment. She did not share Thomas's distaste for it. She could not, as these people had brought her honor.

You were once the same. A thief. Memories assaulted her: the workhouse mistress's accusing shouts, the stern faces of the policeman, the wagging fingers pointed at her. Her false protests of innocence. The white-hot flames licking at her skin as she fell into the fire.

She watched in mute horror as the warriors stretched out Malik's left hand on a block of limestone reserved for this type of punishment. Rusty stains marked the whiteness. Her uncle, his face grim, raised his scimitar. He looked like an avenging angel, his blade sharp and gleaming and righteous in the fading sunlight.

Karida's eyes closed. A sharp thud sounded, and an ensuing howl of pain. More screams as men sealed the wound with hot tar. Her stomach gave a sickened lurch. She loved these people, the Khamsin, but their code was strict and fierce. There was no mercy for a thief proven guilty a second time.

The oath she'd taken echoed through her mind. *I am a woman of honor. I will not cheat, steal, lie or bring dishonor to my name as I endeavor to guard the sacred treasure of the golden mummies. I will keep this ruby safe from those wishing to disturb the resting place of kings. I will never disgrace my name.*

Feeling a gentle pressure on her arm, she opened her eyes to see her father regarding her solemnly. "It is not your fault, daughter," he said.

Malik was helped to his feet. As the thief rose, he saw her. The agony twisting his face vanished, replaced by anger. His moans of pain turned to shrieks of promised revenge.

"Take him away," Jabari ordered grimly, as Ramses gave Karida a worried look.

Malik screamed oaths as two muscled Khamsin warriors escorted him off. An uneasy silence fell.

The crowd slowly dispersed. Karida hugged herself, aware of the inquiring glances. Once an object of pity for her disfigurement, now she was a person to regard with wariness. She had caught a thief, and the thief had been punished. She reminded herself: *It is my sacred duty to guard the map to the pharaoh's treasure.*

She felt for the stone always dangling between her breasts, gripped it for reassurance. The chain Thomas had tied about her neck had to be fixed. She would do so tonight and ensure the ruby would remain safe.

Removing the chain, she held the ruby in her palm and brought it closer to examine in the dying sunlight. Something caught her eye. The small black spot, an imperfection, was gone. The tear-shaped ruby was flawless.

No, she thought in wild panic. It was not the sacred ruby she'd been tasked to guard but a clever replica. Impossible. Malik tried to steal it but she'd taken it back. Thomas had handed it back when . . .

Thomas. She recalled his hands massaging her neck. Thomas, murmuring to her. Thomas, with the manners of a gentleman giving her the ruby she'd thought had fallen onto the ground. He was a thief. Awareness filled her and bubbled into growing anger and shame that she'd been so easily duped. He had gone back to London, which meant the only way she could retrieve the ruby was to journey there. She had to get the ruby back or her vow would be broken. She would lose everything, not least of all her self-respect.

Shouldering her resolve and squeezing the fake ruby in her palm, she went to see her father. He was sitting inside his tent talking to her uncle Ramses and aunt Katherine. The tent flaps were rolled up to allow in the cool desert breeze. Her uncle looked aged, and her aunt clutched his hand.

How could she endure her uncle's grave disappointment? She had been stupid, wanton. She had lost the ruby because of a stranger's touch. Even now she remembered the slow, sensual strokes of Thomas's fingers on her neck, the erotic sensations those caused. He was a seducer who knew all about pleasuring a woman, a thief who knew how to distract with a soothing caress.

The truth hovered on her lips; then she made a decision. Surely it was not a lie if she left out several details. Ramses and her father did not need to know the full reason why she wished to visit England. Slowly, she sat down.

"Father, Uncle Ramses. I have a favor to ask." Burning shame flushed her cheeks as she dipped her head, tracing a line with her finger on the fine Persian carpet. "The wedding, my wedding . . . I cannot stay here with everyone staring at me." True enough. "I wish to get away for a while. Somewhere no one knows me. Until the gossip has died." Also true.

"Oh, Karida." Her father's voice was deep and sad.

"Of course. I understand," Ramses said gently. "To where, Karida? A visit to Cairo?"

"I thought somewhere much farther." Much. "I'd like to visit London."

Silence, one so deep she could hear the wind whispering over the sands outside.

Gathering all her strength, Karida glanced at her aunt. "Maybe there is someone there who would want me as a bride, someone who has not heard . . . of my defect. Men there are looking for brides. I remember hearing how Englishmen in need of money wish to find brides with large dowries. I can use the money paid by Kareem as my dowry. I thought you might help, Aunt Katherine, since you know of such things. We could stay with your father, the earl of Smithfield."

Ramses muttered something dark. Doubt and worry twisted his wife's face. Karida reminded herself that she was Katherine's secret half sister. This was the earl of Smithfield's legitimate daughter. *And I am his illegitimate daughter and he owes me.*

Katherine turned to her. "Well, Father is no longer at his estate in the English countryside, Karida . . . He reopened his London townhouse now that he's remarried, and it's the season in London. You do understand, Karida, considering the aristocrats with whom he's associating, considering his rank in society . . . discretion is necessary."

Discretion, not a shameful secret like his illegitimate

daughter. Resentment bubbled up, but Karida kept a soft smile on her face. "I will be discreet, Aunt. I can be quite discreet." *After all, I have never stepped forward to claim anything from him.*

Katherine glanced at her husband, whose face tightened. "We could do it," she said after a moment. "Father can be your sponsor and arrange for a number of introductions. You could use your English name. He has influence, despite his brief absence from society. I think . . . I think it might be a good idea."

"England," Ramses muttered, while Nuri's brow knitted.

"I do not know. Karida, do you really wish to return there?" her adoptive father asked.

"Yes," she assured him. "I do—for a visit. If I do not meet anyone worthy, I'll be more than happy to return. But I feel I need to escape here. Please, Father."

The deep sigh Nuri issued meant she had won.

Pressing the point further, she said, "I can blend in and dress as an Englishwoman. I was born there, remember. And you know me. I can adapt." How many times had she proved her resilience in the past?

"I will go with you to chaperone," Katherine mused. "Father has written, asking when I can visit again. I'm certain he'd be happy to see you. I'd have to leave the children here, of course." She gave Ramses a level look. "You will have to take care of them while I'm gone."

A heavy sigh sounded deep in Ramses's muscular chest. He motioned to Nuri and Katherine. "Leave us. I wish to talk with my niece."

When the others had left the tent, Karida studied her uncle, wondering if he suspected her reasons for leaving. What would he do if he knew the precious ruby was gone?

"Do you remember when I gave you this?" He gestured to the ruby she clutched in a deathlike grip.

Karida forced herself to relax. "Of course. You brought me to the cave where the map is and told me about Ali, the tomb robber who begged protection from the Khamsin. He desired to break the curse haunting his family since they'd taken the gold of the pharaohs. He was being threatened by other grave robbers."

"Yes. He gave me that ruby, the final piece of the key to finding the map detailing where the treasure is buried, and I slaughtered his enemies." A shiver raced up Karida's spine at her uncle's flat tone, but Ramses just stared at the tent wall. "Now you keep the secret of the map safe, just as the al Assayra tribe guards the hidden tomb. You are the guardian of the east, and the sheikh's youngest son Kareem is the guardian of the west. Do you still remember the combination to the lock I placed on the sarcophagus?"

She recited the numbers, and he nodded. His gaze flicked away.

"You have protected the ruby well these past years. Now you are going to England, back to the country of your birth." Sadness flashed over his face. "You seek to find a husband there. We are losing you, Karida."

"Not for always," she assured him. "And I'm not certain I can find a husband." A familiar tightness squeezed her chest. "I can't have any children, Uncle Ramses. That's what the others say. I'm not as worthy as they are, and just because the English do not know—"

Fierceness glowed in Ramses's amber eyes. "You are worthy, Karida. More so than tongue-wagging girls like Layla. I charged you with an oath when you stole this." He touched the ruby, and her pulse jumped. "You vowed to be honorable, pure, never stealing or lying but acting with honor always, as befits a guardian of the sacred stone. You have lived up to your vow. The ruby is not perfect, but it guards priceless riches." A smile touched his bearded lips. "It is like your heart."

Karida's pulse raced in the quiet as she watched the flame of an oil lamp cast reddish light over her uncle. Smoke curled upward into the thick air, clogging her throat as much as the emotions she felt.

"I was a liar and a thief. I didn't deserve the honor," she whispered raggedly.

Ramses took her hand. "You did, Karida. You are beautiful, inside and out. I know. You were young then, and had known a difficult life. You made some mistakes, but I believed in you. I *believe* in you."

She had a whole family here who believed in her: her adopted parents, their children, Ramses and his family. Karida swallowed hard at the idea of letting them down. In some ways, she already had.

"I gave you the ruby to prove my trust in you and how special you are, and to show my belief that you could change." Ramses's jaw tightened as he stared at the billowing flaps of the tent. "We have all made errors in the past, and they can haunt us if there are not caring people around who see past those mistakes." His gaze dropped to the carpet. "There is something else you should know when you go to England."

His tone was so solemn and disturbing she wanted to change the topic. Would he warn her against trying to seek her father's, Lord Smithfield's, approval?

"How to boil water for English tea?" she teased. "I remember that, as I've missed it."

A half smile touched Ramses's mouth. "You are anticipating this journey."

She nodded. "It will be nice to see the earl of Smithfield again. I remember his house—how large it was, so vast and pretty." Of course, if her real father would acknowledge her, she couldn't care less if he were impoverished. A sigh fled her lips.

Ramses's smile vanished. "He *is* very wealthy, and I am certain he will treat you well. Landon is a good man."

Curiosity finally overwhelmed Karida when her uncle did not continue. "What did you want me to know, Uncle?"

A teasing look entered his eyes. "Do not sit on the floor in Landon's house. The servants will be outraged."

They shared a laugh, and then they left the tent. But as he kissed her cheek and strode off, she wondered why her uncle looked so sad.

No matter. Her duty to guard the ruby remained. Karida put a hand to her neck, trembling with emotion. She stood to lose much if she didn't get the ruby back: her hope, her future.

You bastard, Thomas, Lord Claradon, she thought with dawning fury. *I will get you for this. No one steals from me.*

Chapter Four

"You are such a wonderfully naughty boy, Lord Claradon. I like naughty boys."

The voluptuous redhead on his right lay atop the rumpled linen sheets. She licked her lips and lounged against a bank of feather pillows, her pale flesh gleaming with perspiration that plastered strands of hair to her forehead. Hardened by Nigel's ministrations, two raspberrylike nipples tipped breasts worthy of rapturous odes.

"Extraordinarily wicked," murmured the slender blonde on his left.

The blonde's fingers encircled his restiffening cock. She removed the used sheepskin sheath and tossed it on the floor, then began stroking with enthusiasm. Nigel lay on his back as the redhead kissed him, her tongue keeping rhythm with the blonde's pumping hand. His fingers trailed over her soft flesh, delving lower into the slick folds and slippery channel where he'd sunk his member moments before. The redhead's moans echoed in his mouth as he toyed with her, flicking a thumb over her pearling center.

The blonde's strokes ceased. He felt the warmth of her wet mouth upon him. Nigel hardened fully, and his balls drew up tight as the redhead screamed in climax. Panting, he gave himself over to the roar of pleasure and soon he came in great, spurting jets, hot seed shooting across his flat belly. The blonde sighed with appreciation, as if his performance were that of a virtuoso. As his breathing slowed, Nigel wondered if she would applaud.

"How many times is that for you? Three?" she asked.

"Four, I do believe. I'm not quite certain, for I've lost count," the redhead murmured.

The two women were much sought after by his wealthy peers, who emptied their pockets to adorn them with jewels. The most sexually accomplished among the demimonde, they were exquisite. And he couldn't remember either of their names. The redhead was . . . Amelia? No. Something with an *A*, however. Ann? The blonde . . . ? Something to rhyme with pain. Jane? No, Elaine. Maybe.

"What is a Karida?"

Was it possible for his heart to stop beating? A cold chill draped over him as he stared at Amelia, or Ann, or whatever her name was. "What?" he asked.

"Karida. You said Karida just now." A sultry pout touched the redhead's mouth.

"And last time as well. And the time before," added Jane or Elaine.

Bloody hell. Nigel's heart pounded, his mind seeking a quick explanation for crying out that name he'd tried so hard to forget. What else had he blathered?

"My horse," he muttered.

Jane/Elaine's mouth gaped. Never had he seen a woman look more insulted. "You called out the name of your horse?"

"Both of you offer a lovely ride." But Nigel's teasing failed to coax a smile from either of the women.

Impatience filled him. He sat up, wiped his belly with the sheet, and slid to the bed's edge. Enough of this. He glanced about for his long-discarded clothes. They lay in a heap on the wool Aubusson carpet.

Karida. There was a name he wished he could forget. It burned in his mind like an ember, a fire that refused to be fully put out. Nigel thought of the ruby he'd swiped from her, now securely hidden with the scorpion amulet. As soon as he settled the matter of his inheritance, he'd go back to seek that buried gold. For now, he still pretended to be his twin who held the title.

A blizzard of invitations to balls, parties, teas, and suppers had arisen upon his return in late March. Those of his social rank were eager to welcome Thomas, earl of Claradon, back from Egypt. Marriage-minded mothers were especially quick to extend invitations after he discreetly spread the word he'd changed his mind about marrying Jasmine, the exotic beauty they had snubbed.

Would they have welcomed back Nigel, he wondered, the bad twin who had cheated at cards and seduced their mistresses, or would they wish him back into the empty grave he'd erected for himself? He'd find out soon enough.

Two years ago, after a riding accident, Nigel had decided to play dead. He'd wanted nothing to do with the parents who'd cheated him out of his birthright. Only last year he'd been visiting England under another name and enjoying the fleshly delights of his brother's mistress. Charlotte had been shocked to discover his true identity. Then he'd received that letter, that revelation of a shocking secret hidden away in a filthy, rundown workhouse. It had changed everything.

Masquerading as his identical twin was surprisingly simple. He enjoyed associating with Thomas's friends, flirting with blushing maidens who hoped for a ring on their finger and a countess's coronet. His scheme had worked. So had his other scheme to quietly find proof of the title's true heir. So the masquerade was coming to an end; soon he would reveal to the world that he was the true earl of Claradon, *Nigel* Wallenford.

"You were magnificent, Thomas. Are you quite certain you won't have another?" Amelia/Ann stretched out her long, white arms, asking the question in cultured tones as if offering up a cup of tea instead of something hotter between her legs.

Jane/Elaine crooked a finger in invitation. "We have all night, Thomas."

Karida had honey-gold skin and finely sculpted aristocratic features; her nobility and loveliness rivaled even that of Cleopatra. She smelled as bewitching as myrrh scenting a silken tent billowing in a cool Egyptian breeze. Her skin had been soft and supple beneath his teasing fingers, and he'd kneaded the stiffness from her lovely, long neck . . .

Dirty desert jackal, Nigel accused himself. He scraped a hand over his night whiskers. He reached for his trousers and began pulling them on.

"I've never had a lover quite like you, Thomas." Jane/Elaine began stroking the back of his neck.

He pulled away. "How fortunate for you," he muttered.

"When can we see you again?" the two women chorused.

Nigel paused in pulling up his trousers. The cool look he gave them did nothing to dampen the ardor in the women's eyes. Were they blue? No, brown. But no matter. By tomorrow he'd have forgotten everything about them. Karida had the most exotic caramel-brown eyes, luminous as stars in an Egyptian sky. They were eyes he'd never forget. They'd widened with desire after he'd snatched her from the fangs of that viper, and narrowed in anger when she'd slapped him.

A deep ache seized Nigel, an unfathomable loneliness, though his little masque as Thomas had garnered him scads of friends, more than he'd ever had. He stared at his trousers, flap open, penis dangling heavily between his legs. These women clamored for his company in bed, yes, and their soft bodies gave him temporary solace. They needed him and the exquisite pleasure he knew how to deliver. It felt good to be needed, even if only for this. Certainly no one else in London wanted or needed him. Not as Nigel.

His spirits lifted as he considered the possibility that, when they discovered the truth, when they learned he was the true earl of Claradon and not his twin, Thomas's friends might celebrate with him. He had changed, and he wasn't the same old Nigel they'd once reviled. After all, it wasn't every day that one returned from the dead.

Speaking of which, he glanced down at his flaccid penis. "Sorry, girls," he said in a jovial voice. "The cock shan't crow again."

Two sets of eyes, calculating and shrewd, studied him. Adding up pence and pounds. Nigel knew the look, for he'd seen it reflected in the mirror. His mood dampened considerably. He'd anticipated this. He could not afford the high price of stealing them away from wealthy benefactors, yet he was so damnably lonely since his return.

"You'd best dress. It's quite chilly, and I have no inclination to light a fire." He turned away and fastened his trousers.

"I thought you wanted a mistress," Amelia/Ann wheedled.

"Or two," added Jane/Elaine. "I gave up an afternoon with Lord Brownell to be with you. He promised me an emerald necklace." Her voice was hopeful. "I would continue with you, my lord, if we reach a certain arrangement."

The oak dresser held the price of his pleasure—and the price of its end. Nigel opened a drawer and removed two jade necklaces, taken from Thomas's Egyptian collection. He tossed them at the women.

"Emeralds? Here, these are equally green. As for mistresses, I have no desire to be saddled with whining women who beg for baubles and fight for furs." Nigel pulled on his shirt and began fastening the tiny buttons.

Dismay dawned on Amelia/Ann's rounded face. "But all men of your stature have a mistress."

Nigel turned to her with a chilly smile. "My dear, I killed my last."

Her blue eyes became small saucers, and Jane/Elaine clutched her throat. "You didn't! Why?"

"She never stopped blathering, so I shoved her off a cliff in Egypt," he rejoined. "Does that answer your question?"

Strangled squeaks arose from the women, who scrambled off his bed and stumbled for their clothing. They'd likely never dressed so quickly, Nigel thought with cynical disregard.

At the door Amelia/Ann turned, her red hair in wild disarray, her mouth trembling as if she were debating the wisdom of further conversation. Her whitened fingers gripped the crystal doorknob. "You're a cad of the lowest sort, Lord Claradon. How do you live with yourself?"

Seeing the fear and foiled ambition in her eyes, for a moment he almost felt sorry for her. Almost. Nigel hadn't felt sorry for anyone in an age. Pity was a useless, frivolous emotion, either coming from him, or far worse, for him.

He gave the tart another cool look. "Quite well, thank you. I assume you can find your way out, since you found your way in, Ann."

"It's Sophia!" she shrieked. "You don't even remember my name!" She fled, and the oak door slammed heavily behind her.

The blonde paused in pinning up her hair, and she cast him a hopeful look. "My name is Cecile."

"Get out," he snapped.

Snatching up her necklace, she vanished with a colorful mutter.

Nigel sat back on the bed, spent. "Ah, damn," he said. "What the hell is wrong with me? That wasn't even close to an *A* name. Or Jane."

He rose, crossed the room, unlocked a bureau drawer and withdrew a small rosewood box. Inside, upon a nest of black velvet, was the small scorpion amulet that Thomas had given him. Thrown at him, more accurately. Nigel shut the box, turned it over, removed the false bottom, and shook the gem he'd stolen from Karida into his palm. He closed his eyes, imagining her warmth imbuing the jewel. Imagining those deliciously plump, perfect breasts—

With a snort, he turned the box back over. There was a stickpin and a matching pair of cuff links, each piece sporting a single teardrop ruby. Smuggled out of Egypt, the gems were the only treasures left from his successful thieving. *I wear my fortune on my person,* he thought to himself. *Like gold coins covering the eyes of the dead, they guarantee my passage to a better life.*

He fingered the scorpion, the stickpin, and the cuff links, and then he retrieved the box's final item: a faded photograph showing a solemn face and dark eyes far too old and weary for their age.

Nigel's heart twisted. "Soon, Eric," he said softly. "I promise you, soon. I've been remiss, but I promise I'll come for you. I shan't care if I have to lie, steal, cheat, or kill. Whatever it takes, you'll be with me and will never have to suffer again." Eric would know love and the security of being wanted—unlike Nigel himself, who had been rejected by his parents upon learning of his sterility.

The joke is on them, he thought with cold anger.

"How dare you bring trollops into this house!"

Replacing the photograph, Nigel shut the box and replaced it atop his bureau. He turned with a look of bored indifference as his mother entered his bedroom. The dowager countess had a permanently pinched expression, as if her corset was too tight.

"Countess," he replied. He'd refused to call her mother since his accident. He'd been lying on his bed, arm shattered, that throbbing agony equal to the pain in his heart as his parents looked down on him in cold disregard and agreed he was better off pretending to be dead. He briefly considered tucking his shirt into his trousers but decided the king wasn't visiting today.

His mother's rheumy blue gaze swept the rumpled bedsheets. Nigel leaned against the oaken dresser and folded his arms.

"Careful of your step," he drawled.

Horror sketched her features as she glanced downward. "Oh good merciful heaven, what is *that?*"

He shrugged at the used prophylactic lying on the carpet like a molted snakeskin. "My only protection against the pox. Expensive, but worth every shilling when I consider how it guards the family jewels." He tensed inwardly, waiting for her to make a nasty remark, reminding him of the worthlessness of those particular jewels, but she did not. Instead, the countess screeched at him like an avenging harpy.

"I had thought perhaps you'd changed. Now I see you have not. Bringing those . . . *women* to the house in the middle of the day while pretending to be Thomas! Masquerading as your brother, the earl!" Rage shook her slender form as she twisted a linen handkerchief in her hands.

Nigel affected a bored sigh. "I see you've discovered my ruse. Dare I think your original welcome was genuine?"

She ignored his question. "Does your brother have any idea what you are doing here? How you are ruining his good name?"

"Tommy couldn't care less about his name." Nigel sneered. "He's in love with his Jasmine and has no intention of being earl ever again. Especially since I explained how I am the rightful heir."

Reminded of his parents' deception, Nigel felt his heart shrink inside his chest. "But I've managed to right old wrongs, and now I have the papers to prove it. My real birth certificate, with the time of my birth, produced after a rather forceful persuasion. I have a deposition from Thomas testifying that he acknowledges the rightful birth order and renouncing the title. I've hired an influential solicitor who contacted the lord high chancellor and the chief legal advisors to the Crown. The title is now mine, *Nigel's,* and so are all the lands and this estate." He couldn't help adding, "Soon I shall take my seat in the House of Lords. Your worthless son, a politician, Countess."

Her thin lips trembled with rage. "What did you say to convince the physician?"

"A pistol held to one's temple does work miracles in producing the truth." Nigel felt weary beyond his twenty-six years. "The truth about a birthright you and father denied me and gave to my younger twin. When he heard, Thomas abandoned the title and insisted I masquerade in his place until I found proof I was the legitimate heir. *He* was shocked and happy to see that I was not dead."

"It would have been better if you had continued playing dead." The countess shuddered as she glanced again at the discarded prophylactic. "You have not changed for the better, Nigel. Indeed, you are more scandalous and immoral than ever. How you disappoint me."

The words cut to the bone, but he could not let her see how much. Nigel donned an icy smile. It felt like a mask. Granite, even. He was made of granite, and nothing, not even the sharp chisel of cruel maternal words, could chip away at his composure.

"Fret not, Countess," he drawled. "I'll be gone soon. I'm returning to Egypt."

Ignoring him, his mother replied, "I'm leaving for Scotland to visit Amanda. When I return, you had better live up to the responsibilities of the title or you will rue the day of your birth. I will not see you destroy what your father built so carefully."

Nigel laughed bitterly. "Father? He drained the funds, failed to repair the estate so it's now virtually uninhabitable, let our tenant cottages run down, and nearly bankrupted us. If not for Tommy's shrewd financial moves, we'd be ruined. But be off. Enjoy Mandy's company while you await your new grandson."

"A grandson *you* can never give me."

Another lash, but it couldn't touch his granite heart. Nigel gave an insouciant shrug. "I'll leave that to Tommy and Jasmine. I'm certain they'll make lovely little babies, perhaps as brown as she."

All color drained from the countess's face. Jasmine's Egyptian heritage was the very reason his mother loathed Thomas's chosen bride. "That brown scorpion . . . and your brother."

She twisted her handkerchief and gave Nigel a calculating look. "At least Thomas would never resort to thievery. And don't deny it," she snapped as he opened his mouth. "I saw those fake bills of sale, Nigel. You've smuggled antiquities from Egypt these past two years. You're a libertine no better than a baseborn thief."

Nigel struggled against rising fury and grief. "Why, Countess, thank you. After all that time trying to please the earl by being perfect, I decided it was time to revert to what I truly am: the product of liars and philanderers." He gave a low, mocking bow.

"What are you babbling about?" his mother snapped.

"Your husband, my father. Mandy's and Thomas's father, and father of perhaps a few others. If I am a libertine, then I am only following in the earl's randy footsteps."

"Your father was an honest man!" the countess replied.

"My father was a liar. He had several mistresses. Who knows how many brothers and sisters I have?"

The countess went very still. "If any such child existed, he would be better off to stay in a place suited to bastards."

"Where is that, Mother? The workhouse, that hell for penniless orphans?"

"Don't be ridiculous," she replied, glancing away. Her voice softened, and it reminded Nigel just how duplicitous his mother was. "Our family has been tainted enough, Nigel. First with the rumors of Mandy's increasing before her marriage, then by your brother living with that . . . woman in Egypt, and then the town learning you faked your own death and ran off to live in America. They believe you're still living in the States. I have a duty to keep the family name free from blemish. If your father did have an indiscretion and sired a bastard, such a child would be best placed where he could never cause scandal."

Nigel's jaw clenched. "Well, I think such a child should be acknowledged and cared for in a good home—as all children should."

Satisfaction filled him as her eyes widened in abject shock. "What are you saying, Nigel? What secret are you hiding?"

A hollow ache settled in his chest. Nigel rubbed the back of his neck. "I'm saying nothing."

But speculation gleamed in his mother's sharp blue eyes. Nigel glanced uneasily at her as she lifted her thin shoulders.

"Our family has suffered enough scandal, and I will not bear any more." Her eyes bored into him. "The only child I will care for is my new grandson. His future is all that matters. Perhaps he will achieve all you have failed to become. All those years I despaired that you would amount to nothing . . . and so you have."

Nigel swept her another mocking bow. "My pleasure, madame, to fulfill your expectations. I aim to please, always."

With a sniff of disgust and a twitch of her black bombazine skirts, the countess swept out of the room and Nigel's life. But cold dread filled him. If she knew about Eric, what measures would she take? Tommy's running off to marry an Egyptian girl and the whispers of Nigel's faked death had nearly driven her mad. When Nigel publicly claimed the title that was rightly his . . . would the countess go as far as finding Eric and putting him on a steamer bound for America, or would she do something far more drastic? Of course, maybe she didn't know about the child.

Nigel's head throbbed. He finished dressing and smoothed down his hair. He shrugged into his coat, pulled up its collar. Picking up his bowler, he put it on his head. He looked about to ensure the countess's carriage was gone and she could not follow him; then he walked quickly out of the neighborhood to hail a cab.

The train he caught pulled into Manchester station several hours later, and he headed straight for a stable and the mount he kept there. Nigel stroked Ariel's velvet nose, and the horse whinnied a greeting.

"Heads up, old boy. Have quite a job for you today. We're taking a journey with a few detours."

The trip involved wending through the countryside to throw off anyone following him, but at last he arrived at a modest, thatched cottage. The house might have been charming but for the grease-smeared windows, flakes of paint peeling off the exterior, and the long-dead garden overrun with dead but spindly weeds. Disgust filled Nigel. What effort was it to apply a few coats of paint, polish the windows?

No effort, if there is money, he grimly reminded himself. It is your duty now to see repairs made.

He loathed leaving Eric here at this tenant cottage, but he had little choice. Richards promised discretion—for a price.

The family's London solicitor was discreet also. Nigel had considered asking him to see to this task, but he inherently distrusted the man and preferred handing over the money himself. The fewer that knew of the boy's existence, the better. Nigel's enemies—the men and women he'd cheated over the past two years—might steal the boy away, or they might perform far darker deeds in order to exact revenge. Eric had become ammunition of a human sort and far deadlier than a regular bullet.

Not that he could blame Eric. The boy was an innocent. And if Nigel had one small soft spot in the granite of his heart, it was for innocents. It had taken Nigel much of the money he'd acquired from smuggling antiquities to save the boy and secure him far away from the countess's grasp.

He hitched Ariel to a rotting post and glanced about before marching up the broken flagstone path to the scarred wooden door. His knock was loud, sharp, and impatient. Ushered inside, he repressed a shudder. The interior was filthy, and dust motes danced in the late afternoon light that managed to pierce the grimy windows. Smells of bacon fat and old cabbage permeated the air.

Nigel removed his hat, looking for a place to set it. As usual, there was no offer to take it, nor of tea after his long journey. Not even an offer to care for his horse. Richards did, however, ask for the money.

With a snort of disgust, Nigel removed the bills from his pocketbook and handed them over. Richards licked his thumb and began to count in his slow, laborious way. Nigel bit back impatience. "Where is the boy?" he finally growled.

"Outside." Richards finished counting and shook his head with a heavy sigh. Dread speared Nigel. *Not again, no, not again . . .* "'Tis not enough, milord. Costs is rising. Can't afford . . ."

Nigel's eyes closed as he listened to the familiar refrain. Twice now in the past months the price had risen. He'd barely scraped enough this time and had no desire to steal any more of Thomas's Egyptian collection. The cost of care, silence, and discretion was quite high.

"I can't pay you more," he snapped. "Enough is enough."

"Yes, milord." But a devious light flickered in Richards's eyes.

Nigel clenched his fists. If he removed Eric from this place, where could the boy be put? He lacked sufficient funds to ensure the child's future, and until he had it, he dared not risk bringing him out in the open. Money. He needed scads of money. Money to put Eric in a quiet country home, provide for his schooling and care, far from the clutches of those who would harm him, shame him for being a bastard, or worse, return him to the workhouse.

"I want to see him, and I must water my mount." Nigel strode out the back door. The hinges creaked and groaned like old bones.

Money, money, always the need for more. When would enough be enough? When he had the treasure of the pharaohs. Only then could he relax.

Eric was tending the pigs, slopping them with leftover food. Nigel ducked behind a poplar to watch.

Despite the chilly wind, the boy was bareheaded and in a thin jacket, patches of it worn through. Half his bucket's contents were poured into a long wood trough; then Eric dipped into the pail and brought a handful of the greasy scraps to his lips. He glanced about furtively before gobbling them down.

Nigel clenched his fists. The boy was fed regularly, but old habits from the workhouse died slow; Eric ate whenever and whatever he could. Nigel waited until the boy finished. Then, forcing a bright smile, he stepped from behind the tree and waved.

Eric saw him. Jade eyes pierced Nigel, green as his own. *He does look like me,* Nigel admitted.

The joyous grin the boy gave twisted his heart. He wanted Eric to smile like that always.

"Sir!" Eric dropped the rusty bucket and ran forward. Nigel accepted the furious embrace, his hand dropping to stroke the boy's hair. Alarm filled him as he felt the thinness of Eric's shoulders.

"Where is that lovely warm coat I brought you?" Nigel moderated his tone so that Eric would not sense his fury.

"Gone. They's sold it. Said they needed the money, and that my old one, it'd do fine. I didn't need none of them fancy threads."

"They sold it. Not they's sold it. Those fancy threads. I didn't need *any of those* fancy threads," Nigel corrected, his stomach churning. The longer he left Eric here, the worse his grammar and clothing became.

"You didn't need those fancy threads either, sir?"

Nigel laughed and ruffled Eric's blond hair. "Watch the cheek, lad. Come, help me tend to my horse."

The boy chattered readily in the manner of any seven-year-old denied company for too long. He fetched a bucket and let Ariel have a long drink, and Nigel wiped the gelding down.

As Eric rubbed Ariel's nose, he glanced shyly at Nigel. "I never can thank you enough, sir, for getting me out of that place."

"No thanks is necessary," Nigel managed, his throat closing. "Are they treating you well enough here?"

Bony shoulders lifted. "It's fine."

Nigel picked up Eric's hands, his heart wrenching. Ugly scars crossed the boy's palms, results of wicked beatings at the workhouse. The dank, filthy conditions and the emaciated inhabitants there had nearly made Nigel retch. He now leashed the urge to envelop the boy in a hug, scoop him up onto his horse, and gallop away. Instead, he squatted down so that they were eye to eye.

"Listen to me, Eric. You do what you can to tough it out. You're a fighter, I know it. And one day, I promise, I shall take you away from here."

Doubt lingered in the boy's clear green eyes. "Where, sir?"

"Someplace grand, where you'll get all you want. Whatever you want."

Eric licked his lips. "Meat pies? I had a meat pie once. It was right good."

"More than that," Nigel assured him. "A new house far away in the country, with your own bedchamber. Your own horse. Fine clothing, all the food you want, and school."

The boy's eyes widened, and Nigel saw in them a flickering hope. It mirrored his own. "I've always wanted schooling, sir. I'd like to know reading."

"You shall. You'll go to the finest school, and you'll be the best reader in the class." Nigel hesitated. "It's just going to take a little time. But it will happen. Trust me."

Trust him? The words almost choked him. He was a cad who lied and stole and cheated. No one had ever trusted him.

Not his parents, his sister, or even his twin. But the shining hope in Eric's eyes could not be denied.

"I trust you, sir."

Nigel's nod was curt, belying his passion. No matter what else he did in his miserable life, he'd see to it that Eric had a good home. The boy would never have to endure another beating, having his coat stolen, or sharing scraps with pigs. All it would take was scads of money.

Chapter Five

Taking tea in a stiff English drawing room proved far more complicated than sipping strong Arabic coffee in her tent.

The earl of Smithfield's London home had a quiet elegance and dignity. On a small table was a silver salver covered with lace. Only the plethora of Egyptian artifacts decorating the tables and sideboards made it seem a little like home.

Arranged in a semicircle, the embroidered chairs each held a member of society's upper set. Karida willed her rapidly beating heart to calm as she curled a hand around the delicate china cup. No, that wasn't right. Use the handle. She'd done this before, taken tea, but it was years past—and never while acting as an English lady while staring at the very man who had robbed her. Lord Thomas Claradon. His name was burned into her mind like a brand.

From the gossip her aunt Katherine had gathered, Claradon had left both Cairo and Jasmine, the Egyptian woman he was to marry. Small wonder she did not look at him with favor, but she had grudgingly admitted he was a possible catch while poring over names with Karida and Lady Smithfield. Claradon had become one of the select eligible bachelors invited to their tea.

The earl's suit was finely tailored, and his dark brown chestnut hair uncovered. His jade eyes kept flicking her way.

What a simpleton you are, Lord Claradon. You fail to see who I really am, and all the while you imagine I never realized you stole my property.

True, she looked different than she had in Egypt, where a veil had mostly concealed her features. Her silk gown felt nothing like the traditional kuftan she wore in the desert. Her black hat with its wide brim trimmed with ostrich feathers was ridiculously large, but it proved effective in shading her expression.

At her throat was a fine emerald brooch, a gift from Lord Smithfield. The earl had agreed to be her sponsor. After hearing of the disaster of her failed marriage, he had asked his new wife, Dolores, to take Karida shopping. The woman had showered Karida with gowns, hats, fripperies—all she needed to play the role of an English lady. Karida wondered if Dolores knew she was the result of the earl's former indiscretion. No matter. Her plan was proceeding splendidly.

Her identity was changed. Instead of Karida, the Egyptian girl, she was a visitor newly arrived from Cairo after years of living abroad with her parents. Her name was Miss Anne Mitchell, daughter of good friends of Lord and Lady Smithfield, who had arrived in London to partake in the social season.

Lord Smithfield. He still claims no kinship with me, Karida thought with bitterness.

On the embroidered chairs of the drawing room sat the earl and his wife, Lady Smithfield, plus Karida's aunt Katherine. Five eligible men joined them, along with Lord Claradon. Five men who stared at her with rapturous gazes. But she had seen similar looks on other men's faces before they heard of the defects beneath her layers of clothing.

A white-capped maid brought sandwiches on a silver salver and began serving. Lord Claradon settled into a blue and gold silk chair, his long legs crossed at the ankles. He was elegantly attired in a starched white shirt, black silk tie, and neatly pressed black linen suit.

One of the other guests, Lord Percy, spoke up. "I daresay, Miss Mitchell, it must have been dreadfully dull living in Egypt all these years."

Mr. Hodges picked up a cucumber sandwich and gave it a

nibble. "And yet you survived quite splendidly. It proves that good English blood can weather the harshest of foreign places."

"My good English blood is indeed adept at surviving the harshest of circumstance," Karida agreed as she settled her cup into its china saucer. "I am equally at home with all of you as I am with Egyptians or the humblest working-class people. I have observed how equal we all are, despite the differences of our births." How true the words! Had she not seen an earl behave like a common thief?

"You embrace a radical viewpoint, Miss Mitchell," noted that very man. His keen green gaze focused on her. "As radical as that embraced by the Fabian Society, those avant-garde liberals who sputter that the poor should be given privileges much as the upper class."

"Then, sir, I should deign to know more of them and their principles, for they seem an agreeable group," she shot back.

A small smile touched Lord Claradon's mouth. The other guests exchanged uneasy glances.

Lord Percy stared at Karida with large, liquid eyes, reminding her of a sheep. "Oh, bother, let's not talk of such plodders as those Fabians. I'd rather discuss Miss Mitchell's plans while she's in London. I insist you attend the small supper my mother is hosting."

Two other eager offers followed. Lord Claradon regarded Karida the whole while. Karida took a small bite of scone buttered with rich Devonshire cream and glanced at him. His tongue darted out, licked the corner of his lip with deliberate slowness. The breath caught in Karida's lungs. Her body tingled pleasantly.

After a moment, Claradon tapped the corner of his mouth. Karida touched her lip, which sported a dab of clotted cream. A furious blush raced across her face, and she scrubbed her lips with a damask napkin. The earl gave her a cocky half smile.

She took some tea, and her china cup rattled as she replaced it on the saucer. Karida lifted her cool gaze to her other hopeful suitors. "I shall make time and consider your very generous offers."

"There is the ball tonight at the Hobbsons'," Smithfield hinted. "Miss Mitchell will be in attendance, gentlemen."

Lord Claradon's eyes sparkled. Karida pushed down sudden unease.

"I have an invitation you cannot refuse, Miss Mitchell," he drawled. "A small supper party at my town house." He leaned back, a lazy smile playing about his mouth. "Excellent cuisine, fine wine and, if you join us, exquisite company. If you pine for simple desert fare, I can arrange for us to sit on the floor, Bedu style. To make you more comfortable."

Perspiration beaded on Karida's forehead at the earl's slow, assessing look. "Heavens, that would prove difficult and indecorous in a gown," she said.

The others all laughed.

"True. Egyptian garb better suits their customs. Yet I surmise from your comments that you believe Egyptians to be adaptable like Englishmen. A Bedouin might blend perfectly should you take him out of the desert and put him in other attire—say, English clothing. He might shine at a tea party. Indeed, he might even put on a performance worthy of Shakespearean theatre."

"If Shakespeare spoke Arabic," she retorted.

Admiration shone in his eyes. "Touché," he replied.

As Lord Claradon shifted, adjusting his black necktie, a ruby winked in the light of a nearby lamp and caught Karida's attention. The breath stalled in her throat. Claradon's gold stickpin was adorned with a large ruby shaped like a teardrop—the sacred ruby he'd stolen from her! Her mind raced. His supper party might accord the chance to retrieve it.

"I shall have the invitation sent round tomorrow, for you and your lovely wife and daughter as well, Smithfield," he was saying.

Karida's father frowned. "Katherine, Lady Smithfield, and I have another engagement. I'm afraid we must decline."

Lord Claradon cocked his head. "Then I beg you, please come for tea tomorrow. I have some rather delicious Arabic coffee to remind you of Egypt. Having traveled there several times myself, I wish to engage in conversation with Miss Mitchell about it. I would not bore the others here with such talk, but there are so few, I fear, who truly appreciate her rare beauty. Egypt's, I mean." He gave Karida a meaningful glance.

Lord Smithfield eyed her, too, his expression thoughtful. She hastened to assure him. "Oh, do let's accept."

Smithfield's wife gave a pretty little laugh. "Yes, Landon. I haven't touched Arabic coffee in an age, and we should give Anne all the social opportunities availed to her during her stay. She should be brightly displayed for all to see!"

Smithfield smiled at his wife. "Very well, my dear."

Delight soared through Karida. "Then we accept your invitation, Lord Claradon."

The first stage of the plan was set.

Miss Anne Mitchell was a lovely fraud.

Landon and his wife Dolores had invited Nigel and these other eligible bachelors to afternoon tea to meet her, allegedly just arrived from Cairo after years of living abroad. They had opened their London town house to cautiously test the London season after many years of quiet living at their country estate, all to give their friends' daughter a chance at society. But Nigel's brain clicked and whirred like a clock. The bone china teacup in his big hand felt as delicate as an eggshell. He set it down, bit into a buttered scone, and boldly assessed the lady in question.

Her black and white silk gown clung to delicious curves once hidden by layers of Egyptian cloth. Her hips were rounded and, ah, those breasts! They were as firm and generous as he had wickedly imagined. But what the hell was Karida doing here? He and Karida were both frauds, he thought with dark amusement.

Her cumbersome yet fashionable black hat with its netting

and ostrich feathers was cocked at a jaunty angle. It shaded her pert nose, exotic amber eyes, and silky eyebrows. But that mouth he'd recognize anywhere. A symmetrical wet rosebud, the lower lip plumped in a constant pout.

His erotic dreams had centered on that mouth lately, those full lips parting as he bent to taste their exquisite perfection. He hungered for that. And he would explore further with his tongue, a sensual pirate determined to plunder all her secrets, including those better guarded secret hollows. Would she be like thick, golden honey as he lavished slow, thorough strokes between her legs? Or was she more exotic, a heady spice like cardamom? Or sweet as sin? His sex grew hard at the thought, and he had to shift in his seat.

His gaze affixed to her once more, to her very English striped gown, to that ridiculous hat and the prim mannerisms. Karida thought to disguise herself from him? What pluck! But he could tell her anywhere. All from that wet, reddened mouth and the sensual promise lingering there.

A slow smile touched his mouth as thoughts too indecent for afternoon tea raced through his mind. So, she thought to play games, to perhaps catch him unawares and take back what he had stolen from her.

What I stole from her. His smile faded. No matter what the disguise, she was still a lady, and he was still a thief and a cad. She'd made clear her thoughts of him, of his unworthiness. Her disdain marked him as surely as the scars on his arm. The label she'd given him felt like a hot razor drawn across his skin: dirty desert jackal.

We jackals steal what we wish, my lady, he told her silently. *Beware of our thieving ways, lest you lose more than a ruby.* He longed to steal her virtue, to leave her with memories of erotic pleasure that would heat her body on cold nights long after he'd slipped from her bed. Months after he'd plundered her treasure, Karida would awaken in the dark night and remember his mouth upon her secret places and tremble with want.

The idea thickened his blood and made his heart pound. But as Nigel pondered the thought, he dismissed it. Such passion demanded control. Games he could not play. Karida could never set her long, elegant fingers upon the ruby or the scorpion amulet to which it belonged, and so he would never plunder the hidden riches of her lush, beautiful body. He had too much else at stake. But he had to keep watch over her. She planned something. And when she sprang into action, he would be ready.

Chapter Six

From a small velvet settee in a dark corner, Nigel watched the assembled crowd on the polished parquet floor. London's elite attended the Hobbsons' ball in stiff dinner dress and finely beaded evening gowns. An enormous leaded crystal chandelier dangled over their carefully coiffed heads. The domed ceiling featured a painting of the bluest sky he'd ever seen in London. Many of the ladies resembled exotic hothouse flowers, not the least of which "Miss Mitchell." Though Karida's presence made his blood burn, something else made Nigel's heart race even faster: tonight he would finally cease imitating his identical twin.

He removed a coin from his waistcoat and assumed the courteous, banal smile always worn by his twin. He tossed the coin into the air, caught it.

Out of the corner of his eye, he spotted William Oakley and Tommy's other friends approaching from across the ballroom. Even if he was a half-wit, Oakley was a fun fellow, always drawing laughs and eager for games of cards and sport. He had made sheep's eyes at Charlotte but good-naturedly stepped aside when she'd claimed Thomas.

Ah, Charlotte. The woman had wanted to be more than Thomas's mistress; she had wanted to be Thomas's wife. But his brother's mistress had had the heart of a whore and come straight into Nigel's bed. The dull ache of guilt pounded through Nigel nonetheless. If the ball's other attendees knew a killer was in their midst, what would they say?

I should have realized Charlotte would go to any measures to get

*rid of Jasmine so she could marry Tommy. I should never have trusted
her with my secrets. If I hadn't, maybe she'd still be alive. Maybe I
wouldn't have had to do what I did.*

Secrets and lies, he was living both. He hadn't any real
friends. Not since childhood and discovery of his parents' de-
ceit. Associating with Tommy's mates while masquerading as
Tommy had chased away a little of the loneliness, but the reprieve was brief. He longed for real connection. Didn't everyone?

Flip, went the coin. Flip.

Soon he'd visit Egypt, find the treasure, and return to England wealthier than the king himself. But then? Would he
have true friends? And what of Eric? Once he brought the
boy back to London and had enough money to ensure his future, Eric would find a place in society, but was it a good place
with a disreputable scoundrel like himself?

I can change, Nigel reminded himself. He could become respectable and presentable, the perfect earl. His parents had
dismissed his usefulness long ago, but Tommy's mates, they
were eager for his company. Gone was the lying, disreputable
Nigel who cheated them at cards and mocked them for their
attitudes. The new earl of Claradon had arrived; surely they
would accept him.

Nigel flipped the coin and caught it, turned it over. Tonight marked a turning point. He would not fail, either in his
quest to gain the treasure or a new place in society. He just
had to reveal the truth.

William Oakley and the others greeted him with a hearty
hello. Nigel tucked the coin into his waistcoat pocket.

After making small talk, Oakley mentioned Nigel's supper.

"And, inviting Miss Mitchell to tea tomorrow? Very clever,
Tommy. A proper beauty, she is. I daresay I might pursue her
myself." He grinned.

"Supper shall be a most stupendous occasion," Nigel promised. "The finest wine, the most exquisite fare." He drew in a deep breath to steel his resolve. "Let's adjoin to somewhere private. I've something to tell you fellows. Something you must know."

Five faces exchanged five equally uneasy looks. Nigel ignored them and led the group out of the ballroom, down the gallery to the Hobbsons' music room. He turned on the gas lamp atop the grand piano and sat on the bench, touching one key.

How he'd missed this, the absorption of running his fingers over a keyboard and losing himself in music. Far too long had his talent been silent, his fingers taking, not creating. Nigel picked out a tune, humming along.

Oakley leaned an elbow on the piano and gave him an odd look. "You never were musical, Tommy. When did you learn?"

Nigel ceased playing. His father had frowned upon learning the piano. He'd called such talent "womanly," and as a result Nigel had learned in secret.

"Just toying," he said absently. He looked at the others, leaning on the piano and resembling expectant spaniels waiting for a treat. He couldn't bring himself to speak.

"Bloody hell, don't keep us in suspense anymore, Tommy. Please don't tell us you're returning to that Egyptian chit. I thought you dismissed her."

"Right, Tommy. You *are* over that ridiculous little brown scorpion, aren't you? Tell me you shan't do anything so embarrassing again." Hodges looked truly alarmed.

Nigel chuckled. "I shan't. But I can't account for Tommy. Tommy is in love and will remain so, I'm afraid. But fear not, lads. *I* will never do anything so ridiculous." Emboldened, he plunged ahead. "I'm not Tommy. I'm Nigel. It's been me all along, since returning earlier this month."

Silence descended for a brutal heartbeat; then Hodges broke out in his horselike laugh. "Good show, Tommy. What a joke!

Nigel. Right! He's long gone—to America after he had the gall to fake his death. Remember how you told us? Good riddance, I say."

"America or a coffin. Either is fine with me," muttered Oakley. "Not to speak ill of your brother, Tommy, but Nigel was far from a gentleman. He cheated me of a fair amount at cards. And he was a libertine. A seducer."

Nigel's smile slipped. Silence descended.

"It is me—*Nigel*. Here, I'll prove it."

Shrugging out of his coat, he next unfastened the gold cuff link and rolled up the sleeve of his immaculate white dress shirt. Ugly pink and white scars marred the muscled flesh of his left forearm.

"Good God," Hodges whispered.

"Surgery in America after I fell off that damn Arabian." Nigel rolled down the sleeve, replaced his coat, and explained everything: the fake funeral, his discovery of how his parents illicitly claimed Thomas was the older twin, his eventual desire to return to London and find proof he was firstborn and the rightful heir. Their faces whitened as they studied him and then each other.

"I truly thought you were Tommy. You've acted so jolly and thoughtful; and Nigel was, er, I mean you were always a bit of a selfish bastard . . ." Hodges trailed off.

"That was before. I've changed, fellows. For the good," Nigel assured them.

"Have you?" Oakley's voice sounded strained.

"I have, and I'll prove it. How much did I take from you, Oakley? I admit it was unjust."

The blond man muttered a sum.

Nigel nodded and said, "I'll find a way to repay you, I promise. Soon, I shall have money." His gaze swept over the other incredulous faces. "And anyone else, if I cheated you, I apologize. Come now, let's let bygones be bygones. Shall we? I need your advice. Tommy, when he admitted I was the rightful heir, wanted to ensure changes were made in the tenant cottages. I need to hire an efficient steward to oversee the estate. Have you any recommendations?"

Slowly the group began talking, and quite a few good suggestions were made. Nigel relaxed and smiled. Yes, it was certainly much easier to be accepted. And a leopard could indeed change its spots.

He sprang up, deciding enough had been accomplished for the night. "Shall we return? The ladies are waiting for the pleasure of our company." He returned to the ballroom, expecting them to follow.

At the door, however, he spotted a vision clad in ice green silk and dancing stiffly with a sunken-faced older gentleman, and Nigel's calm vanished. Karida.

Her raven tresses were swept up in an elegant knot, with stray tendrils artfully arranged to frame her heart-shaped face. Pearls woven into her hair gleamed in the overhead light. Cosmetics had altered her appearance slightly, reddening her lips and cheeks, but Nigel could have picked her from a crowd of a thousand beauties. That perfect mouth.

Elbow-length white gloves adorned her long, slender arms, and her gown was embroidered with glass beads and silver thread that set her coloring off to perfection. The bodice tastefully displayed an expanse of golden flesh, and Nigel found himself staring once more at her breasts. This time her considerable assets were highlighted, not hidden.

Emeralds the size of small coins adorned a necklace accenting her lovely, slender neck. Nigel's eyes widened at the sight. Lord, she wore a fortune in jewels!

Her hands maintained a loose grip on her partner. Nigel swallowed hard. Those were such perfect hands, perfect hands with slender fingers that would never willingly touch him, jackal that he was. Anger and lust spurred him on. Though he

knew it best to watch discreetly from a distance, he hungered
to feel her in his arms. Surely she could not refuse the offer of
a dance!

An elegant dinner. Equally elegant gowns with expensive
beading on every dancer. Tiny silver slippers. And dancing
with sour-faced gentlemen smelling of cigar smoke and fruity
cologne. Karida headed for an obscure corner, looking to escape the ball.

Near where she walked, dressed in black evening wear, the
earl of Smithfield sat on a burgundy velvet settee. Karida approached with caution. Oh heavens, would he order her back
to the dance floor with yet another possible beau?

He merely gave her a smile. "Come and sit." He patted a
space beside him.

Karida sat, glad for the reprieve. If she had to accept one
more invitation from a stodgy gentleman who kept talking
about himself, she'd run out of the ballroom. Lady Smithfield
was chatting with several women nearby, and she kept glancing Karida's way with reassuring smiles. Katherine had murmured excuses, wishing to stay home. Karida knew her aunt
had chosen wisely.

"Are you happy?" the earl asked quietly.

She managed a small smile for her unacknowledged father.
"I have much to be thankful for, my lord: my home and my
parents, and all they have given me." Her words held a world
of meaning.

"Good to hear. I always wondered about that decision to
send you to Egypt. It isn't an easy life." The earl fell silent,
looking troubled.

"It's been a good life. And I am loved."

"Do you like those jewels?" The earl smiled and indicated
her emerald necklace. "They suit your coloring."

"Quite beautiful, my lord. But I insist that you are far too generous." Karida bit her lip. That last sentiment was her first lie in ages.

My very existence is a lie, she thought bitterly. *I am your dirty little secret.* Generous? Lord Smithfield? When he'd packed her off to Egypt as easily as a trunk?

Questions burned inside her. Karida clasped her gloved hands together and sat straighter, the pose reminding her of that long ago day when she'd sat in the earl's house, wondering what fate awaited her.

"My real mother," she blurted. "What happened to her?"

Color drained from the earl's face. He glanced around, as if searching for eavesdroppers. His mouth became a tight line.

"Please," Karida pressed. "I have the right to know."

His eyes, so unlike hers, filled with remorse. "Lady Cardew died four years after you went to Egypt. I made inquiries, fearing she might return to demand more money, and heard she'd been confined to a sanatorium."

"Sanatorium? Was she very ill?"

The earl's voice was low. "Consumption."

Karida tried to feel something for the woman who had birthed her. It was difficult.

Seeing her expression, Smithfield patted her hand, an obvious gesture meant to comfort. "I would have helped her financially had I known she was in such dire straits."

"I'm glad you did not," Karida replied. The tone of her voice said it all.

The earl looked away, scanning the ballroom as if desperate for lighter conversation. "Katherine tells me you have a remarkable talent for making jewelry. Tell me about it." He looked genuinely interested.

Amused at the idea of discussing Bedouin jewelry in this high society ball, Karida began explaining the process. Her father asked several intelligent, pointed questions. Hope filled her as he remarked on the valuable pieces he'd purchased himself on his travels through Egypt. He truly seemed interested in her craft. Here was the key to acceptance and respect.

Yet, the question lingering on the tip of her tongue was yet to be asked: Did you send me away to Egypt simply to be kept secret? Are you happy I'm back?

As Karida summoned the courage to ask, a man in distinguished evening dress crossed the ballroom toward her. A striking man. A hank of chestnut hair hung over his forehead, and his confident swagger bespoke an arrogance indifferent to others' good opinions. As she well knew. It was Lord Thomas Claradon.

A shiver wracked Karida's spine. Last night she'd dreamed of Thomas, dark, erotic dreams of pleasures he could deliver with those long fingers as they stroked her neck, then sinfully caressed the space between her legs. Her innocent dreams of Kareem's chaste kisses had faded, burned away by the fiery torment sparked by Claradon's touch, the heated promise in his green gaze. She had awoken deeply shaken, her body aching and feverish.

She stiffened as he approached, gathered her composure.

The formality of his bow impressed even her father, who nodded. As Lord Claradon straightened, his gaze rested on her. "Miss Mitchell. I beg favor of a dance." Thomas glanced at Lord Smithfield. "If it is permissible, Smithfield?"

"Anne is free to choose whomever she wishes."

Lord Claradon held out a white-gloved hand. He was dressed in the manner of all the gentlemen present, in resplendent black dinner dress, crisply starched white shirt and tie, and elegant cuff links. But each cuff link was adorned with a single teardrop ruby.

Karida's heart pounded. Oh, good heavens! How could she tell which ruby was hers? Did he make it a habit of stealing jewels and making them into jewelry?

"Miss Mitchell?" Lord Claradon prompted. His inquiring gaze rested on Karida.

She stood with languid grace, hiding her fury. He clasped her hand and escorted her onto the dance floor.

Thomas acted the part of a gentleman but was a thief at heart. *Insolent ass,* she thought in white-hot anger as she placed a hand on his strong, broad shoulder. But at least Lord Claradon did not reek of overpowering fruity cologne or cigar smoke. He smelled deliciously clean, tinged with a faint aroma of spices reminding her of the sandalwood used by Khamsin warriors.

Claradon waltzed as he did all else, boldly and with vigor and energy, sweeping her about as the string orchestra played "The Emperor Waltz." Karida didn't fret about stepping on his toes, inexperienced as she was; his easy and commanding style merely dictated she follow his lead. It was indicative of his personality, she mused.

She stiffened as Thomas bent his head toward her.

"My dear, delightful Miss Mitchell. You are as lovely as an exotic flower, and as enchanting and mysterious as the Sphinx herself, naked though she may be in the hot desert sand," he murmured into her ear. His hand lightly clasped her waist. He did not attempt to pull her close or touch her in an unseemly manner, but the heat blazing in his eyes said enough. Clearly he was attracted to her.

"Lord Claradon. I should slap your face. Do try to pretend, at least, that you possess some manners. Or is that too much to presume?"

"Your tongue is sharp," he replied, looking unfazed.

They shifted, making a turn, and light gleamed off a ruby cuff link. Karida's breath hitched. She dragged her gaze elsewhere and found herself staring at his mouth hovering near hers in bold invitation. Beneath dark brows, his eyes glinted like the emeralds of her necklace.

"A tongue sharp as, say, a *jambiyah*," he continued. "You're familiar with it, seeing as you traveled extensively in Egypt?"

"A curved dagger. My father always carries one," she mused, unable to drag her gaze away from those full lips.

"Your father is Egyptian?"

Karida caught herself. "A man who is dear to me like a father," she corrected. Flustered, she missed a step and muttered a vague curse in Arabic.

"Manners, manners, Miss Mitchell," Thomas reproved and pulled her along with him to resume the dance.

Karida reminded herself to be more careful but steeled herself to do what she must. "Lord Claradon," she remarked, "I was curious about the rather unusual stickpin you wore today at tea. Might I ask where you acquired it?"

"The ruby is Egyptian, one of the rare antiquities I acquired in Cairo. Not terribly expensive, for it has a flaw, but of sentimental value. That's why I had it made into a stickpin. To keep it close," he remarked.

I'm certain, she thought with rising anger. "What an extraordinary idea."

His smile was wide. "It's rather colorful, and we men can dress so dully. Do you not think?"

"Why not wear it always?" she asked.

He gave a careless shrug. "Some nights it's best tucked away from street thieves. But let's discuss something much more interesting, Miss Mitchell. *You.* Tell me, where in Egypt did you stay all those years abroad? Did you visit the pyramids? Sail the Nile?"

Karida made polite conversation as they continued the dance, relieved to talk about something so ordinary after his initial comment about thieves. He asked her several pointed questions about the ancient step pyramids. However, as the music ended and he led her off the dance floor, Thomas's penetrating green gaze held hers. He lifted her gloved hand to his lips and said, "Do tell me, have you ever visited the Bedu? There is a fascinating tribe called the Khamsin living in the remote Eastern Desert who raise purebred Arabians. Perhaps you have heard of them."

Karida's heart pounded. "I have indeed visited the Bedu,

even lived with them for a while. But who are these Kham-sin?" It wasn't quite a lie. Karida prided herself on her evasion.

Thomas's dark eyebrow arched. "You are not familiar with them? Smithfield's daughter Katherine is married to one."

Caught. Karida nibbled on her lower lip. As she did, she saw Thomas's eyes widen and darken. His gaze rested on her mouth.

"Lovely," he murmured.

Karida frowned. "The Khamsin?"

"What they breed. The females are exquisite." There was a cunning, calculating sparkle in his eye. "I talk of Arabians, of course. But you have never heard of the Khamsin warriors of the wind, despite your sponsor's daughter marrying one and despite your long journeys in Egypt."

Again Karida nibbled on her lower lip. A pulse beat at the base of Thomas's throat. His eyes stayed glued to her mouth.

Awash in hopes of a clever reply, she couldn't help but realize Thomas was intensely attracted to her. Perhaps she had a means to distract him, to divert his attention and steal the ruby. But how did one flirt? Rarely had men shown interest, so she was inexperienced in the art. And Karida was too proud to risk rejection stupidly.

She placed a gloved hand on his arm, a light touch that seemed appropriate. "Such talk of the past is boring me, Lord Claradon. I came to England not to reminisce but to learn. I would rather talk about you."

Most men in her experience puffed like proud peacocks at such a request, began chatting about their many achievements. Lord Claradon was different. His gaze grew distant.

"My accomplishments," he said, "are not as illustrious as those of some other men. You might even find them lacking." The truth—for a moment she sensed he offered it. Then he gave a charming smile that failed to reach his eyes. "Do accompany me as I fetch you a cup of punch. Dancing must have given you quite a thirst."

"I am fine," she replied.

"Are you?" He arched a dark, heavy brow. "You are look-ing flushed, dear lady." He held out his arm, and she reluc-tantly took it.

Orange slices floated in the ruby liquid filling the crystal punch bowl. Lord Claradon poured two cups and then guided Karida to a quiet corner by heavy blue velvet drapes. She took a healthy swallow and coughed.

"Rum punch. It *is* rather strong tonight," Thomas hinted with a smile. "And if you are not used to imbibing, such as Arabs are not, it can have quite an effect."

Alarm ran through her. He had not seen through her guise, had he?

Karida took another sip, mostly to prove him wrong. "Though I have visited the Egyptian peoples, it does not mean I follow all their beliefs." True enough. She did not.

"Of course you don't," he demurred. "And I hope you will see that I am a gentleman and will come to my little supper party even if Smithfield cannot attend. In the meantime, I look forward with great anticipation to coffee." He gazed down at her with the look of a man ensnared by beauty. "Indeed, I would even deign to serve you myself and dismiss those both-ersome servants who lack awareness of Bedouin custom." A twinkle entered his green eyes. "We might sit on the floor as the Bedu are apt to do, recline like wealthy pashas . . ."

"It sounds very hedonistic," she murmured.

"Of course. It would be," he drawled. "But instead I will do my best to impress your sponsor so that you will join my sup-per party. You would be quite well chaperoned if you came without him, I assure you. There will be scads of my friends present. You shouldn't be alone with me for one minute . . . unless you wish it."

"And if I wish it?" she dared.

"I shall do my utmost to accommodate your every desire." He placed his cup of punch on a small table and took her hand. Raising it to his mouth, he pressed a kiss to her gloved knuckles. Through the soft cotton covering, Karida felt the incendiary heat. She remained motionless, knowing she should pull away but compelled to immobility as he hovered over her hand. She resisted the impulse to rub the glove against her cheek, as if to transfer the feel of his mouth to the bare skin there.

As he released her hand, Karida sought to regain her composure. "And how long will we dine at this particular supper party? I must not remain out late. The earl is very strict," she remarked.

"I promise, you shall be in bed at the very stroke of midnight." His dark green gaze smoldered. "We'll dine, engage in sparkling conversation and equally sparkling company, and indulge in a bottle or two of my finest wine. It shall be a lovely evening with you at my side, if I may be so bold. But I shall warn you: I have a tendency to be bold indeed when faced with such exquisite beauty."

He was staring at her mouth, rapt. Karida's breath hitched. Her heart raced with eager anticipation.

Lord Claradon tugged at the index finger of his dancing glove with his teeth and freed his hand. "You are so lovely," he murmured, reaching for her cheek.

Mindful of the last time he touched her, Karida pulled away.

Regret darkened his gaze. "My apologies. I quite forgot myself. I can be a gentleman, despite what others say."

Karida wondered at the pain in his tone. "What do others say?"

His broad shoulders shrugged, raising the dark silk of his jacket. "Shall we forget it happened and start over?"

His eyes reflected anger—and it was clearly at himself. Karida's heart twisted. What a complex man this was, two-sided and two-faced like a coin. Which was the real face? Who was this Thomas, a thief or a gentleman? Or was he merely a cad and the lowest desert jackal? Why had he stolen her ruby?

His fingers were tanned, long and elegant, yet she remembered the soft rasp of callused flesh as he'd stroked her neck in the desert. Gentlemen did not have calluses. They did not work, and their hands were soft and white, not brown from the sun.

Reckless abandon filled her. Karida stared down at her right hand and began tugging off her own glove. Her voice was husky. "Yes, let's start over."

Bewilderment touched Claradon's expression. "Miss Mitchell, what are you doing?"

She did not reply. When her hand came free of its elbow-length glove, she let it fall close to his. Thomas studied it. His long, elegant fingers brushed against her naked ones so briefly it might have been an accident, yet she felt him trembling as if he'd touched a hot iron.

Emboldened, she picked up his hand and turned it over, but again suspicion shot through her. The calluses on his palm were rough and fresh. This was no nobleman and dandy who idled in his club, smoking cigars. Who was he?

Thomas pulled his hand away to slide it beneath hers. He held on with gentle reverence, like he was cradling a small bird. His thumb lightly stroked her palm, making tiny circles in a dance more erotic than the one they'd already shared. He stared at her with heavy-lidded eyes.

"Exquisite," he murmured.

Wonder filled her body like delicious heat, and her loins felt heavy and full. No one had ever looked at her like this.

Voices sounded nearby. Thomas dropped her hand as if it were on fire. He stepped back and pulled on his glove.

Dismay replaced Karida's desire. How had she allowed this thief to steal away her good sense? Hadn't she learned her lesson the first time? Men such as this would strip everything from her: honor, morality. Virtue. They'd strip clean everything and leave her bones bleaching in the dry desert sun.

Her heart pounding, Karida redonned her glove, her hand

quivering so much she struggled to pull the cotton up her bare forearm. Thomas said nothing but grasped the glove and assisted. Each brush of his fingers against her bare skin made her blood race.

When he'd finished, she yanked free of him. "Please, I beg you, do not touch me again," she said in a low voice.

"I apologize for being so forward. I do hope you will not change your mind and will still come for coffee tomorrow." A thin, sarcastic smile touched his mouth as he added, "I promise I shan't dare hand you a coffee cup but will serve you on a silver platter as you deserve."

"I'd be delighted," she murmured.

"Excellent. Until tomorrow." He glanced to his right. "Ah, I see your caretaker is searching for you. I will let you go, before he takes me to task for stealing you away."

Lord Claradon executed a perfect bow as the earl of Smithfield strode up. Karida's father flashed Thomas a dubious look, but Thomas thrust his hands into the pockets of his trousers and strode off. A shiver stroked Karida's spine.

"He'd had you far too long. Are you all right?" the earl queried.

"He's quite harmless," she replied. "I do believe he is nothing to worry about." Karida rubbed the top of her gloved knuckles, dismayed to realize she was lying again. "Nothing at all."

Chapter Seven

The drawing room was comfortable, and the smell of coffee a pungent reminder of Egypt. To Karida's surprise, Lord Claradon began by bringing her and the earl of Smithfield, his wife, and Katherine into the music room and playing a whimsical, skilled rendition of Mozart's "Turkish Rondo." His fingers flew over the keyboard, his brow furrowed in concentration. Gone was any cynical look in those jade eyes, replaced by simple passion. When he finished, his guests applauded loudly, every one.

He apologized for being out of practice. "I usually prefer Russian composers but thought this would match the exotic flavor of our Arabic coffee," he quipped.

Today he wore both the ruby stickpin and cuff links. Karida wondered if he owned ruby hairpins to add to his thick chestnut hair, like a woman determined to flash all her precious jewelry.

The guests returned to the drawing room for coffee. Karida kept a discreet distance but kept her gaze on Thomas.

"Sugar?" Lord Claradon proffered a bowl on a silver tray to each of his guests, finishing with her. "I'm afraid I lack dates to sweeten the coffee, as the Bedu use."

Karida expertly held the tiny handleless cup with two fingers, curling out her pinky. As she took a sip, relishing the cardamom flavor, her English masquerade fell away for a moment, her pretty linen day dress and fancy hat. She closed her eyes, feeling the desert sun warm her cheeks once more, and hearing the distant bleating of sheep and chatter of the boys herding them. There followed an unexpected rush of home-sickness.

But where is my home? she thought with a pang of anguish. *Am I English, or have I turned into a Bedouin for always?*

Karida opened her eyes. The answer gleamed on Lord Claradon's stickpin, reminding her of the heavy responsibility she carried. She had made a promise to keep this treasure safe, and Lord Claradon had stolen the ruby. If she did not retrieve it, she would have failed in her vow. That promise meant everything to her.

Almost everything. Her gaze flicked over to the earl of Smithfield. She wondered if he would ever be cajoled into accepting her as his daughter.

Biting into a honeyed cake covered with almond slices, Karida had to agree it was splendid. She complimented Lord Claradon on his cook.

He shrugged. "I'm afraid I made the cakes myself. Cook is rather narrow-minded. She sees Bedouin fare as lowering, doesn't want to demean her position by preparing 'foreign' cakes. Snobbery exists even among the lower classes."

"I've found there is a great deal more equality among certain Bedu tribes than London society," Lord Smithfield interjected, taking a sip of coffee.

"Indeed," agreed Katherine. "Living among the Bedu has taught me much about what is important. They definitely have a class equality that England lacks. The English could learn quite a bit from them."

"Lady Katherine, you sound as if *you* belong to the Fabian Society," Lord Claradon remarked. Karida remembered him making a similar riposte to her own comments.

Lord Smithfield stirred his coffee, his tiny spoon clinking delicately against the cup. "The Fabian Society, those socialists who advocate such radical ideas as a standard minimum wage. They believe that the common man should all have the same status as the wealthy."

"Yes. Dreamers and optimists, the lot." Claradon laughed.

Karida locked gazes with him, annoyed. "Such principles intrigue me. I believe they carry a great deal of wisdom."

He crossed his legs at the ankle. "Miss Mitchell, gently bred ladies such as yourself would best avoid such liberals. It's politics, and all politics are tiresome."

"I find politics fascinating when revolving around the unjust predicament of others, Lord Claradon. Unlike yourself."

"Anne, mind yourself," the earl of Smithfield chided. "Pray, do not quarrel with our host."

"It's not a quarrel, but a spirited discussion. Wouldn't you venture to agree, Lord Claradon?" she retorted.

Thomas met her gaze evenly, his eyes sparkling. "Quite."

Karida felt old hurts and anger rise to the surface. "I wonder what the Fabian Society would advocate about the workhouses. They must be concerned about these institutions. Of course, a man of your social position would never have set foot inside one."

"I have," Claradon replied quietly, "and trust me, I would not sentence the most flea-bitten mongrel to residence there."

"Heavens, you have?" Lady Smithfield ejaculated. "What are they like?"

His gaze rested on Karida. "I was appalled. A beastly place, stark and dreary. Cold, dreadfully cold. Children were making oakum from old, tarred ropes, picking them apart to be reused. Ghastly work. Their hands were rough and bleeding.

"We witnessed a beating while I was there, I'm afraid. A young boy, no older than five. His master struck his palms with a cane for some minor infraction—but one has to keep strict order in such a place, I was told. The lad was crying, begging the master to stop, but he would not." Lord Claradon stared into his cup with a morose expression. "Such places house the dregs of humanity."

Memories struck Karida like a cane on her own palms. A chill raced up her spine as she remembered her bloodied fingers picking at oakum rope, the constant hunger gnawing at her stomach.

She lifted her gaze to meet Claradon's. "Many in society would argue it's the only way, my lord. What would be the answer if you remove orphans and bastards from the workhouses? Would you clad them in silk and satin, have them attend teas and such?" She spared the briefest glance for her real father. "Or should they be packed away, sent to foreign lands and forgotten?"

The earl of Smithfield set down his coffee cup and gave her a direct look that would chill the hottest desert sand. "That will be quite enough, Anne."

Lady Smithfield looked troubled, and Karida's aunt stared into her coffee cup as if it contained ancient secrets. Lord Claradon simply looked thoughtful.

Karida's stomach churned with anxiety, and sweat trickled down her spine. Arguing was pointless; she'd come here for one purpose and had to see it through.

She stood, the men rising along with her. "Might I inquire as to the whereabouts of your water closet?"

"I'll escort you myself, Miss Mitchell," Lord Claradon replied.

He led her upstairs to a small room. As she went to shut the door in his face, he blocked her attempt.

"Have you no common courtesy?" she gasped.

"No," he replied, grinning.

"You're such a boor."

"But not a bore, as are the other men your uncle is desperate for you to meet. I think you find me utterly charming and cannot resist me."

Karida evaded the truth. "You are arrogant and think much of yourself."

For a moment he looked as remote as the pyramids. Then he gave an insouciant shrug. "Of what else is there to think? Were I to ponder other matters, I should prove as dreary as those who insist on discussing topics such as politics." He gave a wicked smile and leaned closer. "Now, shall I help you with anything? My water closet has all the latest amenities. Do you desire to bathe while you are here? I have a most efficient plumbing system, even pumping hot water into the bath. Would you care to test it out?"

"You are an ill-mannered pig."

"I do my best," he replied, his gaze centered on her mouth. "I must confess that I have been trying to change, but I quite forget myself when faced with you. I revert to my more roguish behavior. So, is it not *your* fault that I am a scoundrel? How can good intentions compete with your beauty?"

An idle flatterer as well as a thief. Karida tilted her chin with pride but couldn't help but ask, "Why do you mock me?"

Genuine surprise flared on his face. "Trust me. 'Tis the furthest action from my mind, my sweet Miss Mitchell. How do I mock you?"

"You call me beautiful," she whispered.

Something shifted in his expression, and Thomas took her hand, lifted it, his fingers caressing her palm in a lazy stroke. "I speak only the truth. Please believe that. You are as lovely as an Egyptian sunrise, with all the promise of a new dawn. You make me contemplate actions that are . . . nothing like me."

Poetic words, designed to seduce. Karida knew she should shut the door on his foot, continue to play the prim and outraged lady. But the sincerity in his voice proved far too tempting.

"And what actions are those, Lord Claradon?"

The expression on his handsome face changed. Its intensity reminded Karida of pictures of satyrs she'd seen in her father's study, romping through the woods in pursuit of shapely nymphs. Thomas leaned forward with a slow smile. "Something quite ungentlemanly. But now is not the time. I'll allow you some privacy." And with a little bow, he stepped back and shut the door.

Karida sagged against the inside, her heart racing and her thoughts jumbled. It took some time to gather herself.

At last she opened the door and peeked out. As no one lingered, Karida exited and explored the upstairs, opening doors until she finally located a masculine bedchamber she suspected was Thomas's. She went inside. But just as she did, she heard a noise in the hallway.

Heart racing, Karida fled to the door and listened. These were no decisive, hard footsteps like Lord Claradon's but softer ones, like those of a maid. Karida opened the door, peered out, and saw a woman in a starched white apron and black dress heading away. A maid, nothing more.

She slipped into the hall, closing the door softly behind her. But barely had she walked a few steps when Lord Claradon emerged from a different door. He closed and leaned against it.

"Did you find it suitable? My bedchamber, that is, the one you were investigating." He folded his arms across his chest.

Karida lifted her chin. "I apologize. I have a rapt interest in Chippendale furniture and must confess to a woman's curiosity, having been absent from England for far too long."

Claradon walked forward, close enough for her to catch the enticing smell of his sandalwood cologne. "The bed is not Chippendale, but it does have a fascinating headboard. Louis the Sixteenth. I do hope you admired it. The bed has proved quite . . . durable." His mouth crooked into a wicked grin. "Or, if you're so interested in furniture, we might venture back to examine the piano. I've never played a duet on it, but I wager the enterprise could coax a rapturous song from that lovely mouth."

Her heartbeat quickened. "I daresay you are too bold. Again. Now, if you will excuse me."

Karida went to push past, but he sidestepped, cutting her off. He studied her mouth with darkening eyes.

"What is the matter?" she demanded.

He reached out and ran a finger down her cheek. "Softer

than the finest Egyptian cotton sheets," he murmured. "Made for the bedroom . . ."

Her eyes widened at the suggestion even as breath fled her lungs. His touch was the gentlest stroke. His naked finger brushed her lower lip, the heat left flaring in its wake a sharp contrast to the featherlight caress, making her body heavy with longing. Feminine instinct that she'd thought long buried in the desert sand flared to life. Karida stood frozen, fascinated and uncertain.

As her lips parted, Thomas reached out and pressed one finger to their side. His warm breath feathered over her cheek and ear. "The piano. I daresay I could teach you a few lessons on top of that particular instrument that would leave you sighing for more."

She nearly raised her hand to slap him. He did not even flinch as she pulled away but regarded her steadily. She struggled to leash both her temper and desire.

"You are presumptuous as well as a scoundrel. I would never consent!"

He arched a brow. "What a shame, to leave oneself untrained. How else but education does one learn one's natural talents? If I had you naked beneath me, I daresay you'd be a quick study."

Breath fled her throat and she stared in outrage. "How dare you!"

He simply smiled. "I apologize, Miss Mitchell. Again, my mouth has run on like a carriage without a driver—or worse, one of those beastly motorcars polluting our streets." But he did not look apologetic. Rather, he resembled a cat toying with its meal.

"You could use lessons yourself, Lord Claradon—in deportment and how to act with a lady."

"Oh, I never act," he replied. "Not in the bedroom, at any rate. It's all me, all the time. You would never need question my passion for you."

Karida's pulse raced. He was a rogue and a libertine, but she recognized he spoke the truth. He wanted her as no other man ever had. And there was something else: he broke rules and didn't give a damn about the consequences. Once she'd been the same.

"These things you say. Aren't you worried what others will think of you? What society will label you?" she asked.

His broad shoulders lifted in a shrug. "Should I?"

"There are certain standards of polite behav—"

"And who sets those standards?" he interrupted. "Anyone I admire? I think not."

Karida's mouth fell open. "You don't care how you appear to society? What about the expectations that accompany your title? You, sir, are an *earl*."

His gaze grew cold. "Miss Mitchell, obviously you care too much what others think. Why live only for what others expect of you? I spent a childhood trying to live up to certain expectations only to realize they mattered not one whit. Therefore I strive to please one person—myself."

"That is entirely selfish!" she remarked.

"No, it's simply rational. I can only please myself. If I try to meet everyone else's expectations, I'll spend my life smacked back and forth like a ball in a game of lawn tennis. I have no intention of doing that."

His comments struck a chord. She thought about trying to impress her father, the earl, and all the members of his society, and about the expectations of her adoptive father back in Egypt. For a moment she was overwhelmed. "I do not want to be a tennis ball, either, whacked about . . ."

To her incredulous surprise, Thomas threw back his head and released a hearty laugh. Deep, rich, authentic. She found herself smiling just from hearing it.

Just as quickly he stopped and held out his elbow in a gallant gesture. All trace of lechery was gone. "I can be civil," he said, "when the occasion calls, and I feel I must oblige a lovely lady and her disdain for my overtures. As well, we have left the other guests wondering where we are. Your guardian will never let you come unescorted to my supper tomorrow if we delay a moment more. So, shall we return?"

He was lethal as a leopard, and every instinct warned he was dangerous to indulge. But Karida was desperate, herself. She'd get no new chance to right the wrong today, so Lord Claradon's invitation to supper tomorrow would have to be accepted; only then could she take back what he had stolen from her. She would have to brave the jackal's den alone.

But I will keep my honor and my virtue, she silently vowed. No one will strip them from me.

No one.

Chapter Eight

The following evening, Nigel hummed as he looked over the dining room. The crystal sparkled, the china shone, and the best linens were laid out. He lingered at the seat next to his. Here he would place the delightful "Anne." She'd sent her acceptance of his supper invitation around by personal servant.

Tonight promised to be most entertaining. Perhaps, just perhaps, he might boldly place his hand on Karida's leg and watch her reaction. He chuckled, anticipating her horrified look: shock mingling with that same erotic awareness as he'd now elicited several times. Perhaps tonight they would even stroll in the park, accompanied by his friends and their ladies, and sneak off behind a tall oak. He'd steal a kiss or two from Karida's lovely mouth. More than that he'd not risk, however. He had a reputation to polish.

Nigel glanced at his reflection in the mirror over the gleaming cherry sideboard. If only one could buff a reputation as easily as servants did furniture.

Waiting, he sat down at the table. The grandfather clock in the hallway chimed half past seven. He was alone.

Nigel's stomach churned with anxiety. He poured himself a glass of wine, a fine golden champagne. It sparkled in the overhead light. *Relax,* he told himself. *Don't tense up, think the worst.*

Sampling the vintage, he rolled it around on his tongue. The taste was delicate, with a hint of apples and smoke. But he couldn't drink too much, lest he consume the whole bottle and leave none for his guests. Surely they would arrive soon. It was like the lads to be late, of course, quite fashionable, even to supper. Oakley probably got caught up in a game of cards at the club and lingered over his glass of port. Hodges was possibly enjoying the delights of his new mistress.

Reeves, the butler, appeared, his white-gloved hands pressed together. "Shall I have Cook wait dinner, sir?"

"At least another half hour," Nigel said smoothly. "They'll be here by then."

He drained his glass and poured another. And then another. An hour later, the bottle was half empty. His stomach grumbled.

When the ormolu clock in the drawing room chimed nine, Nigel swirled the golden liquid in his glass, staring at it dully. Reeves appeared, bearing a small folded note. Nigel brightened. Of course the half-wits were telling him they'd been unavoidably delayed, so sorry about the supper, but perhaps he could meet for drinks at the club? Or maybe it was from Karida.

He tore open the ecru envelope. His mouthful of wine soured like lemons. The note was from Oakley. Three simple words: "Go to Hell." Such ornate, gentlemanly handwriting.

The fine stationary crumpled beneath his trembling fist. He stood and rang the bell. The butler returned. "I dine alone tonight," Nigel told him stiffly. "And open the second bottle of wine."

The supper, served, look cold and appallingly unappetizing on the table. Nigel ate an apple from the sideboard. He started on the second bottle of wine.

Alone at the table, he soon set the half-empty bottle by his plate. Digging into his waistcoat pocket, he removed a coin. Flip, into the air it went. And again. Change? Or not? He flipped the coin once more, letting it fall. It clattered to the polished oak floor. What a fool. He began to laugh. Thinking he could be different, that Tommy's friends would eagerly accept him. Caustic hatred seeped into his heart. He could no more change than a leopard could shift its spots. Impossible. The hell with them. The hell with them all.

A sharp knock came at the front door. Nigel shifted, not daring to hope.

"Miss Mitchell, my lord," the butler announced.

"Thank you, Reeves. You may leave," Nigel said, and propped his head on one fist. With bleary eyes he studied his visitor, a vision in soft white silk.

Oh hell, just go away, leave me be.

And yet, she pulled at him like drink to a thirsty alcoholic. He could not resist her, and his desire would be his damnation.

Karida stared at the drunken earl of Claradon sitting lopsided on his oak chair, ready to fall over. "I came late because I was unavoidably detained," she said, alarmed at his crooked smile and the two empty wine bottles. "Where are your friends?"

"They've been un-nn-navoidably detained," he slurred. "Care for a drink of port or a cigar, since you missed dinner?"

Her little heels clicked on the hardwood floor. "Why have they not come?" she asked as she drew closer.

"Oakley and the others know me for what I am—a charlatan who desired to change. But a leopard can't change its spots. Not even for a beautiful vision." His eyes closed, as if keeping them open proved too tiring.

Karida's heart twisted at the look of him, as defenseless as a child and as forlorn as one denied Christmas treats. What had happened that his friends turned away? Had they discovered that he was a thief and a liar?

"Lord Claradon." Karida slid into a chair next to him. "Why have they declined to come?" She tested out his first name on her tongue. "Thomas?"

He opened one bloodshot eye. "Don't call me that. Say my real name. Nigel. I'm Nigel, damn it. All this time I've been here thinking I could be Tommy, as perfect and witty and charming, and they always knew better. As I should have."

"Oh! But how—"

"Tommy is my twin. He's in Cairo and shan't come back.

He's been in Cairo all this time, happily living with Jasmine, his lady love, making little babies. He always was the good twin, the perfect one, so my parents thought. I tried my best to be perfect, but I'm not quite. Even though I am the true earl and have proof!"

Karida digested that information, her mind racing. Nigel. Not Thomas. Heavens, what a situation. It was Nigel, not Thomas, who'd stolen the ruby.

"Who *are* you?" she asked.

"A liar and a thief and a libertine. A man with a heart carved from cold stone. I wish I could change. But I cannot. Even if I could, none would ever trust me again," he muttered.

Karida studied him, troubled by this unabashed honesty. It was something she suspected he seldom shared.

"Anything is possible," she suggested. "If it is within your heart to change, you surely could. And I do not think you are as cold as you believe."

Nigel's eyes opened wide. He struggled to lift his head, his hand reaching out as if to touch her. "You are like a fair angel," he whispered.

She remained still, waiting and watching. His hand fell away.

"No, I shan't. Angels deserve better than dirty jackals. Go away, fair angel. You don't want to be near me. I am a little . . . cheerless right now." And with a crash his head dropped to the table. His eyes fluttered closed and he appeared to sleep.

Karida's heart turned over. She gently touched his cheek, his flesh chill beneath her warm fingers. She undid her lacy shawl and draped it over his shoulders. For a few moments, she lingered and watched him sleep, torn over leaving him and knowing what she must do. Sharing the dull pain of rejection and abandonment.

Finally, she stood and kissed the top of his rumpled hair. "I am sorry," she whispered.

Her feet made no noise as she glided upstairs. As quietly as she'd done when stealing coins as a child, Karida slipped into his room.

As she'd seen the ruby on his stickpin, Karida made her way to the bureau she'd spotted earlier, the place where he would dress; the sounds of her breathing and the frantic pounding of her heart echoed in her ears. Her eager fingers combed through the jumble of items in his top bureau drawer. Seeing something promising, she withdrew a small rosewood box, tested it. Locked.

She turned and glanced around, looking for a key. Something else caught her eye, something she'd missed in her eagerness to search the bureau drawers. On top of the dresser, looking far too dainty for this heavy masculine room, sat another wooden box. It had a miniature, glass-covered portrait on top, a woman dressed in 1700s period costume. A soft smile graced Karida's mouth. The edges of the box were done in elaborate silver fili-gree. It was dainty, lovely, and something totally unexpected in this masculine bedroom. Certainly Nigel would never own something like this. Would he?

She turned it this way and that, and saw a gold key. Twisting it, she listened. It was a music box, and it played "The Blue Danube." That twinkling, haunting melody filled the silence. Where had he found such a treasure? Nigel seemed the sort to hoard jewels, money and gold, not musical knickknacks. It seemed entirely out of character.

She set it down. Beside the box was a framed tabletop oil painting. She stared at it. Saint Augustine. Her early childhood memories came back. This was the saint who was wicked in his early adulthood and reformed.

First the music box and now a saint's icon? Who was Nigel? Who was he truly? Who did he *want* to be?

Setting down the portrait, she ransacked the rest of the bu-reau. A thin drawer near the top was also locked. Fishing a hairpin out from her topknot, she jiggled it into the lock and twisted. The lock clicked, and she jerked at the handle. The drawer stuck, but she pulled with a grunt. It slid open. It was a drawer of jewelry, mostly empty. Resting atop a bed of black velvet was . . . his ruby stickpin.

Karida picked it up to closely examine it and felt her hopes fall. This was not her ruby. It dropped back into the drawer with a small clink. A hollow ache settled in her chest. Had Nigel sold it in Cairo? Peddled it like a gold coin not knowing its true worth?

Instinct told her he had not. The way he had stared at her, and given the intimate connection they'd shared, he likely saw the ruby as a trophy in place of Karida herself. But Claradon was cleverer than she'd anticipated. He wore that ruby stickpin in the open, but the ruby he'd stolen he did not wear openly, instead hiding it like the precious treasure it guarded.

Her gaze returned upward to the rosewood box. Karida jiggled that lock, too, with her hairpin. After a few minutes, it opened. Carefully, she looked inside. A jade scorpion amulet caught her eye, with markings she instantly recognized. This was the missing key the tomb robber Malik had confessed to selling. Her curiosity grew as Karida also found a yellowing photograph of a small boy. Who was *this*?

She dug through some official documents and read them. Pain rippled through her. These were letters proving Nigel had told the truth. He was the true earl of Claradon, not his twin brother Thomas. He had indeed been robbed of his birthright.

"No, no pity," she whispered. Pity would soften her.

Karida set aside the papers with reverence and looked again into the box. Nothing remained. Disappointment surged then faded. If he had the scorpion amulet, then the ruby had to be here, too. And this interior didn't quite match up with the box's proportions . . .

Turning the box over, she examined the underside. A section appeared loose. She pried at it, and it came free. A false bottom! Her ruby fell into her palm.

Karida put down the chest and stared at the gem. She squeezed her palm shut. The ruby was hers once more; she could return to Egypt.

She could almost smell the lamb kabobs roasting in the fires of the Khamsin camp, hear the jingle of silver coins on the bracelets of the women who prepared dinner. Brief pain pierced her palm from the stone's sharp edge, but she ignored it. Karida replaced the rosewood box's false panel, locked the box and ensured all was as it had been when she'd entered the room. Nothing was out of place.

"Hello, Karida."

The deep velvet voice made her jump. A switch clicked on, and light suddenly flooded the room. Karida gasped. The not-so-drunken earl of Claradon stood in the doorway. Clad only in shirt, trousers, and paisley waistcoat, he looked superbly dangerous. A satisfied smile curved his beautiful mouth.

She was caught but good. What would he do to her?

Chapter Nine

"Why, look what's crept into my bedroom—and after declining all my previous invitations." His gaze was sharper than the edges of the ruby cutting into her palm. "What's this?" He leaned against the doorjamb. "A thief? A lovely thief. Dare I believe you are here to steal my heart?"

"You were intoxicated. I saw you," she protested.

"I never allow myself to become *that* intoxicated. Not since the riding accident that nearly claimed use of my arm. I learn from my mistakes, *Karida*."

He'd used her real name again. He knew who she was. Shock made her knees weak. She licked her lips, willing herself calm as he crossed the room.

"But you passed out on the table. How could you . . . ?"

Nigel crossed his arms. "Forgive my deception, but being duplicitous yourself, you must understand my need for caution." He grinned. "Oh, Karida. Anne. You have so many names, so many identities. Devout Englishwoman abroad, admirer of the Fabian Society, lady of the desert tribes . . ."

Her mouth opened and shut as she struggled for composure.

"Guardian of that ruby," he added softly. "You are a woman of honor guarding one of Egypt's most ancient treasures."

"You know the ruby's true purpose." Panic welled up inside her, but Karida fought it down. This was now no mere matter of the gem. He planned to steal the treasure of the golden mummies.

He snorted. "Of course. I've known all along. Malik told me."

"You were working with him? Of course. He had supposedly hired on as your servant. And you ran off and left him to his punishment."

Satisfaction filled her as Claradon paled. Then he gave a shrug. "Such is the way of thieves—those foolish enough to get caught are punished." He stepped forward and took her hand, very gently unfurled her fingertips. His heat was like an inferno. The ruby lay on Karida's palm, its teardrop base pointing upward like an accusing fingernail. "And you have been caught.

"You are a thief," he continued softly. "You're stealing from me. But here in England we are less cruel than desert tribes. They'll merely send you to prison."

Claradon plucked the ruby from her palm with his index finger and thumb, and Karida's lips trembled as she watched her hopes and dreams vanish into his waistcoat pocket. Her hand stretched out as if to snatch it back. One dark eyebrow arched as he studied her. She let her hand drop, fisted.

"You stole it from me," she accused. "This property is mine, and I am reclaiming it."

"And who would believe you, hmmm?" He began circling her, like a leopard its prey. "You're in my house, pretending to be someone you are not. I am an earl. The ruby is in my possession. That makes you the thief. The police will not believe you."

"Wait." Panic tinged her voice. "I'll tell them the truth. The whole truth."

"And who would believe you? You're here, in my bedchamber, uninvited—though I daresay your presence would normally have been welcomed for another purpose. Say, in my bed. I imagine that would have been much more pleasant than a cold prison cell."

Her heart raced. Childhood memories surged, of being locked in a dark cell, waiting for release, waiting for the police to drag her to a cold stone prison. Claradon was right. They would come, and no one would believe her. They would arrest her. The earl of Smithfield would likely abandon her and her scandal just as he'd abandoned her to live in the desert so many years before. She had no recourse.

All dreams and hope smashed on the rocks of despair as Claradon turned toward the door to fetch the police. A sob rose in Karida's throat. She choked it down. "Stop," she whispered. "I'll . . . do anything."

He paused, a hand on the doorknob, and gave her an inquiring look over his shoulder. Her gaze was riveted to his waistcoat pocket but she dragged it upward. The intent look in his deep green eyes startled her, then gave her back hope.

He'd already demonstrated his desire. If she drew close enough and distracted him with a kiss, she might snatch the ruby back. In some ways she had longed for a kiss. Such feelings were wrong, especially in light of all that had occurred. But it would serve her purpose and help her escape. And when she fled back to the earl of Smithfield's estate without being caught, mightn't the police believe her instead?

Karida steeled her spine and prepared to do what she must.

She'd thought to steal back that which he had taken from her? The irony of her corruption delighted him. Nigel leaned against the bureau she'd raided and smiled.

The cold water he'd splashed on his face had chased away most of the wine's effects. He felt slightly foxed, yet it was more from awareness of her. Anger and desire twined inside him. How dare Karida be so perfect, such a beautiful angel, and look down at him as if he were . . . what he was. But she was the same now: a lowly thief.

"Surely we can work something out, Lord Claradon," she was saying. "You are a man of measure and logic. Tell me how we can resolve this without calling the authorities."

Nigel was sorely tempted. But his guard went up.

"Ah, my sweet, there are always consequences when one

commits a crime. You broke into my room and took something in my possession. Two grave offenses. If we don't call the police, *I* shall have to punish you. Let's see." He tapped his chin with his fingers. "A flogging? No, it will mar that pretty honey-gold flesh of yours. The rack? You are tall enough already, I wager. It will have to be something much more . . . personal."

Karida backed away. "Personal?"

Nigel's blood surged hotly in his veins. So lovely, so poised was his quarry, even now when facing insurmountable odds. Her spirit and fire amazed him, filled him with desire. She was a worthy opponent, noble in all the ways he was not. Honor radiated from her, honor he lacked.

He lifted a hand to touch her face and was struck by an unexpected pang of guilt. She looked as proud and remote as the fairest angel, a vision in pure white condemning him for his sins. Yet, was that all in his mind? No condemnation shone in those startling amber brown eyes. Something else lingered there, the pupils widening, her breathing ragged as she stared back.

He took a quivering breath and dared to touch her—he, the dirty desert jackal! Karida sighed beneath the slow caress of his fingers, and her cheek flushed hot. Her eyelashes fluttered closed, those dark crescents sweeping downward.

Nigel cupped her cheek with trembling fingers and dared to bring his head close to hers. Closer still, his mouth thirsting to taste her. Could one kiss an angel and not be damned forever? Could a libertine and a thief such as himself reach for the very heavens without plummeting like Icarus or Bellerophon?

Angling his head, he dared to try. Nigel touched her mouth with his—the briefest kiss, like a touch of air. Her lips were warm and soft, perfect, just as he'd dreamed.

You have no right to kiss her.

Pulling away, he opened his eyes and stared down at her. Karida gazed up, her lips moist. Dryness rose in his throat. Nigel jammed a hand through his hair, dropping his gaze to his feet. For the first time in his life, he felt ashamed.

And then he heard a soft murmur, beautiful, like an angel calling to him. Startled, he glanced down to see her press against him, and Karida brought an index finger up against his lower lip. He quivered.

Suddenly, Nigel felt pressure on his ribs. Alert, he pulled away, and Karida's hand slipped free from his waistcoat pocket.

Anger and amusement rolled through him. Of course such a perfect creature would never lower herself to willingly kiss someone like him! He drew the ruby out and held it between his index and forefinger.

"Looking for this?" he taunted. He closed his hand and the ruby vanished.

Karida's exotic eyes narrowed at him. Challenge shone in them. Nigel's blood thickened as he relished that look. Too long had his appetite failed to be satisfied. He'd lost friends, but to-night might not be such an abject failure after all. There was much yet to acquire.

Their gazes locked, she stood proud and straight as an Egyptian queen. She held out a palm. "One last time. Give me back the ruby."

He touched her hand, watched it tremble. Ah! So she was not indifferent to him. Yes, this might be the answer. It was worth a try. "I shall not call the police, and you'll avoid prison on one condition." He went to the bureau and put the ruby in the top drawer. Then he turned to see her expression.

"That is?"

"Make love with me."

Karida stared as if he'd asked her to walk from London to Cairo. "Are you mad?"

"When it comes to you, perhaps. You are enough to drive a man mad. And seeing you are now in my bedroom . . ."

She shook her head. "You can't want me. Not like that."

He laughed. "Don't be so modest, Karida. Have you never looked in a mirror? No cheval glasses in your Bedouin tent?"

"I have honor," she replied.

He shrugged. "So you say. You are pure and noble . . . and beyond the passion I clearly feel for you. And you are free. Free to do as you please. For now. In prison, you will not be." He advanced, the blood surging thickly through his veins. The choice he forced her to make was one of the most dishonorable things he had ever done, but desire overruled his conscience. "You shall choose. Do you desire freedom after one night with me or bondage in prison?"

"Go to Hell," she said. But she stood immobile, entranced. Her eyes widened and darkened, a clear indication of her own passion.

"I am already there."

He paused, waiting for her to pull away. When she didn't, Nigel cupped her cheeks, kissed her, tasted her; his lips moved over hers, coaxing and tutoring her obvious inexperience. To his delight, Karida sighed into his mouth.

When he gave his tongue the lightest flick over her smooth lower lip, she made a small startled sound. He soothed her with a murmur and tried again. This time, her tongue darted out shyly and met his. Nigel's body tightened with need. This was the most erotic yet innocent kiss he'd ever experienced. He *would* go to Hell. And so could the whole world, if only he could keep kissing her like this forever.

As the thief and libertine captured her mouth, life roared through her body. Never had Karida felt so ecstatically alive. Her body felt open, yearning, as his thumbs stroked her cheeks.

"Karida," he murmured against her mouth. His fingers trembled much as they had in the ballroom.

"Thomas," she whispered.

He drew back, his green eyes glittering.

"Oh, bloody hell. No. Nigel. I'm *Nigel.*" He held her face between his hands, his eyes blazing. "Say it."

She reeled back, surprised by her slip and by his vehemence. It was just that she'd thought of him as Thomas for so long. But another absurd relief filled her: This was not Thomas, the man betrothed to Jasmine. In the desert, he had been betraying no one—at least, not romantically. He'd been a simple thief and liar.

"Nigel," she breathed. "Ah, this game of identities."

"You will know whom you kiss, Karida. Enough of this entire damn farce, this absurd theater."

He took her mouth again, plundering and ravishing until her limbs threatened to buckle. She wrapped her fingers around his arm for support. Madness! She could not do this, not with him. He was dangerous and would claim more than her body. Karida feared he would claim her soul as well.

He released her. Breath rasped in and out of his lungs. His dark brows knitted together and an odd trembling affected his clenched fists. "Enough games. I want you. Shall you go to bed with me, or shall I call the police?"

Her hands clenched. Damn him. He was relentless, ruthless in his intent.

"You do not want me, I assure you," she said in a low voice.

"You could not be more wrong." His hand reached out, trembling, and briefly caressed her cheek. "You're so damn perfect. So lovely . . . You already know me as a thief. What I want, I take. No shame, no regret. Now, what is your answer?"

Emotion squeezed her throat shut. Surrendering her innocence sent a shiver of fear down her spine, but far worse would be Nigel's reaction to her body. He would see her scarred flesh and pull back in revulsion. She could not bear to witness the shocked horror on his face.

"If I go to bed with you, will you return the ruby?" she asked.

His eyes shuttered. "Perhaps. I promise nothing—only freedom from prison."

Perspiration beaded her temples. Was this the right choice? So be it, she thought dully. And she nodded once, a jerk of her head.

Satisfaction entered his gaze, and Nigel stepped back. "Undress for me. Show me your willingness to enter into our bargain."

This was no bargain but blackmail. Yet he would not want her as much as she wanted him when he saw her naked and glimpsed the ugly scars marring her flesh. Karida's chest felt hollow with shame, and color rose to her cheeks.

She stepped out of her white shoes with their delicate spoon heels. Her white lacy gown was buttoned at the throat. She turned. Nigel's fingers nimbly unfastened the bindings. *He's experienced with women's clothing,* she realized, shivering as his fingers touched her bare skin above the V-shaped white cotton chemise.

He ran a finger between her naked shoulder blades. "Exquisite," he murmured.

Her organdy petticoat rustled as she shifted. Between her legs, her cotton drawers felt damp with perspiration . . . and desire. Desire that was soon to turn to humiliation.

Nigel stepped back. Karida removed her dress, lifting it over her tensed shoulders to toss it aside. It landed in a heap on the hardwood floor, the delicate lace and pretty silk crumpled and discarded.

Like my virginity will be, she thought, *should he still want me after seeing my body.*

"Turn around," he commanded.

A sharp intake of breath followed as his hungry gaze devoured her body, now clad only in chemise, drawers, petticoat and stockings. Karida felt her nipples harden and her breasts grow heavy beneath the intensity of that look. She refused to drop her gaze but stared like a defiant prisoner before her executioner.

Her knee-length drawers had a drawstring tied at the back and had been specially designed because she'd refused to restrict her body with a corset. They gathered at the knee and tied to keep her stockings in place. She'd so admired their delicate lace but had been instructed by Lady Smithfield that one never admired drawers: they were "unmentionables."

Nigel's eyes widened as Karida fumbled beneath her chemise and unfastened her drawers. She sat and untied the drawstrings at the knees, then stood. The drawers dropped to her ankles and she stepped out of them.

Her stockings next. Karida sat and unrolled the pretty white stockings, flicking them aside with a defiant look. Then she shrugged out of her petticoat. All that remained was her chemise, the one barrier between her marred flesh and his heated gaze. Stricken by uncertainty, she hugged herself.

I can't do this. I simply can't.

Nigel stepped forward. Expecting him to strip off her protective covering, she flinched. He arched a dark brow, his mouth pursed, but he merely reached out and plucked free the hairpins restraining her dark curls. Her hair cascaded in a dark cloud past her shoulders, spilled down to her waist.

Karida shivered, feeling as naked as if he'd ripped free her chemise. Nigel selected a dark brown curl, let it dangle between thumb and forefinger. He leaned forward and lifted the strand to his nose, inhaled its scent. His breath soon released on a sigh.

"You smell of exotic spices and desert heat," he murmured.

Karida remained motionless, trying to hold her breath, barely containing herself as Nigel's gaze found the deep cleavage between her breasts. Memories surfaced. How he'd stared at her breasts! Anger boiled to the surface. She let it. Anger was her shield, a barricade between her pride and his forthcoming horror.

Nigel looked at her expectantly. His expression was that of a victorious hunter.

The hell with it, and the hell with him. The hell with all men! With a vicious yank, Karida tore at her flimsy cotton covering. The tiny pearl buttons popped off and shot away, clinking onto the hardwood floor. In the soft golden light of the room, they glinted.

Karida shrugged out of her ruined chemise and let it fall to the floor. Cool air brushed against her naked breasts and caused her stomach muscles to contract. With all her inner strength, she forced her hands down to her sides, fully exposing her body to him. Sweat trickled down her bare backside.

Hunger flared in Nigel's gaze as he studied her generous breasts. Then his gaze dipped lower, to the thatch of brown curls covering her feminine flesh—and to the harsh ridges of the burn scars across her belly and lower abdomen. His green gaze widened with shock. He took a step back.

"Jesus," he muttered.

Her throat squeezed shut. Tears threatened, but she savagely choked them back. *I will not cry before him, I will not cry,* she silently chanted. She clenched her fists and curled her toes.

"What . . . ?" He seemed to struggle with words, jamming a hand through his tangled hair. It stuck up, making him look younger and more vulnerable. Or perhaps the effect was caused by the surprise around his mouth.

"I fell into a fire," she snarled. "They didn't think I would live. I did. I can never bear children."

Karida folded her arms across her breasts. It was over. He would turn, make a choking sound of disgust and flee. The winning card was hers; he had never expected this. She might make a grab for the ruby and run.

She remained immobile, her limbs boneless.

Please. Oh please, don't be like them. Don't turn from me in horror.

A stray tear trickled down her cheek, and Karida closed her eyes. She felt a gentle brush against her skin. Her eyes flew open. With his thumb, Nigel had wiped her tear away.

"You're crying."

She reached up and scrubbed at her face. "I don't cry."

His expression shifted. For a moment the mask dropped and she saw inside the man, a raw-etched and haunted loneliness, something she'd glimpsed back in the desert on what should have been her wedding day. But then his expression shuttered and he stepped back, shrugged out of his jacket and unbuttoned his waistcoat.

Karida watched, shocked. Was he going through with it? Did lust override all? What was that expression in his eyes?

He reached for his left cuff link, unfastened it and tossed it onto a nearby table. "I have something to show you," he said. He rolled up his shirt sleeve.

Karida gasped. An ugly thatching of silvery scars marched up his forearm, as if razor-sharp claws had raked his flesh.

"Surgery. I was thrown off a horse and broke my arm in so many damn places I could not count. The physicians in America did their best," he said quietly. The shirtsleeve flopped loose as he studied her. And for the first time, she saw in his eyes something other men had denied her: tenderness.

Karida blinked, and the look vanished. Nigel strode forward and slid a hand around her neck. His touch was both arousing and soothing. He massaged her stiffened muscles.

He kissed her. His tongue found her lips, demanded entrance. Encouraged by his need, she allowed it. His tongue slid deftly inside, meeting her own with bold strokes. She felt his passion, his crude lust . . . and yearned for it to be fulfilled. No man had ever wanted her this way. No man would ever want her this way again.

With a little gasp of fear she pulled away. Blood rose from her throat to her flaming cheeks, and her nipples grew rosy and hard beneath Nigel's intense stare. His hand drifted over her slender shoulder, caressing her skin, his fingers gentle.

He palmed her breasts, his gaze fierce. He flicked his thumbs over their hardening peaks in small, expert strokes. Karida writhed, a hot throbbing between her legs that grew ever more intense. Oh good heavens, what was this?

"Stop, it's too much," she gasped.

"That feeling you're experiencing is desire," he said softly. "You want me, too. I've seen it in your eyes from the moment you dared first remove your veil."

She could not deny it—especially not when he bent his head and fastened his mouth on a nipple. Karida stiffened, half expecting pain. Instead, there came a gentle suckling, and his tongue flicked over the cresting hardness and swirled. The sharp ache between her legs increased.

Womanizer, thief, he stole all reason from her, his adroit skill making her lose what little sense she still possessed. Karida pressed against him, the covering of his clothing rasping against her body.

Nigel released her nipple. He straightened, a haunted look in his green eyes. "Why did you do that—show me your face? To taunt me?"

Karida licked her lips, desiring the return of his mouth. "Because you were the only man who'd truly looked. I wanted you to see all of me."

"I was looking at an angel," he murmured, and he rubbed his thumb over her jaw. "Now I dare to *touch* an angel, so damn me to Hell for it."

Nigel stepped back, shedding his clothing. Soon he was naked, and her fascinated gaze roved him, his taut, lean body boasting of athletic pastimes, his broad chest, rippling muscles of a flat stomach, and legs dusted with dark hair. Her gaze dropped to the long, thick penis thrusting up from his groin. He was aroused, and she, the ugly and scarred woman whom no Khamsin man wanted, who had been shunned by Kareem, had done it. Karida felt a peculiar mix of anxiety and wonder.

Nigel gave her no time to think or change her mind. He tumbled her backward onto his bed, kissing her, his hands fisting in her hair. A shiver born of sexual awareness seized her as she tested the granite-hard muscles of his shoulders with her fingers. The spark between them caught and flared. She turned her face to where his shoulder met neck, put her mouth on the flesh there, and tasted the tangy salt of his skin. Smelled the musky spice of him.

Nigel kissed the tiny hollow of her throat, the movement

of his mouth increasing the hot throbbing between her legs. She twisted beneath him. His hand drifted to the curve of her hip, feathered over her scars, gently caressed their ridges. She did not feel. She could not; those tissues were long past sensation.

She felt when his hand dipped between her thighs, however. Karida jerked upright in shocked pleasure.

He quieted her with a soft murmur, pushing her down, and she felt his finger slide between her feminine folds. Smooth as silk, he glided back and forth, creating tendrils of coiled tension. She was soon a wound spring, ready to release the fires he stoked with each caress, ready to feel the full burn with erotic pleasure.

He was a devil, flaming in the pits of Hell, and she would happily go with him. A pleading whimper arose in her throat.

"Shhh," he murmured. "Just let go. Surrender to it."

She did just that. All tension within her exploded, and she wailed as it burst from her center and from her throat, shattering her consciousness as if it were glass. And when her eyes fluttered open, she saw Nigel looking down at her with deep satisfaction, and with a hint of male pride.

Shock filled her as he repeated the exercise. After her third release, she collapsed in a quivering heap, perspiration slicking her forehead.

"Now you are ready," he murmured, and pushed open her trembling thighs.

Karida. She was a ripe plum, sweet as sin, slick beneath the surface, drenched and ready for him. Nigel released a low groan of satisfaction. Her own little whimpers of excitement tugged at his heart. This wasn't merely sex, a quick tumble to ease his lust; this was something more, and he knew it. Hated it but craved it. *Needed* it.

He caged her with his body and wrapped his arms around

her, holding her tight as his mouth met hers. The kiss was punishing, demanding, a maelstrom of unleashed lust. He took her mouth with fury, his tongue plunging inside with masterful strokes. Tasting her, taking all and leaving nothing, building her fervent and growing ardor. He intended to strip away everything, grinding her down to her bones. He'd turn her into a woman mindless with pleasure, reckless with need. Make her as wanton and wicked as he was.

A flicker of guilt raced through him, but he dismissed it. All that mattered was getting inside her, invading her fully so that her goodness would sink into his soul and push back the blackness. Just a little. Just for a little while.

He parted her shaking thighs and nudged his lean hips between. The breath caught in her throat. She arched upward, not knowing what she wanted but frustrated and needing *something*. He was in control here, stronger than she, dominating, but a sinful promise lingered in her passion-darkened eyes, a promise that had grown ever since they'd first met, and it was both of their masters.

Nigel lifted the long mass of her dark brown curls and kissed her neck. He ran his tongue over her skin, enjoying the little shivers of pleasure his touch evoked. "Don't be afraid," he murmured. "I promise, I'll take good care of you."

Karida opened her legs wider, the ache between them exquisitely sharp, demanding to be filled. Wide-eyed, she watched Nigel settle closer. The silky hair on his muscled chest rubbed against the sensitive, hardened crests of her nipples. He rose above her, gaze fierce, his shoulders blocking out view of the ceiling. She felt the insistent demand of his iron-hard member against her feminine softness. He would not be denied. She did not want to deny him.

Nigel slipped forward, beginning to penetrate. Karida's virgin flesh quivered in both anticipation and apprehension; her breath stalled. He eased in another inch. Then, with a soft murmur and a powerful movement, he surged forward, breaching and impaling her. Karida bit back a sharp gasp at the sudden twist of pain. Her body stiffened and tensed at the shock. A small whimper fled her lips, and she was pinned beneath the muscled weight pressing her into the soft mattress.

"Shhh," he crooned, kissing her, soothing her with gentle presses of his mouth against hers.

She felt oddly full with Nigel joined to her body, his penis buried deep inside her. There was a burning, but it was far from unpleasant. She'd felt more pain from her accident, and none of this exotic mystery. This was the joining of a man and a woman in the most primitive and ancient of acts.

After a moment Nigel began to move, raising himself up on his hands and pulling slowly out. Sharp disappointment blossomed, and then he slowly thrust back inside. The delicious friction combined with the smoky heat of his gaze. Karida slid her hands around his neck, arching her hips upward in nameless yearning. He obliged, offering more of the languid yet powerful strokes.

She wanted more. Karida wriggled and arched impatiently, wanting all of him, wanting him gasping in need as much as she. He smiled, and his hips began to piston, his sex sliding in and out until his breath became rapid pants. Then he stiffened above her, and Nigel threw back his head and shouted her name, the cords in his neck strained. She felt his warm seed and the ecstatic knowledge that she had coaxed it from him. She, whom no man had ever wanted.

Nigel collapsed with a heavy sigh, burying his face in the pillow beside her. She stroked the sweating, quivering muscles of his back, and her legs cradled him tenderly. When he shifted his weight off of her, Karida instinctively curled next to him, putting her head on his shoulder. Her eyes slowly closed, and her breathing deepened. She, too, felt sleepy and oddly comforted by Nigel's arm about her waist anchoring her to him.

She awoke to his lips nuzzling her neck. The sensation was erotic, and she shifted against him.

"Awaken, sleeping angel," he whispered into her ear.

Karida opened her eyes and saw him studying her. He lay close on the rumpled sheets and touched a finger to her cheek.

"You look like an angel when you sleep. Except for the fact that you snore." His tone was teasing.

She narrowed her eyes. "I do *not* snore."

He gave a deep chuckle. "Perhaps not. And you make lovely noises when you are awake. *Quite* lovely."

Desire pinched her—and guilt. She had dishonored herself, had given her body to a liar and a thief. *I did what I had to do to survive,* she reminded herself. *It is over now. He has gotten what he wants and he will let me go.*

Nigel kept staring with that deep green gaze, however, and it was not what she expected. His was a thoughtful, assessing expression.

"Your scars—they are why Kareem rejected you as his bride."

Stiffening, Karida looked away. Nigel took her chin and turned her face back toward his.

"Sweetness, tell me. I understand what it is to be rejected."

A hollow ache settled in her chest. "Yes, they are why Kareem didn't want me—or rather because Rayya said I could not have children. I'm defective." The close intimacy they'd shared loosened her tongue, that and the hushed quiet of the room and her emotional turmoil. She laughed bitterly. "Kareem insists on making payments to my family, however. The *kalim*, the bride price. I think it's his way of expunging his guilt."

"Bastard," Nigel muttered.

"At least he means well. The others do not. They stare," she confessed, her voice the barest whisper. "They always stare at me."

Nigel rubbed the beginnings of whiskers bristling his hard

jaw. "Do the same. Stare back. Show them you aren't about to let them get the best of you. It's your best defense."

"Defense?" she echoed.

He raised up on one elbow and gave her an intent look. "Think of it as war. There may be no swords or guns, but you're involved in a battle of a different sort. Use the weapons at your disposal."

Confused, she ruminated over his advice. "What weapons do I have?"

A soft smile touched his mouth, making him look younger than his years. He touched her temple. "This—your mind. You're quite clever. And *this.*" One long finger brushed her lower lip. "Your mouth. You possess a sharp tongue and wit. If nattering women strike for your heart, strike back. Don't wait for others' approval or rescue."

Karida fell back into the sheets. "What do you mean?"

"Well, when that chit's mother pushed her daughter toward Kareem and belittled you, it was a perfect opportunity to shoot back."

"I *could* have responded instead of remaining silent," Karida agreed. She wrinkled her brow, thinking. "I could have said, 'No, I cannot have children, but Layla will soon turn into her mother, with the same wrinkled brow, sour expression, sagging belly, and nagging tongue that never stops, even in her sleep. You are most welcome to her.'"

Deep laughter rumbled from Nigel. Delight made his emerald eyes sparkle. "You're a quick learner." He reached down and traced her kiss-swollen lips with his finger. "As I knew you would be."

A flush ignited her body as he brushed his mouth against hers and added, "You have a very skilled tongue, talented in many respects. I enjoy it very much when you employ it."

This quiet intimacy bothered her. They had shared their bodies, but she could not share more. She had already lost too much. For that reason, Karida rolled away from him and raised the sheet to her breasts.

"It is done, and I have kept to my side of the bargain," she said quietly. "Now return the ruby. It is my duty to protect it."

Nigel blinked. "Protect? From what would you protect a ruby, my lovely lady?"

"From those who lack honor," she shot back. "Those who would steal it."

"The ruby has only one real value—and that is to unlock the map leading to the treasure of the sleeping golden mummies."

"We protect the treasure of the sleeping golden mummies, we Khamsin. We let the pharaohs rest beneath the sands as they should. Guarding their resting place is honorable. Taking their treasure"—she pinned Nigel with a severe look—"is not."

Emotion flickered in his eyes, but he gave a casual shrug. "The pharaohs are long dead. They have no need of treasure—unless you believe all that nonsense about the Egyptian afterlife."

She stared at him. "I believe in *this* life. My honor in it has a great deal of meaning."

"I believe in this life as well," he replied. "I believe in the moment—and in using it to get all I can."

"You're a thief," she breathed. "You take what is not freely given."

He brushed back a tendril of hair from her face. "I shall not take from you, Karida. Not again. I will wait for you to give. But will you? Or will you hoard yourself, saving yourself for . . . what? For whom will you save yourself when you can give yourself to me and receive a wealth of pleasure in return? Pleasure . . . and understanding. I want you for who you are."

Despite her anger, their attraction could not be denied. Anticipation licked her flesh as he pressed close, his warm breath feathering over her ear. He nuzzled her neck, dropping tiny kisses there, creating a throbbing pleasure that melted her resolve. Nigel palmed her breasts, flicked his thumbs over her cresting nipples. Her head fell back as she absorbed his passion, his need, stoking the smoldering fire heating her body. The crescents of her nails dug into his arms as she anchored herself to him, this dark thief who stole away all reason and thought with his kiss.

He was not gentle this time but frenzied, sinking deep inside her with long, powerful strokes as if trying to drive himself into her soul. The erotic pleasure built nonetheless and found a heated crescendo where her shrill cries mingled with his hoarse shout. At last they lay spent in each other's arms, his head resting on the pillow beside her and his breath harsh in her ear.

Karida closed her eyes, her thighs sore and aching, the space between them tender. So this was what it was like to be a woman—at least a woman wanted by a man, loved by a man. No, not loved, she reminded herself, and her boneless languor faded. Nigel did not love her. She was mistaking lust for something more.

He kissed her temple, rolled away but draped an arm about her waist as if to link them. The thought proved oddly comforting. And disturbing.

He's a liar and a thief, Karida reminded herself.

The grandfather clock in the hallway began to chime. In horror, she counted to eleven. Karida's palms turned clammy and cold. Her gaze whipped about the jumbled sheets, her dress and underclothing on the floor. Nigel's clothing lay nearby.

She'd lost her virginity to a rake and then been tumbled by him again? The first time might be excused as the result of blackmail. The second? It had been nothing but acquiescence to her lust.

Yawning, Nigel raised his head and gave her a bleary look. "What's wrong?"

"I was late in arriving because I had to gather all my courage to come here tonight. I told the earl I'd return before eleven. He warned me not to be late, for I'd ruin my reputation by being unchaperoned in your home. He'll suspect what we've been doing, and I can't face him. I'll be disgraced, and he'll never approve of me now. He'll be disgusted at how immoral I am and will never want me in his house and . . ."

Hysteria made her babble, and she scrambled out of bed, frantically snatching up the scattered hairpins on the floor. With a vicious yank, she twisted her long locks into a tight knot and then reached for her crumpled dress. Her hands shook so badly that she could barely lift it.

Nigel bounded up. Nude, he stalked over to her with the grace of a pacing leopard. He tugged the dress away, tossed it aside. "Easy, easy," he soothed. "You're shaking."

Her hands trembled violently. Karida buried her face in them, not wanting to see his nudity, not wanting to acknowledge the consequences of her actions. "He mustn't know. He *can't* know!" she burst out, lifting her head and staring up at Nigel with panic. "I'll be disgraced."

Nigel said nothing, only led her over to the bed and sat her down. He fished on the floor for her discarded stockings, drawers, and petticoat. As if she were a child, he dressed her with quiet, calm efficiency. Then he shook out her discarded gown and tugged it over her shoulders, fastening the buttons. As she stood and slipped into her shoes, she numbly recognized his vast experience with this.

"Tell the earl you were caught up in playing a game of whist. It will suffice," he advised.

"I will. Yes, it might—it must. He *has* to believe."

Nigel looked at her steadily. She averted her gaze, staring at the wall.

"The ruby. I need my ruby," she told him.

Silence draped the room for a moment, broken only by the frantic thudding of her heart.

"Nigel, I must have it. My ruby. Give it back. Please."

"On one condition," he countered.

Aghast, she dragged her gaze to meet his. Now what did he want? For her to become his mistress? She might yet hide tonight's debauchery, but what if Nigel demanded more? Would he forever shame her? Would she be forever tempted?

"What?" she asked.

"Marry me."

Chapter Ten

"The earl of Claradon to see the earl of Smithfield. I don't have an appointment."

Nigel handed his crisp white card to the stone-faced butler. The man squinted as if trying to discern the letters. After a moment he escorted Nigel inside, watching him as if Nigel were a semidomesticated snake. He escorted him up the stairs to a lavish study.

"Wait here and do not touch anything, my lord," he sternly warned.

Nigel studied the servant, his brain absorbing small details: a tic in the right cheek, bushy brows, shadows beneath the eyes (a drinker?), and a slightly halting gait. It was always useful to study servants. One never knew when such information might come in handy. He nodded, clasped his hands, and watched the butler walk out the door.

An aroma of cherry tobacco and leather hung in the air. Smithfield's study was wholly masculine and inviting, with its polished maplewood desk and leather club chairs by the fire. Nigel investigated, for old habits died hard. He opened a door in a handsome credenza. A safe sat inside. Nigel's hands itched as he studied the combination lock. Surely all sorts of marvelous money was inside. He needed—

No. No more thefts. He closed the credenza.

Alone with his thoughts, he paced. He had been given another chance and thought long into the night, hours past when Karida left babbling that he needed to seek her uncle's permission. Her hysteria had warned him something deeper was at stake. The genuine panic flaring on her face had alarmed him. It wasn't the panic of a virgin realizing she'd been deflowered without the benefit of a wedding ring, but that of a distraught woman terrified she'd risked something worse. Why was Karida so desperate for the earl's approval? He wasn't even a relative!

Nigel hadn't planned to marry Karida, but seeing her hysteria last night had changed his mind. The decision had been, like many others in his life, made on the spot. Marriage would solve her problems and eradicate any fears of scandal. He could also legally own the ruby this way, seek its treasure, and enjoy the delights of her in his bed. Yes, all his chances to start over again were here in this house. Today he would ask for her hand in marriage.

Nigel's blood heated as he remembered Karida's long, naked limbs wrapped about his as she arched her back to meet his violent thrusts. Passion indeed simmered beneath that morally upright exterior. He wanted her with a burning he'd never felt before. He needed a wife, a woman who would mother Eric and give the boy the gentle but firm hand required. She was everything he was not, but he could change. No more secrets. He would be upfront and honest, including telling her about Eric and his real need for the treasure.

A few minutes later, Smithfield entered. The earl did not acknowledge Nigel's proffered hand but took a seat behind his massive desk.

Nigel stood straight, his necktie perfectly positioned, his hands clasped before him. Sweat trickled down his back. Never had he been this nervous. Or this humble.

"I came to ask for the hand of your ward in marriage, sir." *She is everything to me.*

Of course, she also knows much about the traps inside the tomb, his conscience nagged. *Isn't that your true reason for wanting her hand? You haven't changed a bit.*

He dismissed the thought like a swarming gnat. Conscience was a luxury afforded by wealthier men.

Dressed in severe black, Smithfield perched on the edge of his chair behind the desk. His hands steepled, he did not ask Nigel to sit. His piercing gaze reminded Nigel of a snake ready to strike. Silence filled the room apart from the noise of traffic from the window facing the busy London street.

Nigel tried again. "I know her true identity, sir. Her real name is Karida, and she lived with the Khamsin, the tribe your daughter married into. I believe that—"

"What exactly was Anne doing in your home last night besides having supper? She told me you were playing cards. Until midnight?"

Condemnation in the earl's voice and his quiet disapproving look warned Nigel that Karida's words had not been believed. Nigel felt a disturbing mixture of quiet pride in being her first lover and protective anger at the earl's censure.

"Have you dishonored her?" Smithfield demanded.

Nigel thought of Karida's terror at discovery. He could force the earl's hand and tell the truth: *I deflowered your ward and now we must marry.* Instead he chose to lie. "I'm afraid it's my fault. I apologize. I kept her rather late because we were indeed indulged in a rather robust game of whist."

Smithfield's shoulders relaxed the slightest, but his critical look deepened. "I know who you are. Karida told me you are really Nigel, and I made inquiries about you this morning. It did not take long for me to ascertain exactly who I am dealing with. And what."

"I am the true earl of Claradon," Nigel said with dignity. "The title is rightfully mine, and I have proof for any doubters."

Smithfield waved a hand. "I could not care if you were the king himself. Your reputation is what concerns me. The stories of your debauchery and shameful behavior are disgusting. You, of all people, want to marry her? Nigel Wallenford, London's most notorious libertine?"

Nigel took a calming breath and resisted the urge to raise his voice; Smithfield only stated the truth. "I would never hurt her," he stated. "I know the lateness of the hour she arrived home may have been cause for speculation—"

"Not just speculation but scandal, seeing the women who typically frequent your home," Smithfield interrupted. "When I thought you were your brother things were different, but now that I know who you are . . ."

Nigel held on to his unraveling temper. "I assure you, my intentions in asking for Karida's hand are quite honorable." *Liar,* the tatters of his conscience whispered.

"No," Smithfield said.

Nigel stared. "I beg your pardon?"

Lord Smithfield bristled as he stood from his chair. "I have her parents' authority to act on their behalf, and I refuse your offer. I will not subject her to marrying a cad who would make her life miserable. She deserves better."

Pride straightened his shoulders, but Nigel forced himself to remain calm. He, who never begged, now found himself in just such a position. "I know I am not worthy in your eyes— or perhaps in hers," he said in a low voice. "My reputation is indeed . . . rather tarnished. But please, you must understand, I would never hurt Karida. I would cherish her, and I would see to it that she never wants for anything. I promise this. You have my word."

"The word of the gentleman you are not," came the earl's disgusted reply.

Nigel remained silent.

"Understand this," Smithfield said in a dangerously soft voice. "She will never have anything to do with you."

Hatred seeped into Nigel's heart. Memories surged of his father's study, the earl mocking him for being inadequate and failing to live up to the family name. Always he strove to be perfect, and always he failed.

"I would rather see her wed to an Egyptian peasant farmer than spend another hour with you," Smithfield concluded.

"Or a dirty desert jackal?" Nigel suggested with a grim smile.

"A desert jackal is more honorable."

Stunned, Nigel stepped back. Had the earl coldcocked him, he could not have felt more pained. "You misjudge me gravely, and a gentleman would hesitate before calling names. Especially a gentleman who purports to 'know all about me,' including my skill with the Egyptian dagger called the *jambiyah*. Such an insult should be returned in steel," Nigel warned.

"I would have your blood before you even unsheathed your weapon. Don't misjudge my own ability with Egyptian weaponry—or my influence," Smithfield replied. "If you dare dishonor Karida, I will have that entire tribe of Khamsin warriors on your heels, scimitars raised and ready to mince you."

Nigel grimaced. *You bastard, I've a good mind to take you for everything you're worth.* As an idea struck, he hid a smile. *And so I will.*

Silently he dug into his waistcoat pocket and fished out Karida's ruby, cradled it in his palm. He tossed it onto the desk. It rolled like die toward the earl. "Here is something that belongs to your ward. I advise you keep it in a far safer place than between her breasts."

Smithfield's nostrils flared, but he made no reply. Clearly unsettled, he snatched up the ruby, turned, and opened the very same credenza Nigel had earlier investigated. Nigel watched the earl swiftly spin the dial, unlock the safe, and reveal a stack of pound notes and assorted jewels. Smithfield carefully placed the ruby on the top shelf. When he shut the safe and turned back, Nigel made sure to be staring at the fire.

Smithfield pointed to the door. "Leave. Before I do something I shall regret," he advised.

A soft rapping sounded, and both men stepped back as Karida entered the room. Nigel's breath hitched. She was so lovely, her hair pinned up with a few errant curls drifting down, her body covered by a lavender day dress that picked out the flecks of amber in her eyes. Her mouth parted slightly, and those eyes widened.

Nigel gave a short, polite nod. Smithfield left his desk and went to her.

"Karida, please, my dear. Claradon was just leaving."

"Not before I say my piece," Nigel interjected. He shouldered aside Smithfield and took Karida's hand. "I want to marry you," he told her.

Her hand was soft as a butterfly's wing, and she left it trustingly in his, but he read uncertainty in her gaze as she glanced at Smithfield.

Taking a deep breath, he ventured further. "I promise you, I will always be good to you and do everything in my power to make you happy."

"Don't listen to him if you know what is good for you." Smithfield stepped forward, pulled his ward back, breaking their contact. "Karida, I know of what I speak. He is nothing but trouble and will bring you misery." The man shot Nigel a glance powerful enough to shatter granite. "I am firmly opposed to a match, and you will gravely disappoint me if you agree to his proposal."

Nigel stared at Karida, his heart twisting. "I'm sorry, angel. Apparently your guardian thinks I lack certain qualifications for a husband."

"Nigel," she whispered, and the trembling in her voice nearly shattered him. *"Why* are you asking me to marry you?"

Tongue-tied, he could not answer. Liar he'd been to all others, but with her, prevarications did not come as easily. For a shining moment he saw hope: *You have changed!*

And then: *You cannot.*

"We would make a good match," he managed. "I am familiar with Egypt, as you are, and we have much in common. There is much I would . . . share with you."

A little sigh escaped Karida, like a faint moan. He remembered her moans as she strained beneath him, rising to meet his urgent thrusts.

"You must trust me, angel. I want . . ."

I want to change. Please help me. He would not say these things in front of the earl and risk exposure, however. Or humiliation. Fisting his hands, he silently implored her, pleading with his eyes. *Please believe me.*

"I gave the ruby to Smithfield, the ruby I borrowed from you, so you should see my intentions are honorable. I want you as my wife. I *need* you, Karida. I have made grave mistakes in the past, it is true. I need a good woman."

The earl of Smithfield snorted in derision. Karida glanced his way.

"The grave mistake on your part will be if you marry this cad, Karida," her protector said. "You will regret it, trust me. I will never have anything to do with you again." Smithfield paused and said more gently. "Trust me, I do not intend to be so harsh, child, but it is for your own good. For your future happiness."

Karida's expression shifted, and for a fleeting moment Nigel saw anguish and stark fear. Then she hung her head, defeated. "I can't marry you, Nigel. It's not meant to be," she mumbled.

"You're wrong," he countered, stepping forward, hating the plea in his voice. "Let me prove it to you."

But Smithfield pulled Karida away, putting her behind his body as if to shield her. "You'll prove nothing. You heard it from her own mouth, Claradon."

Anger shimmered inside Nigel like a glowing coal. He restrained his temper with every ounce of strength he had. His body tensed until his muscles ached.

"Karida, please, let us meet again and talk when all emotions have calmed and we can be rational." His gaze flicked to the earl. "Perhaps in a few days."

"I leave for Egypt on the next boat." Her pronouncement was regretful, as if she were saying good-bye. "I have already booked passage."

"Leave," Smithfield growled. "You are not welcome here and will never have her. She is much too good for you."

Nigel glared at the earl, his chest heaving with rage. "I did not take you for a fool, Landon, but I see you are one. Because if you 'knew all about me,' you'd know that I never give up on something I want." His gaze flipped to Karida. "And I want your ward. I will have her, consequences be damned. No Khamsin warrior or your weak, puerile threats can stop me."

Color darkened Karida's cheeks. She glanced at the floor and toyed with her hands.

"I will have you, Karida. Nothing will stop me," Nigel warned.

"Get out," Smithfield snapped. "Before I call the authorities."

"And cause Karida embarrassment? I think not—or I might be a better protector than you." Nigel gave a low laugh and touched his forelock in a mocking salute. "But right you are, guv'nor. I's leaving now. Best mind yer ward, now." And his heels clicked on the hardwood floor as he exited. He didn't bother to shut the door.

"You will never have her! Ever! She's rid of you for good," Smithfield shouted after him.

Nigel swore vengeance.

Chapter Eleven

She was leaving soon, and that was her one happiness.

Katherine saw to it that Karida was busy and took her shopping for anything she wanted, but gowns, lacy lingerie, extravagant hats, and shining jewels held no appeal. Her spirit weary, she desired only to return to Egypt. Had Nigel wanted to marry her for something less selfish than his own purposes? Had she made a mistake in rejecting him because she wanted her real father's acceptance?

No, Nigel's proposal surely held an ulterior motive. He must have learned she'd been briefed on the traps in the tomb. Though new to desire, she was intelligent enough to realize passion did not always join practicality in bed. They had shared an amazing sexual experience—her first, and one where she'd felt vulnerable but cherished—but Nigel was Nigel. Marriage to him was an impossible proposition. He had no true feelings for anyone, and she couldn't ever be certain he'd put her needs first. They had shared passion, but that was all.

No, he could never love her. Even if he dared to profess such an emotion, she'd know him to simply be worse than she'd previously assumed. How could any man love her with the flaws of her flesh? She'd had time to think about it, and Nigel had only wanted her because she represented sexual conquest.

A hollow ache settled in her chest. For one bittersweet night she'd seen the admiration in his eyes, had known the passion between a man and a woman. For one achingly beautiful night, she had known shared desire.

But it was past now, and she had to move on. She was a woman without true marriage prospects. She had to make her own way.

A tiny sigh escaped her as she instructed her maid to finish packing the steamer trunk for the journey back to Egypt. The little maid admired her lace and silk gowns and the delicate silk undergarments. Karida glanced at them with regret. Such pretty things. So very English. Such a shame she would never wear them again after they docked in Port Said.

She took to bed early that night. Filled with a restlessness that would not be quelled, she finally slept. But Karida dreamed of Nigel. He was standing above her, dressed as a butler. Torment filled his gaze as he reached out a trembling hand. His kiss was barely a whisper against her cheek, and when she called his name, he vanished like the wind.

Karida awakened and sat up, chilled suddenly by a cool breeze drifting through an open window. She did not bother to check the tears suddenly streaming down her cheeks, but sleep was fleeting for the rest of the night.

In the morning, as she helped herself to sausage, kippers, and eggs from the sideboard, the earl of Smithfield walked into the breakfast room. Worry pinched his face. "Karida, did you see anyone in the house last night?"

She shook her head, puzzled. "What happened?"

"It's nothing. I . . . seem to have misplaced some money. Perhaps it was my wife on another shopping spree." He gave a small smile. "And so, you are on your way back to Egypt, far from that libertine. It is for the best—though I do not know why you judge all Englishmen by him."

Karida shivered. She'd had to give an excuse for leaving before she found a husband and tarring all of England's peers with the same brush as Nigel was expedient. But the truth was Egypt seemed far safer, a land far from Nigel's ominous threats.

I will have you and nothing will stop me. Nothing.
Even more terrifying was that she wanted to be had.

The lid on the steamer trunk closed with a satisfactory thud. Nigel sat on it. "Good-bye, earl of Claradon. Hello, Charles Porter," he said.

He checked his wallet again and gave a small smile. It was fat with pound notes. "Smithfield, you fool," he murmured, replacing it.

It had been easy enough to obtain the clothing and wig from an ex-lover, an actress. Even easier to steal inside the earl's house at night, disguised as his butler. He'd given his ruby cuff links to Reeves as a bribe to discover Smithfield's butler had a fondness for the bottle; then, at a local pub, Reeves had purchased the man several drinks on the night Nigel designated. The memorized safe combination delivered the cash into his hands. The ruby, however, had been gone.

No matter. He would get it back.

Compelled by insanity or desire, or both, he'd also snuck into Karida's room and stood by her bedside. He could not resist placing a small, chaste kiss on her cheek. Though he'd wanted much more.

Soon, though, he would have it.

Ah, but not for awhile.

Nigel slid off the trunk and went to the mirror to check his appearance. The severe black suit and dull black tie were far more distinguished than his checked or paisley waistcoats. The black wig was cropped short, and the pencil-thin mustache tickled a little. His normally hardy complexion was now pale and sallow, thanks to cosmetics, and his nose was bulbous, courtesy of his friend who'd fashioned him one of putty. Nigel stuffed a little cotton between his upper gums and his cheeks to make them puff out. This felt uncomfortable but was necessary.

He picked up the spectacles from the bureau and slid them

on. They were made of ordinary glass but had a tint, turning his eyes more blue than green.

"My own dear mama would not recognize me," he muttered, adjusting the glasses. "Then again, she couldn't care less."

On his steamer trunk lay a ticket. Karida thought she was rid of him, but as Charles Porter, he would be harmless, bland . . . and stuck to her side. Then, when he had her alone and by his side in Cairo, he would have her naked beneath him.

"No one gets rid of me for good," he said fiercely to the mirror. "You'll see, my sweet. You shall see."

He had one more task to accomplish before leaving, so Nigel stripped off his disguise and dressed again in his usual attire of a dark suit with a paisley waistcoat. He left the town house, glancing over his shoulder. No one seemed to be following him, but he had the eerie feeling someone was. He shook it off.

The journey to the tenant cottage in Manchester seemed to take much longer than usual. As he rode Ariel to his destination, the little hairs on the back of his neck rose.

Why was he feeling so uneasy? Eric was safe. Nothing much could happen to him. But as he dismounted in front of the cottage, dread filled Nigel. The house was far too quiet.

He raced up the broken walk. He did not bother to knock but flung open the door. Darkness permeated the sagging structure. Absently he reminded himself again to hire a good steward to oversee the estate and make the necessary repairs, once he had the money.

Richards and his wife and children weren't there. Nigel called out, his heart beating frantically. "Eric, damn it, where are you?"

The grounds were deserted, too. Nigel sat on a stump, thinking hard. Perhaps they'd taken Eric out for the day and visited a neighbor. He'd just stood to walk back inside the cottage when the back door opened. William Oakley stepped outside.

Now he knew he had been followed. Though his heart thudded, Nigel forced himself to speak calmly. "Oakley, what the devil are you doing here? Out to inspect my properties? I don't recall inviting you."

"Seeing to your tenants' care better than you ever could, Claradon. And your son."

Nigel's heart dropped into his stomach. "What the hell have you done, you bastard?"

"Wrong terminology. I'm not the bastard. He is. Adorable child, well-mannered—much more than you were at his age. Even with the blond hair I could tell he was yours."

"Eric is my *father's* by-blow," Nigel countered.

"That's not what Charlotte told me. She was playing you both for fools, you and your brother. She may have warmed your beds, but she was in love with me. Before your twin left for Egypt with Jasmine, Charlotte told me everything."

Nigel's shock faded to disgust. "Then she was a bigger whore than I imagined, Oakley. And you are a far bigger fool."

Anger darkened Oakley's face, made it ugly. "Charlotte told me there was one thing you valued most—a little boy you sired, a boy you never thought your worthless bollocks could produce."

All blood drained from Nigel. His hands went limp at his side. He wasn't sure how to respond.

"A boy you found in the workhouse after his mother died."

Nigel closed his eyes, emitting a torrent of curse words. This was Charlotte, laughing at him from the grave. Why ever had he trusted her?

Because he'd been a fool and wanted connection. After he'd returned to London in disguise last year, smuggling a very delicate and expensive stelae from Cairo, he'd made the only true mistake of his adult life: he'd gotten mixed up with Charlotte. She'd been delighted to know he was alive and deliciously giddy to keep his secret. She'd been a wildcat in bed, fierce and demanding. And when they returned to his London town house,

Nigel again pretending to be his brother, they'd intercepted a letter meant for him—a letter that proved the Claradon twin Nigel, whom his parents had thought sterile, was a father.

The letter-writer was woman who had birthed a son six years earlier. She was dying and living in the workhouse with her boy, and had begged Nigel to care for his son. He had immediately made plans to do so but had made this mistake of relating them to Charlotte.

Opening his eyes, he studied Oakley's sneer.

"Char told me everything, about the treasure, about how you schemed with her to get back the scorpion amulet from your twin so you could obtain the map. For such a smart man, you made one very large mistake, Nigel. You thought she loved you. But she loved me, not you." Oakley's mouth flattened. "You didn't even go to her funeral, you bastard. Tommy cabled her brother and told him she met an accident while exploring some ruins. They had her body shipped back to England, like cargo, and you weren't there. I always thought you had something to do with it and that your damn brother covered it up. From the look on your face, I'm sure of it."

Black guilt surged through Nigel. He tried to ignore both it and the rapid war drums of his heartbeat. The past was gone. Only Eric mattered.

"Where is my son?" he demanded.

"Safe. For now. A place where he is very . . . productive. Your tenants were happy to get rid of him and gain new employment somewhere else. Their cottage is much larger, and the money I've given them far more than your paltry bribes."

The family was likely on Oakley's family estate. Nigel's mind raced. He could ride there and find Eric by tonight.

Oakley laughed. "Your boy isn't anywhere you will find him. Far too easy. But he *is* in an institution where he is gainfully employed."

Nigel rushed forward, ready to strangle the man. Oakley whipped out a knife.

"You fool, you think I'd come here unarmed? Not that I'd hurt you too badly. We need you too much." Oakley flipped the blade into the air, caught it by the handle. "Eric needs you. Poor Eric. Your one downfall."

"He's a child, Oakley. You would not hurt a child."

"Probably not," the man agreed. "Even as much as I hate you. But there are ships to America leaving frequently from Liverpool these days, or from Ireland, bound for America. Steerage is filled with immigrants. I'm certain someone might take him in hand when he reached shore."

Panic made Nigel's hands clammy. He wanted to choke Oakley until the man begged and screamed for mercy. He would show none.

His brother's friend laughed. "Ironic, isn't it? You, who are so skilled at manipulating people and putting them in ugly spots. How does it feel to be bested? There's a steamer leaving London in a few days. I know you're booked on it, headed back to find that treasure you told Charlotte about. I'll settle for half, leave you a share for all your hard work. Fair, don't you think? But get the treasure and bring it back to London or you'll never see your son again."

Helpless anger engulfed Nigel. He clenched his fists and stared at Oakley with such deep hatred that he knew his soul would be blackened forever. *Change? I do not want to, because I will see you dead, you son of a bitch.*

As he turned, heading mutely for his horse, Oakley called out. Nigel spun back, saw a humorless smile touch the man's thin mouth.

"You'd better watch your step, Nigel. There are many who would delight in slitting your throat and tossing your worthless corpse overboard, and I'm not the only one who knows where you're going. I'd be very careful if I were you." Oakley's mirthless smile deepened. "*Very* careful."

Chapter Twelve

The journey by sea promised to be both relaxing and boring, though Karida dreaded returning to the Khamsin camp. Nuri and his wife would surely be disappointed she'd failed to find a suitable groom.

For the first two days, she kept to her bed on the pretext of seasickness to avoid the crowds of excited, cheery passengers on holiday. The spacious, first-class private cabin was all hers; Katherine had a separate suite of rooms, as Smithfield insisted on acquiring the best accommodations for them both. He also found a woman, Clarice, to act as lady's maid to them both in exchange for her passage. She was on her way to Cairo to be married to her betrothed, an employee with the British government.

The dull hum of the ship's engines echoed in her ears like Khamsin war drums. Karida clutched her feather pillow and buried her face in it. Her stomach churned like the water stirred by the ship's passing.

Smithfield only paid for our cabins because he wants his legitimate daughter comfortable. He cares not one whit about his illegitimate one, only that I am gone and safely forgotten once more.

Sour disappointment filled her soul. At their parting, the earl had acted just as dismissive as the day he'd first sent her to live with the Khamsin. Wild hope had filled her that just this once he might actually hug and smother her with the affection she craved and shout to the world her real parentage. But no, he'd briskly kissed her cheek, wished her well, and hustled her off.

She knew she should be happy; she had the ruby and was returning to Egypt. She could again hope to obtain the money to fund a little jewelry boutique somewhere, even if she chose never to return to London. Why, then, did she feel as if she were sailing back into a cage? And why could she not forget Nigel? In Egypt she'd never have to worry about hands that skillfully stroked and aroused her flesh to extreme heights, hands of a sinfully handsome earl with jade eyes but a thief's heart.

In late afternoon of the second day, boredom got to Karida. She dressed in a lemon yellow gown with a white-yoked bodice and subjected herself to the bindings of a tight corset. Then she went to join Katherine for tea in the first-class lounge.

Small round tables with wicker chairs were covered with fine tablecloths and a silver tea service with bone china cups. Sunlight splashed through the high arched windows, spearing white paneled walls. It all looked very genteel and English. The thought depressed her.

Wending her way through the tables filled with straight-backed women and serious men, she spotted her aunt sitting with a young man and an elderly woman draped in black bombazine. The man, in a dull black suit matching his equally dull black hair, stood upon seeing her, the bluish spectacles perched on his bulbous nose giving him a bookish air.

Her aunt stood and gave her an affectionate peck on the cheek. "Karida, dear, I'm so pleased you can finally join me."

Murmuring hello, Karida sat on the cushioned chair the young man thoughtfully pulled out for her.

As her aunt resumed her seat, introductions were made: "This is Mrs. Rushton and Mr. Charles Porter. They have been asking about my experiences in Egypt. It's a first time for them both."

Mrs. Rushton squinted at Karida with rheumy eyes, her expression as sour as if she'd sucked on several lemons. Charles Porter was a man of prodigious height but had a sallow complexion and a dour air. A thin black mustache set off a mouth that might have been sensual but for the compressed set of his lips, as if he kept secrets well guarded. He looked as fussy as his starched collar.

"Miss Sharif . . ." he began.

"Please, call me Karida."

Behind the spectacles, his eyes rounded to saucers. "Why, I am afraid I cannot be so familiar and call you by your Christian name, seeing we have just been introduced."

It's hardly a Christian *name,* she thought with a sigh.

"Miss Sharif, might I assume you have also seen the splendors of Egypt? I have heard the natives are fearsome and dirty, and caution is advised when traveling among them." He arranged his silverware in an exact pattern, aligned his teacup so it sat perfectly upon its saucer. Nearby, Mrs. Rushton took a liberal slurp of tea. Katherine's smile looked strained.

"Caution is always advised when traveling, Mr. Porter, be it over land in fair Egypt or on a sea voyage." Karida reached for a cucumber sandwich.

To her consternation, the man began nattering about the very nature of caution. It seemed his favorite word, for he dropped it in each sentence until she felt like banging her head on her china plate. Mrs. Rushton excused herself after the tenth usage, but Karida's aunt remained, a polite smile frozen on her face.

"I must admit I never endeavored to journey on such a hazardous trip before, and I am a trifle cautious of the diseases one may encounter. Even on board such a fine vessel, one must be cautious. Why, the very tea I drink I am cautious to ensure it is the good black Ceylon. I consume this each day back at my London flat with my mother. Mother cautioned me to avoid drinking Arabic coffee because I have a very delicate constitution and one never knows with foreign foods! Germs breed disease and I hear that . . ."

Karida's eyes glazed over. She'd never known a man could be such a consummate bore.

Unbidden, memories of Nigel arose: his cheeky grin and

colorful waistcoats, his sense of life. His offering to sit on the floor, Bedouin-style, and drink hot, rich black coffee. His leaping into adventure and daring without a single thought to the aftermath.

His claiming her body with magic hands and a disregard for her scars.

Katherine finally stood, her smile strained. "Please excuse me. I believe I'll rest before dinner. No, no, feel free to stay," she added as Karida pushed back from the table to join her. "You young people get to know each other better."

An oath almost escaped her lips as her aunt walked off, and Karida sank back into her chair, racking her brain for a way to find discourse that didn't involve caution or germs and disease.

"What is the nature of your occupation, Mr. Porter?" she asked.

The man's owlish expression grew even more intense. "Why, banking, of course. The only assured future for a young man on the rise. I began as a clerk to Mr. Samuel Perrington— a cautious ascent as I worked with him, as he's the senior . . ."

Was it possible to drown oneself in a simple cup of tea? Karida eyed her cup, but it was empty. Maybe if she leapt overboard, she could swim to Egypt.

Mr. Porter seemed to catch himself. He actually looked embarrassed. "I beg pardon, Miss Sharif. I do seem to go on and on about myself. I am afraid it is a rather bad habit when I'm in the company of a pretty woman such as yourself. Tend to prattle like a schoolgirl, I do. Would you do me the favor of accompanying me in a stroll about the deck? I promise I will be quiet."

He looked so sincere and earnest that Karida felt sorry for him. Surely it was not his fault that she was comparing him to a man she could not forget.

A man she *must* forget.

Maybe Nigel could be forgotten if she acquainted herself with other men. Here was the opportunity to try.

"I would be delighted," she replied.

A balmy sea breeze and warm sunshine caressed her cheeks as they made their way around the deck. Several lounge chairs had been set out for the passengers, some of whom were bundled in wraps as they took in the air. Karida clasped her hands firmly before her as Mr. Porter walked at her side.

"Do tell me about yourself, Miss Sharif. How did you come to make plans to visit Egypt for a holiday?"

She explained how she lived in Egypt and had been visiting London. He laced his hands behind his back and looked rapt.

"A fine lady such as yourself, might I inquire if you have a beau?"

Her stomach pitched and rolled once more. "No, I am quite unattached."

She drifted over to the railing as he began an account of his bachelor state and how he would eventually marry and have a family when he had saved enough money. Karida clasped the railing as she stared at the azure waters below.

"And no beaus have offered for your hand in marriage?"

Only a libertine who seduced my body and threatened to steal my soul. But he's out of my life for good.

"One did. But I refused him," she said quietly. "He did not meet with my guardian's satisfaction."

"Nor *your* satisfaction?"

A slight sigh fled her. "It was quite impossible."

Mr. Porter pushed at his spectacles. She glanced at him, and for a moment saw his gaze sharpen oddly. A wave of uneasiness washed over her. He looked vaguely familiar. But then his prim mouth compressed, and he assumed his usual prissy expression.

"He probably was not the right one. I am sure there will be others."

"Oh, I'll never get attached." Karida waved a hand, pretending indifference.

"Never say never," Mr. Porter replied. "Because one never knows what the future may bring."

She was so damn beautiful, the ocean breeze playing with loose strands of her dark brown hair. Those caramel eyes were sad, thoughtful, and they stared off at the distant horizon. Dared he hope she thought of him?

You are a fool, Nigel reminded himself.

He'd thought it'd be an easy game, disguising himself as Charles Porter. Nigel had forgotten the effect Karida had on him. The alluring scent of her delicate perfume, the way the light picked out strands of gold and amber in her dark hair, the intriguing cast of her stubborn round chin and her full, ruby-red lips.

The shapely swells of her breasts as she stood in dignified silence made his heart beat faster. Heat filled his groin, and Nigel tensed against rising lust. Charles Porter would not sport a raging erection while escorting even an exotic beauty about the deck. Make an insipid remark cautioning about sea spray stinging her eyes? Yes. Taking her madly in a ship stairwell, no.

But Nigel could not look upon her without remembering her soft body lying in his arms, her tiny, excited cries as he brought her from one exhausting peak of pleasure to another. Or the cold distance in her eyes the day after, when she'd retreated from him.

Bitter resentment replaced his lust-filled awe. Nigel clenched his jaw, glad of the anger. He had to remember how she'd rejected him. She deserved no pity or mercy.

"What of you, Mr. Porter?" she inquired. "Why you are journeying to Egypt? To indulge in travel and adventure before settling down?" Mischief twinkled in her eyes. She rested her hand on the railing, her mouth pursed in amusement. Nigel realized she was teasing him.

He cleared his throat. "You might say. Though I'm not

quite certain what adventure I might have in such a place. Quite dangerous to indulge in adventures. I prefer to play it safe and always err on the side of caution."

She smiled. "You might at least attempt a good cup of Arabic coffee, Mr. Porter. I daresay it will be your greatest adventure yet." She reached out and patted his arm.

Nigel nearly shouted with laughter, and burned with lust at her touch. *Yes, sweet, I find Porter as tiresome as you. Shall we do away with him, stuff him into a closet while you and I take advantage of the nearest lifeboat? You and I would share adventures of a far grander sort than you can even dream.*

But he forced himself to stay in control. He drew back and pushed the glasses up his nose, peering at her as if studying a new species. "Do you say, Miss Sharif? Really, drink Arabic coffee? You do not think it will upset my digestive system? I have a delicate stomach, and I am always worried about trying new things."

"If you add enough milk and sugar, I daresay you wouldn't even notice the difference between it and tea. Oh, do go on, Mr. Porter. Show the world how brave a man can be."

Nigel affected an air of earnestness. "For you, Miss Sharif, I shall. Yes, I shall indeed try—even if I must sweeten it with all the sugar in Cairo."

Inside, he laughed. *Yes, I shall try very hard. And when I have you at my mercy and naked beneath me, you'll see exactly how sweet things can be.*

For the next two days, Karida found herself always accompanied. The man was like sea air. He would be taking tea in the lounge if she went there for afternoon refreshment, and also anywhere else she considered. He dogged her footsteps with a ruthlessness her aunt found amusing.

"I'm sorry for abandoning you, but you did wish to meet eligible English men, and I saw no ring on his finger. He could improve," Katherine pointed out. "Simply get to know Mr.

Porter better, Karida. He seems nice enough, even if it's only for the duration of the cruise. It's easier than avoiding him."

"He hasn't improved. He's a dullard. And he's departing at Port Said like we are. What if I never lose him?" Karida despaired.

"I sincerely doubt he is sufficiently besotted to trail you back to our people. Heaven knows how many foreign dishes he'd be forced to suffer through once there!"

They laughed together in a rare moment of camaraderie, and Karida agreed.

She decided to shock Mr. Porter the next day and bluntly told him of her home, the Bedouin lifestyle, and how she normally spent her days. She expected that her gleeful embellishment of the feasts, and of the slaughtering of sheep, and how eating the eyeball was a tremendous delicacy reserved for honored guests would make him scurry away; she was sorely disappointed.

"The eyeball, so you say? Oh, my! Now *that* is a cuisine I should not indulge in. I daresay I would not ask to be invited to your tribe." He gave a faint shudder, then looked thoughtful. "Though it might help correct my sight, eating an eyeball, if it were an eyeball of excellent health and quality."

Karida stared a moment, but when he grinned at her, she burst into laughter. He wasn't a bad fellow, and she had to stop making comparisons to Nigel. Mr. Charles Porter was simply a dependable and steady sort. He wasn't the type to blackmail a woman into bed or steal an ancient ruby.

After a third day in his company, she actually found herself establishing a routine. They played shuffleboard in the mornings after breakfast— "When the sun is not too terribly hot," he'd suggested—and took short walks on the deck. In the afternoon, they read in the ship's library. He preferred, much to her amusement, books relating to finance and travel brochures about what he could expect on his visit. She indulged in poetry.

They dined together with her aunt each night at the long

tables in the first-class dining salon. Utterly courteous, even when they were alone on their afternoon walks, he made no moves, not even to hold her hand. He became a sadly predictable but almost soothing companion.

Because he was so nonthreatening, she found herself opening up to him. He actually listened, his hands laced behind his back as they strolled the deck, and she talked of her duties and the vow she'd taken to protect the treasure of the golden mummies.

"And what of yourself and what you want?" he queried at last. "It is all well and good to accept such a noble task, but is there anything for you?"

She almost told him of the money she'd been promised, of her little dream to open a small boutique and sell Bedouin jewelry and Egyptian antiquities—and of earning her father's acknowledgement and respect at last. Almost.

"It is enough for me to know I have honor," she replied.

His expression shifted, and its hardness surprised her. "Ah, Miss Sharif, honor in life is not everything. One cannot eat it or sell it when times are hard." Then he chuckled as if making a little joke and nattered on about the practical challenges of commerce.

Karida stared, wondering at the change that had briefly overcome him. He had almost seemed a different person.

A week into the voyage, they sat on wooden deck chairs, enjoying the afternoon sun just before dinner. Mr. Porter, bundled to his chin and resembling an Arab shielding himself against the most brutal sun, surprised her.

"I suppose it is rather presumptuous, but may I suggest a card game in the lounge? You might find it challenging?"

Karida shifted in her seat, stretching her legs and smoothing down her pale pink dress. "What kind of card game?"

"Poker," he suggested.

Carrying on the masquerade of being the boring Charles Porter had proven ever more tedious and difficult. Karida's openness and friendly confidences had lulled him into dropping the pretense at times. She was proving far more intelligent and complex than he'd realized. He found himself longing to share his true nature. He held back, however, knowing the friendship and affection could not last.

It was to put her at a distance, to remind himself of the true rogue he was at heart, that he challenged her in a game that tempted his true nature. He'd cheated at poker for longer than he could remember, indeed, had earned enough money from the sport to keep creditors at bay while financing his smuggling from Egypt.

They sat now in the vessel's recreational lounge at a small square table. Few others were present. Nigel found himself fascinated by the furrows of concentration wrinkling Karida's brow as he explained to her the game's mechanics.

A tiny sigh escaped her. "I fear I am not very good at mathematics, and this seems a game where numbers reign supreme."

"Oh, but you'll do fine, Miss Sharif. Just remember what I've explained."

"Gambling seems out of character for you, Mr. Porter."

He caught the flare of suspicion on her face and quickly changed tack. "It's just a bit of sport, that's all. I never play for high stakes, so therefore it is not *true* gambling. Shall we play for spare change?" Nigel dug into his trouser pocket and withdrew a handful of coins, placing them in precise stacks on the table.

Karida dug into her reticule and withdrew a few coins. She cradled them as if they were treasure and then added them to his stack.

The game commenced. The old thrill raced through him as Nigel studied his hand.

Karida rearranged her cards. "I wonder what my father would think of me playing a man's game. I'm afraid it would lower his opinion of me."

Nigel lifted his eyes to study her, sitting so pristine and erect as an Egyptian obelisk. *Oh for pity's sake, just lean your elbows on the table for once,* he wanted to shout. *You don't have to sit so damn straight all the time.*

Irritation speared him, and he muttered. "You have to be true to yourself. You can't live for someone else's expectations."

"Wise words," she replied. "Do you heed them with your own father?"

Her question took him aback. Nigel answered quickly, "But of course."

Karida gave a small, sad smile that pierced his heart. Then she went back to studying her cards.

He'd said he followed his own advice, but did he? He'd spent his entire childhood trying to please his father and be perfect to regain his affection. Then, after he'd discovered his father's disgust, he'd found himself doing the exact opposite. Nigel had gone from trying to live up to someone's expectations to living against them. He was a man without friends or allies, and trapped in more ways than he realized. And more importantly, he was a man rejected by the one woman who'd made him feel truly alive.

Resentment rippled through him, made him want to shake Karida from the marble pedestal on which she stood. He wanted to tumble her off it and into his world of lies, deception, and greed. He'd done it once before when she had come to his home to steal back the ruby. He'd made her change, corrupted her—if only briefly and for honorable reasons. Could he change as well? Could he become honorable?

I cannot change.

I will not *change.*

Another small sigh escaped her as she fanned out her cards. "I'm not certain if I'm doing this right."

Nigel glanced at his hand. Cheating at cards was one of his smallest sins. He could win this game even if she were better skilled, could win without effort and make her feel defeated and small. She was easy prey, a fish already hooked. Her small stack of pennies on the table was no fortune, but it would be a personal victory. He would take every damn coin she touched, would hoard them like a miser, cherishing the metal warmed by her touch.

Or, he might teach her to cheat. He'd enjoy that, watching her honor corrode, watching her give in to this new temptation and slowly become as corrupt as he.

Dragging his gaze from his hand, he watched her expression. There was no guile in her eyes as she studied her cards, no desperation. Sudden insight flashed: she didn't care as much as he.

"Tell me, Miss Sharif, what will you do if you lose?" he challenged.

Those exotic amber eyes lifted, and she shrugged. "Why, nothing. Except perhaps try again, assuming I enjoy it. Surely the object of the game is to have a good time, is it not? Because it is a game and nothing more, even if a few pennies are involved."

Taken aback, Nigel dropped his gaze. He stared wordlessly at his cards. All thrill of defeating her, of taking her miserable coins and silently crowing over his victory, all joy deflated like a punctured balloon. When was the last time he'd indulged in the pursuit of simple pleasure? Even bed sport had become something resembling a challenge as much as an activity to chase away his constant loneliness.

In a subtle movement, he tucked four cards up his jacket sleeve and traded them for four new cards from the deck. "I call, Miss Sharif." And he laid down his hand.

With a soft noise, Karida displayed her own cards, face up. "I have four of a kind, but no king," she said. She looked up at him in question.

A wry smile touched his mouth. "I concede defeat, Miss Sharif."

The delighted look of astonishment on her face, like that of a child discovering a brightly wrapped gift, touched something deep inside Nigel. He'd seen a similar look on Eric's face the day he rescued the boy from the workhouse. It was such an expression of innocent joy, it chipped away at the hard granite wall surrounding his heart.

Propping his chin in his hands, he regarded Karida with silent pleasure. Her happiness spilled over, and he absorbed it like a sea sponge; it filled the cold empty space inside him.

"Mr. Porter? Are you quite all right?"

Karida waved her hand before his face. A frown wrinkled her lovely brow. It almost seemed she saw past the blue-tinted spectacles and knew him for who he truly was.

Nigel blinked in startled unease. Bloody hell, he'd been eyeing her like a love-struck lad. His disguise had slipped considerably.

Back in form, old boy.

He sat straight and began fussing with the cards, returned to the deck the straight flush he'd concealed in his sleeve. "I do say, Miss Sharif, I had thought I might win. I am always cautious when it comes to playing cards, and of course I caution myself never to gamble. It's such a dreadful sin . . ."

Cold relief filled him as her eyes began to glaze over. She pushed back from the table and said, "I thank you, Mr. Porter, for teaching me poker, but I'm afraid I should look for my aunt now. I must prepare for dinner."

He stood and gave a stiff, formal bow, then bit back an amused grin as she walked off. *I'd get away from me as well.*

"Miss Sharif!" he called, watching as she turned with a stiff smile. He gestured to the small pile on the table. "You forgot your winnings."

"Please, keep them. They're nothing but pennies, after all. We can use them for our next game." And with an airy wave she strode off, her jasmine perfume a whisper scenting the air.

Keep it. Nothing but pennies.

Nigel sank back into his chair, his former thoughts forgotten. Of course. She was a wealthy earl's ward, and pennies were as abundant as grains of sand in the desert. As abundant as the number of people who hated him.

Coins jumped on the table as he smashed his fist down. "Damn you," he muttered. "Damn you and your desert honor." Suddenly weary, he removed his spectacles, rubbed his eyes, and stared sightlessly ahead at the bank of windows looking out onto the open sea.

A round-faced, pudgy man in a rumpled brown suit, his tie slightly askew, stopped and stared. "Nigel Smith? Is that you? Yes, it is, it is! You bastard!"

Oh, bloody hell. Icy panic filled his veins. This man had called him by the name Nigel used in his former smuggling business, but he wasn't familiar. Then again, Nigel seldom remembered the men he'd bilked.

The man vaguely resembled Glen Bachman, his former partner. They had set up a profitable business in smuggling antiquities, Nigel handling the goods and Bachman arranging transport. Unfortunately, Bachman was quick-tempered and a drunk. Nigel had ended their partnership after a disastrous shipment nearly ended them both in jail. The timing of the break was poor, for every penny Nigel earned had gone to pay a sizable debt—or, rather, the sizable gentleman who had come to collect. Last he'd heard, Bachman relocated to the continent.

He quickly masked his surprise. Nigel donned his spectacles again and assumed a blank expression.

"I beg your pardon, but I fear you're mistaken," he said in Charles Porter's most nasal tone.

"It is you! Can't fool me, no disguise can fool me. I was told you were onboard, and that's why I booked passage." The man leaned heavily on the table, his bloodshot gaze piercing Nigel's. "I've seen your ugly face thousands of times in my sleep. Each night I see it I think of how you ruined me, you absolutely ruined me. My poor Nellie would have nothing to do with me."

Who the hell was Nellie? Women's faces sped through Nigel's thoughts like a series of travel postcards. "I fear I do not know this Nellie you mention, Mister . . ."

"Martin. Martin Jones. You know me, thief! My Nellie!" the man shouted. "You philanderer, you stole my love away! You ruined her, absolutely ruined her and then left her!"

The few people in the lounge turned and looked Nigel's way. Sweat trickled down his back. He sat straighter and frowned.

"I am sorry this Nigel person ruined you, sir, but I have nothing to do with him, and I know not this person to whom you refer. He sounds like a disreputable sort, and I make it my aim never to associate with the like." He pushed back from the table and made to escape.

Jones lurched forward, but Nigel sidestepped his fist. His right hand slid up the man's neck, found the right spot, and squeezed. Jones's eyes rolled up in his head. Nigel caught him as he slumped forward.

A steward rushed over. "Is this man bothering you, Mr. Porter?" he asked as Nigel put Jones in a chair.

"The poor chap is quite foxed, and he passed out. He mistook me for someone with whom he's had a quarrel and attempted to assault me," he explained. He pulled out a few pound notes and pressed them into the steward's hand. "Please see to it that he remains far from me the rest of the journey."

"Very good, sir. I'll have him confined to his cabin."

A groan came from the awakening Mr. Jones. As the steward took his arm, Nigel's assailant allowed himself to be led away as quiet and docile as a child.

Nigel glanced around the lounge, deeply shaken. He pocketed the money on the table and went to his cabin.

His first-class accommodations were pricey, but they, like everything else recently, had been paid for with Lord Smithfield's stolen money. The spacious suite boasted a large bed with a brocade spread, paneled walls, polished furniture, and a sitting room with a sofa and club chairs. It even had a private washroom.

Nigel removed his disguise, splashed water on his face, and dried briskly off with a towel. He felt tainted and dirty. His past had followed him onboard. Would it always trail behind, waiting to expose him?

The mirror showed his face stark in the naked light. "You could never change," he whispered to that image. "No matter what. They won't let you."

An ugly thought struck him as he sat down on a red velvet settee: If Jones had recognized him, what were the chances Karida would, too?

"Pull it tighter, Clarice." Karida sucked in a trembling breath as the maid grunted and strained to lace her into the corset.

"Are you certain, miss? Seems like you'd scarce be able to breathe."

"Do it!"

She needed a tight corset. Needed a reminder that propriety and manners ruled and honor guided her steps. That little game of poker this afternoon had greatly unsettled her. The game itself was harmless, even if it was gambling. The man playing the game was not quite so harmless.

She had seen, just for a moment, when he'd pondered her question about expectations, a glimmer of someone else in his eyes. She'd seen her nemesis.

Of course, Charles Porter was no Nigel, but that flash had reminded her of the man. The same vulnerable tilt to his mouth, the full lips loose and slightly twisted, as if he pondered regret. She could not afford to have Nigel in her life in any form.

"There now, miss. Can't pull it any tighter."

Karida wheezed as she released her breath. Goodness, she'd have to limit her courses at dinner! Thankfully she wasn't the fainting type and was accustomed to denying herself little pleasures.

By the time the gong sounded in the first-class dining salon, Nigel had recovered his aplomb. He was back in form as Porter and determined to be as dull as ever.

The walnut-paneled dining room was magnificent. Bowls of fresh-cut flowers adorned each table. Leaded crystal lamps cast pools of golden light on the bone china settings. The tableware was polished, the linen tablecloths and napkins freshly starched. A small string orchestra accompanied the clink of heavy silverware and trill of light conversation.

Spine straight, Karida looked as lovely as ever in a beaded pink satin gown as she picked up a heavy spoon to sip at the watercress soup. But she was quiet. Too quiet. Hell, Nigel hoped word of the ugly incident in the lounge hadn't reached her.

"More wine, Miss Sharif?" He gestured for the steward.

"No, thank you. I fear I am a trifle under the weather tonight."

Damn, she did look pale; her complexion lacked its usual glow.

"Might I suggest a walk on deck after our repast?"

She nodded toward several men sitting nearby. "I would have thought you'd enjoy brandy and cigars like the others are wont to do."

Hell, no; not tonight. He wasn't about to saunter into a room filled with men who might bear him a distant grudge. "I would rather enjoy the pleasure of your company," he replied.

But when the dessert of truffles and chocolate was finished and the men pushed back to head for the smoker, Karida stood. She sucked in a breath and seemed to list starboard, like the ship had been nudged by a giant wave.

"Are you quite well? Perhaps you should retire to your cabin," Nigel suggested.

Karida waved his offer aside. "Fresh air is what I need, Mr. Porter. Please, let us go."

A silver moon hung in the sky. Light glistened off the ocean's mirrorlike surface. If he weren't so intent on looking over his shoulder, Nigel would have enjoyed the quietness and the dreamy romance of the scene.

When was the last time he'd walked in the moonlight with a lovely woman, simply enjoying her company and their surroundings? He could not remember. Usually he was preoccupied trying to get into her bed or manipulate her in some way.

Hoping to coax her out of her unusual silence, he asked Karida how the Bedouins coped with desert summer. She began explaining about their layers of clothing and how the garments allowed air flow through the cotton.

His thoughts drifted to his upcoming desert journey. If the treasure he sought was buried deep in the Sahara, as he feared, venturing there now would be foolhardy. Fierce Bedouin tribes as ruthless as the Khamsin ruled those sands. Temperatures soared past 110, choking a person until each breath seared the lungs. The quest to find the sleeping golden mummies would be like walking into an oven. Only fools and desperate men ventured into the Western Desert past April. He was both.

They found themselves near an alcove with a small but bright lamp. Nigel's heart pounded as Karida lifted her face, shadows and soft light caressing her cheeks.

"The moon in Egypt is so large at times one would think it is sinking into the earth," she remarked on a wistful breath. "It is a land of great romance."

Romance? Moonlight, Egypt, Karida's lovely face and sad mouth . . . Nigel longed suddenly for a kiss. He longed simply for something as pure and innocent as a stolen kiss, nothing more.

The last kiss he'd stolen had been from his twin's beloved. Aching regret and guilt pierced him. *I kissed Jasmine only because I knew Tommy wanted her, nothing more.* The thought made him sick. For once in his miserable life, he wanted something pure and good, a sweet, innocent kiss. He'd dare to steal one now— just a small kiss—and he'd keep it as a treasured memory. This would be a kiss from a proper, upright man, an imaginary construct who had much more to offer than Nigel himself.

His heart constricted. He ached to touch Karida, just once, in this magical atmosphere where anything could happen. He must act before he lost his nerve.

He pushed the spectacles up his nose and touched her arm. "It's a lovely night, Miss Sharif . . . uh, Karida. I know we have not known each other long, but I am compelled to tell you how very lovely you are." She studied him with those luminous brown eyes, and he swallowed hard. "How very much I admire you, from the bottom of my heart. I beg you to excuse me for being so forward, but . . ."

He raised her bare hand and pressed a kiss to her knuckles. Her flesh felt slightly clammy.

Nigel dropped her hand, peered at her face, and was alarmed to see her expression. Her breath came in short, stabbing gasps. She gave an odd noise and suddenly pitched forward. Nigel choked back a shocked curse but caught her. She slumped in his arms, and he carefully lowered her to the deck. Kneeling beside her, he checked her pulse. Weak and thready. Her breathing was shallow. Sick? No, but what else?

His hand rested on her abdomen, found a hardness below the soft velvet dress.

Oh, good God, a corset. The damn contraption . . .

He reached into his back pocket of his trousers and fished out a pocketknife. Drawing it open, Nigel clamped it in his mouth as he rolled her over. Fingers skilled at unfastening women's dresses now unbuttoned Karida's. Moonlight dappled her flesh with silver as he bared her back. He found the laces of the corset and carefully slit them with the blade. The corset made a popping noise like a cork flying out of a champagne bottle. Karida took in a deep gasp and gulped down air. Her breathing sounded like a wheezing pipe organ.

"Easy, sweet," he soothed. "You're all right now."

He pocketed the knife, rolled her onto her back, and fanned her with his hands just as a couple approached, out like he and

Karida had been, enjoying the moonlight. He stood and motioned to them.

"Help! Please fetch the doctor, this young lady's fallen ill!"

They gasped and ran off. Nigel sank back down beside Karida.

Stricken by his depth of relief, he hovered over her. "My lovely girl, trying to be fashionable like an English lady. Don't you realize how beautiful you are no matter what you wear?" he murmured. Unable to resist the softness of her parted mouth, he bent down and pressed a chaste kiss to her lips. "Awaken, sleeping beauty," he whispered. Then he sat back on his heels to watch her.

She opened her eyes. Flecks of caramel danced in their depths. She blinked, her lashes a dark crescent against her honey-gold skin. Tempted to touch her, to stroke her cheek, Nigel fisted his hands.

The moonlighting couple returned with the ship's physician, who knelt down beside Karida. His questioning gaze met Nigel's as the couple hovered above. He had found her knife-severed corset straps.

Nigel put a hand to his chest in exaggerated anxiety. "Dear me. Poor Miss Sharif, she simply collapsed! I was so afraid she would strangle! Oh my, it was horrid. That's why I had those two run fetch you."

The doctor nodded, all suspicion abated. Nigel hid a smile of relief and continued to prattle.

Back in his cabin a short time later, Nigel collapsed on his bed, still in disguise. A close call! Karida had been filled with doubt: the fussy Charles Porter freeing a lady's corset, let alone having the gall to unbutton her dress?

My mother suffered a similar ailment once after dinner, and I witnessed my father apply the very same solution.

His blushing face and stammering speech made the lame explanation just convincing enough.

Lacing his hands behind his head, Nigel stared at the ceiling. "Imagine me doing the same to the countess, my mother. She'd scream and accuse me of trying to do her harm. The old bat would probably rather have the breath choked from her. Perhaps I'd prefer to choke the breath from her."

It was dull pain and an old wound. Try as he might, he'd never reconcile with his mother, would never win her approval. Hell, he could become king, and she'd still look down her nose at him. Not that she wouldn't ingratiate herself to him, then.

I don't need her or Karida or anyone, he reminded himself.

A soft knock came at the door. "Yes?" he called out.

"Charles?"

The voice was low, indistinct. Could it be Karida, coming to thank him for saving her? Karida would put herself into his power? Even the morally upright Charles Porter might be excused for stealing a kiss in this situation.

Nigel sat up, brightening at the thought. "Come in, it's unlocked," he called.

All thoughts of romance and sweet lips pressed against his own fled. Jones entered the room.

"You bastard, I warned you."

Nigel had no time to protest, or even to make a sound. Jones had pulled a knife.

Chapter Thirteen

Nigel's survival instincts kicked in. He rolled off the bed, tumbling to the floor and using the mattress as a shield. His gaze whipped about, searching for a weapon. His guns were all locked in the bureau, but he still had the knife tucked into his pocket.

Jones's voice rang out. "Stand up and die like a man."

The hell I will. I'll stay down here and live like a coward.

A sudden insight flashed, however. This all seemed too convenient, too contrived. A man whose lady love he'd allegedly stolen had just happened to show up on this cruise and see through his disguise? Nigel pressed a hand against his temple.

"How much did William Oakley pay you for this?"

Silence draped the room. Then Jones laughed. "He warned me how clever you are. He wanted you to sport a matching set of scars on your right arm."

Nigel sagged back with an odd mixture of anger and amusement. "I knew it," he muttered. Then he asked: "Who are you, really?"

"Martin Jones—a hired hand. I work for him."

Now Nigel knew the face. Jones was indeed Oakley's man, one known for hard drinking, gambling, womanizing, and a few other sins. Like Nigel himself.

"You might as well come out now. I didn't have to cut you—just was supposed to scare you."

Nigel had just started to stand when someone knocked at his door. "Mr. Porter? Are you all right? I wanted to thank you again."

Karida. Nigel cursed.

The door slowly opened and she stepped in, looking like an angel in her pale lemon dress. Her beauty illuminated the room as she advanced farther inside.

"My, aren't you lovely?" Jones said softly. "Come to warm his bed?"

Nigel stood. He saw Karida pale, swallowing hard. She put a hand to her long, slender throat and backed up.

"I can share. But I come first," Jones leered, stepping forward. He slammed the door before she could escape, leaned close, pressed her against it. "Don't fight, lovely. It's better if you don't fight." He put a palm on one breast and squeezed, and she let out a startled cry. All the blood drained from Nigel as he saw the man's expression shift to crude lust.

For God's sake, do something for once in your sorry life. Karida was everything he was not, everything sweet and good and honorable. Oakley's man believed he could defile her in Nigel's room?

"Don't you dare touch her!" he shouted, and launched himself forward.

Jones whirled, his face an ugly mask. He slashed out with his blade. Burning pain lanced Nigel's left arm, but he ignored it and tackled Jones, toppling the man to the ground. He struggled to wrest the dagger from Jones's grip.

An angry cry came from above. To Nigel's surprise, Jones cringed and yelled; Karida had delivered a well-placed kick to his ribs. His grip on the dagger loosened, and Nigel grabbed it. As Nigel struck a solid blow to his head, the man fell back unconscious.

Nigel rolled off Jones, struggled to his feet, and found Karida removing the pretty sash from her dress. She bent down and trussed the man's hands as if hobbling a camel. Despite the agony in his arm, he grinned in approval.

Blood seeped between his fingers where he clutched his arm. His left arm, the one with all the surgeries. Damn, it figured. He nearly laughed at his bad luck. But Karida was not hurt. At least something had gone right.

Karida's wide eyes met his as Nigel struggled out of his coat. "Oh, Mr. Porter—*Charles*—you're hurt."

He stared at his bloody shirtsleeve. "Never mind me. Get someone before this man wakes up."

Karida ran to the door and upon opening it found two white-coated stewards. "Is everything all right? Someone reported shouting," one of them explained.

"This man attempted to kill me. Lock him up," Nigel instructed, tightly clutching his arm.

"And fetch the ship's doctor, quickly!" Karida added.

The two stewards hauled up the unconscious Jones and carried him out. Karida knelt beside Nigel, frowning at his wound and gently prising his fingers from his arm. "We must stop the bleeding," she remarked. She pulled back his gold brocade bedspread and snatched up a pillowcase, fashioning it into a makeshift bandage. She wrapped it about his arm and pressed hard.

Enjoying her anxious solicitude, Nigel nearly forgot the agony in his arm. Karida's worried expression warmed him. She drew close and clucked over the bloody bandage on his arm. She stroked his hand.

"You saved me," she murmured. "How very chivalrous."

She cares, he thought with jubilant abandon. *She truly does care.*

The ship's physician arrived, and Nigel climbed onto his bed. He was weary and spent, but not too spent to feel alarm as the doctor set a black bag on the nightstand and reached for a pair of scissors. If he cut away the shirtsleeve and Karida saw the mass of ugly scars, she'd know Nigel's identity immediately.

"I beg you, Miss Sharif, I thank you for your assistance, but it's not proper for you to be here when I remove my shirt. I'm quite well, quite well, it's merely a scrape," he asserted.

She was not so easily dismissed. "What in Heaven's name happened? Who was that man, and why was he in your cabin?"

Nigel sought refuge in another lie, but the guileless look on her face and her concern shamed him too much for him to utter it. He took a trembling breath.

"Some lunatic who claimed to know me, or someone I resemble. He was bent on harming me."

Karida's brow furrowed, and she was clearly confused. The truth hovered on Nigel's lips, ready to spill out. He felt weary, wanted simply to end the charade. He wanted to tell her his real name, ask one last time if they might have a chance.

They would never have a chance. Karida had already told him so. What a fool he was. "He was unbalanced, clearly, seeing how he nearly assaulted you. He rambled on earlier, something about me cheating at poker. He must have seen us in the games lounge together. But, please, Miss Sharif, I do beg you, my arm is paining me and the doctor needs to attend it."

"You brave soul, enduring this," she murmured. "After all you did to save me. You are a man of substance, Charles."

Her liberal use of his fake first name and the admiration in her voice sent Nigel's spirits crashing even lower. She was filled with respect for Charles, not Nigel. Charles Porter was a man of honor, who would gallantly save a damsel in distress. Nigel Wallenford was a bastard who would only cause distress. How unfair that they were one and the same.

She gave him a long, thoughtful look. Sweat trickled down his temples, and his arm throbbed. *Please leave,* he thought desperately.

Finally she gave a little smile, reached down, and, to his surprise, kissed the top of his head. Nigel found himself straining toward that perfect mouth as she left, wishing he could feel the warmth of her lips on his own but one more time. The door shut quietly behind her, and Nigel sank back onto his pillows with relief.

The ship's officials appeared one by one, and as they came inside and quizzed him on what happened, he repeated over and over the same lies he'd told Karida. How easily they came to him, those lies. Was his life made up of anything else?

Jones. Jones was the villain here, but the faults Nigel accorded him existed inside Nigel as well. Nigel knew he was no better. He and Oakley's hired goon were cut with the same pattern, albeit from the cloth of different classes. An alarming kernel of self-loathing wormed its way into his conscience. He wanted to retch.

Oh God, I can't stand it, he thought numbly. He quickly downed the opiate the ship's physician proffered, and a sweet numbness stole over him. He looked forward to the blankness with gratitude. As the doctor bandaged his arm and admonished him to rest, Nigel prayed he would find oblivion. Only in sleep would he forget.

Chapter Fourteen

Standing at the ship's railing, Karida felt the brimming excitement shared by the other passengers. Port Said was in view. Her heart beat faster, as it had the very first time she'd glimpsed Egypt's shoreline.

A ways off yet, swept by the sea, the tall, bronze statue of de Lesseps stood on the wall at the entrance of the Suez Canal. Such a great man, who had done great things. Thanks to him, the journey to India was now halved, for the Suez had opened shipping lanes and new opportunities. Great men were expected to do great things. But lesser men, whom no one expected to do anything great, could be just as surprising.

The thought made her glance at Charles Porter. His left arm hung loosely at his side, though his knife wound had mostly healed by now. Eyes brilliant with anticipation behind their bluish spectacles sharpened on her. Yes, even lesser men could become great, if given proper motivation.

His mustached mouth tilted up in a friendly smile. "Well, Miss Sharif, here we are, at the very port where we both shall disembark. Adventures await! Are you prepared?"

Karida deliberately and very gently put her hand over his, ignoring his flinch. His knuckles were slightly scarred.

"I am, Mr. Porter. I am prepared for adventure in every way possible."

Much later, after entering the customs house and being accosted by a parade of fellahin eager to sell novelties and trinkets to the foreigners, the trio boarded the train bound for Cairo. Karida, her aunt, and Charles Porter shared a compartment.

Charles stared out the window and took in the scenery. Cattle yoked together plowed the green fields along the Nile delta. Donkeys trudged along the dirt roads, bearing heads of lettuce in woven bags, and boys with small sticks guided them.

Rapt fascination covered his face, like he was a child glimpsing a treat. "I say, look at this, Miss Sharif! Those donkeys, how ever do they manage such a burden, carrying all those crops?"

"I am certain they are accustomed to their work. I doubt they even feel it. Like people who are forced to bear more weight than they should, they endure. In fact, they would probably be surprised to know exactly how heavy the load is."

When the train pulled into the Cairo station, they shared a ride after Charles intoned he was staying at the Shepherd's Hotel. "I would be most happy to escort you ladies there, seeing you are without a protector," he suggested gallantly.

"Most kind of you, Mr. Porter. We gladly accept your offer," Karida told him. She ignored her aunt's amused look.

After they registered, Charles queried about meeting them for dinner. "I understand if you have friends, family, or other obligations, but since it is my very first night in Egypt . . ." he hinted shyly.

"It will be a pleasure. Seven, then, in the dining room." Karida smiled and touched his arm.

"I'll make the reservations," he said happily. "And if you need me for anything, anything at all, please let me know."

Her room overlooked the splendid gardens of the hotel. Karida opened the window, breathing in the scent of flowers and fresh air. A mosquito net hung over the pretty bed. She unpacked a few things and went into the washroom to freshen up.

A knock came at the door as she was patting her face dry with a towel. Karida opened it to admit Katherine.

"I thought we'd visit the market and do a little shopping until Ramses arrives. We have two days," her aunt remarked, entering.

"If you don't mind, I'd like to visit the bazaar by myself, and the silversmiths. I want to be alone."

None of the Khamsin knew how dearly Karida wanted to return to England and set up shop, and at the bazaar she could get an idea of how much she could charge. She also needed to be alone, away from the woman calling herself an aunt but who was really her half sister. This half sister had laughed so easily with the earl of Smithfield and enjoyed his tender adoration while Karida herself remained in shadow. Katherine, like Ramses and Nuri, had always treated her with affection and love, but Karida couldn't help the bite of jealousy. Karida, the bastard child the earl of Smithfield would not acknowledge.

"Honey, the markets are dangerous. I wouldn't advise it. There are thieves about."

"I was one once. Remember?" she blurted.

A pretty pink flush filled her aunt's cheeks. "That was many years ago. You have changed. You became an ideal daughter."

Ideal. Noble. Honorable. But who *was* she? A woman unwanted by her father. A woman unwanted by any husband except a thief like herself.

"Yes, honorable." Karida gave a bitter laugh. "Wouldn't that have pleased my real father, who first sent me on a ship to Egypt?"

Scarlet flamed her aunt's face. She actually looked uncomfortable. Katherine touched her right cheek and said, "You must believe this. When you were found, all effort was made to right a terrible wrong and send you to a home filled with love. I can't imagine how horrid the workhouse was for you."

More than you know. Karida remembered her chilled, bleeding hands. She wrapped her arms about herself, fighting the memory.

"Nuri and Safa love you, care for you as much as they love their other children," Katherine said.

"But my real father does not want me."

She hadn't meant to blurt it out, but the pent-up emotions gushed free like from a leaky dam. Karida bit her lip, wishing she hadn't revealed her darkest secret.

Shock dawned on her aunt's face, all her color vanishing. "Oh, honey, he does, he truly does, but you must understand it is a delicate matter."

"Having a bastard such as myself, the shame of it," Karida finished.

Katherine was a legitimate earl's daughter, an heiress. She'd given up much of her acceptance in England to marry an honorable Khamsin warrior, fierce, brave, and true. Karida, on the other hand, had been raised in the workhouse. Conceived in the shameful light of an illicit affair, and when found she'd been sent to live in a remote corner of the world. There was little comparison.

So my secret will never be discovered. You can't know what it is like. All I want is for him to acknowledge me as his daughter. Not his ward, not his niece or a distant relative. His daughter, his own flesh and blood. Your half sister. And I want him to be proud of me.

Understanding shone in Katherine's gaze. "You need to be alone from me, don't you? Because of who I am and the relationship I have with the earl of Smithfield."

Embarrassed by her obvious jealousy, Karida stared at the wall. "I love my adopted parents, and I love you and Ramses. But I have a real father, and to him I'm nothing but an embarrassment."

"I wanted him to talk to you. He is not ashamed of you, only his prior life. Please understand, I am not at liberty to discuss it," Katherine exclaimed.

A wall shut down over Karida's heart. "Of course not. And I am not at liberty to disclose my plans. But please know this: I have reason for discretion, just as you have reason."

A heavy sigh fled Katherine. "I wish you'd wait for Ramses to arrive. Just be careful, please. The city is a dangerous place."

"And I know how to take care of myself."

An amused smile touched Katherine's mouth. "So did I once. That was how I met Ramses—who showed me I really did not." She frowned. "If you will not let me go with you, how about Mr. Porter?"

Doubt filled Karida. "To protect me? Against Egyptians and foreigners?"

Katherine laughed. "He is hardly a Colossus, but he is a man, and a man would ward off many forms of unwanted attention. Please, Karida. Take him."

"Very well," she acquiesced. It was not as hard a choice as she might once have imagined.

Charles Porter ceased to bore Karida. Indeed, he soon mystified her. They explored Cairo's markets together, and his obvious interest and fascination won her over. He kept close to her side and looked impressed when she bartered in rapid Arabic with the merchants.

The day her uncle was to arrive, he shyly asked her to accommodate him once more by accompanying him to the Khan el-Khalili bazaar, as he'd spotted a silver box he wanted to purchase but was too intimidated to haggle in English. Karida arranged to meet him at the hotel steps, and as she walked onto the hotel terrace she saw him chatting with a flower girl selling bright blossoms on the street. The girl, a young woman, really, smiled at him. He purchased two roses and doffed his bowler hat in good-bye.

"Charles!" Karida called out, descending the steps.

He turned, beaming. "Miss Sharif, ah, there you are! I bought these for you."

With a shy gesture, he handed her the two red roses. Karida took them, inhaling their heady fragrance. "Thank you!"

However, despite their smell, a dark feeling fell across her. Good God, she hoped the man wasn't falling in love. How she'd hate to let him down. He was a nice man, but she had nothing to offer, and she would never want the staid life she imagined he would eventually lead. She also hoped that he hadn't seen her growing warmth toward their acquaintance as anything to lead him on.

As they set out for the markets in a carriage the hotel porter flagged down for them, Karida realized with dismay that her previous thoughts weren't quite the truth, or at least not all of it. The truth was she couldn't forget Nigel. Nigel, with his brilliant smile, his adventurous ways, his sarcasm. His sensual kisses, the slow stroke of his hands across her bare back . . .

She shifted in her seat, feeling flushed.

Charles gave her an odd look. "Are you well?"

"Quite, just a bit hot, that's all."

Lost in her thoughts, she didn't realize how long they'd been driving until they entered a seedy section of the city. Here, whitewashed apartments squeezed together, their balconies sagging and their windows grimy and dusty.

Alarm filled her. "Where are we going? You wanted to shop."

A woebegone look touched his face. "I'm so sorry, I forgot to tell you. There's an appointment I must keep first. I shan't be long. You don't mind, do you, Miss Sharif?"

He looked so beguiling and earnest, she smiled. "An appointment in this section of town?" It was surprising. "For what?"

"I promised a friend back in London I would pursue a matter of great importance." He removed his bowler and fiddled with it, looking chagrined. "I do apologize, Miss Sharif. It's a matter of some urgency, a debt that is owed. I shouldn't have brought you along. It was wrong of me to make you accompany me to such a beastly area. You are such a lady."

She touched his hand. "It's all right," she said.

His eyes widened behind his spectacles. "You are such an angel." Then he grinned, gave a flash of even, white teeth.

Karida felt a stir of unease. For a moment she studied him, really and truly studied him. The nose was too bulbous, the cheeks puffed out, but that mouth . . . it was beautiful, firm and sensual. Like Nigel's.

Ridiculous! Karida dismissed the thought. Many mouths might look alike.

"Miss Sharif, I must confess that the true reason I brought you here is that you can assist me in the business I must transact. It's a dance with the devil, I'm afraid. I don't know many people who speak fluent Arabic whom I trust, and . . ." Charles looked embarrassed.

Relief swept through her. "Of course I'll go with you." She smiled. "Perhaps I could even protect you, Mr. Porter. Return the favor."

He gave a light laugh, but it was edged with hardness and she wondered again. But again she dismissed the thought, especially as he began nattering away about the horrors of his friend's incautiousness and debt.

When the carriage finally stopped before a row of bedraggled apartments, he gallantly offered his hand to assist her. Karida gripped her roses as she disembarked. To her dismay, as soon as she was out, the driver took off. She called for him to stop, but he drove on.

Charles looked unaffected.

"You should have told him to wait. We'll have a problem finding another in this area," Karida reproved.

The small smile he gave her seemed sly. "It's quite all right. I have everything under control."

Caution returned as he escorted her into a darkened alley. Halfway down, a door opened. A man exited, accompanied by a woman who kissed him deeply. The man was dressed in usual Egyptian garb. The woman wore . . .

Gracious! Her diaphanous gown barely hid her nakedness.

The couple stopped kissing, the man withdrew some money, and the woman tugged him back inside. Karida gasped in sudden understanding. This place was a brothel! What kind of business would Porter conduct in a whorehouse?

"Mr. Porter, we need to leave immediately," she told him.

But he looked at her with a smile unfamiliar, a hard smile edged with lust.

Dropping her roses, Karida turned to run but a muscled arm slammed against her midsection, jerking her backward. She spun around, staring at Porter, his bland smoothness all gone.

"Karida, sweet, don't you know that fair angels should never dance with the devil?" came his husky velvet whisper.

She opened her mouth to scream, but he shoved a rag into her face. A slightly sweet stench warned her of an opiate. She struggled to keep conscious but felt her limbs loosen. The last thing she remembered was a flare of brilliant jade eyes staring in triumph at her over the top of those blue-tinted spectacles.

Chapter Fifteen

A dull throbbing pounded her head as Karida woke. Cool air washed over her body. Why did she feel so chilled? This was Egypt approaching summer. Her arms felt heavy as lead, her legs as well. It was from the drug. Something soft but lumpy lay beneath her. It felt like a mattress stuffed with horsehair.

She went to rub her eyes and found she could not move her arm.

"Open your eyes, my sweet. Open."

The deep, hypnotic voice must be obeyed. Her eyelids felt heavy and glued shut, but she forced them open.

She stared at the ceiling. A murky mirror showed her reflection. She was sprawled on a bed, her arms and legs outstretched. Panic swept through her as Karida jerked at her limbs. They were tied to the bedposts. And that was not all. She was naked.

Oh God, she thought in frantic desperation. Where am I?

Her gaze whipped about, seeking answers. The room was dark; only stray beams of sunlight filtered through the closed *mashrabiya* screens. She smelled sandalwood incense and women's perfume.

Karida blinked again, stared at the walls. Opulent mosaic tiles adorned them, and the floor was covered in a rich red Persian carpet. She spotted furniture. An elegant carved wood bureau, cushions on the floor. A door, leading somewhere. Freedom.

Standing against the closed door was a tall man. Slouched, he jammed his hands into his trouser pockets.

"Finally, sleeping beauty awakes."

She knew that deep velvet voice. Karida's heart lurched as the man crossed the room to stand by her. Gone were the mustache, fake nose, and wispy black wig. The cold, hard stare was all Nigel.

"I suggest slightly more discretion in your dress. You are conspicuous here among the brothels in virgin white—and are misrepresenting yourself."

"Hello, Nigel," she said, willing her heart to stop racing. Fear twined with an odd relief, as his voice held no malice. Their bizarre games had become almost commonplace.

He came closer and opened the screen over the window. Light streamed into the room, touched the lines of his handsome face. He looked weary. As if he'd long ago tired of playing the part of Charles Porter.

"Your cheeks," she remarked.

"Cotton fills them out. An old theater trick taught to me by an actress whose company I enjoyed long ago. Did you like my little masquerade, sweet? For such a cad, as the earl of Smithfield called me, I'm very good at playing noble and good."

"You *are* noble and good, Nigel," she said quietly. "Or at least you can be. You saved me from Jones—and Malik. You are far nobler and more heroic than you think."

He actually drew back, flinched, and Karida's heart turned over. *Oh, Nigel,* she thought, *what happened that you cannot believe anything good about yourself?* She'd wondered this for a long time. She again felt a bond between them at this shared pain.

Cynicism darkened his expression, and Karida knew what he was thinking. Lord knew she herself had thought it several times in the dark night as she lay on the lumpy mattress at the workhouse, and later, in her adopted father's tent. She'd thought it about herself: *I am of little worth.*

"You made a mistake in trusting Charles Porter, that insipid fop. I credited you with more intelligence, Karida."

"I came hoping to save his friend from a terrible debt," she replied. "I'd like to save you as well, Nigel."

He laughed. "Save me, sweet? You'd have to save yourself first."

"You can change," she insisted.

For a moment a light flickered in his gaze. Then his expression shuttered, and he looked hard and cruel once more.

"You think you know me? The armor on this knight hasn't shone in years. I'm as tarnished as one gets. I'm as nasty as Smithfield said. I'm a womanizer, a thief, and a liar. You know the truth as well as he."

"You bought me two roses from that poor flower girl outside the hotel."

"I bought two roses from a former lover. She was a virgin when I met her. Would you like to hear more?"

Karida swallowed hard. "No, thank you."

Silence draped them as he stared at the wall, as if playing the words over in his mind. Liar. Thief. Libertine. *Thief and bastard,* Karida thought. *That was what I was called, but I am better than they originally thought.*

She licked her dry lips. "Let me go, Nigel. My aunt will be worried and start to search for me. My uncle is arriving this afternoon, and he will be frantic."

"Ah, such nobility, such concern about others. But fear not, sweet. I intend to keep you here only the same length of time it would require you to shop with me." His eyes darkened. "But the activities we'll indulge in will prove far more pleasurable."

"Will you force me then, Nigel? Will you rape me and become as evil as Jones or Malik?"

"I won't have to force you," he said softly. "I won't have to. I've seen your passion for me, and you can't help it any more than I can."

"There are many things we can help, Nigel. Untie me and

let's start. You can change; you can become the honorable man you want to be."

His mouth compressed to a humorless line. "Stop your nattering. Wise women do not expect change—and none rhapsodize about my qualities." He paused and his gaze grew strangely blank. "Other than my abilities on the furniture where you now lie."

Karida pressed on. "I'll wager that you can change. I believe in you, Nigel."

He snorted and flipped the knife in his hand. His flickering look of hope seemed forever vanished. "You're as knobby as that Jones fellow. Only believe what you want to believe. Can't see the truth."

"I know what I see." Karida forced herself to lie perfectly still. "Are you afraid of my challenge?"

Doubt flickered in his gaze, and she saw that he wanted to hope but didn't dare. Oh, how she knew that despair.

Nigel sat on the bed, close but not touching her. "Very well, I'll wager with you. But it's my wager, and I'll wager that you have no control." His mouth twisted in a cruel smile. "I know you, Karida. I saw your innermost self, the passion inside you. I watched you in my arms. So I know exactly what it will take to bring you down to my level."

"Why would you do that?" she cried.

"Because I can. And it will be a rather interesting challenge. I haven't been challenged in bed in a very long time. Not even here, in this brothel, where women are taught the most exotic arts."

He named his terms.

Shock widened Karida's eyes. "Good Lord, I can't agree to that!"

"Then I will never let you go," he said. "And I will tear up your clothing. You will remain here as my prisoner." A sardonic smile touched his mouth. "Even if you manage to escape, I will tell your aunt exactly where you have been. In my bed. She will believe me when I show her your clothing, your ruined clothing. Your reputation, Karida—your *honor*—will be in shreds."

"My father will have your head for that," she said, her heart pounding.

Nigel gave a casual shrug. "Or he'll force me to marry you. Either way, I get what I want." His eyes had acquired an odd faraway look.

Karida's mind raced, considering her situation. Nigel could keep her tied to this bed for as long as he pleased. According to his terms, if she won he would let her go . . . but without her clothing! Karida envisioned returning to the Shepherd's Hotel wrapped in a sheet, trying to explain. Rumors would start, and she'd be forever shamed. But if she lost, she'd have to accompany him back to the Khamsin camp and marry him.

Karida guessed his plan; he was encouraging her to wed him either way. He wanted a legitimate escort back to the Eastern Desert, and to the cave containing the treasure map. If he married her, the ruby would be his, for by law their possessions would be joined. He would not be stealing the ruby but gaining it through marriage. A sob of laughter rose in her throat; he was far too clever. She wondered if this was what he'd had in mind all along.

She realized now that Nigel would stop at nothing to get both the ruby and the map and was set upon seeking the treasure. She did not understand his fixation, but she could predict the result. If Nigel continued on this quest, either he or Ramses would die. The tomb's male guardian would not stand idly by, even if Karida herself gave in.

It was a horrid dilemma. Karida's only hope was that one thin fiber of goodness she knew Nigel hid. She would dig to find it.

"Why are you doing this? Because you want to shame me?" she asked, her voice strong and clear. She would not cower before him. "What do you want, Nigel? Truly."

He turned his back to her, but not before she saw a stark longing in his eyes and heard his muttered response, so low she might have imagined it: "You."

Karida knew then what she must do. She held the power; though she was the one naked and bound, he was tied by chains far more binding. Calmness settled over her. "You say you will not let me go, but my aunt will not stop searching for me. My uncle arrives in Cairo today, and he will search for me as well. Do you truly wish to risk that, Nigel—the wrath of a Khamsin warrior?"

His expression shuttered, and Nigel stroked the flat of his knife. "I can handle myself."

Karida shuddered at the thought. "I offer to change the terms. If I win, you will release me, you will return my clothing and me to the hotel. As Nigel. No more masquerade. You will not say a word of this to anyone."

An amused look entered his eyes, and he set his knife down on a small, lopsided bedside table. "And if I win?"

"If you win, everything I just stated—with one exception." Karida swallowed hard. "I will marry you, and we will return to the Khamsin. The ruby will be yours, as you know, for everything I own will be yours by the laws of my people. The difference will be that I will marry you *willingly*, for the terms are now mine."

"Your terms . . ." A new interest sparkled in his eyes—and victory. "I warn you, I will do my utmost to win."

Karida hesitated. *I don't have that kind of control,* she thought in frantic desperation. *Not with him. He knows that.*

Then: *You can do it. You didn't think you could stop lying and stealing, either, and look at all you've accomplished.* Confidence welled inside her. Nearly ten years' experience had proven her strength. *I can do this.*

"You have a very high opinion of yourself. What you suggest is impossible," she countered.

A knowing smile twisted his mouth. "It's very possible that

you will beg me. Were you a cold, prudish woman, perhaps not. But you? With the passion you've already demonstrated in my arms?" He leaned down, and his warm breath feathered over her ear. "I know exactly how to make you plead. I know what makes you tremble with desire. I know how to make you *scream*."

His voice dropped to a husky whisper, and he promised, "Yes, I will make you beg me to take you, to have me inside you. I will make you plead. I am a proud man, but I am skilled at giving women pleasure, and this is the wager I make: If control, as you say, can be learned, if you show that control and remain silent, you have nothing to worry about. You will have won."

A delicate shiver went through her as he nibbled her earlobe then licked it. "But I must warn you, I hate to lose. And I am very determined. And the prize, to merely have you in my bed every night . . ." Nigel nuzzled her neck with tiny kisses, hitting the very sensitive spot he apparently recognized.

Oh God, I am in trouble.

He drew back, his gaze sharp and assessing.

"Well?" she asked.

"I accept your new terms."

He stretched out his arms and cracked his knuckles loudly. Then he went to the bureau and opened a drawer. From it he took a small burner, set this on a table and lit it with a match, then he poured the contents of a blue bottle into its warming dish. A low humming warbled deep in his throat as he stirred the mixture.

"What is that?" Karida asked.

Glancing over his shoulder at her, he offered a sensual half smile. "One of the more inventive charms of this brothel, which is why I prefer it over the others here. Scented, flavored oil. Best when warmed. I prefer cinnamon. Tangy, and quite delicious."

"You'd best have plenty of towels available to wipe it off, or you'll stain these fine sheets," she quipped.

"That's not how I remove it," he replied.

His gaze dropped to Karida's thighs. The space between her legs clenched in a mixture of anticipation and dread. All she could do was wait and watch.

Nigel turned back to the warming oil and continued humming. When he dipped a finger into the mixture, testing it, Karida's feminine flesh ached and throbbed. She drew in a deep breath; she had to remain calm and unmoved.

Sitting on the bed, with a slow caress he anointed her forearm, rubbing the oil into her tightened flesh. His gaze roamed her body and narrowed as it fell upon the ridges of scar tissue upon her belly and abdomen. Though she could not feel anything there, she shivered as he trailed an oiled finger over them.

"Do they hurt?" he asked quietly.

Blinking in surprise, she shook her head. "Only certain places, when I twist the wrong way, and not that much. I have no sense of feeling there, mostly."

She expected a hushed murmur of pity, or a sympathetic gaze. Instead he slid his finger across her skin, stopping at the underside of her right breast. She stiffened.

"You must learn to relax, sweet. There is nothing wrong with accepting and enjoying a massage to ease your tension. Surely that alone will not make you cry out with desire."

Her eyes widened as he reached for his knife, but he surprised her again by cutting her bonds. She stretched and rubbed her wrists with a grateful sigh. Then she sat up, regarding him. "Aren't you afraid I'll run?"

Wickedness tinged his smile. "I think not. You are a woman of honor who will not back down from a wager. Turn over."

Dryness filled her mouth. She stared at him.

He sighed. "I'm merely going to rub your shoulders and back with oil. You're stiffer than a limestone stelae."

She nervously did as he asked. Behind her, Nigel set down the bowl on the crooked table by the bedside. She flinched at the warmth of his oiled hands as they settled on her shoulders.

"You're so tense. But I'll take care of you," he murmured.

Her muscles loosened beneath his gentle kneading. He massaged her upper arms, the scent of cinnamon teasing her nostrils. Karida rested her head on her hands, beginning to relax. But she forced herself to remain alert. She would never surrender to his wicked touch, to the devilish pleasure he delivered. She would not lose this wager.

As she felt the wet warmth of his tongue on her naked skin, Karida gasped with shocked pleasure. She stiffened as he dragged his tongue down the arch of her spine to the small of her back. Nigel gave a low chuckle. His hands stroked the arch of her spine then rested on the roundness of her bottom. He worked oil into the flesh there, and she tried not to move. As he licked it off very slowly, his tongue injecting pure fire into her veins, she dug her fingers into her pillow and muffled a cry.

But when he slid a finger into the delicate crevice between her buttocks, she arched off the bed. Nigel gave a wicked laugh. His hand slipped lower, lightly touching the folds of her womanhood. That bare caress sent hot shivers of pleasure through her. Instinct urged her to arch her bottom in a silent plea.

Disappointment filled her when he withdrew his hand. Karida stiffened, and again Nigel laughed.

"Sorry angel. But I've only just begun. I don't want to win *that* easily."

"Do your worst," she said, her voice muffled by the pillow.

His hands stroked along her legs, oil warming bare flesh. Nigel paused at her feet, tickled her toes, coaxed a laugh from her. That laughter died as he slid his oiled finger between her legs once more, their touch teasing and light. She bit back a moan, resolved to resist. *Remember: this man is a liar and a libertine.*

Nigel turned her over and began stroking her bare abdomen. Distress flooded Karida, chasing away the previous erotic heat as his fingers trailed across her burns. She felt nothing, no arousing caress, and this time it reminded her bitterly of what she could never have: children, a true family. Karida squeezed her eyes shut, wanting to laugh, knowing it would turn into a sob. Her lips compressed to a tight line, pain spearing her as she bit them to fight the raw emotion bubbling up from her throat. Nigel had no chance to win, for all she needed do was think of the stark ugliness of her scars and how other men were right to reject her because of them.

"Ah sweet, you are so beautiful, every part of you," he whispered. And then he bent his head and placed a single, tender kiss on the burned flesh. "You're perfect."

A tear rose to Karida's eyes and dripped down her cheek, splashed to the sheet. She forgot her resolve not to touch him, reached down and placed her hand on his silky hair.

Nigel raised his head, his gaze burning into hers. *I intend to have all of you,* the look said.

He sat back on his haunches, rubbed more warm oil over his hands. He straddled her, then, sitting on her thighs and keeping them trapped. Sliding his palms up, he cupped and massaged her breasts. Beneath the sensual brush of his hands, a rippling ecstasy began to flower in Karida once more. When his thumbs circled them, her hardening nipples crested beneath those slow flicks.

Arousal sharpened into a vibrating hum of need as Nigel kissed his way up her belly, then ran his tongue over her breasts. He took her right nipple into his mouth, his tongue swirling, rasping back and forth. He suckled gently, his wicked mouth winning the wager. Nearly. Soon. If she did not regain control . . .

Karida undulated her hips in shameless need. She'd never realized how much her body could ache, how it could quiver and yearn. It almost hurt, this want, this tension; it dwarfed her resolve to win.

Determination filled her, and she stopped moving. She would not surrender. Keeping very still, she forced herself to ignore the aching throb between her legs that was intensified by the delicious torture of his mouth.

But then he left her breast and kissed his way down her belly and slid off her thighs. He dragged her to the bed's edge and knelt on the floor, opening her legs wide. He draped her knees over his broad shoulders. Fierce heat smoldered in his dark gaze. Then he gently parted the delicate folds of her rosy, wet, and aching center, as if unfurling a lovely flower.

"What are you doing?" she gasped.

"Shhh," he crooned. Then he lowered his head between her legs.

When he blew a soft breath against her flesh, she let out a startled cry, but that was nothing compared to the potent shock of pleasure when he put his mouth on her. He was strong, holding her legs firm as his questing tongue delved between her wet cleft. Long, slow strokes made her writhe against the oil-spotted sheets, made her grind her bottom into the mattress. A heavy, hot pulsing began deep within her.

As he licked the delicate folds, his wicked tongue came close to touching the pearling center of her throbbing. At last he kissed her there—and just as quickly backed off. A frustrated moan tore from her throat.

A dance began, each pull and withdrawal making Karida arch upward in crazed need. Oh why couldn't, why wouldn't he just do it: touch her there, deliver that ecstatic pleasure she craved? She pumped her hips, forgetting everything but the velvet murmur of his mouth against her as he lavished soft praise and sweet words.

Then he stopped, slid a finger deep inside her drenched channel. He lifted his head, eyes burning like green flame. The look of a determined conqueror hardened his face.

"Now," he said.

Nigel lowered his head to the spot where she craved him most. His tongue swept her swollen flesh as he slid his finger slowly in and out of her slick sheath, her muscles squeezing against it. That seductive pleasure was an enticing torment, his mouth working dark magic on her senses as if he were the devil himself. Karida screamed, nearly arching off the bed. The tension built higher and higher. She was reaching for it, almost there, almost . . .

Nigel stopped. He lifted his head, gently stroking his finger deep inside her. "Now Karida, sweet, do you want me inside you? Will you beg me? I can end this, I can ease it for you, I promise."

Left suspended, her body faint and aching, she choked down a disappointed sob. She couldn't resist any longer. She wanted to cry out in helpless humiliation, wanted to plead with him. She craved his hard shaft inside her, filling her completely, wanted to savagely claw out his eyes for the exquisite bliss he'd denied her. Yet surrender was impossible.

Then she looked into his eyes. Tenderness twined with the burning passion, that look holding her captive. Emotion clogged her throat at a longing gaze that mirrored back all her own hidden emotions: despair, wild uncertainty, anguished loneliness. Nigel was a man who had walked too far alone, believing everything everyone said about him. She could see a fear beneath his confidence, desperation behind his desire.

It was time he walked alone no longer. Karida wanted him, not merely his body joined to hers, but all of him. She closed her eyes, knowing the truth. He needed her as equally as she needed him. Together they could be something greater than they were apart. Surrender no longer seemed defeat, but victory.

Her answer was to shimmy back on the mattress and hold out her arms. "Please, Nigel, please take me."

She expected a low purr of triumph, a smug smile filled with masculine satisfaction. Yet only stark relief swept over his face. When he stepped back to undress, she saw the enormous bulge in his trousers stating his urgent need.

Naked he stood by the bed, his swollen shaft jutting from its thick nest of dark curls. Nigel fisted his hands, emotion flaring on his face as he crawled over the bed. She soon felt the impatient nudging of his hard sex at her tender center, demanding entrance. He eased in the slightest, but her muscles resisted.

"Fair angel, relax. Let me in," he crooned.

Karida stared up at his fierce gaze locked to hers. Nigel framed her face with his palms and kissed her, his tongue and lips moving over hers, coaxing a response. She kissed him back with equal desperation.

He pushed forward a little more and she arched her hips to welcome him.

"Take me," he demanded in a low voice. "Take all of me, you can do it."

And as he thrust deep, she knew what he meant: She was to take him, not just his body, but *all* of him, the good and the bad. His groan was a cry from the depths of a soul he thought far too tarnished for redemption, and she was his one chance at acceptance.

Karida accepted. In silent understanding she stroked the tense muscles of his back. Nigel raised himself up, a hank of dark hair hanging over his brow. His gaze was fierce and concentrated as he rocked back and forth, taking her, each delicious inch stretching her impossibly.

He began angling his thrusts, creating a new friction, taking and giving as she took and gave. Her hands curled around his forearms as she arched her spine to the urgent rocking of his hips.

Nigel uttered a groan that sounded almost animal and suddenly sat back. He bent her legs, wrapping them about his waist, and began thrusting violently, his breath rasping in his lungs. He reached between their bodies and touched her.

"Ah, sweet Karida, yes, come with me, come with me now!"

Karida shattered, the building tension exploding like a sudden summer thunderstorm. She screamed, his name a prayer on her lips. He cried out over and over, gasped her name in response. Her eager muscles caressed him, pulled at him, her womb drinking every droplet of his seed like thirsty sand sucking down rainwater.

At last Nigel collapsed atop her, and Karida welcomed his weight, stroking his perspiring and muscled back. He murmured her name over and over and he buried his head in her shoulder. Sweat coated their bodies, the sheets beneath them damp and smelling of cinnamon.

He trembled in her arms then finally rolled off. She feared he would say something sarcastic or crude, but he remained silent, staring at the fly-specked mirror on the ceiling above. Karida glanced at herself in that mirror, a woman whose legs were bonelessly sprawled wide, Nigel's seed trickling out of her, down her thighs, her body flushed with desire, her gaze heavy-lidded and languorous; a woman sated with pleasure and a deeper sense of satisfaction.

She was his.

He was hers.

He rolled over and captured her in his arms, rolling back so she was firmly tucked in his embrace. Karida rested her head on his shoulder as he gently stroked her hair. She toyed with the silky, damp hairs on his chest. The opened shutters let in a cooling breeze. Sunlight flooded the room, exposing all her scars and flaws, but for the first time she felt no shame.

Her hand drifted lower, exploring Nigel's body, feeling the firm muscles beneath her questing fingers, the springy hair on his legs, the length of his softening sex, the sponginess of his testicles as she gently cupped them. She slid her fingers lower on his inside left thigh and felt a line of rough skin. Karida sat up, curious. She leaned over to examine.

Nigel gave her a crooked smile. "Inspecting the equipment?" he asked.

The scar was long, about a quarter inch wide, like a stripe. "This." She stroked it gently. "It looks almost like . . ."

He rolled over, draping her body beneath his. "Happened a long time ago, and it's of no consequence."

"But—"

Nigel silenced her with a kiss.

She'd seen his shameful little secret, the scar he'd hidden away for so long. The scar that hurt the most, even years after his father put it there. It hurt worse than any verbal lashing the man had given. He would make her forget.

He wanted to feel triumph at her sweet surrender, but Nigel felt only drained, as if he'd poured his dark soul into her as well as his seed. Sweet Christ, he needed her more than she knew— and damn it, more than she would ever know. No woman would ever have that kind of power over him. It was too dangerous. The last woman he'd fully trusted was now dead; she'd pushed him and betrayed him, made him lash out in anger. Charlotte, tumbling over that cliff, screaming . . . The blackness of his damned soul smothered him.

Karida stroked his damp hair, her sweet, dulcet voice a soothing murmur that calmed him. It was heaven; he could forget without losing himself entirely.

Nigel set about arousing her all over again, knowing the right places to touch, the little kisses she loved on her throat, the slow stroke of his thumbs on her breasts. He mounted her once more, for his cock was stiff and huge.

He glided inside her. Her swollen tissues resisted at first, then adjusted.

Deeper, he wanted to penetrate deeper still, wanted to be so much a part of her that she could never get him out. He'd be there, sunk into her heart and soul, her memories, her future.

He began thrusting, watched her eyes glaze with passion, watched the rosy blush of her desire, saw the telltale signs of her approaching climax. He was panting; his breath dragged in and out of his lungs in great pulls. Nigel opened her thighs wider and hammered into her as he grasped her wrists, pinning them to the bed, keeping her trapped beneath his weight and imprisoned by his unquenchable lust. The iron bed shook with his thrusts, its headboard clanking against the plastered wall.

Karida laced her fingers through his in a gesture of absolute trust. He'd always remained in control with all the women he'd lain with, but with her, Nigel felt caught up in a violent, animalistic need to claim and consume. To sweep her to the fires of his own private Hell. She was his, and he'd make damn sure she had no other.

She raised her hips to meet his violent strokes, and then she sobbed and screamed his name. He felt her come, and it felt like the darkest heaven, the deepest forbidden pleasure. His balls drew up tight, and he felt the necessity of his imminent release: the heady female scent of her, the moans and cries, the way her tight channel squeezed him as she climaxed.

With a roar he stiffened, spurted his hot seed deep inside her. He kept coming, his cock pulsing, her name a ceaseless prayer on his lips. His body tensed and shook. Then Nigel collapsed atop her, his big body trembling. He gasped into the pillow. Emotion raged through him as turbulent as a boiling river. Stripped bare of indifference, he closed his eyes and opened his heart, whispering so she could not hear his stark confession.

"Oh, my love, you make me want to be good."

Her caress felt like absolution. If he died now, even with all the sins blackening his soul, he would die content.

Chapter Sixteen

Nigel rolled over, shifting his weight as he slid an arm about Karida's limp body. Her eyes were closed, and she lay as if consumed by utter exhaustion. A sheen of perspiration glowed on her soft skin.

He curled next to her, enjoying the feel of pliant female flesh against his hardness, glad he had won—and not merely for the sake of winning. The idea of having this sweet siren in his bed legitimately each night as he performed his marital duties sent a shiver of anticipatory pleasure racing through his blood. Karida was a woman of deep, unbridled passion, more than matching his own desires. No other woman had coaxed out the deep feelings she aroused in him.

Nigel frowned. She roused more than his body, and that scraped at the hard granite of his heart. He relished being unreachable, putting himself out of touch. But somehow, her sweetness and her brutal honesty *had* touched him. Nigel had never before felt such affection, warmth, and intimacy. The emotions alarmed him.

He was endangering himself with such rubbish, such silly feelings that other men—lesser men—harbored for the opposite sex. Nigel vowed they would not trap him. The minute he let down his guard, Karida would prove as cruel and ruthless as anyone else. As coldhearted as Charlotte.

At least Charlotte had a heart, while I have none, he thought with a twist of his lips.

That was what he wished Karida to think, at any rate. If

she knew the truth, how he'd been softhearted with others, like with that flower girl in front of the Shepherd's Hotel . . .

Truth, how ironic the truth! He had not been with another woman since the night he'd taken Karida's virginity. The flower girl he'd bragged of deflowering had not recognized him. Had he not worn a disguise, she would have thrown her arms about him and showered him with grateful kisses. He'd given her ten pounds the night before, after she sobbed out a pathetic tale about needing money to pay the rent or she'd be forced to sell her virginity in a brothel. The money he'd given her had fended off that possibility a while longer—or so he hoped.

Of course, she might well have spent her nights here already and taken him for a fish. That was the main reason he'd instructed her to remain quiet about his gift, to maintain his pride. So he told himself. Not because of Karida or embarrassment at his recent generous instincts.

Karida. Nigel thought again of how she'd demonstrated her passion, heard again in his mind her excited little cries. Against her rounded bottom, his cock hardened. But he fought back his arousal and sat up, regretfully jamming a hand through his hair. He must make arrangements to return her to the hotel, and quickly, lest suspicions be aroused. Such was his promise.

Nigel glanced at the little clock on the table. Two hours had passed, all the time he'd allotted for her seduction. In one hour he must return her to the hotel or her worried aunt would be searching the streets for Karida.

His lips brushed the curve of her cheek. "Wake up, sleeping beauty. Time to dress and face reality."

She rolled over, her lips parting slightly, her face flushed with passion, her manner languorous. Masculine satisfaction filled him at seeing her kiss-swollen lips, the darkening love bite at the base of her neck. These were signs of his intimate and thorough possession. Soon, she would be legally his. For good. Or at least for as long as he wanted her.

He donned his drawers and trousers, and gestured to the adjoining bath chamber. "I suggest you clean up and dress quickly. Your aunt will grow worried." When Karida blinked sleepily at him, he tamped down his lust and added, "You smell of cinnamon and sex, sweet. Your aunt seems a very smart woman."

A grin touched his mouth. "Or we could stay here and begin anew. If you wish. I paid all day for the room."

Alarm sprang into her eyes, along with a becoming flush across her cheeks. Karida covered herself with the sheet, glared at him and went into the bath chamber. The loud slam of the door announced her mood. Nigel chuckled. Marrying her would prove a challenge. He relished the idea, finished dressing, and threw open the outer door.

In a few minutes, he had everything ready. Odd, though. He couldn't understand why Habib, the brothel owner, was so jovial about finding an official who could perform weddings.

"You are marrying Karida, the pretty woman you brought here, Nigel?" Habib had laughed and slapped him on the back. "She will save your sorry skin, that one. I am glad, for I like you. It is good."

When Karida emerged from the bathroom, wrapped in a plain white towel, Nigel stared at her as if seeing her for the first time. Though her hair was combed and her face scrubbed, the love bite was still clearly visible on her neck. Patches of skin were faintly red where his day beard had abraded her soft skin. He frowned, reminding himself to be gentler next time.

Such as on their wedding night.

Her large brown eyes flared with shock as she scanned the room's three additional occupants. "Nigel, what is this?" she snapped.

"Our wedding party, my sweet." He took her elbow and guided her to the sitting area. "I couldn't wait. For a rather large sum, Mr. al-Fasid has kindly agreed to officiate."

His grin deepened at her inward rasp of breath, and she

said, "Nigel, have you gone totally mad? I can't marry you like this!"

Deliberately he misunderstood. "Why, Karida, you look breathtaking. That towel is most becoming."

"In a brothel? With no witnesses I know? I refuse to do this."

"Then grow fond of your covering, sweet. It will be all you wear out of here."

Karida's gaze narrowed. "I agreed to keep my part of the wager, and I shall, but marrying me in a brothel?"

A flicker of cold remorse flashed through him. She deserved a beautiful lace gown, scads of flowers, white lilies and freesia and tiny tea roses, and an opulent cathedral brimming with guests, not this cheerless room where nameless bodies had writhed and sweated in soon-forgotten sex. But he dared not trust her to keep her side of the bargain. Too much was at stake. He needed the ruby and her bound to him.

A dark part of him whispered he needed so much more, such as redemption. His cynical side laughed.

Nigel gave her a charming smile. "Yes, marriage in a brothel. When we walk out of here, we shall be legally wed. I have the license, obtained in London." He cocked his head at her. "Or would you rather I carried out you, still unmarried and naked in my arms?"

The ceremony began, binding them together as man and wife.

Hands clenched in her lap, Karida listened in shock as her new husband spun a tall tale to her aunt and her uncle. The foursome sat on the expansive terrace of the Shepherd's Hotel, and fresh tea and a delicious assortment of pastries was on the table, but no one ate or drank. Katherine looked too stunned, and spots of high color on Ramses's cheeks indicated his gathering emotion.

With gallant enthusiasm, Nigel told his dumbstruck audience how he'd masqueraded as Charles Porter to ensnare Karida in marriage because, "I love her so very much."

The late afternoon sun was warm upon her cheeks at his bold lie. Surely they would blame its heat for her furious blush.

Mischief blazed in Nigel's jade gaze as he glanced at her. "And when I bared my true identity to your niece, she begged me to claim her. So I made her my wife."

Stinging pain laced her lips as Karida bit back an incredulous outburst. *Had you told the whole truth in the beginning, perhaps you would not be in this predicament,* she accused herself. She felt like a fly caught in the sticky strands of a web of lies.

She could have clutched the towel, run from the brothel instead of marrying him; it wouldn't have been the worst thing that had ever happened to her. But Karida had married him. That small flicker of uncertainty in his eyes, and the way he'd turned from her when she questioned him about his desire to change, these things meant more than his lies. She sensed he longed for redemption but doubted he could change.

Yes, he was a lost soul as once she had been; a deep part of her knew the intimate hurt lacing his heart. He would never show that to the world. She had seen his good side, however: the way he'd made her laugh, the clear affection he'd displayed, the number of times he'd physically risked himself to save her. And of course there was the physical attraction between them. They were two souls drifting in a turbulent sea but drawn inescapably together.

Nigel *was* capable of loving her. She believed that wholeheartedly. She'd heard the words he'd meant for her to miss: "Oh, my love, you make me want to be good." And for the first time she believed he told the absolute truth. That was why she'd married him.

His handsome face alight, Nigel explained how he'd been struck since their first meeting and had enjoyed their continued acquaintance in England. This afternoon he'd asked her to accommodate him to a respectable place near the markets where he'd confessed his true identity and his ardent feelings.

"I demonstrated to her the very depth of my feelings, and she told me she was too tied up to make a decision."

Blood flamed to Karida's cheeks and she choked. Tied up? She raised her teacup, gulped down cold tea to hide her discomfiture.

Nigel slid her a sly glance. "But I managed to convince her of my sincerity, and to marry me, and I found an official who was able to perform the deed."

"It can't be legal. You lacked the license," Katherine protested.

Fishing a paper out of his jacket pocket, Nigel slid it forward on the table.

Karida's aunt's eyes widened. "A special license?" she asked.

"Procured in England by my solicitor, and since Egypt is governed by England, it's legal here as well!"

A low growl rumbled in Ramses's chest. Karida shivered at the menace glittering in his eyes. Katherine placed a hand on her husband's arm and squeezed gently. He calmed.

"You married my niece without awaiting our permission? While you deceived her and my wife by pretending to be someone else?" Ramses asked.

"In light of the fact that my father, Karida's sponsor and chaperone, refused to grant permission for you to marry her back in London, your actions are questionable, Lord Claradon," Katherine added.

Upon hearing this news, Ramses grew red-faced with fury, and Nigel looked at him beseechingly. "I know, Lord Smithfield thinks I am not worthy. I confess, I did seize advantage of the situation because I was doubtful how you would receive me." He turned to Katherine, giving her an imploring look. "Seeing Lord Smithfield denied me, I could not risk being turned down again. I beg you, do not look upon me with displeasure because I hid my identity or what I have done in the past, but see my intentions now for what they are. I cannot bear for your niece and myself to be apart."

"You are Nigel. Thomas's brother. His twin brother," Ramses said slowly. "It was you buying horses and there at the wedding capture, not Thomas."

Nigel nodded, meeting the Khamsin warrior's gaze. "Your people were friendly with my twin. I thought it better to use his influence."

"And so, you are a master of disguise. What are we to believe? Who are you? One who hides his true identity is hardly trustworthy. You marry my beloved niece in haste after her London guardian denies his permission . . . ? That is an act without honor." Ramses put a hand on the hilt of his scimitar.

Distress filled Karida. Her uncle did not touch his sword lightly. That razor-sharp blade could part Nigel's head from his neck in an instant, and the thought twisted her insides. She would not see that cheeky, roguish grin forever vanish.

Pasting a bright smile on her face, Karida turned to Ramses and said, "He did have something to hide, Uncle. His feelings for me. He was afraid of showing them." She placed her palm over Nigel's, which trembled slightly. Lifting her chin, she swept both her aunt and uncle with an imperious gaze. "I agreed to the marriage this time. I did not in London because it was all too sudden, and I failed to see certain qualities in Lord Claradon—the feelings for me he had not yet expressed."

She glanced at Nigel, and shock flared in his expression. His brilliant green gaze burned like fire-lit jewels. "Yes. When I first met Karida, I knew I would never forget her, try as I might."

Warmth ignited her. He told the truth. But what did it prove?

Ramses's gaze did not leave Nigel's, but his hand dropped from his sword hilt. Suspicion glinted in his amber eyes. "And so you are married. Without the approval of your parents or any relatives. There is only one option left, Karida. We must set out straightaway for the Khamsin camp."

The breath hitched in her throat, and she could almost sense Nigel's innate satisfaction . . . and then his dismay when Ramses added, "Nuri, Karida's father, will need to meet with you, and Jabari, our sheikh, will need to approve your union. Jabari's approval is very important for all of my family, including my extended family."

No emotion showed in Nigel's expression as he nodded. "It would be my honor, sir, to meet Karida's family. Truly, I am not such a bad sort once you get to know me—and it's not like I bring nothing to the table."

As Nigel rattled off the details of his earldom and family lineage, she could almost hear the irony. She interjected, "Yes, he isn't *such* a bad sort, Aunt Katherine, Uncle Ramses." She gave Nigel a fond look. "And as we know, people can change for the better. I intend to work very hard with my new husband. I'll bring out qualities he never realized he had."

Alarm flickered in Nigel's steady green gaze, and Karida gave him a sweet smile. *I can change you. And I shall. You will see, Nigel. You can reform, and now that we are legally married you don't stand a chance.*

A dark frown drew Ramses's brows together, and he pinned Nigel with a menacing look. "Since yours is not a legal union in the eyes of our tribe, you will not be acknowledged as husband and wife until you are married by Khamsin ritual. My niece will not be staying with you tonight in your room."

Surprising Karida, Nigel nodded.

Her aunt gave a small smile, but her uncle's level gaze warned that Nigel danced close to the sword's edge. Too close.

Chapter Seventeen

A chorus of barking dogs heralded their arrival at the Khamsin camp; the setting sun painted the jagged black and gray mountains with deep violet and saffron hues, and the purple shadows deepened on the cliffs as they reached the clearing in the desert. The camp was rows of black goat hair tents on a flat plain nestled between rough ridges of mountain. Tall date palms, acacia trees, and yellow and green vegetation peppered the tawny, pebbled sand.

Nigel resisted the urge to shift in the saddle. The Arabian he rode was sturdy and sleek with a steady gait, but it might as well have been an old nag. His ass hurt dreadfully after the hours-long journey from the Nile. Never an excellent rider, he'd spent weeks fighting to overcome his trepidation of being in the saddle after the accident that had nearly killed him. Horses were like women: fickle, temperamental, likely to toss you aside when you least expected it.

Yet, his bride was not like that.

Nigel glanced at Karida, serene atop her pretty white mare. He sensed she had her own motivation for marrying him: she thought she could change him for the better.

He gave a snort. Redeem *him*, the man everyone detested? Not likely. Like an angel trying to coax a demon to reform.

As they rode through camp, disquiet filled him. It seemed the same as his last visit, women hovering over cooking fires, boys herding sheep, and warriors keeping watch. But something was different. They were staring at Karida.

Nigel glanced at her, too, and was shocked to see the proud lift of her chin droop. She bent her head, studied the ground.

They . . . know about my scars. That was why Kareem rejected me, because the women convinced him I could not have children. I'm useless. The words she'd shared as they lay in bed together still haunted him. Now he saw and felt firsthand the consequences.

A strange, dull sensation settled in his chest. He wondered what it was and then realized he was feeling grievous pain. Not for himself. But for her.

Nigel tried to dismiss the ache, but it remained as a vise squeezing his heart. It gave him pause. He was becoming dangerously vulnerable because of Karida.

He stiffened his good British spine as they dismounted and greeted the Khamsin sheikh. He could summon enough acting skill to convince the potentate he had deep feelings for Karida. *Enough to marry her and achieve your goal, even if your affection is false,* he whispered to himself.

Liar, his conscience replied.

And much later that night, in his quarters, emotion coursed through Nigel as he thought of Karida sleeping in her father's tent a short distance away. This marriage had been a last, desperate measure. He'd wanted her, and now he had her. But now he needed her. Need was not the same as want. The thought plagued him as he finally fell asleep.

He woke the next morning, filled with determination as he washed and dressed for the day. Shortly after a breakfast of dates, yogurt, and camel's milk, Karida formally introduced him. Her adoptive father coolly studied Nigel until he was summoned to the sheikh's tent.

The many-poled, expansive home was cool and airy, its flaps rolled up to allow in natural light. Jewel-like Persian carpets layered the ground. Breeze-billowed silks separated the main room from the sleeping quarters.

Jabari sat on the floor, hands resting on his knees, spine straight as the edge of Nigel's razor. Nuri, Karida's father, was sitting to Jabari's left, and Ramses was on Jabari's right. None of the men looked pleased to see Nigel. Ramses fingered the hilt of his long scimitar.

Nigel resisted the urge to put a hand to his throat. Instead, he faced the men evenly, gave them a cool assessing look in return.

"Sit, Lord Claradon. Here, in front of us."

The sheikh gestured to the floor. Nigel sat, facing them. Sweat trickled down his back, plastering his white shirt to his skin. He forced himself to assume a blank look.

An interrogation began, a volley of harsh questions coming from Nuri, Karida's father. Nigel answered each, lying as he needed, telling the truth where he could. When her father asked if he truly cherished Karida, Nigel responded truthfully.

"She is more to me than you will ever know."

Jabari kept studying him intently with his coal-black gaze. Then the sheikh lifted his broad shoulders, his mouth relaxing beneath his short-trimmed black beard and mustache.

"Enough, Nuri. It matters not if his intentions are honorable. I suppose it is best Karida marries a foreigner. Her chances of finding a groom here are slim, for she is considered inferior, since she is not of Egyptian birth." The Khamsin sheikh leveled his dark gaze at Nigel. "She came to us from England, and her parents were not married. She is what is known as a . . ." Jabari frowned, as if searching for the term. "Ah, yes, a 'bastard.' She is a woman of little worth, especially since she can never bear children."

Shock became violent rage. Nigel thought of the rude stares the Khamsin women aimed at Karida, and of her quiet dignity when Kareem rejected her. He sprang to his feet, ignoring the stern warning of Karida's father.

"You bloody sod, sitting there and passing judgment on her. How the hell would you know what her worth is?"

Jabari merely arched a dark eyebrow. "You wish to confront me, Englishman? You dare to contradict *me,* the sheikh who rules here?"

"You're damn right I will," Nigel snarled. "And I couldn't care less if you rule over the whole damn country! You've insulted my wife."

Enraged, Nigel lifted his fists and beckoned the Arab to stand up. Hell, sparring with this bastard would prove enjoyable, and he'd survived more than a few scrapes in seedy Cairo bars and the back alleys of London. But as he moved forward to attack, he crashed into a solid, muscular chest. Ramses had stood and blocked his path.

"This is between us, Ramses. Stay out of it."

"I am my sheikh's guardian and will not allow you to injure him. And you are wrong, Claradon. This is between *us.*"

A blow crashed into his face with the force of a locomotive; Nigel staggered back in pain and tasted blood. He brought a hand to his lip. His fingers came away red. He regained his balance and struck back. The punch caught Ramses's right eye, but the warrior barely flinched, and his next blow found Nigel's solar plexus.

Wheezing with the pain, Nigel resisted the urge to double over. Instead, he threw an uppercut that would make the most hardened pugilist proud. Ramses grunted with surprise and reeled.

"Caught off guard, eh? Jabari insults your niece, and you attack *me?* What kind of relative are you?"

"One who cherishes her more than you ever will know." Ramses drew back his fist to throw another punch.

"Enough! Ramses, stay your blow. He has proved himself." Jabari stood, smiling. Bloody hell, the bastard was smiling! He extended a friendly hand to Nigel. "You have proven yourself worthy of Nuri's daughter, Lord Claradon. Any man who would lay his life on the line—for that is what you do by assaulting me here, in my tent—to defend her honor is a man of true worth."

Nigel said nothing. He was too stunned. What the hell was wrong with him? He, who thought honor an archaic concept, had nearly given the sheikh a facer and would likely have taken a sword blow. All for Karida.

Nuri grinned and slapped Nigel on the back. Nigel shook the sheikh's sun-darkened hand. Ramses gave a respectful nod, his right eye beginning to swell and turn purple.

Beaming faces regarded him as if he'd pulled off some tremendous feat, but he had no honor. He was a thief and a liar and a desperate man. Yet he'd gone sailing into a fistfight, provoked by a simple insult.

Nigel stretched out his hands and stared at his raw, bruised knuckles. He didn't like what he was feeling, didn't like the backslapping and the congratulations. *This is not me,* he wanted to argue. *Stop trying to shape me into something I am not, like I'm a bloody sand castle.* Because sooner or later the tide would come crashing in, the sea with its turbulent froth, to destroy everything. All that would be left on the sand would be wreckage. He'd seen it happen before, with his father, who had briefly needled him into playing the part of the perfect son. Nigel had failed, however, and everything he worked so hard to build was smashed.

I will never go through that again. I'm not a goddamn product of someone else's expectations.

Another thought took him, a reminder that he was in control. A cool, detached smile touched Nigel's mouth, and pain speared out from his cut lip. He would simply lie. He could play the part of the eager and loyal groom. He was no more loyal than a kicked dog, but he could act it.

"If you're all finished congratulating me, I suggest we get on with the wedding," he suggested. "Let's do it quick, before I change my mind."

Nuri laughed, and Jabari assured him the wedding would commence at sunset. Only Ramses stood in thoughtful silence, his amber eyes watchful as if Nigel were a viper. It was as if his wife's uncle could see straight through him.

Karida's afternoon sped by. Nigel refused to explain why he sported a swollen, cut lip, muttering it was nothing. Something had happened. The slight mocking look had faded from his gaze, and he acted distant.

She thought about the open, breezy attitude he'd acquired on their journey to camp. Nigel had been uninhibited and frank, and Karida actually found herself enjoying the trip. They'd argued about England's dominion over Egypt, discussed some principles of the Fabian Society and their mutual fondness for steak and kidney pie, and laughed about many other things. She, who'd had few companions, had found a close one. But now he'd shut himself down, saying little. Had the journey all been an act? Who was the real Nigel—the liar and thief, or the charming, unguarded friend? Karida pondered this question as she walked to her father's tent to prepare for her wedding.

She nearly stumbled over Rayya, Layla's dour-faced mother, who carried a goatskin bag of water. Clear droplets splashed onto the tawny sands like teardrops as the woman stopped. Karida tried to ignore her, but Rayya caught up, bag sloshing.

"So, you found a suitor who married you. How much has he been paid that he would discard a future with sons of his own—for we both know *you* will never bear them."

Karida lowered her gaze, too wounded to reply. Then Nigel's advice came back to her.

She centered her gaze on the hostile woman. "How much did your father pay your husband to marry you and free him of the curse of that endlessly wagging tongue? I'm wagering he thinks it's not enough now. All the treasure in Egypt would not be enough, unless he were given gems to stuff into his ears to shut out your voice."

Rayya's jaw unhinged. She lost her grip on her bag, and it

plummeted to the ground, the water inside splashing everywhere. The woman's mouth opened and closed like that of a fish gasping for air. Karida smiled and strolled on, her step lighter.

The source of her inspiration was sitting outside her tent, absorbed in examining some silver jewelry she had on display. Chin propped up on one fist, he held an anklet up to the light. A hank of dark hair spilled over his forehead, sunlight picking out gleams of copper and gold in the strands, and she felt an absurd urge to brush it away to see his eyes—to truly see his gaze upon her without lust or mocking intent. She wanted to see a candid glimpse of authentic tenderness.

He glanced up and set the anklet down. "What have you done? You look like the cat who ate the canary and then nibbled on its brother for dessert."

Odd, how he could instantly assess her so accurately.

"I had words with Rayya, that mother who urged Kareem to marry her pregnant daughter."

Nigel broke into a wide grin, flashed gleaming white teeth. His smile warmed her like the sun. "I take it she was left stunned."

Karida nodded. "Wordless, probably for the first time since she left her mother's womb."

A deep, amused chuckle resonated from Nigel's throat. He touched his forelock in a respectful gesture. "Well done, my lady." With his boyish grin and relaxed manner, he looked open and honest.

Nigel jingled the anklet. "Did you make these? Why is all this on display? What did you plan to do with it?"

She squatted down and took the chain from him, palming it with a wistful sigh. "Sell it someday, perhaps. I'm to get a bit of money when I turn twenty-three. I once dreamed of opening my own little shop in London." She stopped then, dismayed, realizing she'd told him far too much, certainly more than she'd ever told anyone else.

Nigel took the anklet back and set it down. His gaze was knowing. "You wanted to create, to give to people—to win their approval by the beautiful things you make."

How well he understood her, just as she thought she understood him. But what good was understanding without trust? "It is possible. Anything is possible. People can change."

As she'd feared, Nigel's look shuttered. Once more he hid behind a granite mask. "You'd best get ready," he told her.

It was a curt dismissal. But as he left to return to his quarters, a lingering residue of joy refused to leave Karida, along with an insistent whisper in her mind: *He can change—and he will with your help.*

They married at sunset. Dressed in the white robes she'd worn for the marriage capture, Karida kept stealing anxious glances at Nigel. In his neatly pressed khaki suit, oyster striped waistcoat, and polished boots, he looked more solemn than she'd ever seen. No mirth twinkled in his jade eyes, no cocky grin twisted his full mouth. He almost looked as if he were being sentenced to prison as he grimly recited the Arabic words of the ceremony.

But when Jabari congratulated them both and pronounced them married, Nigel turned to Karida. He lifted the gauzy veil shielding her lower face and very gently, almost reverently, pressed a kiss to her mouth. He whispered against her lips.

Karida blinked in astonishment as he dropped the veil. It wasn't the fine pressure of his kiss that had caused her to gasp, either, but his words. For as his lips found hers, Nigel had whispered the most incredulous thing, his voice so quiet that she wondered if it was the desert wind scraping across the sands: "I don't deserve you, but maybe someday you'll learn to care for me. Just a little. Because I sure as hell care for you."

Her husband picked at his food at the wedding feast. He acted jovial enough in response to the usual light teasing offered by the Khamsin warriors about the wedding night, but Karida sensed a change in him. Tension gripped her body, and she could barely eat anything, either.

Relief filled her when Nigel finally stood, extending a hand. He said, "If you will excuse us, my bride and I need to retire for the evening."

He firmly gripped her slender fingers and they walked to their tent. This was a moment she'd dreamt of, but it was tainted by circumstance. Gone was her fantasy of love, of a close-knit marriage, of children scampering at her heels; gone was any surety of living with a man who honored her as he honored himself, who loved her with every breath he took.

She'd thought Nigel had been lying when he murmured those words as he'd kissed her during the marriage ceremony. But maybe he had not. His actions this afternoon had filled her with incredulous hope. She'd learned he'd nearly cold-cocked the sheikh in her defense.

The interior of their spacious tent smelled of jasmine and sandalwood. Luxurious Persian carpets had been laid down. There was a mahogany chest from Lebanon, a table containing a pitcher and glasses, a looking glass, and small wardrobe. Dominating the tent was a huge bed. Crimson and yellow silk pillows were scattered atop a handwoven yellow and violet bedspread.

As he shrugged out of his jacket, she went to Nigel, placing a palm against his waistcoat, feeling his body's heat beneath the thin silk. "My father told me what happened in Jabari's tent this morning."

Nigel scowled. "Your father is indiscreet."

"I can't believe you challenged Jabari! The sheikh, you actually attempted to hit him? Because of me?"

He winced and rubbed his knuckles. "He deserved it for what he called you," he muttered.

She kissed his sullen mouth, careful of the healing cut on his lip. Nigel looked surprised. She kept kissing him, urging his mouth to soften beneath hers, willing away his frustrated anger. Finally his lips moved against hers.

"Mmmm, you taste delicious," he murmured. Then he broke away, staring at her with a tormented look.

"Maybe it's best we take it slow tonight," he ventured. "Or even wait."

Karida's mouth dropped open. This from the man who had blackmailed her into surrendering her virginity, tied her up naked in a brothel and ravished her until she screamed?

"On our wedding night?"

Nigel half turned, the scowl back on his face. "These tents aren't very private," he muttered. "You can hear everything."

She gave a light laugh. "That's what my mother told me. She said sometimes the camp can tell if it will be a happy marriage or a troubled one based on the wedding night sounds."

Nigel cocked his head. "Your *adopted* mother, you mean."

Karida's pulse kicked up. "What do you mean?" The cynical twist of his mouth made her shiver.

"I know, Karida—Anne. I know your real name and how you came to the Khamsin." He closed the space between them, jamming his hands into the pockets of his khaki trousers. Pearls of sweat dotted his temples despite the night's relative coolness. "You were born in England and sent here to live with the Khamsin by an Englishman who is probably your real father. You spent the first twelve years of your life in a workhouse. You met with a terrible accident there. That's where you fell into the fire. Not here in Egypt."

"How . . ."

"I asked the sheikh this afternoon. He told me."

Karida struggled to regain her composure, but it felt like snatching at the wind. She met Nigel's gaze evenly.

"Yes, it's true. I'm a bastard. Is there anything else you'd like to know? Anything else you wish to lord over me?"

Nigel's expression changed. He cupped her face with overwhelming tenderness. "You could have been born in the gutters of Whitechapel and you'd still be better than me—and if I could find the bloody sod who put you in the workhouse, I'd thrash him for abandoning you. How could a father do that to his child?"

A tumult of feelings washed over her as his thumbs stroked her cheeks, making little circles. The action calmed the churning of her stomach.

"My mother," she muttered. "My real mother put me there. Not my father. He didn't even know of my existence until she brought me to him. And then she . . ." Her cheeks burned. She put her hands over Nigel's and tried to pull away. He would not let her.

"She what, sweet?"

Lies tripped to the edge of her tongue. Karida swallowed and reconsidered. The truth hurt, but it was far better than lies. There had been enough of lies and secrets regarding her birth; she would no longer hide behind them.

She raised her eyes and said, "She sold me, sold me to my father for a sum of three thousand pounds."

Nigel swore and leaned his forehead against hers. "A paltry sum for acquiring *you,* love."

Words gushed out in a torrent. It felt almost a relief to spill them. "My real father is a highborn aristocrat. He bought me like a horse or an artifact. He sent me here, away from him, because he was ashamed that I'm a bastard and his secret. He sent me away because I wasn't good enough. That's why I want my own shop. I want to take the money I'll receive on my twenty-third birthday, money I'll get for guarding the tomb of the sleeping golden mummies, and return to England. I'll open a shop and sell my jewelry, make a name for myself to prove to him that I'm not just a burden. Then maybe, just maybe . . ." Her voice dropped to a raspy whisper. "He'll call me his daughter." Tears clawed up from her burning eyes, but she refused to let them come.

Nigel's face twisted in anger. His hands gently cradled her

cheeks. "Karida, love, it had nothing to do with you, trust me. If he sent you away, it was because your father felt guilty for letting you wither for years in that workhouse."

She tried writhing away. She was feeling irrational, furious. "No, you're wrong. It's not his fault. He's above reproach; he didn't know of my existence. I want to be like him, perfect and good. Why should he want a burnt, thieving brat who can't even—"

A low curse spilled from Nigel's mouth, and he released her. "Perfect? No one is perfect, Karida. Why are you fixated on what's wrong with you? You're the one who always says people can change. You spit that out at me and then canonize your father?"

She was taken aback, forced to review her dreams and goals. It was one thing to expect her husband to accept and improve himself, quite another to abandon her own feelings of despair. It was frightening, also, abandoning the ideal she'd clung to for the past ten years. She closed her eyes, seeing the misty London streets, hearing the *clip-clop* of horses' hooves as carriages rattled past. A numbing fog descended over her as she hugged herself, forgetting everything but her memories.

"I just want to be close to him, to get him to finally realize I have worth. I can be someone he'll like. All I need is to go back to London, to start that shop, and I will earn his respect."

"Who? Who is it, Karida?"

His voice was sharp, and broke into her ruminations. Karida's eyes flew open, and the words spilled from her lips before she thought. "Lord Smithfield."

"Him?" Nigel looked doubtful. She'd expected him to sputter in outrage and curse, not adopt this puzzled, thoughtful look.

"Did he tell you he was your father?"

"He didn't have to. He paid money for me. Doesn't that say enough? And then he sent me away, burying me in the desert like a problem he wished to hide." Karida paced to the bed, stared down at it. How many times had her father slept with the woman who was her mother? Once? Twice? Presumably they'd felt something for each other, but she doubted it was love. Her conception had been the result of a tawdry affair.

His two hands settled gently on her shoulders and turned her back to face him. "Not a problem. A treasure. That's what you are. And I suspect he didn't send you away for the reasons you think, but for something far more important. Karida, look at me. *Look* at me."

She did, and the tenderness in his gaze broke through her self-control. Tears spilled down her cheeks. He kissed them away, his mouth feathering warm pressure against her chilled skin.

Nigel bent his forehead to hers. His voice lowered to a trembling whisper. "Listen to me. None of this was your fault. Your father, maybe he didn't know, and maybe when he found you, however he found you, he felt horrified at all you had to endure. He only wanted to make up for everything, but he felt so guilty, and maybe he felt terrible as well that he feared he would fail you, because he had failed you for the first part of your life." His voice cracked. "And maybe . . . just maybe . . . he doesn't want to fail anymore."

Suspicion filled her. Nigel hid a dark secret, himself. But he wasn't ready to reveal it. Not to her.

Then his mouth slid down to hers, applied a tender pressure. His kiss was gentle and coaxing. Karida clutched his hands, clinging to him in desperate hope. She licked his lips, tasting the juice he'd drunk with dinner and the dates he'd eaten for dessert. His soft groan of appreciation made her smile against his mouth. Sandalwood, cloves, and jasmine mingled with Nigel's scent of clean skin and the faint aroma of leather and horses. Karida's hands slid over the taut muscles of his back, her nails skimming his flesh as he nuzzled her neck, dropping tiny kisses over the long column.

"I thought you didn't want this," she managed, gasping as he nipped at her skin.

"Damn it, you always chase away all my sense."

She held him to her, as if holding him could chase away all the darkness and meld them together. Nigel made a low sound and tore the covers off the bed with one hand, shedding his clothing as she undressed.

He made love to her with a sweetness she'd not expected. Nigel treated her with reverence, stroking her skin softly, murmuring heated praise when she responded to his ardent touch. When he pushed inside her, joining their bodies, melding them from hip to chest, he raised himself up. His eyes met hers. Some turbulent emotion blazed in their depths then vanished.

He began moving inside her, the slow, delicious friction building pleasure to a delicious crescendo. Karida clung to him and, as she climaxed, Nigel kissed her deeply, capturing her excited cries in his mouth.

When he shuddered against her and lay still on her body, his head pillowed on her shoulder, she stroked the trembling muscles of his back. Karida felt something warm and wet trickle down her skin.

She ignored Nigel's tears, however, and held him to her, her heart rent in half. Finally he slid off her, buried his face in the pillow as if ashamed.

Karida knelt on the bed and began massaging his shoulders, kneading the tense muscles, saying nothing, letting her touch soothe as his touch had comforted her after she'd confessed about her father. When she finished, Nigel turned over, capturing her in his arms. He began loving her again with a fierce intensity. This time he did not muffle her moans and cries but let them echo loudly with his own.

A long time afterward, as they lay in each other's arms, sweat cooling on their bodies, Karida studied her husband. His long body was relaxed after lovemaking, his expression softer than she'd ever seen. He'd let down his guard and shown a side she knew was hiding deep within.

"You're wonderful." She traced the fullness of his lower lip.

A scowl twisted his mouth. "I am not what you think, Karida."

"You are what you are, Nigel. And what you are is a man capable of great love and honorable action. I believe this, or I would not have married you." She sat up, pushing at the long fall of her tousled hair. "You may think I had no choice, but if I had not seen the man you will become, I would have run out of the brothel naked rather than marry you."

He turned to her. His face had shifted from serene satisfaction to the familiar granite mask, and his voice was cool. "Don't talk me into something I can never be. If you want a noble, honorable man, go find my twin. Go sing praises about him, for God's sake."

His curtness should have hurt, but strangely, Karida felt only a wrenching pity. She sank back onto the bed as he turned his back. "I'm not singing anyone's praises, Nigel. I'm only pointing out what you plainly cannot see."

Nigel watched. Karida slept like a child, one hand curled beneath her head, her lips parted. A rosy flush from their lovemaking lingered on her cheeks, and Nigel's heart lurched.

I am no hero. I am a thief.

Regret and desperation clashed like warriors on a battlefield. He'd only desired to comfort her after seeing such desperate grief, but he should have left her alone. Making love with her had fulfilled his deepest desires—and his darkest fears. He could no longer ignore his feelings. With every kiss, every stroke of her silky skin, his heart engaged; and that organ, harder than the firmest stone, had begun to crack. When would it break? When would she realize the depth of his emotions for her?

No woman will have that power over me again, he'd

vowed. But somehow, Karida had found a small crevice and wriggled her way inside.

Nigel stared at Karida's ruby. She'd set it on the bedside table. Light from the lamp played over the crimson stone, giving it an eerie glow.

Sliding out of bed, he picked up the gem and went to his rucksack. Fishing out the scorpion amulet, he fit the ruby into the charm's tail. It clicked into place.

The amulet: the key to his future riches. He could have it all now.

He again grabbed his rucksack and withdrew a fake ruby necklace, this one with a small black dot exactly like hers. Weighing each in his palm, he stood motionless, studying the gems. One was the key to unlocking great riches, the other false as he. He glanced at his sleeping bride. For a wild moment he wanted to toss both stones to the floor. He wanted to forget all and climb back into bed with his bride, awaken her with loving kisses and find surrender and peace in her arms.

But then what? When she discovers the truth about you, how base you truly are, will she stay with you? the mocking voice inside him asked. *And what of Eric? Oakley's not about to let you off paying.*

Nigel swallowed hard, pushing aside the pain settling on his chest like a boulder. He placed the false necklace on the bedside table and, taking paper and pen, quickly scribbled a note. Then, packing his things, he silently left the tent like the ghost of a man he was.

The gentle mare the Khamsin had given him as a wedding gift was sturdy. By the light of the creeping dawn, Nigel carefully guided her toward his destination—the cave where the map was locked.

He had been this way before, but only during the day. Grayish light filtered over the majestic limestone mountains all around and slowly grew stronger. Nigel rubbed his forehead, sweating despite the lingering chill of the fading night air, and he dismounted as he recognized the rock markers designating the mountain with the cave entrance. The scorpion amulet sat snug in his trouser pocket.

Pebbles crunched beneath his boots as he made his way down to the entrance. The cave was set at the bottom of a small ravine, and as he climbed down the large boulders he kept an electric torch in hand to light the way.

Inside the cave, he set his torch on a nearby rock and gazed around, inwardly marveling at the rich textures of the ancient stalagmites dripping from the cavern's ceiling. A small depression in the sandy floor indicated an old water source. Karida had told him how the Khamsin, like other Bedu, filled such a hollow with water by digging down. This particular basin had probably been kept dry due to the secret it guarded.

Two extinguished torches set in iron sconces flanked the doorway. With a pounding heart, he approached the rock wall and the small ankh carved into its surface, a door to a chamber carved out many years ago. He removed one of the torches and lit it with his lighter to add more light to the cave.

Nigel next fished out the scorpion amulet. His hand trembled as he brought the key to the matching indentation on the wall. His torch flame cast wavering light over the rough surface.

For a moment he faltered. He saw Karida's honest, trusting face. Then he blinked and saw Eric's honest, trusting face. Both had suffered greatly in the past. But Eric was a child; Nigel could not leave him to fend for himself.

Nigel closed his eyes. "I'm sorry, love. Forgive me, Karida, for being such a bastard—again."

The key fit perfectly. He pushed at the rock door, and it swung open slowly, giving a creak and a groan that echoed through the small cave. Nigel entered the room holding his torch in front. The chamber smelled of ancient dust and old bat guano. He looked around, a chill draping him.

You dishonor the dead here. The thought came from nowhere.

He pushed it aside and turned, sweeping the flaming torch in a circle.

On a small rock sat a rectangular box. Nigel set his torch in a nearby iron sconce, went to the box, and saw the same indentation matching the ruby's teardrop shape. He removed the ruby from the scorpion amulet, fit it to the box, and heard a click. What was inside made his heart still.

Expecting to only find a rolled papyrus map, Nigel stared at the plain wooden box's contents. Light flickered over an emerald the size of a large coin. The gem glistened in the orange torchlight as he scooped it up.

The box also contained the expected rolled parchment and a small piece of papyrus with words printed in neat Arabic. Nigel frowned as he peered at these. He understood very little. But as he turned the papyrus over, he saw words in English, as if the author had anticipated someone like him seeing them. His heart sank.

"Take this jewel as compensation for guarding the rest of the sleeping golden pharaohs. If you dare remove this map to recover the kings' treasure in the Western Desert, you will be haunted all your days. Cursed is the greedy thief who quests for more. Your thirst will remain unsatisfied, as that of a man drowning in hot sand."

The papyrus slipped from his grasp and floated downward. Nigel sank to the ground on his knees.

He recognized the emerald for what it was: a chance to change his mind. He could take the gem back to England, sell it, and split the difference with Oakley. Oakley might just accept that this was all the treasure there was, as long as there came no other displays of newfound wealth from Nigel. It was worth perhaps four thousand pounds. With his half he could get Eric back but would still lack money to do everything he wanted for the boy. Eric would have to live in London and be a source of speculation for the cruel gossip surely to come his way for being the bastard son of . . . a *true* bastard.

The emerald spilled through Nigel's fingers and back into the casket. A roar of sound bounced off the rock walls as he threw back his head and chuckled. The chuckles turned to laughter, and the laughter turned to a scream. Finally he ceased, wiped his streaming eyes. Bloody hell, when was the last time he'd cried? After making love to his new wife.

Nigel struck a fist against one hard thigh. Given a choice, he knew what he must do.

He scooped out the map, unfurled it. The directions were written in Arabic, but the map clearly outlined key landmarks he fully understood. So now he knew exactly the location of the sleeping golden mummies.

He tucked the map into his inside jacket pocket, picked up the emerald, thumbed it. "Sorry. I'll take my chances with the pharaohs," he told the gleaming stone. Then he dropped it back in its casket, which he locked, and pocketed the scorpion amulet and the ruby.

As he stood and grabbed his torch, a sudden gust of cool wind flew past, extinguishing it. He shuddered but clenched the now-dead stick in his sweating palm. Turning on his electric torch, he did not look back as he left.

Chapter Eighteen

Karida spoke little on their journey back to Cairo, except to ask her husband why they were rushing back. His muttered reply about escaping the prying eyes of her family for more lovemaking made her heart sink. He was lying to her again.

She'd vainly hoped he was hunting deep in the desert when she'd awakened yesterday, as his note claimed. Her ruby necklace looked the same, and when Nigel returned in early afternoon, two grouse dangling from his saddle, her heart had soared. Now she realized it had all been a clever ploy to disguise his real intentions.

They checked in at the Shepherd's Hotel with money given by Nuri and her adoptive mother, who'd encouraged them to take a real honeymoon. Nigel paid the porter a handsome tip and shut the door behind him. He shoved a hand through his dark, mussed hair. "I've got to go out in the city for a bit. It's rather hot. Why don't you stay here and rest?"

A canopy of mosquito netting draped the enormous bed. Pushing it aside, Karida sat, toyed with the fabric. "Why don't you tell me the truth for a change? Why you really brought me here."

Nigel spread his hands out in an innocent gesture. "Would you rather return to the brothel? I can get us a room there, if you wish."

Ignoring his sarcasm, she fingered her ruby necklace. "This isn't real. I can tell. You see, after nearly ten years of wearing it, and holding it, I've come to know everything about the gem.

One side isn't worn quite so smooth. The real stone is slightly smoother on one side from my always touching it. Even the hardest rock can be worn down over time, Nigel. Like a heart that seems as hard as stone can, too, if handled right."

Her words hung between them. His body tense, Nigel looked as desperate as a trapped gazelle she'd seen her father hunt once in a wadi. "Your philosophy means nothing to me," he grunted. "I have to go."

"So, you have the map and now you're going to purchase supplies," she said. Something flickered in Nigel's eyes. He started to speak, but she waved her hand. "No, no more lies. Go and do what you must, whatever it is. I just can't take another lie. Not right now."

A low curse escaped his lips. He fled to the door.

As he reached for the doorknob she called out. "Wait! Just one question." She summoned all her strength, her heart racing. "The words you spoke to me after Jabari declared we were married. Tell me the truth: were they a lie?" She had to know, because if he did lie, then everything she'd hoped for would crumble into dust.

Tell me it wasn't a lie, that you are capable of loving me. Please. It's all I need for now. I can live with the fragments of hope, as long as you did not lie. Karida held her breath, waiting for his answer.

He turned, his hand on the doorknob, and looked directly at her. The bleakness in his eyes told her of a deep shame, and also that he had told the truth. "No, that was not a lie."

The door slammed behind him like a thunderclap.

Nigel descended the hotel steps, accompanied by the hotel porter and the porter's two sons, whom he'd hired to help haul his purchases back. At the bottom of the stairs outside the hotel flowed a steady stream of humanity. Dust rose from all the passing carriages. The braying of donkeys mingled with the street traffic and the bustle of pedestrians. Flies buzzed around baskets of raw sugarcane sold by dark-eyed vendors. Women passed, their swaying hips accommodating heavy baskets balanced on their heads.

He scanned the street, wondering if that little flower girl had finally married and settled happily, or if she now plied her trade at another hotel. Dismissing the thought as sentimental, he flagged down a carriage.

On the ride through the city, he made a mental list of supplies: a shovel, a pick, other tools . . . dynamite. Descending from the carriage, he frowned as he gazed down an alley in Cairo's business district. No, he would not use dynamite and excavate the way explorers had in the last century, destroying history in their eagerness for wealth. If he could, he would leave the tomb intact.

A grim smile twisted his mouth. Was it possible he was feeling the revival of a long-dead conscience?

The antiquities shop where he had smuggled and traded treasures over the past several years was discreet and tucked away in an alley. It also was an excellent place to get supplies. Nigel pushed the door open, and he and the porter and his sons entered.

Inside the musty, cramped store, a man was poring over a limestone stelae with a magnifying glass, his face absorbed as his fingers traced the markings. Dressed in a simple khaki suit, he sported a large diamond ring on his pinkie. Nigel absently labeled him: a wealthy American touring the Mediterranean, an easy mark shopping for antiquities.

Impatient to acquire his items, he selected a few off the shelves and dumped them on the counter. "All this, and I'll take one of those large canvas tents."

The store owner went to fetch the items from the back. As he did, Nigel cast the American an indifferent glance. He looked vaguely familiar. Nigel had sold a few smuggled items to his kind, maybe even to this particular man.

The store proprietor came back with Nigel's tent. Nigel opened his wallet and paid. He glanced at the eager porter and gestured to the acquired merchandise. "Take all this back to the hotel, immediately, and there will be a handsome *baksheesh* waiting for you." The porter barked an order to his sons, who scrambled to collect Nigel's purchases.

The proprietor hustled over to the American, realizing he was a hooked fish. He was right, as the American said, "I'll take it," in an accent Nigel recognized from New York City. "Beautiful specimen. From the eighteenth dynasty, you say? Akhenaten's reign?"

"Yes, yes." The proprietor beamed. "Genuine treasure. Very good price, sir."

Nigel shook his head as the store owner named a price that would have fed a village of peasants for a full month. He himself had smuggled artifacts, but he'd always charged a reasonable sum. Out of sheer curiosity, he glanced at the stelae. Then he laughed. There was a time he wouldn't have spoken out, but for once he felt compelled to tell the truth and save the poor sod from being taken for a fool. "That much? For that piece of rubbish?"

The owner bristled, and the American glanced at Nigel. "What are you talking about?"

"It's a fake," Nigel said. He took the man's magnifying glass and ran an index finger over the markings on the limestone. "No copper, see? The ancient Egyptians used copper to carve out their stelae. Whoever did this used a steel chisel."

"My God," the American said softly. "I would never have noticed. That's right."

The proprietor, sensing a lost sale, stammered out a string of protests and angry accusations. Having been called far worse, Nigel ignored them and handed back the magnifying glass.

He added, "Say what you wish, but your blustering won't change the facts. Next time, use copper if you wish to fool someone into paying an exorbitant amount. The very least you can do is try to fake it *well.*" Nigel pinned the shopkeeper with a censuring look, then nodded to the American.

As he left the store, the little bell over the door jingling merrily, he heard the American call after him. More curious than anything, Nigel turned.

"I know you," the American declared.

Nigel's heart dropped to his stomach. "I doubt it," he muttered and turned to leave.

"Please, wait! It's Nigel, Nigel Stone, isn't it? That was the name you used when I bought a Roman amphora from you, the one you found in the Eastern Desert. A fine antiquity. I paid too little, probably because it came without the sanction of many government agencies." The American's eyes gleamed.

"Maybe," Nigel said, guarding his words.

"Well, I did want to thank you for saving me just now from spending a lot of money on a fake. Worthless trash," the American growled.

Nigel shrugged, amused. "It's not exactly *worthless*. The limestone itself is genuine. Worth a few shillings, perhaps."

"It doesn't matter." The man reached into his jacket pocket, withdrew a shiny gold case and opened it, and handed Nigel a card. A pristine white background bore elegant black lettering that read *Walter Rockford*. Nigel nearly whistled as he read the listed New York address. Residents in that district were wealthy people who used dollar bills to light their fires.

"Very nice."

"Look on the back."

Flipping the card over, Nigel saw a hand-scribbled London address.

"I have a business proposition. I usually winter here in Cairo and purchase antiques for my collection, but my daughter is marrying an English nobleman, so I'm moving to London to be closer to her. I'm moving my entire collection there and plan to expand it. I need a sharp eye to organize all my antiquities and advise me on future purchases so I don't get cheated. If you'll come work for me, I'll pay you."

Rockford named a salary that made Nigel's eyes bulge.

The man was willing to pay him that much to avoid fakes? He almost didn't believe it. In fact, he didn't. It was too good to be true, and in his experience things that were too good to be true, weren't.

"I'm very flattered," he said. "Thank you, but no, I'm terribly busy." And Nigel started to hand back the card.

The American shook his head. "Keep it. If you ever decide to reconsider, you know where to contact me."

The man's palm was outthrust. Nigel stared at it, confused. *Gentlemen* shook hands. Jabari had done the same, considering him a gentleman. What fools.

He shook Rockford's hand and scurried away, stuffing the card into his pocket. But as he stepped out of the narrow alley and started toward a nearby cab, a man bumped him while hurrying past. Nigel scowled and turned.

"Pardon me," said a low, mocking voice.

Nigel glanced down at the man's hands. Shock made him immobile; a sickening nausea roiled through him as he realized the man's left hand was missing. Nigel dragged his stunned gaze up to meet a familiar but angry sneer.

"Carry your packages for you, sahib?" said Malik. "Launder your garments? No, I can't, not with this!" He shook his stump at Nigel. "You were supposed to watch my back."

Recovering his customary aplomb, Nigel snorted. "And you were to stay away from Karida. I warned you I would remove your fingers if you stole, Malik. The Khamsin went one step beyond."

Malik leered. "She is pretty, that Karida. Perhaps I should have taken her there in her tent instead of going for the ruby."

Fury engulfed Nigel like white-hot lava. He whirled and reached out to grab the man by the throat and shake him like a dog, but then he stopped himself. He stared at his outstretched hands.

Malik laughed. "You would not like that, would you? The

English with the stone-cold heart has given it away. That is good. Very good." Malice gleamed in Malik's onyx eyes.

An unflattering comparison between Malik and a donkey's behind came to Nigel's mind, and he voiced the thought. Malik's smile faded. From inside his jacket pocket the Arab removed a knife.

Nigel stepped forward, crowding him, showing him he was not afraid. "Try anything and I won't be as merciful as the Khamsin. I'll cut off your damn balls and feed them to the vultures while you lie there screaming and bleeding."

The blood drained from Malik's face as he glanced down at a dagger pressing very gently against his crotch. He muttered something, throwing up his arms in surrender. Then he backed off into the alley.

Nigel's heart beat like Khamsin drums as his old partner chose as a destination of flight the very store he'd just exited. Stripped of a profitable sale, the proprietor would be only too happy to tell Malik of Nigel's purchases. Malik was stupid as a sheep, but even the dumbest man could put two and two together, information such as how Nigel had bought items for a long journey through the desert and tools to excavate a tomb.

Nigel headed in the direction of the brothel. He knew what he must do. Habib was a short, large-bellied sort with a laugh like a stuttering hyena, but sly as well. He was smart, and Nigel had done him favors. Habib owed him, and it was time to get repayment—with weapons from Habib's gun collection.

An hour later, Nigel returned to the hotel, a long sack strung over one shoulder. Upstairs, he paused before entering. He felt as if he were about to leap into a giant, yawning canyon. He'd either crash and break every bone of his body or by sheer good fortune land on something soft. He didn't know what to expect.

But this had to be done. Karida had to know where they were going tomorrow, and of the fact that Malik had spotted him. He wished he could leave her here, free to enjoy a shopping trip, free to spend money on whatever baubles and fripperies women enjoyed. The journey across the blazing heat of the Western Desert promised to be taxing and dangerous, and he did not want to subject her to it. But he knew it had to be.

Karida was curled up in a stuffed chair by the window, reading. She didn't look up as he entered and gave orders to the hotel porter's sons regarding where to place the items. After he'd paid them and they'd left, beaming and assuring him they would be happy to help again, she finally glanced up.

"Shopping, husband?" Her gaze swept the tools and canvas tent. "Or are these wedding gifts? The shovel will come in handy when you venture into the tomb of the sleeping golden mummies. The tomb. The mummies. The map you took with my necklace."

He clenched his jaw, refusing to acknowledge the truth though just a moment before he'd intended to come clean. He didn't like that she already assumed the worst. He didn't like it because she was right.

Karida shook her head. "If you opened the casket containing the map, you saw what was inside. That emerald is quite valuable. You can do marvelous things with what it brings you."

"No. I can't. It isn't nearly enough," he mumbled.

She stared at him. "Are there debts you must pay? Do you owe?"

Her soft concern nearly made him crack, but Nigel folded his arms across his chest. Thoughts buzzed in his head, stinging and angry. "I paid off all my debts—which put me in this predicament, having no cash. I need money for . . . I need it."

"I see." She looked sad. "So you will take what is not yours. Like in this story."

Out of the corner of his eye Nigel saw Karida thoughtfully stroke a finger across her book's title. He stiffened. It was *The Book of the Thousand Nights and a Night*.

"Interesting reading, sweet. Ali Baba and the Forty Thieves?" he guessed.

Karida shrugged. "Very tragic, what happened to Cassim in his greed. He wanted to take more of the treasure than Ali Baba, but he forgot the magic words and was trapped inside the cave. The thieves killed him and chopped him to pieces."

Nigel's pulse quickened, and he dropped his chin to his chest. He jerked a thumb at the shovel propped against a chair. "I assure you, if the same happens to me you can make good use of that shovel—for my grave."

She sprang out of her chair and strode over to him with lithe grace, jabbed a finger at him, poking him in the chest so hard he drew back. "You're always so damn cavalier about everything, even your own bloody demise! Be serious for once!"

Blinking in surprise, he couldn't help but smile. "I've never heard you swear before."

"You forced me into it. Because you're so stubborn. Listen to me, Nigel. You don't know what you're getting into."

"I do know exactly what I'm getting into. I just have no choice in the matter."

Suddenly he felt too weary to argue. He shuffled to the nearest chair and collapsed, pressing a hand to his forehead. The beginnings of a dull headache began to pound inside his skull.

A delicate fragrance of jasmine enveloped him as Karida sat on the chair's arm. Her soft fingers began massaging his temples. He leaned back with a groan of pure relief.

"Please, Nigel. Tell me the truth. Why do you need the treasure?"

"Why must you ask so many questions?"

"When did you plan to leave?"

Nigel sighed, giving in. "I must make arrangements first to rent camels and hire porters." He pushed aside her hands. "And there's one more thing. Malik is in Cairo. I saw him. We must be careful. You especially."

The blood drained from her face. Karida rubbed her left

wrist and swallowed hard. "This is an obstacle, but he can be handled. I'm more concerned about the desert. It's nearly June, and the temperatures will be climbing. We'll need plenty of food and water."

"You're willing to help me?" he gasped. Then, as she went to check the supplies piled by the door he added, "You're not going. I've just now made up my mind. Tell me where the tomb's traps are and I'll handle them by myself. I shan't risk your life by taking me with you. You don't deserve that."

She shook her head. "Your chances of coming out of the tomb alive are better with me."

Nigel sprang out of his chair and joined Karida, tempted to shake sense into her. He gripped her shoulders, feeling both thin bones and soft skin beneath his fingers. "Listen to me. This is not a game. Malik surely knows by now what I intend. I partnered with him to find this treasure on the condition he didn't steal the ruby. He attempted to take it from you when my back was turned. I'm certain he'll be following me—and not to share tea and crumpets."

"All the more reason you need my help," Karida said. "I know the desert, and two are a better defense against one."

Nigel's grip eased, and he began to knead her shoulders in a light, soothing motion. "Karida, please don't do this. Just tell me where the tomb traps are and let me go."

"I won't let you go. You're my husband, and where you go, I go."

At her ardent declaration, something constricted in his chest. No one had ever been so loyal to him, not even his twin. He rested his cheek against her head. "You are stubborn, woman. Stubborn and willful. What have I gotten into?"

"It's called marriage," she said.

I don't deserve this devotion. Torn, he stared at her beautiful face, feeling like a leopard trapped in a gilded cage.

"Tell me, husband. What do you plan?"

Nigel went to his trunk and opened it, fingering Charles

Porter's spectacles. "My plans have changed. I think it's time for you to finally meet someone very close to me."

Nigel left, instructing Karida to wait for him in their room. Minutes ticked by. Karida glanced at her small gold timepiece. She began to pace and wonder about his motives. His secrets. What was Nigel hiding that made obtaining this treasure so important?

After two hours, Karida stopped pacing. Where was he? Had he decided to abandon her as well, like her father had? They were truly married in the eyes of the Khamsin, but the papers had yet to be filed. The sour taste of fear and anxiety flooded her mouth.

Karida dressed quickly, choosing a lemon yellow gown with a scoop collar and white lace sleeves. She brushed her curls and swept them back in a loose chignon. Light brown eyes stared back at her in the looking-glass. Her face was pretty enough, with its soft roundness, full mouth, slight nose, and dark lashes. But the rest of her was not. She pressed her hands against the abdomen that would never grow round with his child. Had Nigel changed his mind about being with her?

She went downstairs to the lobby and settled into a chair. About fifteen minutes later, a tall, broad-shouldered man in a khaki suit walked into the hotel with languid grace. He clutched a small rucksack. It was Nigel.

Karida raced forward and threw her hands around his neck. His eyes widened to saucers as she dragged his head down for a lingering kiss. As he gently pulled away, her heart raced. The kiss had felt wrong, all wrong. What had happened?

"Excuse me, do you mind telling me why you're kissing my husband?"

A petite, dark-haired woman in a lace dress with a square yoke stood nearby, hands on her hips. Her stomach was rounded.

Karida reeled backward. Oh God, this girl was pregnant?

Had Nigel kept more secrets and lies from her? Was this why he needed the treasure and what he was loath to tell her? She put a hand to her throat and stared at the woman. They were about the same height, had the same hair coloring, but the woman's face was exotic and lovely. She had dark skin hinting of Arabic parentage.

Nigel slid an arm about the woman in a protective gesture. He looked slightly amused. "Jas, I think this is the woman you're supposed to mimic. At least I hope so, and that my brother hasn't been . . . more like he used to be."

Karida bit her lip hard to control her quivering emotions. "Is this the secret you've been hiding from me, Nigel?" She gestured to the woman's belly. "Is this why you need the treasure, because she can give you what I never can? So your marriage to me was another lie?"

The amusement fled Nigel's face, replaced by concern. "I've gone and upset you. I'm dreadfully sorry. I thought you knew. I should explain."

"Tommy, what are you doing to my wife?"

Another man walked briskly toward them. He was a man dressed in a khaki suit, his dark head uncovered, with the exact same height and features as the one standing before her. Insight slammed into Karida. Nigel. Thomas. Twins.

Hastily she scrubbed her face, humiliated at the tears burning behind her eyelids. She managed a crooked smile. "I forgot you had a twin," she blurted as Nigel kissed her on the cheek.

"Sweet Karida," he said gently. "I told you I'd be back. I wouldn't abandon you—not like Kareem did."

"Nigel, you brat, you didn't tell her anything and now look how you've upset her." The strange woman gave Karida's husband a censuring look. She came over and gently touched Karida's arm. "I'm Jas, Jasmine, Thomas's wife. Nigel's sister-in-law."

"Let's go upstairs, where it's private." Nigel slid a supportive arm around Karida.

In their hotel room she sat in a chair, her gaze whipping from Thomas, seated in a chair beside his wife, to Nigel, who was standing against the door. They were duplicates, mirror images. Yet in Nigel's eyes was a bleak hardness Thomas lacked.

The plan took shape: Thomas and Jasmine had agreed to stay at the hotel as decoys to divert Malik, with Karida accompanying them as if she were a visiting relative. Jasmine would dress in the same type of shapeless black *abbaya* as Karida's standard and veil her face. When Jasmine and Thomas left the hotel, Malik would follow them, not Karida. Since they were about the same height, it would work.

Karida glanced at the couple, their adoration of each other apparent as they held hands. Would she ever have the same?

"Why are you doing this?" she blurted.

Jasmine glanced at Nigel. "Because Nigel is Thomas's brother. Family. And I owe him dearly. He saved my life."

"Balderdash," Nigel muttered.

Jasmine looked surprised. "You know Charlotte would have shot Thomas and myself if you hadn't—"

"Enough. Can we get on with this?" Nigel interjected.

"I wish you wouldn't do this, Nigel," Thomas said. "Not only is it desecration, if you believe in Egyptian religion, but it's damn dangerous. Digging around old tombs can get you killed."

Tautness showed in Nigel's jaw. "I wish I had a choice. I wouldn't have asked you to do this if I wasn't so worried for Karida. I trust you to look after her, Tommy. Karida can act the part of your visiting sister, and with Jasmine dressed exactly like her, it will confuse Malik. Just make sure to keep an eye on her."

Nigel handed Jasmine a ruby necklace exactly like Karida's, and Karida knew it was the real one—the one her husband had stolen. Jasmine fastened it around her neck.

"How are you getting to the tomb?" Thomas asked. "You should travel with a caravan as far as you can. It's safer that way."

Nigel nodded. "I did some checking, and there's one leaving tomorrow from the Giza plateau."

"We won't be accompanying them," Karida interrupted. "That will take too long—and out of our way."

"Karida," Nigel warned. "You're not going."

"The Cairo route is ten days in the desert. The Darb al-Bahnasa road is faster. Postal caravans bring the mail that way. We'll join one of them. We'll go to al-Minya and get the rest of our supplies there, and rent camels. We'll leave from Beni Mazar. It will take only four days across the desert to the oasis that is our destination."

Thomas slid her an admiring look. It was a startling contrast to Nigel's stormy scowl.

"You," her husband repeated slowly, "are staying here with Thomas and Jasmine."

"I am not."

Karida's heart raced as she faced down Nigel, but she had to do this. If she let him set foot in the desert alone, he would never return. This was her chance to find out why he was so desperate to get the treasure—and to change his mind.

"What reason do you have for visiting the oasis?"

When he remained mute, she cocked her head. "I thought so. If Kareem sees you, he'll grow suspicious as he does of any stranger near the tomb. He will cut off your head. If I go with you, it will help. He trusts me." Karida sucked in a deep breath, hating the shame creeping over her like a London mist. "I have a good reason for visiting him, you see. I'll tell him we are married now and he must stop his *kalim*."

She ignored the questioning looks Thomas and Jasmine exchanged and added, "When we reach Bahariya, we'll ask Kareem for hospitality. It's the Bedouin way. It will not make him suspicious, since I will have a valid reason to see him." *And maybe I can change your mind by the time we arrive. Oh God, please let me change your mind.*

Nigel made a low sound in his throat and pushed at his hair. "Fine. We'll leave for al-Minya tomorrow. But I've already made reservations for tonight at the Mena House hotel in Giza, so let's get dressed and leave."

Relieved he had capitulated, she plucked at the folds of her gown. "What do you call this?"

"The wrong type of clothing. Tommy brought us the right type. Now, go with Jasmine and get dressed. I want to leave before it gets dark."

Karida and Nigel emerged from the hotel as a scowling, bearded Arab in flowing white robes with a light blue turban and a Bedouin woman in a black *abbaya* and a half veil shrouding her face. They took a tram to Giza and headed for the Mena House hotel.

Sitting in cane chairs on their private terrace, they sipped tea while watching a brilliant orange sun slip behind the Great Pyramid. Light played on the shimmering sands, caressing the silhouetted palm trees as the rose pink sky gradually darkened to a deep indigo.

"You like to travel in style. I hope you don't expect such grand accommodations on every part of this trip," Karida remarked to Nigel, watching him nibbling the edges of a warm sugary pastry.

"I wanted to give you a proper honeymoon for at least one night," he replied. His eyes said he spoke the truth.

They had changed into their western clothing now, in private. Nigel was clad only in a starched white shirt and pressed khaki trousers, and Karida wore a lacy white dress. He finished his treat and licked his lips slowly, causing a shiver to slide down Karida's spine as she remembered the hot deliciousness of his tongue tracing every inch of her skin. He stood and rested his hands on the railing, staring at the sunset.

She wanted him, and this was their last night together in private, so she went to him, sliding her hands over his shirt. Her fingers nimbly unfastened the buttons and she slid it off his shoulders, admiring the smooth play of muscles. She pressed her mouth against his collarbone, tasting his skin's tangy salt.

Nigel shuddered beneath her light, teasing kiss. She felt his fingers slide around her neck, gently stroking, then caressing her nape.

"You didn't even feel it," he murmured.

Flummoxed, she drew back. Shock made her speechless. Her ruby necklace dangled from his fingers. He swung it back and forth like a pendulum.

"This will always come between us, won't it, Karida? Because you will always think I wanted this more than you."

"No, it won't," she denied, touching her bare neck.

He simply dropped the necklace into her palm and folded her fingers over it. She could feel that he'd returned the real necklace to her care and wondered when he'd switched them. Then he walked into their hotel room to check several supplies. Karida bit back her frustration, deciding she would just wait until later.

But later that night, as they prepared to retire to the opulent, canopied bed with its intricate carved headboard, Nigel seemed restless. He told her he was going to stroll the perimeter of the hotel, "Just in case." He did not come to bed until two hours later, sliding between the sheets quietly and then turning his back.

Disappointment as sharp as a scimitar sliced through Karida. For the first night since they'd married, he had not made love to her.

She fell asleep deeply troubled and awoke to the fragrance of jasmine. Her sleepy gaze took in a man dressed in Arab robes at the open windows overlooking the gardens, gazing out at the rose and burnt orange sunrise streaking the tawny sands. The Arab half turned and she saw it was Nigel, sans fake mustache and beard.

"Go back to sleep, love," he said quietly. "It's early yet."

Suspicion filled her. Karida sat up, scanning the room. Canvas tents and supplies were near the door, along with Nigel's rucksack.

"You're leaving without me." It was a statement.

She slid out of bed and scrambled to dress. He stopped her. "It's too dangerous."

"It's too dangerous without me. For once listen to reason, Nigel, and stop being so stubborn. You need me. You knew you needed me for this when you married me, so why are you changing your mind?" An attack of conscience? Or something more? She didn't dare hope.

Nigel pulled off his turban and let it fall to the floor. "It doesn't matter. Not now. Go on, freshen up. We'll leave for al-Minya after we've breakfasted. I'll make arrangements."

The door shut quietly behind him, as firm as the barricade her husband had erected between them.

Chapter Nineteen

The sun blazed down. His flowing white robes and blousy trousers helped cool him, and the turban provided shade against the harsh reflection of the sun on the endless white sand, but Nigel cursed the camel beneath him. Desert travel had never suited him.

They had taken the train south to al-Minya and stayed there with a distant cousin of Karida's, waiting for the postal caravan to depart. Now, five hours into the journey, he was heartily glad Karida insisted on this route. Being in a camel saddle for ten days would have been torture. He might have simply given up and dropped dead on the white sands, the sun bleaching his bones. Except he had responsibilities now. Eric—and Karida.

Karida. In her dark robes and with that veil half shielding her face, she looked serene atop her camel.

They were on the well-traveled postal route, used for delivering mail to and from the oasis. Ten merchants carrying everything from brass urns to clothing had joined them. They sang, laughed, and told bad jokes in Arabic to pass the time.

Nigel was glad of their company. It broke the monotony of his tortured thoughts.

When Ali, the caravan leader, stopped for a rest, Nigel sighed with relief. He slapped his camel on the neck. The stubborn beast hissed but obeyed and sank to its knees. Nigel slid off, resisting the urge to rub his sore butt. He grabbed his goatskin of water, a small straw mat, and unfolded it on the sand. Nigel sat on the mat, resting against the camel. As the others in the caravan gathered together and chatted, he remained apart, staring at the far horizon.

Nigel took a long drink. A shadow draped him and he shaded his eyes to see Karida. He'd spoken little to her, afraid of what he would say. Afraid of saying too much.

Despite the water he'd just swallowed, his mouth felt dry as she joined him. God, he needed her as much as he needed the water but didn't dare show it, didn't risk letting her get close to all his dark, dirty secrets. He'd already made one horrid mistake in confessing everything to a woman, and look at what a mess had resulted.

Again, guilt pierced him. At least he was still alive. Charlotte was dead, pushed over that cliff, screaming and screaming. He could still hear her cries echoing in his mind.

You're a thief and a killer, and you fathered a bastard who spent the start of his life in a filthy workhouse. Karida would run in the other direction if she knew what you really are.

He'd tried to be honorable for once in his damn life, tried to do the right thing and ensure Karida's safety by leaving her behind with his brother and Jasmine. Nigel hadn't counted on her stubbornness equaling his own.

It was selfish of him now, but he was glad of her company. Last night when the desert wind billowed the canvas tent flaps he'd lain awake. In the wail of the wind, he heard Charlotte's eerie cries as he'd pushed her off that cliff, tumbling to her death. The past ghosts of his other sins echoed as well. Nigel had turned over and embraced Karida, allowing himself the comfort of her warm body to lull him finally to sleep.

I am what I am.

He was not impervious to regret and guilt anymore. Now they seeped through him like water trickling across parched, cracked land.

He stood, brushing sand off his long robes. He attached the goatskin and straw mat to his saddlebag and shaded his eyes as he gazed at the western horizon.

Karida gestured to him. "I have a salve that will act as a sunscreen." Wind swept across the desert plain, fluttering the hem of her robes. Her fingers were gentle upon his quivering hands. Nigel tensed beneath her soothing touch; when she touched his cheek in a gentle gesture, he flinched like she'd struck him.

"Let me," he said roughly. He took the pouch and scrubbed the mixture over his face, rubbed it in with the heel of his hand.

Silence quivered between them as he gave her back the pouch. Karida fingered it, her clear brown gaze searching his. Nigel looked away. Despite the heat, a chill stroked his spine. She was truth, and goodness, and he had dragged her down into the mire with him. Nails bit into his palms as he clenched his sweating fists. But nothing would stop him from seizing the treasure. Not even her.

Yet, she did have a right to know one reason why the treasure was so important to him. Maybe if she knew she wouldn't think he was such a dirty desert jackal. Or maybe she would. Nigel avoided her gaze.

"I need the money for a house. To buy a grand house in the country, far away from London." He gave a short, bitter laugh. "And from those who know me and my reputation, such as the earl of Smithfield. I need a home where no one knows about my rather tarnished past. The emerald would not have been enough for that house and all that must go with it."

He wanted a real home for his son, a home fit for a king to make up for all Eric had previously endured. He wanted a grand school with the finest education, teachers who could overlook Eric's questionable parentage and afford him the status he deserved.

He fell silent, looking down at his feet. Words escaped him. For a man who kept everything locked up inside, he'd told far too much. He felt dry as the sandy dust, empty as the plains stretching before him.

A slight pressure squeezed his arm. Nigel glanced up to see

Karida regarding him. "Why are you running away, Nigel? How long have you been running?"

He could not reply, could only turn away in silence.

The pace was killing him. Nigel wanted to race to the tomb, to do what he must and return. But his camel's gait was steady, and the journey slow. The burning yellow sun beat down upon him, just like the wind whipped at his robes. To keep dust from his nose and mouth, he now followed the Egyptians' example and draped the trailing end of his turban around his lower face.

Karida glanced over at him, only her large, exotic eyes showing above her veil. "You're so quiet. If you talk, it will pass the time."

Nigel was loath to converse. He was too apprehensive of what he'd say. Karida had a gentle way of coaxing out the truth. Only with her could he feel fully himself. She didn't expect anything of him and let him be. He didn't know why it was, or how, but the attitude made it hard for him to resist confiding more in her.

"How did you learn to play piano?"

The question startled him into blurting the truth. "You might say I stole the music." He was silent a moment, idly flicking his reins. "I have a music box on my bureau. You probably saw it when you were rooting through my drawers, looking for the ruby."

Her gaze slid downward, and she looked embarrassed. God, if she thought *that* was embarrassing . . . He was the thief.

"The music box belonged to my sister, Mandy. You might say it's the first item I ever stole."

"And you kept it? Why, to remember her? Is she dead?"

Nigel snorted. "No, she's married and quite alive. I keep the box to remind myself what a degenerate I am. The box had a most lovely melody. It enchanted me. When it was late, and everyone was asleep, I'd sneak into her room and take it downstairs, picking out the same on the piano."

"You're self-taught? Nigel, that's simply amazing. You're quite good."

There was no point in false modesty. He shrugged. "Not as good as professionals. I like playing, but my father frowned upon it. So I'd take the box, and I'd always return it before morning." He paused a moment. "I stole it for good on the day I locked Mandy in the hay bin. I locked her in there and she screamed and cried. I went into her room and played the box to shut out the sounds of her screams."

Karida stared in blank astonishment. "Locked her in the . . . Why would you do that?"

He gave an angry look, though he was truly angry at himself. "Life is cruel, sweet. I discovered it in those early years. There are two types of people—those who are shut in hay bins and those who do the shutting. I was never going to be the former again."

"How could you lock her up like that? It must have been so dark. She must have felt so alone." Karida almost sounded as if she knew the experience.

Anxiety churned in Nigel's stomach. He thought about a lie but did not utter it. "She was pampered by my father. He'd given her a gift that day. Father never gave me any gifts. Amanda kept nattering about the new bonnet my father bought her. He called her his perfect princess and wished I could be as perfect." Nigel's heart raced in the heat. "He told her this as he looked at me, shaking his head. I locked her in the hay bin so she would shut up about her gift. Because she . . . just would not shut up. I didn't want to hurt her, just wanted to get her to stop taunting me and . . ."

Sympathy filled Karida's gaze, and she muttered a dark oath against his father.

Nigel laughed slightly. "Yes, I thought the same."

"So, you kept the music box to taunt your sister in return?"

Suddenly ashamed, Nigel ceased chuckling. "No, I gave it back after Tommy freed her. But she wouldn't take it."

"Because she knew you needed it more than she did," Karida realized. "It was her way of forgiving you."

"She should not have done that. I kept trying to give it back, but she refused to take it. She told me to play it and remember she was thinking nice thoughts of me."

"Did you?"

Nigel averted his gaze. "No. Never again."

They stopped talking. Only the sweep of the wind, the quiet laughter of their fellow travelers, and the occasional snort of a camel broke the silence. They covered many miles.

"The desert is changing," Nigel noted as they approached a long stretch of an orange sand dune.

The Egyptian leading their caravan looked back, showed a wide smile full of gums, and shouted. "Ghurd Abu Muharrik!"

Nigel lifted a brow. "Same to you," he jested.

Karida's light laugh reminded him of the rapid, joyous melodies he'd played on the piano—melodies she claimed to want to hear. She pulled her veil free and wiped her mouth. "He thinks this sand dune is the longest in the country, but I wonder. Either way, we're going to ride on top."

"Good. I like riding on top," he teased, enjoying the blush tinting her cheeks. In fact, that's what he wanted to do at that very moment. If only there weren't so many strangers around . . .

"Nigel, keep your wits about you," she scolded. "Ali says he thought he saw a group of Bedouins in the distance. They may not be friendly."

Raiders were a large concern, and one he'd contemplated. He reached for the dagger and pistol tucked into his robes. "I wish you had remained back in Cairo with my brother," he muttered.

"I can handle myself," she replied.

Sand blew in small clouds around their camels' hooves. Karida reattached her veil as they plodded along the dune, hot wind and sun mingling. Nigel bore it quietly. Loud laughter from the others slowly died, replaced with concerned mutters.

Glancing to the right, he felt alarm arrow through him as he saw what they did. Approaching was a large party of dark-robed Bedouins. The leader of the caravan called a halt.

"Karida, bring your camel to the left of mine. Now," Nigel ordered. Thankfully, she did as he asked. Nigel kept a wary eye trained on the group as they neared.

The leader of the party pulled up and exchanged polite words with Ali, the head of the caravan. When the others dismounted, Nigel and Karida did as well. Nigel did not let his guard down, however, even as he realized the Bedu had recognized the postal caravan and would let it alone; he and Karida were still in danger as foreigners. He sensed this. They regarded him curiously, as if wondering what a foreigner was doing wearing Arab robes.

Suddenly, one swaggered toward Karida, hand on the hilt of his scimitar. The Bedouin stared at Karida as if he liked what he saw. A chill raced through Nigel's blood despite the burning heat. Though she had tucked the necklace inside her robes, a small length of chain showed, glinting in the sunlight. It matched the greed gleaming in the Bedouin's eyes.

The man reached for the necklace, his dirty fingers like claws. Karida clasped her neck and stepped back.

"Leave her alone," Nigel warned in a dangerously soft voice. He placed himself between the two.

The Arab continued to stare at Karida. "Give me the necklace and I will leave her and not take her with us."

Nigel bristled. "You're not touching her or her possessions."

"Taking tribute from caravans is a time-honored tradition among us," the man replied roughly. "The necklace," he demanded. "Or fight for it like a man, if you are so determined. I am Aziz, and I have taken lives for less. Give it to me or draw your weapon."

"No guns!" called the Bedouin leader sharply. "Blades only. This is a matter of honor."

Honor, Nigel's ass. But he'd fought over much less. For Karida's honor . . .

He turned to Karida. "Get over to Ali and stay there," he warned.

Barely had he turned back when he heard the whisk of a *jambiyah* unsheathed. He dodged a blow and danced out of reach as he withdrew his own dagger from the folds of his robe. But then the fight commenced, a harrying fight, for the Bedouin was toying with him. It was a fight in which Nigel was getting very few attacks. The Bedouin grinned, showing gleaming teeth white against the darkness of his skin.

Suddenly, the Egyptian's eyes bulged. His mouth opened in a silent scream. He toppled.

Karida had felled him from behind with a solid kick between his legs. The Bedu shrieked, his scream echoing over the dunes.

"That's for trying to take my necklace and thinking you can abduct me," she declared.

The caravan travelers all laughed. "Felled by a woman," one chortled. "This one, she has the spirit of a jinn!"

My woman, Nigel thought with astounded pride.

As the Bedouin straightened, his eyes were like hot coals. He faced Karida, dagger held aloft as if to throw it. Her eyes widened in horror.

The hell with honor. Nigel withdrew his pistol from the folds of his robe. He fired, deliberately grazing the man's arm. The Bedouin dropped his knife and staggered, a harsh rasp of pain escaping his lips.

Nigel raced forward, his heart pounding. He grabbed the man about the throat and grated, "I told you not to touch her."

He applied pressure at the vulnerable hollow of the Bedouin's throat. The man began to choke and gasp. Nigel pressed harder with his thumb. In one move, he could kill.

There was a time he wouldn't have hesitated. But as he looked into the man's eyes, he paused, heard Charlotte's screams echoing through the valley.

The Bedouin deserved to die. He was a thief, a raider, and a killer. Scum.

So are you.

Sudden insight made his hands shake violently as if caught in a windstorm. Nigel eased his grip, shoved the man. The Bedouin toppled forward into the hot sand.

"Get out of here, before I change my mind," he snapped. He kept his gun trained on the Arab. "Your practices are not mine, and you deserve no tribute."

His foe gasped, rubbed his neck, and joined his compatriots. Some of them were laughing at him. The group all rode off in a cloud of dust.

Ali and the others in the caravan studied Nigel with new-found respect, but nothing mattered to him now but Karida's opinion. He was afraid to look at her. When he finally did, he saw no revulsion for the violence he had nearly committed, only curiosity. That bothered him more than if she had been repulsed.

In their tent that night, he suffered a nightmare. He had killed the Bedouin after all, and the man's voice called over the dunes, accusing him in a chorus with Charlotte's.

Murderer!

A hand pressed his arm, shaking him awake. Nigel sat up, rubbing his eyes. Karida lit the lamp. In the dim glow of the lantern, he knew what she saw: a man haunted by his past.

"Are you all right?" she asked.

"Go back to sleep," he muttered.

Karida gazed at him thoughtfully. "Tell me something, Nigel. Why did you spare him, when so clearly you wanted to kill him?"

Nigel met her eyes. He could not voice the words, but he knew the reason: *Because I looked into his eyes and saw myself staring back. Killing him would be like killing myself.*

Instead, he shrugged and said, "It was too hot, and I only kill on weekends and holidays."

She did not laugh. "Just tell me the truth, Nigel. It's not hard. It's all I ask from you."

"It's not easy."

"It wasn't easy for me, either, at first. And then I learned, gradually, that the truth is easier than lies. Because lies you always have to cover up, and tell stories and again and again and try to keep them straight until they twist and turn in your head like snakes and you can't control them."

Shadows danced across her face in the flickering light of the kerosene lamp. The caramel flecks in her eyes glittered like amber.

Awareness slammed into him. "What are you talking about? It wasn't easy for you, either? You've never told a lie in your life. Not an important one."

The light, musical laugh warbling from her lips startled him. "Oh, Nigel. I am no saint—quite far from it."

Nigel folded his arms, feeling wholly displaced, as if she were a mirage and he was hallucinating. Dumbfounded, he listened as she told him of a life filled with thefts and lies—until her Uncle Ramses charged her with the task of guarding the ruby and a pledge to change her ways. Until someone believed in her.

The light pressure on his arm from her fingers seemed to wake him from an absurd dream. His vision wavered of her as always honorable and perfect, replaced by living, warm flesh and blood, as if she'd finally jumped off a stone pedestal. She was more attractive than ever.

"What caused *you* to steal?"

Her expression fell. "The workhouse . . . I stole when they beat me, to get even. I had hoped to escape, someday. When I came to Egypt to live among the Khamsin and they teased me, I kept at it."

"How much did you steal?" he asked quietly.

She looked ashamed. "Ten pounds."

Such a small amount. He had stolen much more—and for less understandable reasons. "You had good cause," he mumbled, stricken by a rare bout of conscience. "I was brought up in privilege, wealth . . . I never needed for money while growing up."

"One can have wealth but an empty life," she gently corrected. "That is why we steal. Now, Nigel, why did you spare the Bedouin?"

Nigel flexed his fingers. "I spared him because of . . . myself."

"Because you saw something of yourself in him?"

Startled by her understanding, by the quiet way she found truth, he fell silent. Wind rattled the tent flaps, shaking them like ghostly fists. Nigel shivered, wrapping his arms about himself.

"I hate the damn wind," he muttered. "It sounds so . . . lonely."

Karida studied him. "I suppose," she agreed, "though it's never bothered me since coming to Egypt. 'Lonely' for me was being thrust into a dark cell crawling with rats."

"You deserve so much better," he said hoarsely. "Deserved it even more as a child. God damn them for ill-treating you."

He brushed back an errant strand of hair from her face, marveling at her inner strength. So physically beautiful, and yet her real beauty was inside: her ability to survive such horrors and not be a fractured soul bent on taking and hurting others. That's what he had become.

"I suspect you deserved better as well, Nigel," she said quietly, her fingers brushing his. "If you want me to help you, if you're going to trust me to guide you past the traps in the tomb, you'll have to trust that I'm with you all the way. For that, I need to know why we are taking such a great risk."

Emotion clogged his throat, making it difficult to talk. Oh God, he wanted to trust her, wanted to confide in someone. He'd been alone far too long. But telling her the details of his life meant risking her scorn. What he'd suffered was nothing compared to what she'd endured. His sorry past did not excuse the sorry man he'd become.

"You, especially you and what you've endured, won't like it." *Or me. You'll hate me, and I don't know if I can bear that right now.*

"Nothing you tell me will change my feelings for you, Nigel," she said gently. "I'll still care as deeply for you as I do now. Haven't I remained with you this long?"

The simple declaration shouldn't have made him feel such absurd joy—but it did. Nigel stared at her in stark wonder. He'd treated her horribly, forced her into marriage, and yet she cared. If only he could risk the same. Or rather, risk admitting it.

No, he could not tell her about Eric. Too much was at stake. But she deserved to know the rest about his past and what drove him.

He stood and paced the rounded tent and began to tell his story in slow, halting sentences. It found freedom like water from a sputtering faucet: How he fell sick at age eight and the doctor told his parents he would never father an heir. How he'd overheard his parents bribing the doctor to change his birth certificate to make his twin, Thomas, firstborn.

"They lied. I was eight, and they lied. The first of many lies," he muttered. "I became desperate to gain his approval, force my father to see I was the more perfect son. I grew to hate my brother because of what he'd been given that was mine. I hated my sister as well because they loved her and she didn't have to do a thing."

Nigel fell silent again, nausea making his stomach roll and pitch. Then he spoke further, listening to the wind brush against the sands outside, the fluttering of the canvas tent accompanying the monotone of his voice. He talked until his throat grew dry as the sand but did not stop, telling Karida about the accident that crushed his arm two years previous, how he'd bargained with his parents to pretend to be dead if they gave him enough money for a fresh start.

"My father told me I was better off dead." He glanced at her. "You asked about the scar on my thigh. It was a gift from my father. I was about nine, and I confronted him in the stables. He was putting away his whip. He liked to crack it in the air over the horses to make them run faster. I told him I knew he'd lied about Thomas being firstborn; I wasn't going to stay quiet anymore. His face turned purple, he was so enraged. He picked up the whip and pushed me to the ground and then . . ." Nigel drew in a shaky breath, heard the sickening crack of the whip, the horrifying whistle as it sailed through the air.

He dragged a hand through his hair. "He stopped after he saw the lash cut me. Told me to clean myself up and never breathe a word about it or what I knew. Because if I told, he said, he'd use the whip on my bollocks next time—and he would not stop."

Her inward gasp of breath, accompanied by a clap of her hand over her mouth, made Nigel glance away. He would not meet her horrified gaze.

His body felt like granite, his face stone cold. "What he did next was far worse. He told me if I tried harder, if I was better, more perfect, it could change. If I proved to him that I was worthy to be his damn heir." Nigel turned. "Fool I was, I believed him. He was only playing me against Tommy, getting Tommy to be tougher, to live up to the model I set. We were both duped."

He stopped speaking, waited for her to react. He waited in silence, listening to the wind flap the tent like the wings of a large bird. When she responded, her voice cracked.

"Who . . . who else knows he whipped you?"

Nigel's stomach gave a lurch. "No one. Not my twin, nobody. My former lovers, I told them I got that scar in an accident. You're the only one I've ever told."

Silence descended over them. Nigel felt as if he would crack like granite under the force of a heavy hammer. His heart thudded madly in his chest, even harder than when the Bedouin raider had challenged him.

When Karida went to touch him—either in sympathy, camaraderie, or even, oh God, love—he drew away. He could not look at her. For he was afraid if she saw his eyes, she'd see the coward lurking there deep inside.

"Nigel, please look at me," she said.

He made no reply, but she took his face in her soft, warm hands and turned him toward her. She kissed him, a coaxing brush of her mouth.

He kissed her back as if he'd lost himself in a terrible sandstorm and she was guiding him home. They lay down again, Nigel holding her in his arms. He stroked her hair, her dust-coated hair, as she rested a palm against the scar on his thigh.

Tonight, the wind could screech, but his ghosts would stay quiet. He would not let them howl anymore.

Chapter Twenty

They arrived at Bahariya in late afternoon, trudging into the narrow streets of the tiny village of Hara. Villagers streamed out of their houses like ants from a nest, chattering, laughing, and running to greet the caravan.

"Getting the post must be a tremendous event here," Nigel laughed.

After they were shown a place to freshen up and take care of necessities, the travelers were all directed to a cluster of shady date palms. Carpets were set on the ground. The caravan sat, and Nigel sensed they were to be pampered.

A man left his small mud brick house bearing a basin, a jug filled with water, and a towel with which the others cleansed and dried their hands. By the time the water jug reached Nigel, it was almost empty. He bit back a sigh as he dipped his hands in the dirty water and dried them with the threadbare towel. Karida was last and smiled her thanks at their host.

After returning the basin and towels to his house, the man reappeared with a basket filled of figs.

"You'd think with all the water in this bloody place, he'd bring enough for all." Nigel sighed and tried not to notice how some of the figs were rotten. He ate his way through one that had the fewest bad spots.

Karida gave him a look. "Sometimes small gestures show more about who cares than more extravagant ones. These gestures should be all the more welcome for that."

Nigel didn't have a response.

Finally, Karida signaled it was time to leave. She and Nigel stood and thanked their host, parting company with the rest of the caravan with hearty good-byes. The two then rode off through the dusty street, their pack camel tethered behind Nigel's mount. Karida led.

"Where are we going?" Nigel asked as they left the village.

"Kareem's house is a short journey away," his wife said softly. "We should go there."

Doubts hammered him, though he knew it was a smart choice—the only choice, if he didn't want a sharp scimitar aimed at his throat. Kareem would certainly kill him if he suspected Nigel's intentions were to steal the ancient treasure. It would be better to beard the lion in his den and misdirect him.

"Of course," Nigel admitted. Then doubts surfaced. "Are you certain he'll welcome you?"

"He is very wealthy and will treat us like honored guests. He will have food—likely a hot lamb stew, rice, warm bread, and chilled fruit juice. He will give us a large room with soft cotton sheets on the bed and a private place to wash with a bath large as a sheikh's tent. He will welcome us with hospitality; it is the Bedouin way. Even to a woman he rejected as a bride." Her voice was flat.

The idea of a hot meal made Nigel's mouth water. The fig had done nothing to curb his hunger, and the food on the journey had been lackluster to say the least. He grunted. "Let's hurry. I'm exhausted and famished. I need a bath, and I'm bloody tired of riding this beast."

He dug his heels into his camel's sides. Food, a bath, a shot of whiskey . . . Blast it, Kareem was Muslim and probably didn't drink. Well, he'd settle for fruit juice. He'd sleep in a damn bed for a night, then give a lot of thank-yous and be off. A quick, brisk hello and good-bye.

He glanced down at his grimy hands. God, what a mess he was. Both he and Karida were travel weary and sunbaked from trudging through the desert; they looked like Hell's refugees. He looked a fine state for an earl. But who would really care here? The Bedouin would understand.

Nigel looked at his wife. Her shoulders were shaking. Tears streamed down her dusty cheeks, leaving tracks like camel hooves through the sand. Nigel watched. Karida kept weeping silently. He said nothing but began to scan their surroundings; he could not take her to Kareem's like this.

At last he saw what he needed. A small, tidy limestone lodging house was just beyond the village, offering some privacy from inquiring eyes. A woman in a modest black *abbaya*, her eyes darkened by kohl, lingered outside. Gold bracelets jingled on her arms. The woman glanced at Karida as he slid off his camel. Nigel murmured a few words and slipped the woman some coins. He left their camels in her care.

The room he'd purchased was in the back and had its own entranceway guarded by two skeletal trees. It had one window and was not large at all, but it was clean, with a narrow bed, a chair, and four clothing pegs on the white walls. There was even a small water closet with, miracle of miracles, indoor plumbing. He stared in rueful amusement at the low, tarnished brass chandelier hanging from the ceiling.

Karida kept crying as he guided her into the room and dropped their packs on the floor. He stripped off her clothing. Nigel gently pushed her down on the bed, removed her dust-caked soft leather boots with their pointed toes that were now blunted like the tines of a well-used fork. He left her then to enter the water closet, filled the pint-sized tub with water.

When the tub was full, he picked Karida up and deposited her inside it. A small cake of soap sat in a dish next to a bottle. He uncorked the bottle and inhaled a delicate floral scent. Setting the bottle back down, he let the cork drop into the water. It bobbed merrily, a miniature boat in a calm ocean.

Nigel picked up the soap, ran it over his wife's slender

shoulders, and scrubbed away the desert from her neck and back. The grimy sleeves of his robe dipped into the warm water. Impatiently he rolled them up. His hands soaped her breasts, lingering a little, trembling as he stroked her nipples. She kept crying noiselessly, staring straight ahead at nothing. At no one.

He washed between her legs with brisk but gentle efficiency, then her thighs and calves. Nigel picked up each foot and scrubbed it. He tickled her toes briefly. Tears dripped down her cheeks, splashing into the tub in a salty rainfall.

He washed her hair next, using the floral shampoo, careful to keep suds from her eyes. When he rinsed, he shielded her dirty face and her eyes with one hand. Then, as her tears streaked the desert dust, he gently washed her face.

He helped her stand. A washcloth and three towels hung from nearby wooden pegs. Two towels were soft and sun dried; the third was thin and rough. Nigel picked up the third towel and saw light streaming through it. He set it aside and dried her with one of the soft towels, then used the second to dry her hair. He lifted her again in his arms.

She was quiet as he sat her naked on the bed. He began to untangle her hair using the pretty tortoiseshell comb in her pack. He said nothing, only hummed quietly. The humming seemed to soothe her, relaxed the rigid tension in her shoulders.

He finished combing her hair and settled her on the bed, pulling a clean sheet over her. Then he pulled up a wood chair and watched her sleep, determined to guard her rest.

Karida awoke to the sound of water splashing. She sat up, rubbing her eyes, taking a quick assessment of her surroundings. Sunbeams strayed through the *mashrabiya* screen behind the bed. Beyond an open door, she saw Nigel in the tiny tub, scrubbing himself. He was shivering. She lay back down, pretending sleep.

He stood and climbed out of the tub, all long, athletic limbs.

As he entered the main room, he banged his head against the brass chandelier and muttered a curse. It swayed as if caught in a sandstorm.

Nigel had snatched a towel off a peg. It was the third, as the other towels were damp; he'd used them on her. The towel made scratchy noises across his flesh as he tried to dry off. He set it aside, his skin still gleaming with moisture.

Karida watched as he rubbed a hand over his wet hair. Those dark brown chestnut locks stood up in spikes. He shook, like a dog, spraying droplets everywhere, and finger-combed his hair. Then he turned and saw her watching him. His scowl turned into a soft smile.

He sat on the bed. "Hello," he said quietly. "Have a good rest?"

She nodded.

He pointed to a small tray on the room's lone chair. "The boarding house's owner brought us fresh fruit from her garden. Otherwise, it's bread and water, I'm afraid."

His fingers trailed over Karida's now-dry face, and he cupped her cheek. "We can stay here tonight if you wish. All night, and tomorrow even. Or we can camp out in the desert again; we have enough supplies. You . . . you don't have to go there."

And then Karida realized what he'd done, what he was willing to do. He didn't want her to have to face Kareem, the groom who had rejected her, to lie and betray her vow of honor for him, even though she'd volunteered without any prodding. He had correctly interpreted her unspoken pain.

Karida closed her eyes, turned her cheek toward his palm like a flower seeking the sun. They simply sat there in silence.

After a moment, Nigel rose and went to his pack. He rooted about and withdrew a small gold band. He took Karida's left hand and slid the ring onto her finger. An emerald the size of a pinhead was at the center.

His expression was apologetic. "I bought this in Cairo—with my own money; I swear I didn't steal it. I sold my ruby stickpin to purchase it. I just wanted you to have something. It's not much, I know. I can't . . . I haven't the money for the kind of jewels you deserve." His voice trailed off.

Karida turned her finger so a stray beam of sunlight through the screen caught the gem. It sparkled like a green teardrop. She took his hand and kissed each finger, one by one. He smiled at her.

Nigel brought over the tray of food. Naked, they sat on the bed to eat, their legs dangling off the side. He sliced an orange with his dagger, the flesh shining wetly. He brought a slice to her mouth. She ate, and some juice dribbled down her chin. He brought an index finger to one stray droplet and then put it in his mouth, sucking. Karida blushed.

They ate in silence, grimacing as they tested the hard bread, finally dipping small pieces into the water jug to soften them. When they finished, wiping their sticky faces and fingers with small, threadbare napkins, Nigel set the tray back on the chair. He looked at her, saying nothing.

Words she wanted to say stuck in Karida's throat like the rock-hard bread. She took her husband's face in her hands and kissed him instead. His mouth was warm, giving, beneath hers, and when she drew back, gazing into eyes that sparkled like the tiny emerald on her ring, she finally found the courage to speak. Her voice crackled like broken glass.

"We'll go to Kareem's."

He nodded, brushed back a strand of damp hair from her face.

"Help me to forget . . . everything," Karida whispered. And then she kissed him again.

His lovemaking was slow and tender, as if he cherished her. Karida reveled in that. Nigel feathered tiny kisses over her breasts and hips, spending extra time on her scarred abdomen, pressing his mouth on burned skin that could not feel. She stroked his dark hair as he did. Then he pushed her thighs apart and loved her with his tongue, making long, lazy intrusions through aching wet flesh. Swirling, flicking, each stroke triggered warm pleasure until Karida went rigid and cried out, shaking and bucking off the bed. In the clean little room he'd rented, his mouth made her forget everything that was wrong with the world.

When he finally entered her, Karida threw her arms around him and urged him deeper. Her heels dug into the thin mattress. His thrusts were long and slow, his breathing sharp little rasps, like when that rough towel abraded his naked flesh. Damp hair hung off his forehead along with pearls of sweat. One dripped like a tear and splashed onto her cheek.

He cleansed with each bittersweet stroke, the loving both joyful and a sad reminder that this body would never give birth. His seed spurted, warming her, drawing away her pain even as he filled her with himself. This was a benediction of an empty womb that would never bear fruit, but at long last Karida at least knew she could feel joy.

Chapter Twenty-one

Kareem's house was a short trek away, on the north corner of the oasis and nestled amid a forest of lush, cool date palms that eradicated any view of the harsh white desert they'd crossed. A flock of glossy ibises foraged alongside the banks of a quiet lake mirroring the harsh blue cloudless sky. One bird paused and tilted its head to regard the newcomers.

In her camel's saddle, Karida shifted sticky thighs. She had not washed but had retained the fruits of their lovemaking as a veil of protection. She and Nigel both had changed into fresh clothing, however.

Nigel had discarded his Arab robes for a khaki suit and white shirt. The suit was wrinkled and the shirt collar rumpled. Wind ruffled his dark hair. He was slightly burnished from the sun and looked a bit mussed and very English, and very out of place among these exotic surroundings. She had never loved him more.

Karida stared at her husband, gauging his reaction as they dismounted. Kareem's opulent limestone house had domed archways, outdoor courtyards, and rooms open to a cooling breeze from the small nearby lake. Date, apricot, and lemon trees peppered the four-acre garden, replete with lush vegetable crops, desert roses, and jasmine.

"Kareem's father built all five of his sons homes like this," she told him.

Nigel cocked his head, resembling the curious ibis. "Hmmm. Rather modest," he said finally. "Are you certain there's enough room to accommodate both of us?" At her burst of joyous laughter, a wide grin touched his mouth. "Come on, love, let's go see Kareem. Shall we burst in like rude Westerners, or do we wait for the big, strapping, scowling keeper of the harem to answer our knock?"

Karida sputtered. "Big, strapping, scowling keeper of the harem? Kareem's?"

Nigel hooked his arm through hers and laughed. "In these places, there's always someone guarding the women. Fear not, though. I can handle him. I've had lessons."

They did not have to knock. A burly man in a shining white *thobe* and turban came out of the house. A scimitar and dagger were strapped to the red sash about his waist.

"The harem keeper," Nigel whispered, and Karida stifled a fit of giggles.

They were escorted inside by the guard, his face wreathed by a wide smile upon recognizing Karida. Nigel vaguely recognized the man in return; it was Saud, who had accompanied Kareem to the Khamsin camp for the marriage capture.

The man kept chattering as if she were an old friend. He settled them in a large room, its cool blue and white tile soothing to the eyes. Nigel and Karida saw low cane chairs with plush cushions. Nigel eased onto the softness with a loud sigh.

"Wait here, and I will fetch my master." Saud bowed deeply and left.

"Remarkable fellow. Very chatty. I suppose he's spent too much time among the women," Nigel commented, waggling his eyebrows.

Karida's smile died as she gazed around the room. Memories flooded her. Upon her last and only visit, Kareem had been very attentive. They had talked for hours, Ramses a vigilant if indulgent chaperone. She had not seen Kareem since his rejection. What would he say to her now?

She knew he had entered the room even before she turned and saw him. He had a way of taking up all the space in a location. In his flowing purple and eggshell-white robes, with the white keffiyeh on his dark head, he looked majestic. Imposing. Royal.

Nigel rose with an equally commanding presence. These were two equals, she realized. She was glad of it.

Tension fled as she remembered Nigel's lovemaking, his tender whispered words. Courage filled her. She met Kareem's curious look with a bold one, lifted her chin high and murmured the traditional Arabic greeting.

She gestured toward Nigel. "This is my husband, Nigel Wallenford, earl of Claradon."

Kareem did not look surprised at her little announcement. He approached, bent over, and took her hand. His palm was warm as he lifted it to his mouth and kissed it, and congratulated her. Then he straightened and held out a hand to Nigel, who shook briskly.

"Welcome to my home. I am most glad of your company." Kareem settled into a low cane chair. Only a square sandalwood table separated them. A glass vase filled with lilies sat upon it. Dimly Karida thought about how much she loathed the smell of lilies. Kareem had presented her with a perfect lily when he'd visited the Khamsin the first time. Their cloying scent would always remind her of that souring experience.

Servants, directed by Saud, brought silver trays with a jug of fruit juice, glasses, a dish of ripe figs and pitted dates, and almond bread coated with sugar. They set out three plates and napkins. Karida had no appetite.

She, Kareem, and Nigel made small talk for a few minutes, between small bites; then she wiped her fingers with one of those fine napkins. Damask, she noted absently. "Thank you for your hospitality," she told her host. "We came to Bahariya to visit because . . ." Words failed. She knew she should say: *I am here to visit to let you know that I am happily married and you are absolved of all your responsibilities.* Her gaze riveted to the lilies, however, and the words clawed at her throat.

"Blame me," Nigel interjected smoothly. "It's my fault, in a

way. We got to chatting about history. I was nattering away
about how fascinated I was by Alexander the Great, and she
mentioned how she'd been here to the oasis and that it held the
only temple erected by him in Egypt. Well, I'm such a stubborn sort that I insisted on trekking all the way here to see it."

Kareem studied Nigel calmly. "Interesting."

"Yes, I'm in the antiquities business. It's a bit dodgy at
times, but I have a client who has great interest in Alex's temples, and this man commissioned a miniature replica of this
temple."

"Ah, yes, I understand how you Europeans adore monu-
ments built by your tremendous egos. The Greek's temple is
not quite as well preserved as other temples in Egypt. Unfortunately." Kareem kept his face expressionless, yet Karida
sensed beneath the calm a cobra ready to strike if he must.

Nigel must have sensed his danger as well, because his own
smile flattened, and he changed tack. "And while we are here,
there's the little . . . ah, actually, the rather large matter of the
kalim you insist on paying."

Kareem stiffened ever so slightly. "It is a matter of honor."
He glanced at Karida, and she felt her cheeks heat.

Nigel shrugged. "I can provide quite nicely for my wife.
Your payments will stop immediately, whether you feel guilty
or not."

Anger flared in Kareem's eyes. Karida knew no one told
the prince what to do—and worse, no one told him why he
did anything. Her stomach churned, but Nigel looked calm,
as if he'd suggested nothing more consequential than taking
tea. The two men stared at each other for a long time.

With a heavy exhalation, Kareem finally nodded. "Very
well." He clapped his hands, and Saud appeared. "Saud will
show you to your quarters. Please, feel free to stay as long as
you wish, and come and go as you please. If you need anything,
ring the bell in your room. I am leaving for Cairo at dawn, so I

would be honored if you join me for dinner, promptly at eight." His gaze met Karida's. "I would indeed be very honored."

"Thank you," Nigel said smoothly, taking her arm. "I suspect we'll be leaving on the morrow as well. Your hospitality is much appreciated."

Their bedroom boasted an imposing platform bed piled with crimson silk pillows embroidered with gold thread. Persian hangings decorated the walls, and the carpets were antique. An archway led out into a garden, its open doors allowing for a breeze that billowed the bed's hanging silks. A waist-high dresser of finely-grained wood was against one far-off wall, and before it on the floor was a thick sheepskin rug as soft as a cloud.

Nigel watched two servants place his and Karida's rucksacks on sandalwood tables. He dismissed them and then gazed around with a wry expression. "Where do we erect our tent in this wilderness? Or will Kareem have his servants carry us the miles to the bed on a litter?"

Karida felt as if her muscles were stone. "You lied to him for me," she said softly. "Thank you for doing so."

He smiled, a genuine smile lacking any cynicism. It made his face appear younger and lit up his eyes. "In a manner of speaking. I did intend to see the temple—especially in its proximity to the tomb."

The tomb. Ah, yes. It stood between them like a rock wall.

Karida sighed and decided the time had come for another plea. "Nigel, I beg of you to change your mind about the tomb. The treasure of the ancients will only cause you grief. Whatever your need, the curse will make things worse."

Nigel's smile dropped. He leaned against a bedpost and folded his arms. His eyes were flat and unemotional. "Don't question me on this, Karida."

She played another card. "Kareem is not stupid. He'll suspect something, no matter what we said. Our lies will help but . . . how do you plan to smuggle out the goods? Right beneath his nose?"

Nigel laughed. It was a cold sound. "There's a trick to smuggling. Those packs on the camels I brought containing useless junk? They'll take their place in the tomb, and I'll use the sacks to smuggle the treasure out. I made sure that Kareem's servants feel free to inspect them."

"You plan to take the entire tomb that way?"

He gave her a cutting look. "Don't be silly. I don't intend to take everything."

Dryness filled her mouth. Karida felt as if her world were spinning. "Why, Nigel? Tell me why you are doing this. Why won't you trust me with the truth?"

His jaw tensed as he shoved a hand through his hair. "I want to but I can't," he muttered.

"You expect me to enter the tomb with you, violating everything I know and honor, and you won't tell me why you need the money? Don't you fear I might tell Kareem? Couldn't I have already done so? Maybe this was why I demanded to come along." She walked toward him, crowding him, forcing him against the far wall; this time she would not back down. Ironic, how he'd encouraged her to stand up to people. Karida placed a palm on his chest, feeling his heart beat rapidly beneath her splayed fingers. "Answers, Nigel. Now. Why won't you tell me the truth?"

Blood suffused his face. "Because the last woman I trusted betrayed me—just like you are insinuating you would do. I pushed her off a cliff. Do you understand, Karida? I killed Charlotte. I pushed her off a damn cliff when she pointed that gun at my brother, but another part of me knew I'd told her too much to let her live, that she would betray me again at the next opportunity. Is that what you want? For me to trust you entirely and know you will have to be destroyed?"

Shock made her speechless. Karida remained frozen, her hand still resting on Nigel's chest as his fingers encased her neck. He did not squeeze, but she knew his capability, had seen him nearly choke a man to death just a few days before.

"Is that it?" he asked softly, his fingers stroking her throat. "Do you want to know what it's like to feel Death coming for you? To tumble off a godforsaken mountain, screaming until your lungs run out of air and your body is crushed, knowing the man you made love with only hours before is the one who pushed you?"

Her heart pounded a crazy beat and sweat began to form at her temples. Still, Karida didn't dare take her eyes off Nigel, the tortured wildness dancing in his gaze.

"You blame yourself for Charlotte's death, but I saw gratitude in your brother's and his wife's eyes. You *saved* them. But you loathe that gratitude, don't you? You don't want it because it makes you the hero, not the scoundrel you believe yourself to be. Is that what you want, Nigel—for me to think you're as terrible as everyone else says you are? Because I won't. No matter what you tell me, no matter what you do, I won't change my opinion of you, at least of your core. I know what you are at heart. You just haven't been given a chance to show it. No one ever gave you enough of a chance. I came with you, and that demonstrates my trust. I would never betray you."

The pressure eased at her neck. Nigel backed away, looking disgusted and horrified. He turned to the door.

Karida waited until his hand rested on the knob. "Why did you speak to Kareem for me?"

The haunted look on his face nearly did her in. "I didn't want you falling on the sword of your sacrificed dignity. Not to him. Not to anyone. You're much better than that."

"Why did *you* do it for me, Nigel?" Her voice came out as a croak, a whisper, a plea. She wanted him to recognize what he was, what he felt for her.

His mouth worked. "Because . . . because it meant you would hurt less. If it means you hurt less, I'll lie and keep lying until my dying day. For me to lie is less of a sacrifice."

"You see? You can be selfless. You can be a hero. You just won't admit it." She could not take her eyes off him, searching for emotion.

He showed none. "God damn it," he finally said. "I'm going for a walk."

The door slammed behind him.

Karida's emotions were all in a lather. Everything she'd once sworn to uphold—truth, honor, and morality—teetered on the edge of a yawning chasm. Everything she believed was in the air.

Kareem was a starkly honest man. He was honorable and upheld the same code that she did. Yet his words and actions had hurt her deeply. Kareem had rejected and shamed her.

Nigel had accepted her and honored her, though he unquestionably was a lying thief and corrupt libertine. He had killed his own mistress. Yet he'd acted for a good reason, to save his brother. Lying was wrong, and yet Nigel had done it for her, to keep her from being hurt. He'd put his fingers around her neck and stroked, but he had not hurt her. She knew now that he never would hurt her again, not if he could help it.

She herself had allowed Nigel farther in his quest for the sleeping golden mummies than he ever should have gotten. She had not warned Kareem, had not reported Nigel for his wrongdoings. That in itself was wrong, but she hoped there would be a happy ending—if a happy ending was possible. The strict black and white of good and bad was blurred, leaving shades of dark gray.

"Nothing much makes sense anymore," she whispered, curling her fingers around one of the bedposts. She wondered if it ever would.

Nigel and his wife dined with Kareem that night, the predicted sumptuous feast of lamb stew brimming with rich gravy and fresh vegetables, a heaping platter of rice, fruit, fresh bread, and endless sweet tea and fruit juice. Nigel's earlier irritation returned as he watched Kareem chatting easily with Karida. He shifted on his plush cushion. For all the palatial elegance in this house, why did their host insist on sitting on the floor?

Karida laughed at something Kareem said, and the Arab smiled. He glanced at Nigel. "You have quite a treasure, Lord Claradon. I hope you realize it."

Nigel realized he'd had quite enough. "Changing your mind about my wife, Kareem? Have you decided to steal her back?" He laughed a tad bitterly, broke off a piece of flat-bread, and scooped up the lamb stew.

Karida's laughter faded.

Kareem studied him. "Men here are honorable. We do not steal. When a thief is caught the first time, he is carried about on the back of a donkey, paraded through the streets, and called names."

"A punishment certain to prevent a second offense," Nigel rejoined.

"No, public humiliation is not usually a successful deterrent. It is what happens on the second time the thief is caught . . ."

"What's that? You make the man carry the donkey?"

"We cut off his left hand." Kareem's gaze fell upon Nigel's hand, which was resting on his knee.

Nigel sipped more sweet tea and shrugged. "A good thief never gets caught, so unless you have an abundance of stupid thieves, I'll wager you seldom have to use that scimitar of yours. Otherwise I'm sure I'd see a stack of hands lying about like cordwood."

Karida gasped softly and put her hand to her mouth. Nigel kept his gaze locked on Kareem. The Arab looked grim; then suddenly beneath his black beard, the mouth softened. He threw back his head and laughed.

"Tell me something, Kareem." Nigel ran a finger around the edge of his cup. "Would you punish a child?"

The man frowned. "What do you mean?"

"If a child stole from you a small amount—the equivalent of ten pounds, let's say—so she could escape a horrible situation, would you punish her? Would you lock her up, threaten her with jail, even though she stole because she believed she had no other way out?"

Karida made a strangled sound.

Kareem looked puzzled. "Of course not."

"Why?"

"Because such a crime is born of desperation. Like a leopard caught in a trap, the child will do whatever she can to be free of her misery. The just punishment belongs to those who inflicted the suffering she seeks to escape."

Nigel glanced over at Karida, his gaze soft. "I agree."

The sheikh's gaze hardened. "But an adult who steals is far different. He is not helpless but greedy. He knows better and should suffer punishment."

Cold sweat trickled down Nigel's back. He merely offered a smile to hide his discomfort.

Karida didn't know exactly what to make of her husband's odd line of questioning. She and Nigel finished dinner and thanked Kareem, and their host bade them a good night. He lingered over pressing her hand, far longer than was polite. He'd been overly attentive at dinner as well, as if apologizing without words. Karida could tell it bothered Nigel.

In their bedroom, her husband closed the door and leaned against it, his eyes glittering like green fire. "Kareem certainly was friendly with you."

She shrugged. "He is that way with all women."

"He still wants you. Perhaps more now that he knows he can never have you." Nigel kept watching her.

Karida made a derisive sound.

"Before he wanted *and* needed you. The need has gone; the want will not have. I'm a man, and I see it in the way he looks at you—as if he'd like to be the one in your bed tonight."

Emotions awhirl, Karida scowled at Nigel. "Kareem would never disgrace himself by seducing another man's wife."

"Wouldn't he, angel?" Nigel moved toward her with an intent look. "Of course not. Because he's so noble. The wealthy sheikh's son who can have any woman he wants."

Karida stepped backward as Nigel forced her against the wall, and he placed both hands on either side of her face, caging her with his body. His gaze burned into hers. "Any woman but you," he vowed. "He may be principled and rich and all those damn things women sigh and moan over, but he'll never have you. You're mine."

He stroked a finger down her cheek, and desire raced through her. His moist, full mouth was close to hers, his sweet breath fanning over her lips as he leaned close.

"Do you dream of him making love to you beneath stars, angel? Do you fantasize about him taking you in every way a man can have a woman, servicing your every desire?"

A strangled gasp of pleasure escaped her as Nigel cupped her breast, teasing her nipple through the fine fabric of her kuftan. She could not speak.

"Or is it me in your shadowy dreams, bringing to life every single erotic fantasy you could ever imagine?"

"Yes," she gasped. "It is you. Since we met."

He lightly pinched her nipple, and she moaned. "Of course. Because he is not like me, a libertine who seduces away all your sense," Nigel whispered. "Yes, I am a thief—and I shall steal away every memory of him." His mouth descended on hers, roughly, his kiss inflamed and filled with dark intent. He kissed her as if to seal off every mention of Kareem's name.

Karida made a sound against his mouth, bit his lower lip, and ground her hips against his. Anger and passion warred within her, for she wanted him and no other; and yet he still would not trust her with his motives. She loved him with every breath in her body, but he would steal away that breath and that love, lock it away without ever sharing anything in return.

He kept kissing her—deep, almost punishing kisses, his tongue dueling hers as if they were in a battle and he wanted to dominate her, force her to surrender. But she was not at the mercy of this powerful, sensual man, as she'd been at the brothel. He was at her mercy instead. Deep inside, she recognized the frantic plea in his assault, the question behind the intent in his eyes.

Can you truly love me, even though I am not worthy?

Karida pulled away, panting, fisting her hands in his shirt. She baited him, because she needed this reassurance; damn it, if she could not have his love and trust, then she'd settle for his unquestioned passion. It was a start.

"Is that what you want, Nigel—to steal me away only for yourself?"

"I won't share," he said roughly. "Not you. Not ever."

Fisting a hand in her long hair, he kissed her ruthlessly, his erection grinding against her. His tongue worked magic. A low moan tore from her throat.

Nigel broke the kiss and stared at her, his eyes wild, a big vein throbbing at the base of his throat. The sounds of their ragged breathing filled the room. "I can't wait," he said. Her kuftan nearly tore as he tugged it over her head. Beneath it she wore nothing, and his eyes widened with pleasure and worship.

Nigel shed his clothing. His rigid phallus was thick and impossibly engorged; a shining droplet of moisture glistened on the rounded red knob. Daring seized Karida, and she took him awkwardly in her hand and touched the wetness, rubbed that over his shaft. Her heart thudding frantically, she dropped to her knees and took him in her mouth. As she swirled her tongue, Nigel shuddered and gripped her shoulders. Her movements were hesitant and inexperienced, but she let her love for him guide her.

Nigel made a low growl of approval but then gently broke the contact. Karida stood, looking at him with uncertainty until she felt his hand come between her thighs, stroking, coaxing moisture from her. She whimpered and gripped his arms as he teased her, one finger sliding between her slickening folds.

"You're so wet for me. Now you're ready, fair angel," he whispered. "Brace yourself. I'm going to have you, and I can't be gentle. I may . . . lose control."

She could only hope so.

He led her to the waist-high dresser and turned her around. "Bend over," he commanded. She did just that, shaking with anticipation and excitement, her hands pressed against the dresser's surface. It was a shameless, wild, and wanton position, and she felt vulnerable and exposed.

Shock surged through her as he parted the moist petals of her feminine center and slid a finger deep inside. "Yes, open to me, fair angel," he said in a velvet whisper. "Feel me inside you. I'm going to take you hard and fast, and when I'm done making you scream and making you sweat and pleasuring you until you collapse in sheer exhaustion, I'll be branded on your soul."

Nigel withdrew his finger and ran the wet digit down the arch of her bottom. Karida shivered as she felt his hands grasp her hips. In this position she could not move, however, his hands checking her escape. He meant to take her from behind, like two animals.

She felt the impatient nudge of his arousal pressing. Then Nigel surged forward, thrusting deep inside as he uttered a low groan of satisfaction. He began to deliver on his dark, erotic promise.

Nigel hammered into her, his flesh slapping hers. She recognized his primitive need to brand her, to mark her as his own, and this was not the action of a thief stealing another's soul, but a husband claiming what was rightfully his. Nigel sought to win her; he would make her remember this wild rapture, the bond forged between them in flesh, and imprint upon her very soul the scent, the very feel, the utterly dark torment of the erotic pleasure he imparted.

He forced her to cry out, to wail, the sounds of her desire echoing through the chamber and filtering outside to the starry night. He made her forget everything but him and the tormenting repetition of his shaft filling her, the wetness of her arousal, the devilish pleasure of his hands upon her skin. She arched her bottom as he reached around her hips to where they were intimately joined and caressed her bud of pleasure.

Sweat glistened on her body, her heart hammered wildly in her chest, and she gulped down air and frustration, a climax building inside her until she slapped her palms against the wood and wailed. Then he gave one more hard thrust and she climaxed, screaming.

Nigel slid free of her, leaving her empty and trembling. He sank onto the sheepskin rug, lying on his back and beckoning to her. "Here, this way," he instructed, breath still rasping in his lungs. He pulled her atop him.

Karida straddled him, her hands pressed against the silken, moist hairs on his muscled chest. Slowly she sank down as her husband guided her, impaling herself on his still rigid length. Shock rippled through her, and she let out a startled cry as he filled her completely.

"Ride me, my fair angel," he demanded.

He taught her the rhythm, clasping her hips to lift her as she squeezed his rigid length, sinking down and rising up. Sensations flooded her, scorching pleasure filling every cell, and an incredible feeling of being in control of this dangerous, unpredictable man who loved her with such wild passion. Nigel removed his hands and palmed her breasts as she increased the pace. He stroked and kneaded, flicked his thumbs over her cresting peaks as she began to pant with renewed urgency, tension building in her loins.

"Let go, angel, let go. Surrender to it," he told her.

She screamed as another orgasm shot through her like a bolt of white-hot lightning, her body shaking, her hands digging into the thick muscles of his arms. Nigel gave a purr of satisfaction, then just as quickly sat up and rolled her onto her back, his big body covering hers. Gulping, she looked up at him in dazed wonder.

They began anew. This time it was a battle of wills, however, a fierce and wild mating. He intended to mark her with his passion? She bit his shoulder, sinking her teeth into the hard muscles, marking him in return. He hissed and pinned her with his weight. Karida dug her heels into the sheepskin and raked her nails over his back as he slammed into her. A desperate intensity flared in his gaze as he took her, over and over, his member swelled to impossible size within her.

At last, Nigel crouched back and parted her legs wide, angling his thrusts deeper for more intense strokes. Karida clutched his forearms, digging her fingers into those muscles as she felt once more a gathering tension in her loins. Then her husband surged over her, cupping her face in his hands and forcing her to meet his gaze.

"Look at me, love. Look at me. No one else but me. Say my name," he demanded.

"Nigel," she choked out in a desperate sob.

"Yes, Nigel—your Nigel, the only one for you. You're mine, and I shall never give you up," he rasped.

Then he pushed forward in a last, violent thrust, and he shook with his climax, shouting her name to the very heavens. She shattered, clutching him to her: her Nigel, her dark thief of delicious promise, her husband. He was branded on her soul as she was branded on his. She would never give him up.

They dozed in the bed, the cool lake breeze drying the perspiration on their bodies. Karida lay in Nigel's arms, looking peaceful and innocent as a lamb. She'd been a tigress, however, matching his own wild passion. He would never give her up. And it was time to tell her the truth. Finally. He'd realized there was no other option.

Nigel rolled over, switched on the gas lamp. A soft glow of

light filled the bedroom. Very gently, he jostled her awake. Her exotic golden eyes opened, blinked sleepily at him. He sat up.

Wiping his perspiring forehead with the sheet, he said, "Karida, I need to tell you something—the truth, the honest truth. In case something happens and I don't make it, I need to ask you a very important favor." He dragged in a breath, hating this, hating himself. He should have trusted her earlier, should have explained this before he'd realized he needed her.

She sat up, touching his arm. "What is it?"

"If something happens to me . . . I need you to go to London—with your father or your uncle or someone—and arrange to find Eric, and arrange for his care." At least then the boy would be free of his father's stigma. He knew that if he was dead the earl of Smithfield would be kind to the child.

"Eric?"

Nigel's stomach gave a sickening lurch. "My . . . son. He's illegitimate." He could not look at her but heard her sharp intake of breath. "I didn't know of his existence until a year ago. I was told I was sterile and could never father a child. I found him . . . in a workhouse. Where he ended up because I didn't do my duty by him." He realized she must think he was a horrible person. He'd feared telling her this for so long, knowing she'd see him as uncaring as her own father had been. He'd made so many mistakes in his life.

"And you're caring for him now?"

He looked at her. Stark admiration glowed in Karida's eyes, not loathing. She gazed at him as if he cradled the entire world in his palms, and she wanted to be cradled there as well.

Suddenly she gasped. "The treasure, that's why you want it! Not for yourself. You . . . it's because you're broke and you want to do right by him, away from all the people who would call him a bastard and be unkind?"

A deep sigh of relief escaped him. Karida understood! "Yes. But there are complications." Nigel's heart squeezed. "A rather nasty fellow has Eric. He took him so I would give him half of the treasure."

Overwhelmed with gratitude, Nigel began to tell his wife about Eric, affirming her guesses and explaining how he'd hidden the child away in order to build him a good home in the country as soon as he could, away from his sordid London past and everyone who hated him. It was then that Oakley found the child.

"Promise me please, Karida, that you will help Eric if I can't. I know I'm asking a lot for you to return to London and find him, but the thought of that scoundrel sending my boy to America in steerage . . ."

Karida raised two of his fingers to her lips and kissed them. "I promise, on my honor, I will do as you ask," she whispered.

Nigel's eyes closed. Sharp relief flooded him, and he began trembling wildly. He could not even summon the strength to disguise it.

He went to thank her. She kissed him instead, cut off his words. They made love into the night, the sounds of the desert rising around them.

Chapter Twenty-two

The burning yellow sun baked the ruins of the temple of Alexander. Date palms and grass peppered the tawny sand, that greenery a stark contrast. While Karida explored, Nigel sat on a boulder, sketching columns. It was a good ploy in case anyone spied on them. Most of the structure was low sandstone and mud-brick walls, but Nigel had found a scene of Alexander offering gifts to the god Amun. It was this which he sketched.

Clouds scudded overhead but did not provide any relief from the heat. Karida inhaled, feeling the dry air fill her lungs, wring the moisture from her very mouth. But at last she and Nigel had spent enough time at the temple to suggest it was the true reason they'd journeyed here, and they set out for the tomb.

Her husband regarded Karida as they set off. "Are you certain you want to do this? I don't want you to have to break your vow," he said quietly. "At least, not any more than you already have."

She gave him a sad smile. "I recognize why you do this. I only wish we could find another way. It seems that Heaven should provide."

Nigel made no reply.

The tomb's location in the tawny sand was marked by a simple pile of rocks. Karida and her husband dug in the sand with the small shovels Nigel brought and uncovered the door she knew was there. Sweat streamed down their faces.

During the work, Karida sat to rest several times, bothered by her low energy. *The heat,* she decided. It surely was the heat, and perhaps even guilt over the crime she was about to commit.

Finally, they found the door with a round knob securing it shut. Karida turned the knob. There came a click, and a latch sprung up. Nigel lifted the door. It opened with a loud groan, the echo of her breaking heart.

She stared down into the yawning darkness, and at the sandstone steps leading to the burial chamber. Long ago the mummies had been buried here. Mummies of all shapes and sizes, mummies with golden masks. They lay several feet beyond the steps.

I am disturbing the dead.

By descending these steps and helping Nigel pilfer these riches, Karida was dismissing everything she'd ever embraced. She was becoming a thief, turning her back on the woman she'd become, the upright, honorable woman whose behavior made her adoptive parents so proud. But what choice did she have? She'd sworn allegiance to her husband to the bitter end, had realized that only her unqualified love might save him. She'd seen the reason for his intent and had seen his own love in return, his tenderness. Did their end justify these means?

Her foot tentatively touched the top step.

"Karida, sweet, do you want to turn back?"

She looked up at his solemn, suntanned face. "No. We're moving forward. It's the only direction for me from now on. For us. Others have told me that stealing is wrong. I believe that, but what we can do with these valuables is right for Eric. His welfare comes first. Heaven must provide, or we must provide for ourselves."

Swallowing all her misgivings, taking the electric torch he held out, she descended into smothering darkness.

The chamber was indeed filled with mummies.

Dust motes danced in the electric torchlight. The air smelled musty and foul. Nigel squelched his dismay and shock at seeing so many dead bodies. These were mummies with gilded masks, mummies whose wrappings were exposed, faded, and dirtied with time. The bodies were piled atop each other like cordwood, though. Adult mummies. Small mummies of children. Nigel swallowed hard, thinking of Charlotte and her screams as she tumbled off the cliff. This wasn't a tomb. It was a damn nightmare.

"The first trap. Follow me and don't vary from where I walk."

Karida moved forward effortlessly, gliding like an angel, her white kuftan making her look like a ghostly bride as she lifted her electric torch. Nigel followed, a hand to his mouth, his own torch raised as they wended their way through the bodies.

Karida halted before a rock wall. She turned and saw him. "Nigel! Don't move. Stay there!"

He froze, his heart pounding.

She approached, her torchlight illuminating grotesqueries all around. "Take my hand." He did so, and she guided him past a small seal in the floor. Her eyes were huge. "The well. If you stepped on it . . ."

He understood and gave her a reassuring smile he did not quite feel.

They skirted one cluster of mummies. Karida came to a rock wall at the chamber's far side and pushed a lever. She raised her electric torch and shone it into the revealed chamber. Shadows played over the rock walls, over ominous hieroglyphics carved into sandstone. Karida froze, her face mobile with awe and doubt.

Nigel saw the fear in his wife's eyes, the anguish flickering there. He was making her act against everything for which she stood. He paused, curling his fingers around his electric torch.

Karida entered the chamber. Darkness slid over Nigel like a slimy blanket as she did, and he forced himself to breathe slowly and evenly. He wasn't afraid of the dark, only of dismal failure yet again. All his life he'd failed. He could not do so now. He was doing this for Eric.

He entered the chamber. Karida beckoned for a lighter, then

lit several wooden torches in iron sconces on the walls. What Nigel saw made his jaw drop in wondering awe. Gold glinted in the soft torchlight. Gold, everywhere. A chest brimming with rings, earrings, bracelets, armlets, anklets.

There was a beaded *wesekh*, a collar worn by ancient Egyptians, set with semiprecious stones of turquoise, carnelian, and lapis lazuli. "I know someone who would gladly pay a thousand pounds for that alone," he murmured.

Gold *ushabti* figures were stacked in a corner. A lone sarcophagus rested on the room's far side. Karida made her way over to it gingerly, Nigel in tow, cautioning him to step over a small protrusion on the floor. A rather modern combination lock was on the sarcophagus.

"Only Ramses and I have the combination. Ramses had the lock fitted to the coffin after Ali told him about this treasure," she said softly. "I wanted you to see it." With her twist of the knob, the catch slowly released.

Nigel lifted the stone lid. What he saw inside made his heart go still. A solid gold mummy mask glittered in the light of his torch.

Karida looked at him solemnly. "Whatever you do, don't touch it. It's the last and most deadly trap." She gestured to a crevice in the wall above the coffin. "If you lift the mask, the blade will decapitate you—or cut your body in half, depending on your height."

Nigel swallowed hard. "I'd venture to say I've seen enough."

They replaced the lid and retreated back to the treasure trove. Nigel knelt before a large painted chest featuring Horus and Isis. He lifted the chest lid and made a choking sound that bounced eerily off the chamber walls. Inside the casket were gems. Dozens, no, hundreds of emeralds glittered in the torchlight. Karida moved over to investigate and ground to an abrupt halt, gasping in awe. Nigel reached inside and withdrew a fistful.

Karida shook her head. "All this is new. There was nothing

but some gold jewelry in this chest when I came here years ago with my uncle." She gave Nigel a bewildered glance.

He let the emeralds fall back into the chest. "I'd venture to say that someone *else* has been using this tomb as a storage facility. I think we've been duped, Karida. And whoever it is, they've continued with this perfect ruse. They're using the tomb's curse—and now also your guardianship and Kareem's—to keep this a perfect hiding place. But only you, Kareem, and Ramses know where the traps in this tomb are." Nigel stood up and looked at his wife. "It must be Kareem, smuggling the emeralds in here."

She shook her head. "Kareem is trustworthy. Honorable. He would never do such a thing."

"How do you propose these got in here?"

Karida couldn't answer Nigel; she was too stunned by their good fortune. Heaven had provided! She dug her hands into the lake of emeralds. "So pretty," she murmured. "And there are so many. They'll fetch thousands of pounds, hundreds of thousands! They're easy to smuggle out, and it's not like taking the treasure of the pharaohs. It's not the same thing at all."

It wasn't. Not to her. She could maintain her vow to protect the treasure, for this was not the same as the ancient treasure of pharaohs; this was something else. She didn't want to consider what.

Karida stroked the smooth surface of one emerald the size of a camel's eye. Her real father had denied her birthright, just as Nigel's father had denied his. They'd both been denied wealth, opportunity, so many things that should have been theirs. This was the chance to truly turn their lives around!

She grabbed fistfuls of stones and began shoving them into her rucksack. They clinked like small coins. When the bag was full, she dragged it up the steps. Nigel followed and watched her struggle to load the sack onto her camel. He did not help, only watched as she returned with a second sack. As she bent over the chest of gems once more, he gave her an odd look and made a strangled sound.

"No, don't. Just, don't. Leave it." Nigel tugged her hand away. "Don't do this, Karida. I've changed my mind. Put it all back. I don't want it. I don't want any of it."

Blinking, she stared at him as if he'd turned into one of those long-dead and mummified pharaohs. "What?"

"I don't want the treasure." When she stood mute, he repeated the phrase again.

"What about Eric? What about me?"

He seemed to struggle for composure, raked a hand through his dusty hair. "I'll find another way. I must, I can, I will." He fisted his hands. "I know with my estate locked up I'm nearly penniless as a pauper, but I'll find a way to care for you and Eric. Something, anything! It's for you. I can't stand this, seeing you look like this. You're my angel. You're goodness and honesty, and I shan't see you corrupted like I am." He set down his electric torch and gathered her hands in hers. Emeralds spilled back into the chest. "Come away. I won't see you do this. Please, angel."

Nigel dropped to his knees, brought Karida's hands to his mouth and kissed them. "It would kill me to see you do this," he whispered.

She touched his head, won over by his surprising change of heart. "Nigel, I love you."

The stark honesty in his gaze brought a lump to her throat. "I love you, too."

"How very touching."

Nigel sprang to his feet, and Karida turned. A harsh light played over both of their faces. Saud stood there, a cruel smile marring his visage, holding an electric torch. At his side was Malik, armed with a pistol.

They were trapped.

Chapter Twenty-three

"I knew you'd come down here, Nigel. And I trusted Karida would guide you. What a benefit to have her working for us." Saud approached, a dagger in his hands gleaming in the torch-light.

Nigel stepped in front of his wife. "Leave her alone."

Saud's smile was flat. "Karida has what is now mine—Kareem's emeralds. *My* emeralds."

Nigel swore softly as Malik inched closer. "Kareem treats you fairly. He trusts you, and this is how you repay him?"

"Why should I not?" Saud laughed. "They are but a pittance, the tiniest portion of my master's wealth. I've served him for years, and he has rewarded me with so very little."

Malik gave Karida a baleful look. "I should cut off your head for what you did to me."

"You did it to yourself when you tried stealing my necklace," she shot back.

"And you thought it would stop me from seeking this treasure. It only forced me to find another way. You're as foolish as my father. He believed in the tomb's curse and told me he would never reveal the hidden traps to me because the treasure brought our ancestors nothing but grief." Malik glanced at Saud. "I bargained with my friend here, and told him if he provided me with the tomb's location and the traps, if he could get it out of Kareem somehow, I'd split the treasure with him. It was a good choice."

Saud nodded, staring at Karida as if she were fashioned from gold. "My master trusted me and showed me all the tomb's surprises. Malik didn't realize what a mutually beneficial arrangement our partnership would turn out to be. I had already stolen some emeralds from Kareem but needed a good hiding place. In turn, he promised he would get the combination to the sarcophagus." His gaze went to Nigel. "You should thank your wife for saving your miserable life, Englishman. I would have had you killed in Cairo if not for her."

"What the hell are you talking about?" Nigel demanded.

"You weren't a threat when you went back to London. It wasn't until you returned that you became a problem. Malik hired spies all over Cairo to find out if and when you came back, because we knew you'd come straight here to steal the treasure."

"Why do you think I praised the virtues of Habib's brothel above all others, Nigel?" Malik gave him a sly look. "Habib is my cousin. He's kept an eye on you all along. And when he told me you married Karida in his brothel . . . well, you ceased to be a problem and became a benefit. We knew you'd bring her here to guide you past the traps. And Kareem told Saud she is the only woman with the combination to the sarcophagus."

Torchlight cast flickering shadows over Saud's face. "I want what's inside that coffin."

Nigel shook his head. "You greedy bastard."

Malik's dark eyes glittered like chips of onyx. "You couldn't resist the treasure in this tomb any more than we could, Nigel. You're just like us." The Arab sneered.

Karida pushed past Nigel. "My husband's not like you and never will be," she burst out. "Let us go. You can have it, all of it! Take the emeralds and go."

"No." Saud's gaze rested on the sarcophagus. "Not just the emeralds. Give me the combination to the lock."

"Go to Hell." Karida pronounced each word slowly.

Kareem's servant stared at her. "What is your honor worth, woman? This coffin is what you were sworn to protect, but everything has a price. You and your uncle are the only ones with the combination. Give it to me."

She refused again. Nigel felt a surge of pride.

Suddenly Malik held a pistol to his temple. "I'd enjoy blowing his brains all over," he warned. The man was staring at Karida with a loathing that made Nigel's gut twist. But Nigel shook his head; he'd rather be killed than see her give in. He finally realized what was important in life, and his wife had known it all along.

But she surprised him. Shock and fear crossed her features, and then a spark of something else. An expression of surrender crossed her face . . . and then she gave up the combination. It was the real one.

"No!" Nigel cried, but she silenced him with a look. There was a serenity in her eyes—and suddenly Nigel understood.

Saud opened the coffin. He struggled to lift off the lid but, when he did, his dark eyes widened. "At last, the sacred mummy mask!" He turned to Nigel and Karida. "Do you know that legend says the one who places it on his face will inherit all the pharaoh's power and wealth? That alone is worth taking it. But I know someone who will pay hundreds of thousands of pounds for this, and that's worth it, too." The man laughed heartily.

"I wouldn't," Nigel warned. "Greed can make a man lose his head."

Beside him, Malik made a small noise that was tough to interpret. He lowered his pistol and eased away from Nigel. "My father told me that mask carries a curse of death for those who steal it. Saud, wait. I think . . ."

But it was too late. Saud grabbed the mask and lifted it, his thick arm muscles bulging. "It's mine!"

"No!" Malik shouted simultaneously.

Saud raised the gold mummy mask out of the coffin. An ominous roar echoed through the chamber. Nigel heard the *snick* of the blade before he saw it. He pulled Karida to him, shielding her eyes, but could not save her ears from Saud's terrified scream. A dull thud followed, and the loud clatter of solid gold falling back into the coffin. Saud's head rolled on the ground, his lips frozen in shock.

Malik stumbled backward, dropping his gun with a look of shock. "No!" he cried again.

Nigel's eyes widened as he realized his ex-partner was stumbling toward a hidden trap. "Damn it, watch out!" he yelled.

But it was too late. After a terrified scream, silence followed as Malik fell into the newly opened pit, his body pierced by spears. And there was more, besides. Sudden openings appeared in the rock walls and sand began pouring into the chamber.

"Oh, sweet mercy! Run!" Karida screamed.

Nigel didn't need an engraved invitation. Grabbing his wife by the hand, he ran through the back burial chamber. To his horror, sand was pouring into the first room as well. It was already ankle deep.

Because they couldn't see, they were now in danger of stepping on the well and falling to their deaths. Karida went first, inching forward, showing Nigel the best path. But sand now flowed up to their calves, making progress difficult. He knew she was no longer sure of where she was stepping.

Karida. His wife would damn well not die here. Not here, not now. If anyone was going to die it was him. He deserved it; he'd brought them both here. Stupidly. She did not. He pushed her in back of him and went first, slowly and muttering prayers.

He heard a cracking beneath his feet and bellowed a warning. Throwing his weight backward, he managed to avoid the ground that gave way, but Karida teetered, dangerously close to the edge. Heaven alone knew what awaited her, whether it was more spears or something worse. For that reason, Nigel grabbed her and pushed her to safety as they spilled to safer ground.

She sobbed and clung to him, and he nodded. They weren't dead. But as she rose, he tried to stand as well and realized his foot was caught beneath the sand, probably trapped by a broken board. She saw his face and tried to pull free his leg, but it was hopeless. The sand kept pouring in.

"Go," he rasped through swirling dust. "Run, angel. Please." The incoming sand continued to pour over his lower limbs, .dusting him up to his torso. He struggled to free himself. "Go," he gasped. "Hurry!"

"Nigel! I can't leave you." She pulled at his arm.

"Leave me, please. You can't wait. If I can't get free . . . *look after Eric*," he explained. He tried to say everything with his eyes, but then he added, "Karida, I love you."

He felt the urgent pressure of her lips upon his hand. Then, with a sob, she was gone.

Shadow covered him as the staircase to the tomb entrance began to fill with sand as well. Nigel twisted his leg and summoned all his strength. "Come on, damn it. Come on!" He thought of Karida, who'd dared to take a chance on him. Of Eric, who trusted him. Of his brother, who had forgiven him all his sins. And then he thought of his own anger at himself for all the things he'd done wrong and how he wanted to make up for all of them. With a vicious yank he pulled. He felt a searing pain—but he was free!

The sand was up to his waist now, however, and even though he could slog forward it was a struggle to make his way toward the dim light of the tomb entrance. He coughed in the swirling dust. Sand had reached the level of his upper chest, squeezing his lungs. He could barely move. His vision grew dim, and he thought again of all the miserable things he'd done, all the badness.

He also remembered the joy he'd known. The love he had for his son, and the deep love he had for Karida. *I wish . . . I wish we'd had more time together. I'm sorry, love. I'm sorry I brought us here.*

Of all the indecorous ends; he'd never envisioned dying in a tomb covered by sand after doing the right and honorable thing. But this mattered not. Suddenly he was too weary, too numb, and the tremendous compression of the sand upon his chest demanded he finally surrender. Nigel closed his eyes, keeping the face of Karida before him. It would be the last memory before he went to his just reward: Hell, where thieves and murderers and libertines all went.

Light burst over him. Pure and blinding light, burning through his eyelids. He instinctively reached out for it, heard a dim roar of voices and a firm, authoritative command. Angels or demons were coming for him.

Suddenly hands were pulling him free, the horrid pressure on his chest easing. His body scraped against the sand, scraped against something else rough and hard, and it felt like he was sliding upward, higher, toward the fury of the white light that was making his eyes tear. A melodious whisper sounded in his ear, the voice of an angel, pure and soothing. Nigel turned toward the source, longing for it, needing it. Was it possible he'd found redemption instead of damnation?

A soft hand caressed his cheek.

"I'm . . . not dead," he gasped.

"Not for a good many years if your wife has anything to do with it," came a deep, amused voice, the same voice of authority so recently yelling instructions in Arabic.

Kareem.

Blinking furiously, Nigel struggled to focus his watery vision. The face of an angel came into view, an angel with matted dark curls, a smudged face, and a scrape on one cheek. She had exotic, beautiful caramel-flecked brown eyes.

This was his angel, Karida.

Nigel collapsed in her arms, finally letting the darkness take him.

Chapter Twenty-four

Fire. His throat was on fire, his body burning. Hot sand washed over him, a molten wave, the heat so intense he wanted to scream. Nigel opened his mouth but dry sand poured out. Nigel tossed and turned, anything to get rid of the feeling that he'd been stuffed into a clay oven and baked.

A cool cloth passed over his forehead. He turned into it, his hands grasping. Gentle fingers lifted his head, pressed a glass to his lips. He gulped down the proffered liquid.

"Easy," came a low voice, as melodious as an angel's. "Slow, drink it slow."

Obeying, desperate to hear more of that voice as cool and refreshing as the water, he sipped. The cloth passed over his eyes, his face, and then another swiped down his body. Exhausted he fell back, letting himself fall asleep.

For two days, fever seized her husband. The cut on his foot from the broken boards was infected. Karida hovered over him, bathing him, making him drink. Kareem had also hired four women from the village, women with knowledge of healing and herbs. The treatment at last worked; Nigel's fever broke.

When he was again conscious and coherent, they talked. Nigel left the decision up to her. Karida at last came to one.

She asked Kareem to meet with them. Insects hummed in the gardens outside, and the splash of water in the pretty mosaic fountain accompanied the meal they shared. Kareem sat on the silk couch across from her and her husband, and there was a question in his eyes.

Karida swallowed hard. This was so difficult: being honest about all that had happened, about how she had broken her vow. She had given him a peremptory explanation about why she and Nigel were at the tomb, and how Malik and Saud appeared and demanded the treasure, but Kareem had known there was more. He had not pressured her, however. Would the man treat her the same as they had in the workhouse once he found out the truth? She had stolen—not ten pounds in coins this time, but thousands of pounds of rare gems. She had stolen from the very people she'd vowed to protect.

Nigel slid his palm over hers and nodded. He loaned her his strength in a gentle, assured touch.

Karida gestured to the rucksack at her feet. "These belong to you." She loosened the drawstring and dipped her hand into the sack. She withdrew a fistful of gems, and as she opened her hand a waterfall of emeralds spilled out, clattered like bullets on the table. "I stole them. I'm sorry," she whispered. "I thought I was more honorable than that, and I have disgraced your house." Tears blurred her vision.

Nigel squeezed her palm. "Please, Kareem, don't blame my wife. It's my fault, for leading her here."

Kareem gave them both a long, thoughtful look. "You belong together, you two. I can see it in your eyes. But I must tell you, Karida, that an action is not stealing if the object you take belongs to you." The young Arab picked up an emerald, a rueful smile playing across his mouth. "Yes, such treasure." He took the emerald, placed it on the floor and picked up a large marble bust of Horus. "Stand back, please. Both of you."

When they did, Kareem smashed the emerald. It shattered, shards flying in all directions on the floor.

Nigel bent over, picked up a small, jagged piece. Laughter exploded out of him. He kept laughing and laughing as he dropped it. "Glass!" he sputtered. "Worthless green glass!"

"I suspected Saud was stealing from me when I noticed small items disappearing. I had trusted him with my household.

When he kept making inquiries about the tomb and how he should know its location to protect it when I was gone on business, I grew even more suspicious. To test his loyalty, I took him to the tomb, showed him the traps. He failed. I arranged to have my emeralds replaced with glass. The real ones are in very safe hands." Kareem glanced at her. "Your *father's* hands. I knew I could trust him with your bride price."

Karida stared at him in mute shock.

"They are but a small part of my wealth, Karida," the Arab said very gently. "Worth only forty thousand pounds. But I wanted you to have them, to make up for my dishonorable actions. I shamed you, thinking only of my ability to have children. To act so in front of our tribes . . ." Kareem dusted off his hands, looked at them and shook his head. "If you wish, I will hire porters and guides for your return journey to wherever you go. I'm afraid I must leave as well. For good, this time." A shadow passed over his face. "I was being truthful when I told you I must depart for Cairo. My brother the sheikh is dying in the hospital."

"I'm sorry," Nigel said. Karida could tell he meant it. It seemed her husband had gotten over his jealousy.

"What happened?" she asked softly. "Is he ill?"

Turmoil filled Kareem's dark gaze. "The physicians do not know. They have conducted all manner of tests, and he continues to slip away. He just turned thirty-four a month ago and had no children. Like my older brother who died before him, Zayid will die shortly after his birthday."

The soon-to-be sheikh took another glass shard, played with it between his fingers. "My family is cursed," he said finally. "All of my father's sons are cursed to die without children shortly after we reach thirty-four. I did not believe this—not until Zayid fell ill and there was nothing we could do to heal him."

Kareem stood, and Karida and Nigel stood with him. Kareem made a gesture to sit. "Please, enjoy the dinner my chef has prepared. Feel free to remain as long as you wish. Consider it my wedding gift to you, the full use of my palace."

"Thank you," Nigel said. He stuck out a palm, and Kareem shook it.

"You have a treasure, Nigel. Do not forget it."

"I won't," Karida's husband promised.

Kareem looked straight at her. "I have never lain with a woman. You would have been the first," he blurted. "I wish you to know this, because I shamed you and that is unforgivable."

Speechless, she studied him. Beside her, she saw Nigel's eyes widen. "What about Layla?"

Kareem laughed, mocking himself. "I wanted my first time to be with my bride. I thought Layla was oddly distracted and her mother too anxious as well. That fear grew as we traveled. We stopped in the village, where I ordered an elder's wife to inspect my bride. Before the woman could refute her virginity, Layla confessed the child she carried in her belly." He sighed. "I will not marry for a long while now. It is imperative that I find the right wife, a very special woman."

His onyx gaze met Karida's, and it was the gaze of a man staring at death. "The only one who can break the curse." Then he gave an elegant shrug, and his familiar arrogance slipped back over him. His white silk robes whispered sadly as he left.

They left soon after the soon-to-be sheikh, eschewing Kareem's offer of time spent in his palace, and their trek across the desert was more arduous than any of their previous travels, despite the porters and supplies Kareem had given them. Karida's husband kept a constant wary eye on their surroundings, and she knew he'd been loath to travel the postal route to the Nile Valley because of the Bedouins they'd encountered.

Nine days of enduring the heat. By the eighth day, Karida was so weary that she wanted to drop on the sands and die.

Nigel urged her on, however, kept her spirits up. He laughed, talked, even sang. He told wild, incredible stories of his travels in Egypt that made her sputter in disbelief. She'd never felt so physically ill before, had always been a hearty person who endured the heat. But now she ate little and in the mornings retched upon waking.

Nigel was very patient, and if he was worried, she did not see it. He fashioned a small tent and erected it on his camel, and then she rode with him, dozing against his back. The heat was brutal, sucked the moisture from their lips. But they fought back by coating their mouths with salve and taking small sips of water.

Finally, late on the ninth day, Karida saw a sight that made her weep: the Great Pyramid of Khufu, rising on the plain. They had made it to the Giza plateau.

"We'll rest here before going into the city. You need the rest," Nigel decided.

He paid Kareem's porters a generous tip from the reserves of Lord Smithfield's money and gave them money to bring back fresh food and water from a nearby village. Then Nigel settled Karida in the shade of the pyramid, spreading out a camel blanket on the sand. She sank down, grateful to stretch out.

When the porters returned, bearing baskets of fresh fruit, bread, and cheese, and jugs of water, Karida had never seen such a wonderful sight. Nigel gave the men another generous tip and they set off with many handshakes and hearty well wishes. Then she and Nigel ate on the tawny sands and sipped gratefully at the cool water.

Nigel flashed her a grin as he dragged the back of his hand across his mouth. "We did it!" he laughed.

Dirt and grime covered Karida, but she had never felt so thankful—if tired—in all her life. "We made it," she croaked.

Nigel sighed and nodded. He wore a thoughtful expression.

Karida looked at her husband, his cheeks darkened by rough bristles, his eyes glowing jewels in a sun-darkened face. "I love you," she blurted out, needing to confess it after the ordeal they'd endured. The words felt necessary with the bold relief of the pyramids.

"I know," he replied.

Karida stared. "I just said I love you, you dolt! I love you, and that's all you have to say?"

"What did you want me to say?"

She wound up for a tirade before she saw the teasing light in his eyes, the mirth in his expression. "Oh you insufferable . . ."

"Come here," he ordered. He pulled her into his arms, and his mouth met hers in a hard kiss. She knew what that kiss meant: All he could not say. The regret. The sheer relief, the gratitude. The love.

He smiled at her. Then Nigel laughed, an emphatic burst of jovial boisterousness. It filled her heart to bursting.

Her husband reached over and clasped her hand, his warm palm encasing hers in a comforting grip. Then they were kissing, the shadow of the giant structures draped over them.

Suddenly, what seemed like a legion of Cairo's finest rode up on horses, surrounding their impromptu picnic. "Stay right there," one policeman ordered in rough Arabic. "You are both under arrest."

Chapter Twenty-five

She was in a cell with iron bars. After all these years, her worst nightmare had again come true.

They had been taken to a prison facility just outside Cairo. The charge was "theft." Nigel disputed it and argued for Karida's release, but the authorities had not paid any attention; the proprietor of the shop where Nigel purchased their supplies had leveled the charges against them both. As soon as the porters had appeared in the village to purchase supplies, chattering about the Englishman and the pretty lady named Karida who had come from the oasis, the authorities were notified.

Anxiety churned in her stomach. To be jailed for a crime they hadn't committed struck her as terribly ironic, considering all they'd actually done. She sank now to the floor, burying her head in her hands. *I can't do this, I can't . . .*

Memories peppered her like shotgun pellets. The scowling face of the policeman, the smug triumph of the workhouse mistress. The small, dark cell. Her fists hammering to get out, blood streaming down her injured knuckles.

Panic engulfed her. Karida jumped to her feet and ran to the iron bars. Her fingers wrapped around them. With all her strength, she shook.

"Let me out! Let me out now! Please, someone let me out! *Let me out!*"

Her cry was a litany mixed with throat-clogging panic. No answer came but the crude insults from other cells. Then a deep voice echoed nearby. Nigel. He was in the cell next to hers.

"Talk to me. Karida, *talk to me.*"

She ignored him, kept shaking the metal that would not yield, the bars that showed no mercy, kept her penned like a wild animal in a cage. She was trapped and would never go free again.

"Karida! Sweet, talk to me. Talk to me."

He kept repeating the words in his deep voice. She stared at the whiteness of her knuckles, her hands grasping for freedom. Again and again her husband's words came, insistent and soothing, slowly countering her panic. It permeated the thick fog of her terror, reached down to gently pull her free of the mire of fear. He was trying to tug her back to the here and now.

He was separated from her; her rock, her lifeline. Karida slid her grasp from the middle cell bars and followed his voice, thrusting her hands out to blindly root for his. She felt the warmth of strong, calloused fingers. They pulled her back to reality. He was here. Her rescuer. Her devilish rescuer, the one she'd gladly follow to Hell if only she could be with him once more. He was not perfect, but he was hers. She loved him more than anything.

"Oh, please tell me all will be well," she said in a choking sob.

His fingers slowly stroked hers, the contact an anchor in this whirling madness.

"Trust me, sweet. All will be well. I will not let anything happen to you. I'll let them put me to death before I let them convict you. Easy now," he soothed.

She kept a grip on his fingers, remained touching his strength. "You wouldn't look very good dead," she managed. "Very few people do."

He laughed, and suddenly she believed all would be well.

"It's us together, love," he said softly. "Hang on, and you'll be fine. You're my angel, and nothing bad can happen to angels."

They were still holding hands when a blustering voice bellowed down the hallway. "Where is he? Get him out here immediately! I insist!"

To her shock, a guard unlocked their cells as a scowling man in a white suit stood behind him. Nigel stepped out of his cell, and she ran to him, wondering what new fate awaited them.

Her husband hugged her tight and smoothed down her hair. "See now? Didn't I tell you?" he whispered. He seemed less nervous than she.

"Wallenford. That's your right name," the stranger accused.

Nigel gave him a sheepish look.

Karida stepped out of her husband's embrace. "What, sir, may I ask, do you want with us?"

"Hello, my dear. My name's Walter Rockford." The man took her hand, pumped it vigorously and released it. "Happen to know your husband here. I was there when he bought those supplies. I've been making inquiries. I'm a stubborn sort who gets an idea in his mind and refuses to let go. I wanted to ask you again to work for me." The American gave Nigel a searching look and whispered, "There is, ah, the little matter of the small *ushabti* the shopkeeper says you sold him on your last visit, the one you stole from a tomb in the Valley. But I gave the appropriate parties proper compensation and assurances you would never do such a thing again, as you'll be working for me from now on." He named the same considerable sum as before, plus expenses while traveling to Egypt.

Nigel stepped back, shocked.

"Well?"

Nigel glanced at Karida. "Yes. I'll do it. A respectable job, one that will provide well for my wife. She deserves it. Gladly. If you really mean it, thank you."

Karida knew what it cost his pride to agree, to become a working aristocrat. But he'd clearly learned his lesson and had higher goals in mind than ever before, and she also knew how he could overcome the snobbery of his peers. No longer was either of them a thief or dependent upon the approval of others. Together they were going to see to Eric. Together they were going to be happy. She squeezed her husband's palm.

"Let's get out of here." Rockford led them past the guards. His warm gaze twinkled as he clapped Nigel on the back. "Have to get away from them, you understand. They understand English better than I do Arabic, and they might not approve of everything we talk about. Not that I want you smuggling, Nigel, but I won't prohibit you from doing what you feel you must. You're quite good."

"Yes," Karida's husband said. "I was. But that career is over now. I'm making a new life for myself. I have good reason." He squeezed Karida's hand. "My days of crime are over. For good."

They left Cairo with a promise to return in two weeks to join Rockford on his yacht and sail to England. Karida wanted to say good-bye to her family—and to retrieve her emeralds.

Nigel had been so attentive, nurturing with a quiet tenderness. Before they left the city, they had stayed with Thomas and Jasmine for two days. Nigel had loved her, tenderly satisfied her over and over until finally she gave a little sigh and cried, "Enough." They'd rested in each other's arms.

Now they ate dinner with her family at the Khamsin camp. Nigel was quiet. He'd been quiet since their arrival. She wondered if he was thinking about the dilemma awaiting him in England, about how he would get back Eric. Karida had assured him she would help, but of course he knew that. She would do anything for him. *Anything,* she'd told him. What mattered most was that they were all together.

When dinner ended and the music ceased, they walked back to their tent. The desert wind scraped against the sand, sending eddies swirling at their feet.

Inside, she went to the low sandalwood table. A fat goatskin was there, tied with a strip of leather. She handed it to Nigel.

"Uncle Ramses brought these today. Keep them for me, husband. Sell them. We can put them to good use when we reach London. We can use them to get Eric back and to buy a nice home in the country."

"And a shop for you to sell your jewelry," he suggested.

Karida shrugged, and she felt her spirits fall. "It would be nice, but it doesn't matter. That was just a dream." In London was the earl of Smithfield, her father. No matter what sort of shop she set up, there was no way he was going to recognize her as his own. Not now. "My father, my real father, he won't be pleased by our marriage. Not after he deliberately condemned it. I can't live according to what he expects, though. I'm my own person and have to find my own joy—with you, my love." And this she meant.

"The earl of Smithfield," Nigel said slowly.

He was silent as he untied the bag and looked at the gems inside. He tightened the drawstring again, weighed the bag in his palm, and then switched it from one hand to the other. When he looked at her, his gaze was troubled.

"Karida, how much do you want your real father to accept you?"

She considered lying, telling him that the earl's approval no longer mattered. Then she reminded herself that honesty was the beginning of all good things. "More than anything," she whispered. "But I'm not like Kareem's false emeralds. I won't shatter like glass. I'll get by. London is a large city, and if the earl wishes to avoid me, he may." She went into Nigel's arms, holding him tight.

He set the bag down and rested his cheek atop her head. She felt his breath warm her scalp. "I'd do anything to make you happy . . ."

They went to bed, and he made love to her, gently, tenderly. It was exquisite, as always. She fell asleep in his arms.

In the morning, when she awoke, he was gone.

Chapter Twenty-six

He had left her.

Nigel trudged up the steps of his home, the home he detested, the home where he'd seldom seen any true affection. He had taken his wife's emeralds and fled, leaving her with her family. He'd fled like the dog he was, leaving only a terse note. He hoped to be reconciled with her again at some point, but he knew he could not depend upon it.

He had not wanted to leave her. Nigel had wanted to stay, to watch her laugh, to see her smile for the rest of her life. But he'd left instead. It was for the best. He had complications to work out. And so did she.

Nigel knew it would make her cry that he'd left. It would make her cry, and the one who was haunted most by her pain would offer comfort. And maybe, finally, the truth. Nigel hadn't been able to deliver the truth himself, though he'd recently discovered it. Karida needed to know the truth and to reconcile herself to it. She could not leave Egypt until she did, or it would always be a pall over their lives. Eric could not wait for that.

It had been a pleasant journey on Rockford's sleek yacht, a leisurely sail back to England. He'd had his own cabin, a plush bed, and the food was exquisite. He'd longed for the simplicity of a desert bed, Karida in his arms. But he'd told his new employer that his wife had decided to stay behind. He supposed he was still a liar at heart.

Upon reaching London, Rockford helped him sell the emeralds. He recommended just the right building for a small shop, a perfect location. The leftover money was immediately placed in a bank for Karida. Nigel did not spend one farthing on himself. The money was meant to make her dream, not his, come true. He would not take from her. His days of thieving were over.

Rockford loaned Nigel a generous advance on his salary. He was taking his family to visit Bath for a few weeks, but as soon as he returned, Nigel would start working for him. Nigel sent most of the money to the earl of Smithfield's house by means of his solicitor. He included an unsigned note that simply read: *I'm sorry.*

But he had nothing left to give Oakley, and he pondered his options as he opened his bedroom door and collapsed on his bed. *Nothing.* But if he had to pound and kick the bastard to get his son returned, he would.

Hearing a noise at his door, he stirred. His mother stood in the doorway, staring at him. Cold anger washed over Nigel. The countess studied him with as much weariness as he felt.

"You're back," she said, and her voice held a strange note.

"Yes, I'm back," he burst out. "And I'm leaving shortly to get my son back. My bastard son. And when I get him, wherever William Oakley is hiding him, he's coming here. I don't care what you think. Or your friends, or anyone else. Eric is staying here, with me. And I'll do my damnedest to ensure he has a happy life. I can't guard him from all scandal, but I'll do whatever I can to make sure he's happy."

"You've changed, Nigel," she said.

"Yes, I suppose I have. Not that it matters." *Not one bit. Not without Karida.*

Too weary to argue, he let his head fall back on the pillow. His mother left without another word.

He slept for a full day. When he awoke, sunlight streamed through the lace curtains. Nigel stumbled to his water closet, relieved himself and then splashed water on his face. As he left his room, he heard voices downstairs. He ran a hand through his tousled hair. *Bloody hell, visitors at this time?* The countess could entertain them; he didn't give a damn.

Nigel went downstairs, rumpled suit and all, and ground to an abrupt halt at the downstairs drawing room entrance. His mother—God, his *mother*—was sitting on the striped settee, showing a tow-haired boy the cat's cradle. They both looked up upon hearing Nigel's vulgar exclamation.

"Don't swear, Nigel. It's a bad influence on the boy," the countess said softly.

Nigel ran over to his son, put shaking hands on the thin shoulders now covered by a linen suit. "Eric, how . . . ?"

Words failed him. Nigel bent over and hugged the boy tightly. He glanced at his mother, who stood up, smoothing her skirts.

"Eric, why don't you go into the kitchen and see if Cook has any of those delicious pastries she promised?" she told him.

With a glance at Nigel, who nodded, the boy went. His son. Alive and present. The boy was well and dressed in clean, expensive clothing. Nigel rubbed the back of his neck, totally flummoxed.

The countess set down the string she'd used to demonstrate the game. "William Oakley is a fool. He is blustering and arrogant, but I threatened to have him arrested for stealing away a child belonging to my family—his own family would never brook such a scandal. He laughed at me until I told him if he did not bring Eric to me by the day's end, I would see it to that his good name was blackened in society and he'd never marry a suitable woman." The countess gave a sly smile. "I still have the influence to ensure it would happen."

Nigel's mouth worked. "I'll be damn . . . er, darned." Then he forced out the words: "Thank you." He slid her a suspicious look. "Why, after all this time?"

Her smile faded. "You changed, so I can change as well. I'm getting older, Nigel, and I don't know how many years I have left. I will not waste them with regrets. I am sorry—for all that you had to endure with your father, and that I lacked the strength to stand up for you and your brother. Your father was a forcible person."

She walked over to the mahogany desk with a Tiffany lamp and picked up a piece of paper. Nigel read it as she handed it over. He stared at the birth certificate, conflicted, wanting desperately to disbelieve the stark words printed there:

Father: James Wallenford, earl of Claradon

Eric was not his son but his brother.

"You're lying, just as you lied when you delivered my brother and I!" Nigel crumpled the paper in his fist.

"The earl wished for Eric to be kept hidden away. He arranged for a sum of money to be given to the boy's mother in order to do so. I didn't discover his treachery until the woman came to me, begging for help. The money had run out, and they were both in the workhouse. She was dying and wanted someone to care for Eric. Your father laughed in her face and threatened to send for the police."

The countess smoothed her black bombazine skirts, as if she could wash away the past with every stroke of her fingers. "So Eric's mother begged me. Begged me to visit the place where they were forced to live. I did and was horrified." Shame crept over the countess's face. "Yet I dared not risk a scandal. I didn't know what to do. And then you came back to London and provided the answer—my son, who was hiding his true identity, whom everyone thought was dead, would be perfect at hiding a bastard as well."

His mother's face seemed harsh in the dim light filtering through the dingy lace curtains. Nigel remembered the day he'd returned and snuck into the house, pretending to be his twin, and she'd caught him on the stairs. The bowler hat. He'd always worn it, and Thomas disdained the style. She must have known then.

"I waited and watched and arranged for all of us to be gone. The day you were alone in the house with Charlotte, I sent a letter purporting to be from the woman. I knew you'd not remember her among your"—the countess's voice dropped to a half whisper—"many lovers, but the words would convince you that Eric was your son. And you would do anything, anything, to care for him because you'd been told you could never sire a son."

A cold chill fell over Nigel. He felt a great space opening between them, as if he and his mother were miles and miles apart. "You set me up and lied to me, all so that I would look after my father's child?"

"I had to!" Her voice rose, and he studied her in amazement. The countess almost never raised her voice, never allowed herself to become this agitated. "I had to do it, Nigel. I couldn't afford anyone knowing. The scandal! But the boy . . . I wanted to do something for him. He looked so frail. He was only a child and—"

"I was a child once," Nigel interrupted.

Sorrow filled her rheumy blue gaze, and she lifted her eyes to him. "I know. And I know I never saved you from your father. But I could save Eric. If you found him, I knew you'd take him away, hide him, care for him—but only if you thought he was yours."

Eric wasn't his son. Oh God. Nigel wanted to sink to his knees and bellow in despair. But a small part of him kept insisting, *He is blood. You are all he has. Will you forsake him because he is not your seed? He is your son in spirit: handed over to a workhouse like a dirty little secret, never to know the comfort of a warm bed, good food, or even the slightest affection.* Like him, Eric had been betrayed by a father who thought him worthless. A father who did not care about his welfare.

Eric trusted and relied on him. Eric needed him.

He is your brother. That is enough.

"Can you forgive me? Just a little?"

Once Nigel would have laughed cruelly at the countess's broken, pitiful voice. He would have turned on his heel and walked out, washed his hands of the whole mess. It had nothing to do with him. Once he'd thought he could never love a woman, could never give Karida his whole heart. Once he'd thought he could never, ever change.

Nigel looked calmly at his mother. "Eric will need a home, and this is as good as any until I can hire a steward and make repairs on the country estate. He'll need affection and a sturdy hand to guide him past the gossips who will surely look at him with disdain. There will be scandalous talk, and you will be ostracized by your highborn friends. How committed are you . . . Mother?"

An emotion he couldn't quite decipher flickered in her eyes. "I'll do it. I will help you with Eric."

He stared at her. "Just one thing. No more lies. No more secrets. Eric will know the truth of his origins, and he must know you are not his blood."

She nodded. "It's best he knows the truth."

Nigel didn't know what to do. He didn't want to hug his mother or express affection. Perhaps in time that would come. Perhaps one day he could learn to forgive and, eventually, forget.

For now Karida came first. With the terrible fear of losing Eric out of the way, he now needed only to make a few more arrangements and then find a way back to her. Back to his heart, safely tucked away in Egypt's desert. He hoped she had worked through her issues with her father.

Her real father.

Karida could not stop crying. Nigel had run away again, taking her emeralds, had left her with only a note and a vague promise of return. But, return when? Why had he not trusted her to help him recover Eric, which she knew was his first priority? Had she done something wrong? She knew he had.

Nigel had promised not to steal. He had said so in his note, writing that he'd make good use of the gems, "For you, love." He'd broken his promise. He had stolen when he left: he'd stolen her heart. Did he ever plan to return it?

She slid a palm over her scarred abdomen, and a surge of terror and joy shot through her. Her mother had beamed this morning when Karida had confessed her suspicions. She, who had been once called barren and unmarriageable, was carrying Nigel's child. Nigel, her husband who had abandoned her.

Karida was downright scared for another reason. Though the doctor in Cairo assured her the burn scars weren't so deep that it would prohibit her belly from properly stretching to accommodate the baby, she wasn't certain.

Her adoptive mother and her mother's brother's wives fussed and marveled over her and promised to help with lotions and creams that softened the skin, but Karida wanted Nigel at her side, Nigel clutching her hand as they both absorbed this miracle they'd created. And she did not know if he would ever return.

Tears streamed down her face. She scrubbed at them as she sat in her tent fashioning an earring, the silk walls billowing in the breeze.

"Karida? Is it true, your husband has left you?"

Ramses stood at the entrance to her dwelling, looking uncertain. Karida wiped her face as he came inside. Her uncle squatted down and touched her chin.

"He made you cry," he said tightly. Anger twisted Ramses's handsome face. "The jackal, I will cut out his heart for this. Have you not endured enough sorrow?"

Karida struggled to contain her emotions. "He said . . . it was best that I remain here until everything was settled for me. He would be back."

"Did he take your emeralds?"

She toyed with the earring she was crafting, reluctant to answer.

"A man should *never* abandon his wife—especially when she is carrying his child!"

Ramses looked away, a muscle twitching in his jaw. "When a man becomes a father, he has responsibilities he must not disregard."

"He will come back for me. I know it. And then, when he does, we'll have a home. Maybe then . . ." Karida looked away, her eyes watering. "I need to go to London, to tell my real father that he's going to be a grandfather. I don't feel like I need his approval anymore, but he should know. He won't be happy, as he drove Nigel away, saying he wasn't good enough for me. But he should know." Her gaze whipped over to Ramses. "Nigel *is* good enough. He's more than just good. I'm sure he believed he was doing what was best. I love him, even when he does something so foolish. I always will. Something my father will never understand."

Ramses stared at her for a moment, then said, "The earl of Smithfield is a good judge of character, but he is only a man, and he makes mistakes—as we all do. There is something I must tell you." He stood and paced, his hand on the hilt of his scimitar. Karida had never seen him so agitated.

"Uncle Ramses, what's wrong?"

His eyes closed, then opened. His gaze was filled with haunting sorrow—and grim resolve. "The earl of Smithfield is not your father."

Shock made her speechless. Clutching her earring, Karida walked over to the bed and sat. She fisted her hands in her lap. "I don't understand," she finally whispered.

He would not look at her but stared at the tent walls as if they contained a thousand secrets. "The earl of Smithfield paid that money to Lady Cardew to release you. He did it because once he too fathered a child out of wedlock, long after his wife died. When he discovered your existence, he promised he would do all in his power to see you safe from that woman. It was too late for his child; she had died. By saving you, he was assuaging his own guilt." A pained whisper threaded through Ramses's voice. "But I never assuaged mine."

Dryness squeezed Karida's throat. She could not talk, could only wait, the frantic beating of her heart a thudding in the stillness. A growing dread gathered.

Ramses's gaze dropped to the scimitar hilt he clutched so tightly. "Before my marriage to Katherine—*long* before—I was . . . ah . . . with many women." His skin grew darker with apparent embarrassment. "I reveled in seducing English-women who were wintering in Cairo whenever I went there to conduct tribal business for Jabari. It was a game with me. The women meant nothing."

Karida closed her eyes, her hands curling ever tighter in her lap.

"I especially enjoyed seducing them while their husbands were gone. I was very careful never to impregnate any of them." His flush deepened. "I used certain methods to prevent it. Except, I grew reckless with one woman, a lovely but haughty aristocrat who proved too tempting for me to resist." He stole a quick glance at Karida. "Her name was Edith. She adored spending money on herself. Her husband was an aging earl in the last years of his life. Lord Cardew."

An answer at last. Karida found it impossible to breathe. "What, what are you telling me?"

Ramses faced her. "Your mother. Lady Cardew. We had an affair. It lasted four days. I was smitten with her beauty, but she laughed at me in the end because she thought I was a simple desert warrior without money." Ramses looked grim. "I left, never to see her again. Until she heard I was in London, staying with my new father-in-law, the earl of Smithfield. The very wealthy earl of Smithfield. And she brought you there to sell you like a camel because her debts had overwhelmed her."

"Oh, God." Tears blurred Karida's vision. "You. It's been you all this time."

He bowed his head. "I am your father, Karida. Not the earl."

All these years, thinking Smithfield was her father. All those lost, wasted years, longing for acceptance, craving it. It had all been a lie, when her real father lived less than one hundred yards from her own damn tent. Shock gave way to white-hot rage. She took her pretty silver earring and flung it at him.

"You . . . *thief!*"

"Karida," Ramses said.

"No. Stop it, just stop it." Karida stood and paced the tent. "You've stolen from me all these years I could have known who my real father was! I've longed to have my real father accept me, even if he were the poorest fellahin. And you've been here, right here with me, and never told me. All the years wasted, when you could have acknowledged me, told me I was your daughter!"

"I was ashamed," he muttered, looking away. "Ashamed of my actions and failing you as a child. That you were forced to endure such horrors."

Forcing herself to calm, she blurted out the question that had haunted her for ages. "Why did my mother put me into the workhouse?"

Ramses raised his gaze to hers. "She would not say at first, not on the day she brought you to the earl of Smithfield. I demanded an answer. She finally told us that her husband was not capable of giving her a child and knew it. When she discovered she was pregnant, she went away discreetly and then abandoned you at the steps of the workhouse with a note stating your name. She was not willing to give up her position in society or risk her marriage." His voice dropped to the barest whisper. "I am so sorry for all you had to suffer. As a child—"

Pain speared Karida's palms as she fisted her hands so tightly the nails bit into her flesh. "I could forgive you that! You didn't know I existed, so how could you help? But after? When you knew? Was it because of Katherine? Were you afraid of her condemnation?"

A heavy sigh fled him. "Katherine knew as soon as I returned to Egypt with you. She was a little angry, but she forgave me. She was the one who kept insisting I tell you, but I did not want to spoil your happiness. I thought it would be easier for you to remain my niece and for you to keep your full English heritage."

"My English heritage! Do you think I gave a damn about blood?" Bitterness filled her. "My English relation put me in a cold, filthy workhouse!"

Ramses hung his head, looking miserable. "Again, I am sorry," he said in a low voice. "I never meant to shame you, and if you knew I was your father, not a rich earl . . . The day when you first came to us at the earl's, when you held out your arms to him, you looked so happy, so proud to be his child."

Sudden insight struck her. Ramses was ashamed. Ashamed not only of fathering a bastard, but of what he was: a desert warrior and not a wealthy aristocrat. How long had he harbored such thoughts? Had they begun when Lady Cardew first rejected him, or were they even deeper-seated?

A lump rose in her throat. "Did you think I could not love you?" she asked brokenly.

"I am sorry, Karida . . . Anne." Ramses turned away, his broad shoulders sagging. "Tell me what I must say to make up for it. I have loved you from a distance as much as I could and guided you as best as I could. I only wanted for your happiness."

Just call me one name, she thought sadly, watching him. *Just that one word I've longed to be called all my life, from my real father, that one word of acceptance: daughter.*

Karida waited. Rames remained motionless as a statue.

At last she gave up. She settled on a bold, outright lie. "There is nothing. I'll be fine. Truly, there is nothing you can say." She shrugged her shoulders and looked at the wall.

He did not say a word, only sighed again and left the tent. Karida flung herself on her bed and wept—for herself, for Nigel, for Ramses, and all that the three of them had lost.

She also wept for her unborn child, whose future remained uncertain.

Nigel arrived at the Khamsin camp. Oddly, the same women who had mocked Karida and smiled at him now scowled; they glared as he rode into camp and dismounted from his sturdy mare.

He wiped his damp palms against his trousers. Perhaps it wasn't such a grand idea, having cabled ahead of his arrival. Maybe he should have simply walked in unannounced. He spotted Ramses striding toward him, the man looking as dangerous as a tiger.

Nigel offered a smile. Ramses pushed him to the ground.

The Arab withdrew his sword and laid the blade at Nigel's throat. He placed one booted foot on Nigel's chest. Nigel didn't dare breathe lest his throat be cut.

"Give me one good reason I should not remove your head for leaving her and making Karida cry," the Khamsin warrior demanded.

Nigel stared up at him with cool eyes. "Because I just bought this suit, and it would be a damn shame to get blood all over it."

Something flickered in the warrior's eyes. Humor? Anger? It was hard to tell. For once, sarcasm didn't work as an easy escape. So, Nigel settled on the truth. He locked gazes with Ramses.

"Because if you do, you'll be killing your son-in-law."

Odd, how shock changes a person's face, Nigel thought as he watched Ramses remove the sword from his neck. He stood, ignoring the Arab's tormented look.

"How . . . ?" Ramses cleared his throat. "How did you know?"

Pity filled Nigel at the older man's slumped shoulders. "It was easy enough, once I saw—truly saw—my Karida. Her beautiful eyes are exactly like yours."

Ramses sheathed his sword. He gestured to a distant tree. "Go to her. She is there. Make her happy if you can. She deserves to be happy."

Nigel walked in the direction the man indicated. Sitting beneath the sprawling shade of an acacia, Karida was reading. When he stood a few feet from her, Nigel looked down at his wife. "Hello, my love."

She did not glance up.

Drawing in a deep breath, he said the words he'd rehearsed for hours on the ride here.

"Karida, I want you to come with me back to London and live with me as my wife."

She lifted her face to his. It was devoid of all emotion. "Why should I bloody well care to do that?"

Nigel licked his lips. He felt the presence of a crowd gathering behind him. Glancing over his shoulder, he saw a cluster of women and Khamsin warriors, and they were staring not at Karida but him. This was all so damn public. What he had to say . . . Well, he would not humiliate her. Or Ramses. All that mattered was her feelings. He would bare his own.

He sank down onto his knees before her. "Because you make me a better man. Because I've been so terribly lonely without you. Because you are all I can think about. You're my oasis, and I will die without you." His heart was beating frantically.

His wife said nothing, only gazed at him with calm indifference.

He kept his gaze trained on her, seeing only her, worshipping her with his adoring gaze. "Because I love you, and I'm a horrid, rotten cad. I can't promise I'll change. I'll probably always be a horrid cad and do things that make you want to scream at me, but I promise I'll try my best to make you happy." It was the most honest he'd ever been, he realized with a rueful smile.

She set down her book, drummed her fingers on it. "You *are* a horrid cad, Nigel Wallenford."

"The worst."

"And what you did was unforgivable, dumping me here like an old saddlebag you no longer had use for. Not taking me with you? After all we've been through together?"

"I should be thrashed. If it makes you feel better . . ." Nigel glanced over his shoulder, seeing Ramses. "He can do it, if you wish." He had never seen a more miserable man.

Katherine joined her husband, sliding an arm around his waist. Nigel nodded at her, and Katherine nodded back. There was a silent understanding between them. Ramses would need her love and understanding in the coming days. How well Nigel knew what the man was feeling.

"I have a better punishment in mind. You're going back to London and taking me with you—to Eric and our new family. I'm going to punish you by forcing you to make up for it the rest of your life," Karida told him. Then she smiled.

"No lie?"

She shook her head. "Truth only. For both of us from now on." Her smile dropped away. "Why did you do it, Nigel? Couldn't you trust me?"

He glanced around, decided he could risk this much: "I did it for you," he said honestly. Later he would tell her the full truth, in the privacy of their tent when all eyes and ears were not turned toward them.

"I took your emeralds and sold them, and bought you a pretty little shop in London. I put the rest of the money in a bank account in your name. I didn't use any of it for myself. It's your money. Now you can sell your jewelry just as you wished. I needed to get Eric back and get everything settled for you to come back with me. I wanted to get everything perfect for you. You deserve everything to be perfect."

"Nigel . . ." She sighed and struggled to her feet as he reached down to pull her upright. "Don't you realize I don't need perfection? Life is never perfect. There will always be messes to straighten out. The important thing is, we need to face everything together. And we need to be truthful with each other, no matter how much it hurts . . . or how much we think we know best for the other."

Her gaze went to Ramses, and Karida's voice rose so that he could hear her clearly. "Because the truth is not always as it seems, and those who keep secrets because they fear they'll disappoint us are always wrong. We love them because of who they are, not what we expect them to be."

Ramses walked over and hugged her. "Thank you," he said thickly. "You are a treasure greater than any the pharaohs ever buried."

Nigel knew then; Karida had discovered the truth—and had reconciled herself to it.

Ramses released his daughter, and Nigel gave him a long, assessing look. The warrior returned the gaze and then stuck out a palm. "Take good care of her. I trust that you will. You are a man of honor."

Nigel shook. Then he turned to Karida, catching her up in an embrace. He kissed her warm, soft lips, crushed her against him.

She laughed, put a hand on his chest. "Careful, you'll hurt the baby."

He couldn't have heard right. Nigel released Karida and stared at her stupidly. "What baby?"

"Your baby, you ninny. I'm carrying your child."

The soft, tender smile touching her mouth, and the glow in her rosy cheeks echoed the thrill in her voice. Nigel stumbled backward, his mouth hanging open. His throat constricted painfully and when he spoke, it was a small, hopeful whisper.

"You're pregnant?"

"Yes." Very gently she took his trembling hand and placed it over her belly.

Something wet and warm filled his eyes, trickled down his cheeks. Nigel kept staring at her, unable to speak past the thick lump in his throat. He slid a palm down her abdomen, imagining the new life growing there, and it filled him with renewed hope.

"Are you all right? Are you well?" he finally managed.

She nodded. "I went to see a physician in Cairo. He said my burn scars don't seem too deep and there is a slim chance that when I increase the skin will have trouble stretching, but there are salves that the Khamsin women use."

"I'll find the best physician in London. I don't care what it takes, you'll have the best possible care!" he promised.

Her hand rested on the slight swell of her abdomen. "You're going to make a perfect father."

"Forget perfect. I'll settle for being the best I can. Just like I love you, and always will. You're my fair angel."

Her smile curved upward in a secret amusement. "Not always," she murmured. "I do feel a bit devilish at times—around you."

Secrets and lies had nearly destroyed both their lives. Never again. Nigel took her into his arms and kissed her, not caring who stared at them. Not caring about anything but to have her in his life for always.

And that was the honest truth.

Epilogue

Music drifted through the open door. Nigel was at the piano in the music room, writing a new composition.

Karida—who was going by Anne again, both for the sake of English society and as a gesture of acceptance of her origins— gazed out the sparkling window of the upstairs drawing room. In the estate gardens below, her mother-in-law showed Eric how to trim the rosebushes. The weather had turned warmer, a promise of spring in the air.

The dowager countess straightened and glanced upward. A smile touched her mouth as she spotted Anne, and she waved. Anne waved back. Life in the country agreed with all of them. As soon as the country estate was repaired and renovated, they had moved, Nigel's mother as well. She and her son, once bitterly separated, had reconciled, and she now was a good influence on Eric. The woman had even reconciled with Jasmine, when Jasmine and Thomas had visited last year. The two women were civil to each other, as Jasmine and Thomas's twin daughters had softened their animosity.

Nigel had ceased working for Walter Rockford. After a year the man had moved back to New York, claiming he missed "good American food." He still proved to be a good friend, however, advising them in business matters. Nigel had sold a few songs and made a bit of money, but most of the Claradon estate's income came from Nigel's investments—and from Anne's London shop. Surprising them both, many aristocrats were eager to acquire her jewelry, keeping her busy designing unique creations for each of them.

Anne made her way down the hall to the music room. As she entered, she saw the nanny upon a nearby chair, smiling at the duo at the piano. Nigel bounced their two-year-old daughter on his knee. Her dark chestnut hair, green eyes, stubborn chin, and sense of daring adventure were all his. Anne had complained to Nigel about that, telling her husband that their daughter did not resemble her.

"Yes, she does. Jenny's an angel, just like you—except when it comes to bedtime," he had gently teased.

If they were blessed with another child, so be it. But Jennifer and Eric—whom they were raising as a son—were miracles enough.

Nigel stopped tinkering on the keys and let their daughter bang on them. He looked up, a tender smile touching his mouth. When Anne leaned down, his kiss was as passionate and welcoming as it was on the day he'd married her for the third time, this time in a London church.

Three times makes it perfect, he'd declared.

"Anne, love, have you come for your music lesson?" he teased softly. "You make such lovely melodies—as I always knew you would."

She smiled shyly and blushed at the memory of the words he'd said so long ago, when they were both thieves caught in an intrigue with a ruby key, and then she returned the smoldering look in his eyes. Last night, while everyone was sleeping, they had crept into this room and made love on the piano. It had been miraculous, like everything else they did together.

She sat on the bench, but her smile faded. "He'll be here soon. The cable said he was in London and making his way here."

Jenny frowned, her little face scrunched in concentration as she pounded on the keys. "Papa, pway!"

Nigel laughed and kissed the top of his daughter's head. "Later, poppet. Go see Nanny now."

He set the girl down on the floor and Jenny toddled off

toward her nanny. Anne's throat tightened. *Papa.* What a lovely word.

He stroked her hand. "Are you nervous?" At her nod, he kissed her cheek. "He loves you, and everything will be fine."

But she could not be certain. Would he, after all these years, finally call her the one word she'd longed her entire life to hear? She'd kept hoping he'd do it before they left Egypt to return to England, but she had been disappointed.

She touched a key, the soft *plink* echoing in the enormous room. "I haven't seen him since after Jenny's birth."

"Give him a chance, love. He feels guilty and probably still ashamed at neglecting you all those years—and at what you had to endure."

"He has his own family, his real family in Egypt. But just once, I wish he would call me his daughter."

Nigel took her into his arms and held her. Anne dropped her head on his shoulder, relishing the simple comfort he offered. Perhaps this was enough. No matter what, she had the love of her life. She could never forget that.

The door chimed downstairs. She stiffened.

Nigel touched her cheek. "You can do this. Go to him, sweet. And remember, I'm here for you. I love you."

The simple declaration he'd once been loath to make flowed so easily now. Glad of it, she kissed him and left, her steps heavy on the wide staircase.

The butler was heading for the door. She called for him to stop. "I'll answer it," she explained. She smoothed down her skirts, knowing she looked very English and nothing like the last time her father had seen her.

Anne Wallenford, once known as Karida, the desert girl, former thief and lover of a libertine, protector of desert treasures, and woman of honor, took a deep breath. She opened the door and saw the black-bearded man standing outside, his amber eyes so much like her own. Anxiety swam there, as if he were unsure of his welcome. Tears misted her eyes.

"Father," she said thickly.

Ramses's own mouth twisted, as if he struggled with his emotions. "How long I have waited for you to call me that. Hello, my beloved daughter," he whispered.

She fell into his opened arms.

Bonnie Vanak

"Vanak has a gift for creating exciting stories, memorable characters, and a passion hotter than the Middle Eastern sun...."
—*Romantic Times BOOKreviews*

The Scorpion & the Seducer

Jasmine Tristan was no stranger to the upper crust of London society. And yet, she knew the cruel sting of bigotry. When she took revenge, a new fear was voiced: Was Jasmine truly bad at her core, like her sultan father from whom she and her mother had fled? How could she be, when she'd known a moment of pure beauty with Lord Thomas Claradon? Their kiss had been scorching as a desert sun. But like a sandstorm, it was misdirecting: Thomas's loyalty to his family and duty put him forever out of her reach. Only a return to her birthplace, a quest to find her roots, would bring Jasmine answers—and also prove that true love could triumph over ignorance, passion over prejudice.

ISBN 13: 978-0-8439-5975-8

Trish Albright

Author of *Siren's Song*

"Exhilarating adventure." —*RT BOOKreviews*

Lady Olivia Yates enjoyed a wide array of scholarly pursuits. And she had an astounding vocabulary to prove it. Thanks to her archaeologist father, she also knew just about everything there was to know of ancient Egyptian artifacts—including a code no one else had yet deciphered. But she had no idea what to do when it looked as though someone was trying to murder her.

Samuel Stafford understood only about half the words that came out of the woman's mouth. But he didn't mind—so long as he had a chance to watch those luscious lips at work. Too bad he wasn't paying more attention, because suddenly Olivia was dragging the shipping captain halfway around the world on a perilous treasure hunt. From fighting Barbary pirates on the high seas to exploring centuries-old tombs, only together could they unlock the…

Siren's Secret

ISBN 13: 978-0-8439-6087-7

KATHRYNE KENNEDY

Author of *Double Enchantment*

Enchanting the Beast

~Relics of Merlin~

"Really fun and imaginative." —Eloisa James

Grimspell castle. With its dark, imposing stone walls, it certainly looked haunted. As a ghost-hunter, Lady Philomena was accustomed to restless spirits. But she found the dark, imposing nature of the castle's owner far more haunting than any specter. London Society might not approve of shape-shifters such as Sir Nicodemus Wulfson, but firmly-on-the-shelf Philomena rather enjoyed the young baronet's sudden interest in sniffing around her skirts. She'd even consider giving in to him altogether if not for a murderer on the loose—a beast that might just be Nico himself.

"Simply delightful."
—*Publishers Weekly* on *Enchanting the Lady*

ISBN 13: 978-0-505-52764-6

☐ **YES!**

Sign me up for the Historical Romance Book Club and send my FREE BOOKS! If I choose to stay in the club, I will pay only $8.50* each month, a savings of $6.48!

NAME: _____

ADDRESS: _____

TELEPHONE: _____

EMAIL: _____

☐ I want to pay by credit card.

☐ **VISA**   ☐ **MasterCard**   ☐ **DISCOVER**

ACCOUNT #: _____

EXPIRATION DATE: _____

SIGNATURE: _____

Mail this page along with $2.00 shipping and handling to:
Historical Romance Book Club
PO Box 6640
Wayne, PA 19087
Or fax (must include credit card information) to:
610-995-9274
You can also sign up online at **www.dorchesterpub.com**.
*Plus $2.00 for shipping. Offer open to residents of the U.S. and Canada only.
Canadian residents please call 1-800-481-9191 for pricing information.
If under 18, a parent or guardian must sign. Terms, prices and conditions subject to change. Subscription subject to acceptance. Dorchester Publishing reserves the right to reject any order or cancel any subscription.